The Reluctant Savior

Etherya's Earth, Book 4
By
Rebecca Hefner

Copyright © 2019

RebeccaHefner.com

For those of us who are a bit broken inside...
Who learned how to build walls and soldier on...
May you one day find your Kenden, whomever he, she or they might be.

Table of Contents
Title Page and Copyright
Dedication
Map of Etherya's Earth
Prologue
Chapter 1
Chapter 2
Chapter 3
Chapter 4
Chapter 5
Chapter 6
Chapter 7
Chapter 8
Chapter 9
Chapter 10
Chapter 11
Chapter 12
Chapter 13
Chapter 14
Chapter 15
Chapter 16
Chapter 17
Chapter 18
Chapter 19
Chapter 20
Chapter 21
Chapter 22
Chapter 23
Chapter 24
Chapter 25
Chapter 26
Chapter 27
Chapter 28
Chapter 29
Chapter 30
Chapter 31
Epilogue
Acknowledgements
About the Author

ETHERYA'S EARTH

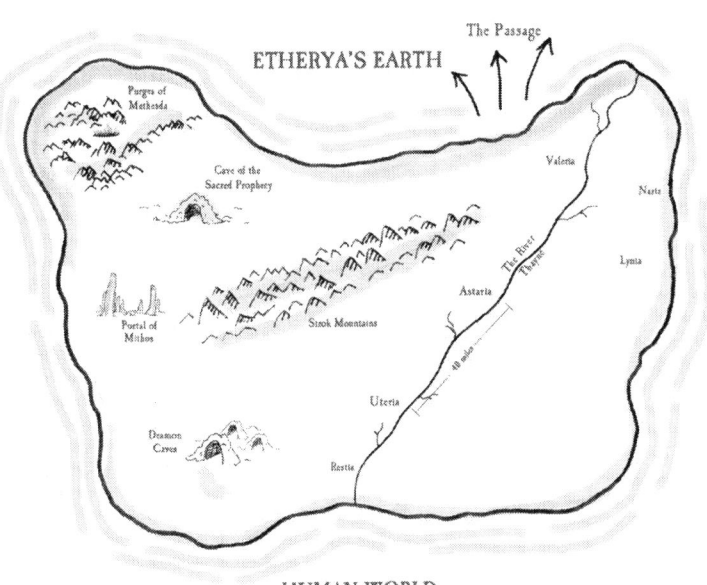

The Passage

Purgea of Methenda

Cave of the Sacred Prophecy

Portal of Mithos

Sizok Mountains

Valetta

Naris

Lynia

Astaria

The River Thorpe

40 mile

Uteria

Deamon Caves

Restia

HUMAN WORLD

Prologue

Several Years After The Awakening...

The goddess Etherya materialized into the dark lair of the cave. In the murky light, she saw the child. Small and pale, the newborn baby slept upon the dirt-covered blanket. Rina had borne her in this lair, where she slept when the Dark Lord wasn't torturing her. Knowing that he was doing that right now, Etherya's broken heart beat in her airy body.

Darkrip would be with them, his father forcing him to watch the savage cruelty inflicted upon his mother. Crimeous had grown so strong. Although she wanted to save her precious children, she could not. But she would do her best to ensure that the Dark Lord would perish one day. Many centuries from now, the babe that slept before her would possess the power to end him.

Etherya sighed as she contemplated the tiny girl. A battle already raged within her. Although she was barely three weeks old, the goddess felt the struggle. She was much more evil than Darkrip and therefore extremely powerful. Crimeous' paramountcy had grown exponentially in the years since Rina had birthed Darkrip, and every extra shred of malignity was embedded in their daughter. Although Etherya could see much, Evie's future was unclear. Many centuries from now, she would be faced with a choice. Terrified, the goddess prayed to the Universe that she would choose righteousness over malevolence.

It had to be her, since her powers were so substantial. Sadly, no one else had the prepotency to kill Crimeous. Of course, Evie wouldn't realize this for many decades. Her early life would be filled with so much pain. It would be agonizing and demoralizing. Hurting for her, Etherya ran her cloudy hand over the baby's dark hair.

"I'm so sorry, my darling girl," she said, her tone filled with sadness. "Please, remember that I love you with all I am inside."

Gently, the goddess placed the sharp tip of the nail of her index finger over the vein pulsing in the sleeping child's neck. Closing her eyes, she extended the nail into the vein. Transferring as much of her energy as she could, she let it bleed through her finger into Evie's body. It would only make her stronger, which was desperately needed to defeat her father. Etherya knew that the Universe would be displeased with her action, since she was forbidden to help the immortals. They were supposed to live and die by their free will. But the prophecy had already been forged, and she'd lost too much to worry about upsetting the balance. The Awakening had shifted her world so severely that she wondered if it would ever piece itself back together.

Lifting her lids, she observed Evie's hair turn from raven black to her own shade of bright red. Understanding that the energy transfer was complete, she withdrew her nail. The tiny wound bled onto the babe's snowy skin but it would heal quickly enough. If only all of the sweet child's future wounds would be so small.

"I've done what I can, little Evie," she said, stroking her soft cheek.

The girl opened her eyes to stare up at Etherya with her stunning olive-green irises. It was as if her precious Valktor was looking into her soul. Inhaling a huge breath, Evie began to wail. Knowing that she must go, Etherya blew one last kiss to the crying baby.

Dematerializing, the goddess transported to the Passage. A beautiful fountain sat within the grounds, water flowing under the gorgeous blue sky. The stone structure was adorned with angels and demons, monsters and sirens, plumes of water shooting from the eerie creatures' mouths to rest in the pool below. Valktor stood by the fountain, watching the liquid circulate in its endless pattern. Floating over to his side, Etherya regarded the once-magnificent Slayer king.

"It is done."

Valktor's emerald eyes darted over her face. "And you feel that she will be the one?"

"It is unclear," Etherya said, gazing down at the translucent water. "But she has the power to kill him. Only time will tell."

"Thank you," Valktor said, his eyes welling with tears. "I'm sorry that it has come to this. It's all my fault."

"No," she said, her voice sounding so faraway. "It is mine. But that is a story I long-ago stopped sharing. Go sit with Markdor and Calla and continue to send your energy to the Earth. Your children are all so important if we are ever going to see peace again. It is imperative that you keep willing it to happen."

"We will. I'm so thankful for their forgiveness. Now that they are in the Passage, they could choose to hate me for eternity. It is a magnificent gift that I don't deserve."

"Markdor and Calla understand that you were trying to save Rina. But yes, it is quite amazing that they were able to forgive your transgressions against them. They love their children as much as you love yours. They understand that every ounce of energy needs to be amalgamated in order to reunite the species."

Valktor nodded. "Yes. I will go to them and spend every second willing it to happen. Miranda is strong, and so are Sathan and Latimus. Although it might be futile, I still have a seed of hope, my goddess."

"As do I." Placing her hazy hands on his cheeks, she pulled him to her, giving him a soft kiss upon his brow. "Now, go."

He vanished, leaving behind the scent of his resolve to do everything in his power to restore the world beneath them to greatness. Trying not to let hopelessness choke her, Etherya contemplated the gurgling water of the fountain. Tears fell to mingle with the clear liquid.

Perhaps she cried for a small eternity; perhaps only for a moment. Once the wetness dried, she lifted her face to the galaxy above and disappeared. Keeping watch over her planet, she waited...

An Excerpt From the Forgotten Fairytale of the Soothsayers...

Once, many moons ago, when the planet was still so new, the beautiful woman sat upon the grass, inhaling the vibrant scent of nearby wildflowers. Eyes closed, her ears perked as she heard the rustling behind her. Turning her head, she saw the man step from the forest.

"Hello," she said, her voice so soft and sweet. "It is so rare that I see another. And what are you called?"

"I am Galredad," he said, his voice as deep as the nearby ocean. "I rarely see others upon this planet as well. It is quite lonely. Perhaps we could become acquainted."

"Perhaps we could." Gesturing to the grass beside her, she said, "Sit down and let's see if we can make conversation."

He sat, crossing his legs as he regarded her. "You are quite beautiful."

The woman gave a shy grin. "And you are quite handsome."

White teeth glowed from his brilliant smile. "We seem to be conversing quite well so far."

"That, we do," she said, lips fully curved as she gazed upon him. "That, we do..."

Chapter 1

Evie threw back her head, laughing at whatever the man was dribbling on about. Although quite handsome and a Vampyre soldier, she was bored to tears. Immortals always seemed to do that to her: endlessly bore her out of her ever-loving mind.

There were only a few who could keep her attention. One whose attention she was trying to procure at this very moment. Surreptitiously searching the large banquet hall, she wondered if he was observing her with the hulking man. Just in case, she slid her palm over the Vampyre's broad chest, eyebrow lifting in a silent invite to ask her to dance later.

The Vampyre smiled, his fangs glowing in the soft banquet lighting. She couldn't remember his name but didn't really care. Names seemed to have meaning to everyone for some damn reason. Didn't they know the futility in that? Why the inhabitants of this awful planet thought that their lives had any significance was beyond her. What a waste of time. It would be easier if everyone realized that their existence was squalid and pointless.

Sipping her drink, she chewed the crunchy ice as her eyes darted around the room. Her brother had gotten married earlier today. The idiot was so in love with the spunky Vampyre princess that she fought not to barf in his face when he was reciting his vows.

Darkrip used to be quite evil, as she'd seen firsthand during her early years in the Deamon caves. Having their father's blood course through his veins ensured his malevolence. But he'd also had such goodness, trying to keep their father from raping and torturing her and her mother, Rina. Although he'd been unsuccessful, she appreciated his pithy efforts. Evie guessed she was happy for him. If he wanted to attach himself to one vagina for the rest of his life, good for him. Wrinkling her nose in distaste, she reminded herself of her vow to never settle down. How positively uninteresting.

Not to mention that she didn't really buy into the whole "kids and family" reverie these immortals seemed to be increasingly employing. Her half-sister Miranda was head-over-heels for the Vampyre king, the warrior Latimus had turned into a lovesick sap over his bonded mate Lila, and now, her brother was in love too. Good grief. They'd all gone mad.

Evie loved adventure. Living in the human world for the last eight centuries had afforded her lots of that. Along with handsome men, great sex, luscious wine and beautiful excursions. Why anyone would want to tie themselves to another person for eternity was beyond her.

Oh, and then there was the little tidbit that any children she spawned would have her father's villainous blood. No, thanks. She had enough shit to deal with, controlling her evil half, already. Bringing another progeny into the world would be extremely foolish.

Narrowing her lids, she regarded Arderin as she danced with her brother atop the wooden dance floor. Lord, he was terrible. Thank god the spirited beauty was leading him. Her abdomen was slightly distended in her gorgeous white gown, causing Evie to shake her head. Darkrip was a fool to procreate with her. But it was his life, so she let him be. Hopefully, the little brat wouldn't be as depraved as their father. Only time would tell.

"Did you scare Draylok away?" a baritone voice asked behind her.

Hating the shiver that ran down her spine, Evie turned to gaze upon the man she'd previously been searching for. "Was that his name? I couldn't remember. I was too busy admiring his other...attributes."

Coming to stand beside her, Kenden arched a russet-colored eyebrow. "He's known to be quite a catch. Not only is he one of our best soldiers but he's single and looking to settle down."

Evie scrunched her features. "Thanks for the warning. I'll make sure to avoid him at all costs."

His velvet laugh surrounded her. "Yes, we wouldn't want you to get emotionally involved with anyone you seduce."

"Oh, Kenden," she said, turning to face him fully. "You think you have me pegged. It's so ridiculously unbecoming. Perhaps that's why you never get laid. I think you need a nice woman to fuck this serious streak out of you. It's quite unattractive."

She was lying through her teeth, of course, as she found the Slayer commander insanely gorgeous. There was something about his mop of chestnut-brown hair, angular features and blazing white teeth between his full lips. And those eyes. They seemed to melt like milk chocolate left on a hot stove. More often than not, she found herself drowning in them.

Determined to keep the upper hand, she licked her lips, slowly and seductively.

"If you want a fuck-buddy, just ask me. I'll come looking for you once I'm done with the Vampyre soldier."

Those striking eyes narrowed. "That's the difference between you and me, Evie. I don't do fuck-buddies. I believe in monogamy and relationships and *feelings*. You use seduction as a weapon. It's off-putting and extremely unattractive to me. So, I guess we're both repulsed by each other."

"I guess so," she snapped, breaking her gaze from his to stare at the dance floor. Sipping her drink, she contemplated his lie. He was fiercely attracted to her—this, she knew to be true. As the daughter of the Dark Lord, she could read images in others' minds. Kenden had so many images of fucking her that he could probably start his own porn site.

She had no idea why he fought his desire to sleep with her, knowing that he wanted it so badly. It seemed futile to her. They obviously would do the deed one day. Two people who possessed so much pulsing energy between them were bound to. She'd learned this over her many centuries of seducing men.

Never had she had to work so hard to get a man in her bed. It infuriated the hell out of her. What a cruel joke the Universe played on her, instilling such intense yearning for a man who was determined to fight his attraction to her so vehemently.

But Evie was nothing if not resilient and she loved a challenge. She would have him in her bed and inside her deepest place one day soon. Getting the upper hand on men had become an obsession of hers. It somehow allowed her to process and move on from all the grief and pain from the rapes and violations in her youth.

The arrogant and handsome Slayer commander had another thing coming if he continued to delude himself. Determination and will were her greatest strengths.

Gathering her wits and giving him her most glorious smile, she said, "Well, now that we've established our revulsion of each other, do you want to dance?"

White teeth gleamed as his full lips curved. Chuckling, he took the drink from her hand and set it on the nearby table. Clutching her hand in his firm grip, he said, "Why not?"

With his muscular frame, he led her to the dance floor.

* * * *

Kenden pulled Evie close, loving how perfectly her lithe body molded into his. Her slender, five-foot, six-inch frame fit to him like an expertly-crafted puzzle piece. Inhaling, he smelled the fruity scent of her flame-red hair. Feeling himself grow hard in his suit pants, he spun her away from him. Pulling her back in, she gave him a blazing smile. Goddamnit, she was absolutely fucking gorgeous.

"How did you become such a good dancer?" Olive-green eyes sparkled with mischief and desire as she looked up at him.

He shrugged. "I was an aristocrat before I was a soldier. We used to have lavish parties before your mother was taken. Dancing was required learning for me."

"Hmmm..." she said, arching a perfectly-plucked brow. "Makes me wonder if your moves are as good *off* the dance floor."

Chuckling, he shook his head. "Guess you'll never know, since we've decided we repulse each other."

Those magnificent almond-shaped eyes narrowed. "We'll see."

Holding her close, he swayed with her to the human pop song. After a moment, he said, "I'm not interested, Evie. I need to be clear about that."

The heat of anger flashed through her thin frame. "The images in your mind would suggest otherwise."

"I have a lot of images in my mind. Very few of which I act upon."

"How absolutely boring," she said, perplexion in her gaze. "Don't you enjoy getting laid?"

His irises darted back and forth between hers. "I'm ready to settle down. I want a wife that I can build a home with and lots of children. You've been very clear that you don't want any of that. That you'll return to the human world after you fully commit to fighting your father and hopefully fulfill the prophecy. We don't want the same things, and I'm not willing to waste my time."

"Good god," she said, rolling her eyes. "All of you are completely insane. Whatever happened to having a good fuck and moving on? I don't know what the hell is in the water over here, but it's utterly annoying."

Kenden couldn't stop the smile that spread across his face. "Sorry to disappoint. I'm a serial monogamist. I only sleep with women that I'm in a serious relationship with."

Disbelief marred her expression. "What about when you were young? Surely, then—?"

"I've slept with nine women in my life, Evie. That's it. I'm not nearly as experienced as you. All of them were like-minded women whom I dated for no less than a decade. Some of them for several decades. As the commander, I was never able to settle down, so they eventually married and started families, but I assure you that once we defeat your father, I'm ready. The next woman I sleep with will be my wife."

Her scarlet eyebrow arched, making her look so sexy. "Is that a challenge?"

"It's just a fact. I'm not a bullshitter, Evie. You know that by now. I don't want there to be any doubt as to where I stand."

"Oh, fine," she said, scrunching her features. The faint freckles across her nose moved under the pale light. He'd always thought them so appealing. "Go on and be a damn monk for all I care." The song ended, and she stepped back. "I'm going to find the Vampyre and get laid. Some of us actually like sex." Lifting her chin, she pivoted and stalked away from him.

Kenden couldn't stop his chuckle. Man, she was something else. He wondered if he'd ever been as attracted to a woman as he was to Evie. Contemplating, he realized that was unlikely. But attraction didn't mean love or caring—this, he knew to be true. Evie was a master of seduction and used sex to manipulate men for power and control. Vowing to never succumb to her charms, he crossed the dance floor to speak to his cousin.

"Hey," he said, approaching Miranda where she stood against the wall of the ballroom. "I think I'm heading out. I want to get back to Uteria since I have to train the troops early in the morning."

Miranda regarded him, mischief swimming in her olive-green irises. "Looked like you were having fun dancing with Evie."

Kenden rolled his eyes. "Enough with the matchmaking. It's not happening. I told you that." Leaning down, he gave her a peck on the cheek. "See you in a few days."

"Hey," she said, grabbing his wrist as he began to walk away. "I love you. I realized recently that I don't say that to you as much anymore, and I need you to know. You were there for me before I had Sathan or Tordor or anyone. You'll always be such an important person in my life, Ken. I just need you to know that."

Love for his amazing cousin coursed through his muscular frame. They'd only had each other for so long. Thrilled for the wonderful life she'd built, he pulled her into his embrace.

"I love you too," he said, kissing the top of her silky hair. "You're my person, Miranda. You always will be, even though you leave me all the time to hang at this pretentious Vampyre compound."

Clutching her arms around his waist, she chuckled at his teasing. "You're my person too. But one day soon, you're going to find a new person. A woman who can challenge you and love you as much as Sathan loves me. And I'm betting with everything I have that it might just be Evie."

Laughing, he pulled back and regarded her. "If this queen thing doesn't work out, I think you need to open a courting service. You're relentless."

"Yep," she said, biting her bottom lip as her emerald irises swam with gaiety. "I'm pretty awesome at it. Just ask Latimus and Lila."

"You're awesome at anything you set your mind to. We all know that." Giving her one last soft kiss on the forehead, he squeezed her hand. "See ya later."

Heart full, Kenden walked through the darkened hallway of the castle, through the barracks warehouse and out to the train platform. Walking down the concrete stairs, he boarded the train. During the thirty-minute ride, he reflected on the night. The ceremony had been beautiful, and he was very happy for Arderin and Darkrip.

Once at Uteria, he climbed in the four-wheeler that he'd parked there earlier in the day. Hopping in, he reveled in the wind whipping his hair as he drove through the warm night under the bright moonlight. Pulling up to his four-bedroom home, he cut the vehicle's engine and trodded up the porch steps. Locking the large front door behind him, he headed upstairs to his bedroom.

He'd built the home recently, anticipating that he would settle down soon, once the army of immortals defeated Crimeous. Wanting lots of kids, he'd built four bedrooms, knowing he could expand down the road if needed. Turning on the bedside lamp, he removed his suit and set about brushing his teeth.

Naked, he slid under the soft covers, pulling them up to cover his chest. Staring at the ceiling, he couldn't stop the image of Evie's face from blazing across his mind. His feelings for her were rather complicated, and it frustrated him that she could read his inner musings. Consumed with a deep well of compassion for her, he understood that she'd been raped and tortured by her father as a child. No matter how complex his opinion of her, he firmly believed that no child should ever have to suffer such trauma.

The fact that she'd returned to the immortal world gave him hope. She insisted that she would enlist in battle with the immortal army if she could identify something she deemed worthy of her effort. Kenden admired her gumption and knew that, if they could convince her to fight, she would be a powerful ally indeed.

If they lived in another world, where they wanted the same things and had visions of similar futures, he would be honored to court her. She had Rina's blood in spades although she always tried to deny it. Evie had so many of the qualities that he admired in a woman: intelligence, humor, confidence, frankness and, of course, her undeniable beauty. For one moment, he let himself imagine the life they could build together. It would be filled with passion and desire, frustration and compromise.

She wasn't an easy person, but that suited Kenden just fine. He loved nothing more than a challenge and building a life with the fiery redhead would certainly present one. But he also wanted children, which she professed to never consider. It was too bad, really, since he wanted it all: the messy meals, playing with the tots in the meadow outside his home, the school productions and talent shows. Kenden had always craved those things and was smart enough to realize that he would never have them with Evie. Shelving his attraction to her, he forced himself to push her from his thoughts.

Reaching over, he clicked off the light. There, in the darkness, he lay in the home he'd built for his future family, knowing that one day it would come to fruition.

Closing his eyes, he smiled in contentment.

As he drifted off to sleep, he could've sworn that he was enveloped in the fragrant scent of Evie's shampoo. Giving in to the notion of holding her, he fell into his dreams.

"So," the woman said in her lilting voice, "How did you come to be on this planet? I was so sure I knew of all the creatures the Universe instilled here."

The man absently picked at the flowers beside him with his long, tapered fingers. "I was born in the Elven world, not too far distant when one walks through the ether."

"How lovely," she said, giving him a wistful smile. "Is it a beautiful place?"

"More beautiful than anything I've ever seen," he said, his expression becoming one of longing.

"Oh, please, do tell me about it. I love hearing of far-off lands."

"Well," he said, grinning, "where do I begin? There are so many stories to tell…"

Chapter 2

When the faint light of dawn slid through the curtains of her cabin, Evie awoke. Stretching, she yawned and ran her legs over the soft sheets. Recalling the previous evening, she scrunched her face. She'd been set to bone the Vampyre and wake up in his bed. That is, until she'd danced with Kenden, alleviating the desire to have any man's hands on her but his. Bastard.

Sighing, she lifted from the bed to get ready for the day. Once dressed in her expensive, tailored, forest-green khakis with silky drawstrings at the ankles, a white V-neck sweater and Valentino Garavani sandals, she headed to the main castle to find Miranda.

Evie absolutely loved luxurious and high-priced clothing. Not only was it a powerful tool in seducing men, but she wore it like a suit of armor. Men were visual creatures, easily led by a confident and well-dressed woman. They were quite content to focus on her beauty and glamour. Her attire was a potent armament that ensured men wouldn't think to look deeper inside, at the girl who had been tortured and defiled so many centuries ago. No, that girl was long-dead, and she'd be damned if anyone dredged her up. Ever.

She decided to walk to the castle instead of dematerializing. It was a warm morning with a soft breeze, as most were on Etherya's Earth. The immortal world exhibited a temperate climate with few rainy days. While some might thrive in that environment, Evie sometimes missed the unpredictability of the weather in the human world.

Feeling her lips curve, she reminisced about the large beads of rain that would fall during the powerful afternoon thunderstorms under the darkened clouds in Western North Carolina. The drops always reminded her of tears being cast down to Earth by an angry god screaming in the sky, with claps of thunder and bolts of lightning.

She also missed the snow. There was a wholesome purity in the white powder that reminded her that things could be clean and pristine. A welcome acknowledgement that the dark part inside her detested but still somehow craved. Skiing in the mountains of Japan and Colorado had been one of her favorite pastimes.

And, oh, how she had loved the hot, humid nights along the Amalfi Coast of Italy. The breeze of the immortal world always swept away what little humidity existed.

Although many detested the sticky air, Evie always loved the sheen of sweat that formed on her skin as she sat under the stars in the dense blanket of heat.

They all called to her, these comforts of the place she'd built her life in for so many centuries. She wouldn't go so far as to call the human world "home," for she'd never really had one of those, but it certainly was the closest she'd ever come to one. Longing for the familiar enveloped her as she trudged along the open meadow.

As her sandals crunched the grass, she noticed Kenden's pretty house off in the distance. It was only about a five-minute walk from her cabin, and she found herself wondering if he was training the troops. He'd been extremely focused on preparing them to fight her father, and she admired his tenacity. Score another one for Mr. Perfect.

With an inward eye-roll, she continued to the castle near Uteria's town square. Nodding hello to Sadie as she passed her in the foyer, Evie headed to her sister's royal office chamber. The door was slightly ajar, and Evie could see her sitting in the high, leather-backed chair behind the mahogany desk, feeding Tordor from her breast.

"You're here early," Evie said, pushing the door open and approaching the desk.

"Yup," Miranda said, gesturing for Evie to sit in one of the chairs across from her. "Sathan is training with Latimus and the troops at Astaria today, so I figured I'd come home early and get started on some paperwork. My favorite."

Evie chuckled, knowing Miranda detested the administrative portion of the queen's duties. "So, Sathan will be fighting with the soldiers?"

Miranda nodded, her expression filled with vague worry and frustration. "I've tried to talk him out of it, but he's determined. And although everyone says I'm stubborn as hell, my caveman husband is about as pliant as a rock when he's made up his mind."

Studying her, Evie shook her foot atop her crossed legs. It was an absent habit that she employed when she was contemplating. "Will you be fighting as well?"

Exhaling a breath, she shook her head. "Sathan and I discussed it and we need to make sure one of us holds down the fort. I wish I could though. I want to beat the shit out of that maniac. If not for what he did to Lila, then for what he did to our first child." Gently, she feathered her fingers over Tordor's soft black hair. "Isn't that right, little man? We're gonna kick that bastard's ass for hurting our family."

Something akin to guilt speared through Evie and she brushed it away. "I was as responsible as my father. You should hate me as well."

Inhaling a breath, Miranda's green eyes bore into her. Good god. It was if her mother was staring her down. "As we've discussed, although your actions spurred the battle earlier than we anticipated, I blame your father for our baby's death."

Evie gazed at her, struggling to tamp down the self-loathing that always reared its head when she thought of the child who had perished. "I don't deserve your forgiveness."

Her sister's expression softened a bit, filled with the compassion that she possessed so much of, and that Evie rarely merited.

"You know, you're going to have to try harder to convince me you're a bad person, Evie," Miranda said. "You claim to be so evil but you're one of the most candid and straightforward people I've ever met. Not really qualities that wicked people possess."

Evie arched a brow. "Then, I'll make a more fervent attempt. Because I'm a conniving bitch."

Throwing back her head, Miranda laughed. One of the loud, throaty laughs she was known for. "We'll see. Regardless, I know you would've acted differently if you'd known I was pregnant."

Tordor chose that moment to detach from his mother's breast and spit up all over her chest.

"Well, shit," Miranda said, wiping the gunk off with the towel that sat draped across her shoulder. "Just when I think having kids is awesome, the bugger pukes all over me." Pulling up her shirt to cover her breast, she began to burp her son. Hitting one of the buttons on the phone that sat on her desk, she said, "Dahlia? I'm ready for you to come get Tordor."

"Sure thing," the nanny's voice chimed over the intercom.

The sweet girl came into the room and swooped up the child, cooing to him as she departed.

"She's good with him," Evie said of the straw-blond caretaker. "But very young."

"Yes," Miranda said, standing to stretch. "Aron knows her family and trusts her immensely. She's twenty and hasn't gone through her change yet."

"When did you go through your change?" Evie asked, annoyed that she was curious. She was coming to like her sister very much. It made it hard to keep the distance that she so often imposed on people.

"When I was twenty-six. You?"

"Twenty-eight," Evie said. "At least, I think so. The years all ran together in the caves."

Sympathy permeated her sister's expression, causing Evie to straighten her spine. She didn't have time for emotion. How absolutely illogical.

"I've come to inform you that I've discerned something I want badly enough to fight with you all. I would like to meet with you, Sathan and Kenden to discuss it."

"Okay," Miranda said with a nod. Lowering into the chair, she rested her forearms on the desk. "If it's within our power, we'll do it. We need you, Evie."

"I know," she said, hating how her heart quickened at the words. "It's a strange feeling, since no one really ever has."

"I'm so sorry," she said, slowly shaking her head. "My father was cold to me but he still loved me and did the best he could. You deserved better. I promise, now that I've found you, we're family for life. I'm never letting you believe you don't deserve to be loved, sis."

"Sweet but unwarranted. Nevertheless, let's see how you feel after I name my price. I have a suspicion you might think otherwise, but who knows?"

Miranda grinned. "We'll see. On another note, how are your sessions going with Darkrip?"

"Good," Evie said with a tilt of her head. "He's picking up on the human dark magic very quickly. Although I haven't committed to fighting my father yet, I don't mind helping Darkrip learn. Wielding black magic is quite enjoyable and it's nice to have a reason to use it again."

"Thank you," she said, her gaze full of determination. "I appreciate you dedicating the time to train our brother. I've become close with him and I hope that you and I can do the same. I want to get to know you, Evie."

How could one possess such genuineness? Evie had no idea. Her sister was a damn saint. Rina must've passed all those genes on to her and Darkrip, leaving none behind for Evie's wasted entrance into this pissant excuse for a world.

"We all want a lot of things, but they rarely happen." Standing, Evie narrowed her eyes. "When can I expect to meet with the three of you?"

"Tomorrow at lunch should be good, here in my office. If that doesn't work, I'll text you, but I think it should be fine for Ken and Sathan. Thanks for coming to a decision. We're excited that you're part of our team."

With a caustic glare, Evie pivoted. "For now," she said, strolling from the room and closing the door behind her, the sound a soft, ominous click.

* * * *

Aron smiled and lowered the hand that had been lifted in a wave goodbye to the nice Vampyre couple. The newly married pair—or *bonded*, he should say, since that was what Vampyres called it—were lovely. Content, he began to put away the folding chairs.

Today, he'd held an orientation for the fifty Vampyres that were moving to Uteria next week. As Miranda and Sathan continued to unite the species, it was imperative that members of both tribes inhabited all six of the immortal compounds.

Aron had volunteered to orient the new Uterians during the last combined council meeting. Descended from one of the oldest bloodlines of Slayer aristocrats, his ancestors had lived long before the Awakening. He considered it his duty to bring peace to Etherya's children and was honored to help in some small way.

If he was honest, it also allowed him to support Miranda. Their queen was a magnificent ruler. Strong, steadfast and immensely intelligent.

Oh, and there was one more thing. Aron was completely, mindlessly in love with her.

Sighing, he continued to fold and stack the chairs. The meeting had been held in the ballroom of Uteria's main castle, and he took his time restocking the chairs in the wide closet near the entrance. Once finished, he headed out of the compound's large mahogany doors into the mid-afternoon sunlight.

The sounds of Uteria's main square whizzed by him as he walked. Dogs barked, children squealed as they played, birds cawed as they flew above. The place he'd always called home was buzzing with its always-present energy, causing his lips to curve into a grin as he walked.

Finally, he arrived at the gallery and entered. Moira was standing to the left, showing a painting that sat affixed to the wall to one of their regular patrons. Knowing Moira, the man wouldn't leave without the canvas boxed and paid for. She was a phenomenal salesperson, and Aron was thrilled that she seemed to thrive at the gallery.

Heading to stand behind the sales counter, he absently leafed through the mail as he heard her answering questions in the otherwise quiet gallery. Although she had no knowledge of fine art before her stint at the store, she'd learned quickly. Impressed by her ability to retain such dense and intricate information, he listened.

"Absolutely, sir," she said confidently. "It reminds me of a Dali as well. I know he's your favorite surrealist. Unfortunately, I can only offer you a ten-percent discount, good through close of business today. We have an event this weekend, and I'm sure it will sell at full price once our patrons see how exquisite it is."

The man's features drew together. "I'll only purchase today for a twenty-percent discount, Moira. We discussed this."

"That was before we received an additional thirty RSVP's for this weekend's engagement. I never consented to twenty-percent, although I do appreciate the effort, sir."

"Stop calling me 'sir,'" he said, giving her a light-hearted glare. "You make me feel like a washed-up old snob." Eyes narrowed, teeming with deliberation, he studied her. "Ten percent and dinner with me at Maltese's," he said, referencing the fancy Italian restaurant that adorned Uteria's town square.

Out of the corner of his eye, Aron saw Moira's sly grin. It wasn't the first time a customer had tried to negotiate a date with her. To his knowledge, she'd never accepted.

"I'm flattered, Tobias," she said, "but it's ten-percent flat today. Or I'll sell it on Saturday so fast you won't remember it was here."

Tobias shook his head, his tawny brown hair staying perfectly in place, coiffed like a proper aristocrat. "Fine. But can you at least personally deliver it? I'd love your opinion as to where to hang it at my home."

"Sadly, no. It's against our insurance policy for me to touch a painting once it's left the store. If it sustains damage, I can't prove that I didn't cause it. It's too much of a risk. Let me get this boxed up for you. Aron can ring you up," she said, jerking her head toward the front counter. "Excuse me."

Lifting her thin arms, she proceeded to grasp the piece and abscond with it to the back warehouse.

"Your girl is wily, Aron," Tobias said, approaching him at the counter. "Sometimes, I think you just hired her to swindle me out of my money."

Aron breathed a laugh. "That, she is, although she's anything but my girl. In my mind, she'll always belong to Diabolos. May the goddess have peace on his soul."

Tobias arched a chestnut brow. "Still loyal to Etherya after all these centuries? I thought you'd long given up on that."

"I'm loyal to many things that I think are just and true. That's why it was so easy for me to support Miranda becoming queen. The blood of Valktor runs strong through her."

"That, it does," Tobias agreed.

Aron completed the transaction with his old friend, and they chatted as Moira boxed the painting in the back room. Once finished, she appeared, a broad smile dominating her pretty face.

"You're all set, sir," she said. Her tone dared him to scold her for using the formal address. "I look forward to seeing you again soon."

"As do I, my dear," he said with a nod. Clutching the artwork, he retreated from the store.

Aron couldn't stop his chuckle as Moira's azure eyes swam with elation. "Son of a bitch, that felt *amazing*." Stretching out her arms, she twirled around, head tilted back, graceful as a ballerina. Coming to a stop, she trained her gaze on him. "He still thought he could get twenty percent out of me. Some people never learn."

"You're ruthless, Moira," Aron said, winking at her. "Hiring you was the best thing Preston and I ever did."

Red splotches appeared on her cheeks, showing her embarrassment at his compliment. Blond hair fell in a wave from behind her neck and shoulders as she contemplated him. "You know, Preston didn't want to hire me at all. He thought a laborer's daughter would be too stupid to understand fine art. I only have this position because of you. I'm so thankful you stood up for me."

"Of course, I stood up for you, angel," he said, employing the nickname he'd called her since childhood. "You're the wife of my best friend. It's my duty to protect you and look out for you. It's an honor that I take very seriously."

Ocean-blue irises darted between his own as she regarded him in silence.

"What?" he asked.

"Nothing," she said, dismissively waving her hand. "It's just...Diabolos has been in the Passage for seven centuries. I know it's hard for you to acknowledge that sometimes, since you two were so close, but he's gone, Aron. I'm not his wife anymore. I'm not anyone's wife."

"I know," he said, the ache of his friend's passing gnawing his gut as it usually did. "I just miss him. He was a good man. I want to do right by him and by you."

Those huge doe eyes brimmed with emotions he couldn't decipher. Chalking it up to her grief over losing Diabolos, he tried to lighten the moment. "That was a good one about the insurance policy. Did you make that up on the fly?"

"You bet your ass I did," she said, lifting a brow. "Tobias is sweet, but I'm not in the market for a husband. I find that I like my independence just fine."

"That's good to hear. But one day, you'll want to have children, no?"

Laying her pale hand on the counter, she looked to the ceiling. "I'm not sure. Maybe. It's not something I've spent a lot of time thinking about."

"Well, if and when you do decide to marry again, he'll be a lucky man. You're one in a million, Moira."

"Thanks," she said, her tone soft and sweet. "You've always been so kind and supportive of me. All those centuries ago, when Diabolos proposed to me and his parents threatened to disown him, you came to my defense. They only reconsidered because of you."

Aron thought back to those days, so long ago. Moira was the daughter of his family's housekeeper, Celia. Widowed when her soldier husband was killed in the War of the Species, Celia and Moira had moved into Aron's family's large estate. Being one of the oldest aristocratic dynasties, Moira used to tease him that his house was bigger than Uteria's castle. She hadn't been far off. The home was massive.

Diabolos and his wealthy family were Aron's neighbors. Less than a year apart in age, the three of them used to play as children in the grassy meadows that surrounded their homes. His friend would always watch Moira with an intense gleam in his eye and profess his desire to own her one day. Aron had always thought that quite strange, as one couldn't own another person, but he figured that his friend just meant to marry Moira when they grew into adulthood.

As she evolved into womanhood, Moira matured into her beauty. Aron spent many wistful nights as a young man imagining his hands upon her soft, pale skin. But he was a polite man, perhaps too much so, and Diabolos had always been so ardent in his pursuit of her. As soon as she went through her immortal change in her mid-twenties, he'd asked for her hand in marriage.

Aron could still remember the burn, deep inside his chest, when he'd learned of their engagement. Knowing that he'd never caress her silky skin, he'd wished them well, sincere in his desire for their happiness. He'd become quite an expert in that over the centuries—wishing women he pined for bliss with other men. It was rather unfulfilling. Perhaps, for once in his life, he could actually fall for a woman who wasn't in love with someone else. It would be a major improvement on the sad state of his romantic existence thus far. Giving himself a mental shake, he disengaged from the dreary thoughts.

"I wanted you to be happy, Moira," he said, smiling down at her. She was at least six inches shorter than his six-foot frame. "I'll always fight to make that happen. Diabolos was distraught when you disappeared. We had no idea that you thought he was abducted and murdered, nor that you fled to Restia to hide from the war. He wanted to find you so badly."

"I'll bet he did," she murmured, her nostrils flaring. "Well, I'm safe now. And truly happy for the first time in centuries. I'm so glad we reconnected."

"Me too. You're a great plus-one for all these weddings we seem to have lately. I had no idea you were such a fantastic dancer."

White teeth toyed with her bottom lip. Aron found the act quite charming. "I used to hide and watch you and Diabolos take your dance lessons. Then, I'd practice in my room at night. Guess it paid off."

"Sneaky little thing, weren't you?" he asked.

"You don't know the half of it." Running her hand through her hair, she surveyed the room. "I think Tobias was the last customer we're going to have today. Want me to close up?"

"Sure," Aron said, heading to the cash register to total it for the day. "Why don't you square everything away, and I'll walk you home?"

"You don't have to do that. My apartment's on the other side of town from your castle."

"Stop teasing me, wench," he said, winking at her again. He hoped the nickname or the gesture didn't piss her off. They had an easy rapport, and he felt so comfortable around her. "You know I'd lose my gentleman card if I didn't walk you home. Let me just tally this up."

"Okay," she said, placing her hands in the pockets of her black slacks. "Give me a few minutes to clean up in the back."

His gaze cemented to her backside as she sauntered to the warehouse, the sway of her hips mesmerizing. Mentally scolding himself, he remembered that she was his dead best friend's wife. That made her extremely off-limits. Aron was a stickler for morality and decorum and would never disrespect his friend's memory by making a pass at his wife. Shaking the image of her slim waist and curvy body from his mind, he set about balancing the day's transactions.

A few minutes later, they locked up and began an unhurried walk down the main street toward Moira's one-bedroom apartment. Aron knew the landlord and had helped her secure the lease. The man had been hesitant to rent to her, knowing that she had no assets, so Aron had secretly given him a generous security deposit on Moira's behalf. Knowing how proud she was, he didn't want her to see it as charity.

When they were children, she would always stare wistfully at the sky and tell him of her intentions to make a better life than her mother had. She was embarrassed to be the child of a servant and was determined to rise above her station. Aron had always assured her that she was his equal and capable of doing anything she set her mind to. Being born a servant didn't make one less than, just as being an aristocrat didn't make one extraordinary. He firmly believed that one must strive to the highest morals and ethics at all times. In his opinion, that was what dictated one's worth. Moira had those qualities in spades. He was intensely proud of how she'd rebuilt her life after returning to Uteria.

Arriving at the front door of her building, she turned to face him. The sun had fallen behind the far-off mountains, and her face glowed in the dim light of dusk. Tilting her head back, she licked her pink lips. Aron felt himself grow thick and hard in his expensive tailored trousers.

"Good night, angel," he said.

"Good night," she said, her lips glistening with the saliva that her tongue had lathered there. "Thanks for walking me home."

"You're welcome." Placing a brotherly kiss on the soft skin of her forehead, he rotated and walked toward the large mansion he solely inhabited. His parents had passed centuries ago, leaving the large compound to him, the solitary heir. Willing his body to relax, he inhaled deep breaths filled with the scents of impending nightfall.

And so he told her, the magnificent woman beside him, about the lush world of the Elves. Tall trees, with leaves of evergreen at the crest, covered expansive forests. Below the hulking redwoods and oaks, there were rolling hills dotted with flowers of every color and size.

The Elves were a simple people, building homes with nary a space between them so they could become close with their neighbors. Many raised livestock behind their small homes, cultivating the pigs and cows to be so fattened that the meat was never short of succulent.

"I can still taste the meat from my neighbor's bounty," Galredad said, closing his eyes. "I have never had food like it in centuries."

"So, you must've been here a long time."

"Yes," he said, his gaze turning sad and lowering to the ground. "I left my world behind when it was destroyed..."

Chapter 3

Kenden entered his cousin's office chamber the next day starving for lunch. A spread of sandwiches and wraps sat on the long conference table, and he thanked the gods. Grabbing a sandwich, he began adorning it with mustard and mayonnaise.

"Hey," Miranda said, entering. "Aren't you going to wait for us?"

Kenden smiled at her as Sathan entered behind her. "Sorry. I'm famished. I've been training the troops since seven a.m. Do you mind?" he asked, lifting the food in anticipation.

"It's fine," she said, coming to look over the spread. "Do you want anything?" she asked her husband.

"No food for me," Sathan said. "I've never really developed a taste for it like Arderin has. Although, since she's pregnant with a Slayer-Deamon, that might be increasing her appetite."

"How's she feeling?" Kenden asked.

"Good," Sathan said, sitting at the large table. "Her morning sickness has abated quite a bit, and she seems happy now that she's bonded with Darkrip."

"That's great," Kenden said, swallowing the large bite. "I'm really happy for them."

"Me too," Miranda said, sitting at the head of the table. "I love that Darkrip fell for my husband's sister. It's a family affair all around."

Kenden chuckled. "Yep, it's awesome." Finishing the sandwich, he deposited the paper plate and napkin in the trash. Coming to sit at Miranda's left, he asked, "Have you heard from Evie? She said noon, right?"

Miranda nodded. "She should be here soon. I wonder what her price will be for fighting with us. She says I might not like it."

"No use in speculating," Kenden said. "Evie plays it close to the vest. Guess we'll find out soon enough."

No sooner did the words leave his mouth than she breezed into the room.

"Well, hello," she said, the ever-present mischievous grin on her full lips. "I see everyone's here."

"Hey, Evie," Miranda said, gesturing to the chair beside Sathan. "Have a seat."

"Thanks, but I'll stand." Sauntering to the chair at the other end of the long table, she regarded them. With lean fingers, she clutched the top of the leather chair in front of her.

"I realize you all are busy, so I'll cut to the chase. I've finally decided on something I want badly enough to fight with you. If the request is granted and fulfilled, I will be ready to train for our cause immediately afterward. If not, I'll return to the human world. Those are my terms. Understood?"

"Yes," Miranda said. "What is it? We'll do everything we can to accommodate."

The corners of Evie's lips curved, her green eyes simmering. Strolling to the window, she fingered the thin white curtains and looked out over the meadow.

"There have been very few things I haven't been able to secure in the past eight centuries. I'm an extremely resilient and confident person and can usually manipulate those around me with ease." Turning, she regarded them.

"However, there is something that I haven't been able to procure, and I'm tired of wasting time with futile attempts. Therefore, I find myself forced to take action."

Approaching Kenden, she stood beside him, her irises searching his. "I want the Slayer commander in my bed. Three nights together, and I will consider the demand satisfied. That is my stipulation."

Kenden felt his eyebrows draw together as he gaped up at her. "Excuse me but what?"

"You heard me," she said, scowling down at him.

Surprise coursed through Kenden, compounded with flashes of anger. "You want to sleep with me? *That's* your demand?"

"Don't look so shocked," she said, waving a dismissive hand. "It's obvious we both want what I'm asking for. You're too much of a prude and a saint to act on it, so I'm forcing your hand. Three nights in your bed, and we're done. It's nothing."

Exasperated, Kenden looked at Miranda. "Am I taking crazy pills here?"

"Wow, Evie," Miranda said, her olive-green eyes wide. Kenden found himself pissed that they were also filled with amusement. "That's a very interesting request. I don't...um...well, Ken? What do you think?"

"What do I think?" he asked, incensed. Standing, he stared down at Evie. "Are you fucking insane?"

"Good grief," Evie said, rolling her eyes. "It's not as if you're a quivering virgin. We're both consenting adults here. It might be nice for you to actually get boned for once in your life."

Fury, strong and true, filled every fiber of his core. "You've got a lot of nerve, Evie. And let me tell you something about consent. It requires two people."

"Don't tell me about consent, you arrogant prick," she said through clenched teeth. "I know more about that word that you'll ever begin to fathom." Placing her hands in her pockets, she slowly began pacing around the table as she talked. "To me, this request is simple. Kenden and I both want what I'm proposing, but he's determined not to act on it. I'm simply expediting something that, in my opinion, is bound to happen."

Lifting her arms, she gently ran her hands over the smooth fabric of the leather chair that sat at the opposite end of the table from Miranda. "I imagine you all think I should be embarrassed, asking for something that you consider salacious. But I assure you," she said, her tone becoming pensive, "I lost the ability to feel embarrassment centuries ago. Perhaps the first time my father raped me. Perhaps the first time multiple Deamon soldiers held me down and did the same. Who knows?" she asked.

Gazing at the floor, she lifted her hands to rub her upper arms. Kenden thought the gesture so tragic, as if she was attempting to soothe herself from the transgressions she spoke of. Through his anger, he felt a wave of empathy. Although she was infuriating half the time, no one deserved to be violated in the way she had.

"There has to be another way, Evie," he said, ensuring his tone was calm and understanding. "This request is about control. I won't let you have it, and you want to take it from me. Let's think of something else you want. I'll do everything I can to make it happen."

Those almond-shaped eyes narrowed, her irises shooting daggers at him. "I've made my decision. It's futile to argue with me. I'll give you a week to decide. After that, I'm gone."

"This is ridiculous," he said, shaking his head. "There has to be something else—"

"No," she snapped. "I won't let you make me second-guess myself." Walking around the table, she came to stand in front of the office door. "One week. I would suggest you contemplate quickly. I find myself missing the human world." Arching her eyebrow, she made eye contact with each of them. Giving a nod, she opened the door and strolled through, closing it behind her.

Miranda blew out a breath, the air fanning the hair above her forehead. "Holy shit," she said, stunned.

"This is absurd," Kenden said, running a hand through the brown hair at his temple. "Is she for real?"

"It would seem so," Sathan said, eyeing him, his expression weary.

"Who knew you were so irresistible, Ken?" Miranda asked, mirth swimming in her eyes.

"You do *not* get to make a joke of this," he said, pointing at her. "This is not funny!"

Unable to control her laughter, she covered her mouth with her hands, shoulders quaking.

"Goddamnit, Miranda!" Kenden said, exasperated.

"Okay, okay," Sathan said, training a scolding glare on his wife. "I know it seems funny, but Ken is obviously upset." Addressing Kenden, he asked, "What can we do to help while you consider her demand?"

"I can lend you some erotic novels from my bookshelf so that you can study up," Miranda said, doubling over with laughter in her chair as she snorted.

Kenden scowled and regarded Sathan. "She does know that I'm not laughing, right?" he muttered to the Vampyre king.

"Oh, don't be such a stick in the mud," Miranda said, wiping tears from her eyes. "It's obvious you want to bone her. Just do it already. If that's all she needs to fight with us, it seems like a small ask to me."

"Well, it's not you who has to fulfill her request. This is absolutely ridiculous. I don't have time for this crap." Stalking around the table, he looked down at his cousin. "Don't tell anyone about this, you hear me?"

"Yes," Miranda said, struggling to contain her giggles, mock innocence all over her flawless face. "Although it might be hard, since you're so...*alluring*." Laughter burst from her throat as she doubled over again.

"She's exasperating when she's caught in one of these giggle-fests," Sathan said, standing to address Kenden. "Believe me, I know. I usually have to mentally restrain myself from strangling her."

"Hey!" Miranda said through her snickers.

"Let me know what you need, Ken," Sathan said, his demeanor much more serious than his wife's. "If this is something you won't contemplate, we need to know right away so we can strategize on how to tell Evie."

Sighing, Kenden rubbed his forehead with his fingers. "Let me just think for a bit. She dropped a damn bomb on me. God, she's infuriating."

Sathan lifted an eyebrow. "That, she is. Take some time but let me know what I can do. We need to move this along."

Kenden nodded. "I'm going to head back and finish up the afternoon training session. I'll be in touch." Sparing one last glare at Miranda, he stalked from the room.

As he headed to the training field, fury and indignation threatened to choke him. Who in the hell did Evie think she was, demanding something like that of him? Sex was a tool for her, used to manipulate men to her will. And she'd found a way to use it against him, even though he'd sworn she never would. If he wasn't so damn pissed, he'd actually be impressed. She'd gotten one over on him.

Kenden had always prided himself on his ability to strategize and see every angle of a situation. The fact that she'd been able to spring a surprise demand of this magnitude vexed him. He'd underestimated her. Vowing it would never happen again, he brainstormed his next move as he plodded under the afternoon sun.

* * * *

Evie stalked from the royal office chamber, blood coursing through her supple frame. Nerves threatened to choke her, but she held firm. Confident that she hadn't relayed any of the insecurity she was inwardly experiencing, she headed down the stairs to Sadie's infirmary.

The Slayer physician was applying some sort of serum to her forearm. As her thin fingers massaged her scarred skin, Evie realized it must be some of the burn-healing salve that Arderin and Nolan had created for her.

"Hello, Sadie," she said softly, not wanting to startle her.

"Oh," she said, lifting her head. "I didn't see you, Evie. Can I help you with something?"

"I need you to do a physical on me," Evie said, "but I can come back."

"It's fine," Sadie said, screwing the top back on the tube of salve and sitting it on the counter. "Have a seat on the table."

Evie arranged herself on the bed, the white paper crunching underneath her.

"So, why do you need a physical?" Sadie asked.

"I'm anticipating taking a new lover. Although I've always used protection in the past, I don't wish to do so with him. So, I want you to check me out, make sure I'm healthy and complete a full STD-screening panel. I also had an IUD implanted a year ago and it should be good for another four years, but I'd like you to confirm that."

"Okay," Sadie said, her eyes widening a bit. "It's refreshing to speak to someone so candid. I'll be happy to help. Let me just start a chart for you."

Evie regarded her as she pulled out a yellow folder, used a hole-puncher at the top and placed some blank papers inside.

"In the human world, physicians mostly use electronic records now."

"I know," Sadie said, giving her a shy smile. "But Nolan and I are the only physicians in this world, and we both prefer paper. I guess we're dinosaurs." Pulling a gown from the cabinet under the counter, she handed it to Evie. "Go ahead and fully disrobe, the opening of the gown in front. I'll be back in a few minutes."

The Slayer left and returned a few minutes later, after Evie had shed her clothes. Fingering the gown, her legs hanging off the table, she answered Sadie's questions as she sat in front of her on the rolling stool. Medical history, sexual history, history of illnesses.

"Have you ever been a victim of sexual assault?" Sadie asked.

Evie couldn't control the laugh that escaped in a puff from her throat. "Yes. Repeatedly, for the first few decades of my life."

The Slayer's eyebrows drew together, her face a mask of compassion. "I'm so sorry."

Evie shrugged. "Water under the bridge. I got over it centuries ago."

Pretty hazel eyes studied her, making Evie uncomfortable. "I'm glad to hear it. Just so you know, I'm well-versed in human psychology. I would be happy to schedule a session with you if you want to talk."

Evie's lips formed a frigid smile. "Thanks, but I don't really think of those times anymore. I saw multiple psychologists and therapists when I lived in the human world. In the end, one has to get over these things on their own."

Sadie blinked a few times. "Okay. Well, just know that I'm here if you change your mind. Ken most likely put my number in your phone when he programmed it."

Evie nodded. The examination continued, Sadie performing a gynecologic exam and then drawing blood to run the various tests. Afterward, she placed the chart on the counter and faced Evie.

"You're all set. I should have the test results by Thursday morning. Nolan and I will be running a health screening in the main square on Thursday, but I'll take a break and meet you here in the infirmary to give you the results. Want to meet me here at noon on Thursday?"

"Sure," Evie said. "I don't mean to pry, but I can read images in others' minds. Is it too presumptuous of me to inform you that I see the thoughts you have about Nolan?"

The unburnt side of Sadie's face flushed. "Probably. But maybe I shouldn't squander the opportunity to pick your brain. No one's ever been attracted to me before. It's a bit scary. I don't know the first thing about sex or love or any of that stuff."

Evie gave a throaty laugh. "You don't need to, honey. Believe me, I've seen the images in his mind too. They were quite overwhelming when he was dancing with you at Darkrip's wedding. He wants to bend you over and do all sorts of scandalous things to your pretty little body. Mark my words."

Sadie bit her lip. "I'm anything but pretty, but thanks for the pep talk. You're so confident. I wish I was."

She slid from the table, holding the robe closed. "It took me a long time to become so. When I was young, I was a doormat. Useless and broken. You'll get there. I think Nolan is the perfect person to help you on your journey. He's quite handsome."

The Slayer grinned. "He is. I'm flattered that he's interested."

Evie lifted her brow. "Oh, he's more than interested, sweetheart. Trust me."

Sadie chuckled, her multicolored irises roving over Evie's face. "You're pretty cool, Evie. I think you might not want people to know it, but you are."

"Don't tell anyone. The last thing I need is more friends. Miranda already wants to inscribe matching BFF tattoos on our foreheads."

"Well, Miranda's awesome too, and when she's determined, she usually accomplishes her goal."

"Yes," Evie said, "it's quite irritating. Are we done here?"

"Yup," Sadie said with a nod. "I'll let you get dressed and I'll see you here on Thursday."

"Great, thanks."

Before closing the door behind her, Sadie pivoted. "You deserve people who care about you, Evie. I'm sorry you don't believe that. I hope you'll change your mind one day." With one last soft smile, she closed the door behind her.

Alone, Evie donned her clothes, considering the Slayer's words and hating that she wished they were true.

"Oh, I'm so sorry, my friend," the woman said, wracked with sorrow as she lifted her hands to her cheeks. "How did your world die?"

Galredad sighed. "There was a great flood, one that washed away all that existed. And then, a great fire that burned every trace of my realm to the ground. It's all gone," he said, wrapping his arms around his knees, "as if it never existed in the first place. And now, I feel so lonely."

"What a terrible story," she said, gently caressing his arm. "I have never heard its equal."

"Oh, you will," he said, his tone ominous, "for I have learned that the Universe always lies in wait, calculating the perfect time to destroy one's happiness..."

Chapter 4

Three days later, Kenden stood outside his home chopping wood for the fireplace. He'd built one so that he could indulge his love of relaxing by a warm fire each evening after he trained the troops. Lately, he'd been exhausted from the grueling sessions and was thrilled to have the day off.

Under the glowing orb of the afternoon sun, he plunged the axe through the log that sat upon the stump, splintering it in half. Picking up one of the halved pieces, he sat it upright and proceeded to divide it again.

It was grunt work, mindless and draining. It cleared his head so that he couldn't focus on Evie or her ridiculous demand. Or on the fact he'd been avoiding her like a damn coward. Gritting his teeth, he thrust the axe into a new stalk of wood.

Kenden wouldn't even begin to delude himself that her request was about anything other than manipulation and control. Although he knew she desired him, that was most likely an afterthought for her. No, Evie thrived on power and dominance, on being able to dictate her own terms, and anyone who was unlucky enough to be stuck in her path was doomed.

Breathing a bitter laugh, he took a break to run his forearm over his face, wiping away the sweat. It ran down his neck, onto his chest, bare above his gray sweatpants. Sighing, he set the axe down to lift the water bottle and consume several continuous gulps.

She materialized in front of him as if he'd willed her there. Lowering the bottle, he swallowed. "Hello, Evie."

"Well, hello," she said, her voice sultry and sure. "And what do we have here? My god, you're a fucking Adonis, aren't you? Who knew you had a perfectly chiseled six-pack?"

Rolling his eyes, he threw the empty container on the ground. "What do you want? I'm busy."

White teeth threatened to blind him as she smiled. Approaching him, her irises wandered over his sweat-covered chest, unabashed and slow. "I can't wait to lick every single crevice of you, sweetheart."

He clenched his teeth, forcing himself to remain calm. Staring down at her, he struggled to keep the anger from his voice. "I'm not sleeping with you, Evie."

Full red lips pursed as she made a *tsk, tsk, tsk* with her gorgeous mouth. "Now, Kenden, let's not be hasty. I think you've avoided me long enough. I never pegged you for a wuss." Lifting her hand, she slid the pads of her fingers over his pecs.

"Stop it," he said, grabbing her wrist. Holding it in a vice-like grip, he pulled her closer. "I won't deny that I want you, but not like this. I told you, I don't do casual sex."

"You're literally the only man who has ever said those words to me." Yanking her wrist from his grasp, her eyes narrowed. "Fine. Then name your terms. Perhaps I'm willing to negotiate."

"Name my terms," he said, his tone flat.

"Come on," she said, lifting her arms, sounding exasperated. "You just admitted you want me. Begrudgingly, but we both know I can read the images in your mind. So, tell me. What will it take for you to grant my request?"

Inhaling a deep breath, he pondered. "I would want to court you, like I would any woman I make love to."

"It's called 'dating' in the human world."

"Fine," he said, annoyed at her correction. "I'd want to date you. Get to know you. The thought of sleeping with someone I don't know anything about isn't appealing to me. I like to have a connection with women I'm intimate with."

Laughter bounded from her throat. "My god, you really are a boy scout. It's absolutely unbecoming."

"Then, leave me the fuck alone," he said, incensed by her. "If it's that off-putting to you."

Compressing her lips, she regarded him. As the silence stretched between them, he felt himself growing more uncomfortable. She looked so sure and confident in her expensive clothing. Next to her, in his sweat-soaked pants, he felt like a scrub.

"I don't have time for this," he muttered, lowering to pick up the empty bottle. When he attempted to breeze past her, she grabbed his forearm.

"Wait," she said, her voice quiet. "Let me think for a damn minute."

Heart pounding at her touch, he stared down at her. She was several inches shorter than his six-foot-two frame but her eyes threatened to suck the air out of his lungs. They were so wide, so deep, that he felt he might drown in them if he didn't escape.

"It's never been this difficult for me before," she said, blinking as she held his gaze. "Men mostly want to fuck me and move on. I don't understand your reluctance to do the same."

Compassion swamped him, although it was unwelcome, causing him to think of the first time he'd spoken to her in the hotel in France. She'd sworn that there was no one she'd ever loved; no one who'd loved her. Empathy pulsed in his gut. What a lonely existence she must lead. How did one live so long without affection?

"I can't speak for anyone else but myself. I want more than just a good fuck, Evie. It's something I've come to expect and feel that I deserve." Unable to stop himself, he lifted his hand to palm her cheek. Rubbing the pad of his thumb over her soft skin, the tiny freckles across her nose seemed to glisten in the sunlight. "Maybe you deserve the same. You won't know until you try."

Expelling a long breath, her irises darted back and forth between his. They were filled with curiosity and deliberation and, if he had to guess, a slight bit of fear. Steeling herself, she straightened her spine. Wrenching from his touch, she distanced herself several feet.

"So, if I let you date me, you'll sleep with me afterward?"

Mulling her question, he stared into her grass-green eyes.

"Yes," he said finally, giving her a firm nod. "Three dates followed by three nights together. If you agree to those terms, I'll concede."

Red lips curved into a sexy smile. As she stood before him, he reveled in her splendor. Inwardly admitting that he'd never met a woman more beautiful, he waited.

"Fine," she said, smirking. "I agree." Holding out her hand, a manila folder materialized onto her palm. Closing the distance between them, she slapped it onto his chest. "For you to look over. I had Sadie perform a physical on me, and we met earlier today to discuss the results. I'm clean. I don't want to use protection with you, so I'd urge you to get tested if you have any doubt as to whether you're clean too."

Good god. She was the most straightforward person he'd ever known. "I'm clean. I get tested regularly and haven't been with anyone in several decades."

The perfect features of her face scrunched. "How absolutely dreadful. Thank goodness I've come along to remedy that."

His nostrils flared. "And if you get pregnant?"

She shrugged. "I have an IUD. Won't happen. Get ready, big boy. We're going to have some fun together." She waggled her scarlet eyebrows.

Against his will, he chuckled. "Good lord, Evie. You're something else."

"You bet your goddamn ass I am," she said with a nod. "So, when's our first *date*?" she asked, making quotation marks in the air with her fingers.

He couldn't stop his grin. "Saturday. I'll be done training the troops at five. I'll pick you up at your cabin at six-thirty. Wear something pretty."

"Oh, were you under the impression that you could boss me around now that I've negotiated with you? Don't delude yourself, Kenden. I'm in control here. You'd do well to remember that. Ta-ta for now." With a puff of air, she vanished.

Shaking his head, he muttered to himself, frustrated. Flipping through the folder, he read her results. Clean as a whistle. Well, damn. Craving a shower and a bit of peace, he headed inside to contemplate what in the ever-loving hell had just happened.

* * * *

Nolan watched Sadie address the couple that stood inside their booth at Uteria's main square. The afternoon sun flirted with the distant mountaintops, foreshadowing an end to the pretty day. Thanking Sadie, the couple walked away, hand-in-hand.

"They're trying to get pregnant," Sadie said, smiling up at him. Her gorgeous, multicolored hazel eyes were magnificent in the sun's dying rays. "I hope it takes. She had trouble with her first husband, who was abducted in the raids centuries ago. Hopefully, this time will be easier for her."

"Hope so," he said, his lips curving into a grin. Such was her way, always wishing others happiness and hope. He'd never met a person more caring and selfless than Sadie.

"Should we break this down?" she asked, gesturing around the booth. "I think we're about done here."

"Sure," he said with a nod. They chatted as they worked, disassembling the various medical equipment and tent components. Nolan made sure he did the bulk of the heavy lifting. Not only because she was so slight but because a proper gentleman would never let a lady do manual labor when he was perfectly capable of doing that himself. His dear mother had ingrained that in him centuries ago.

"Well," she said, fisting her hands on her jean-clad hips, under her white lab coat. "I think we did it. Ken said he'd send some soldiers over in four-wheelers to transport everything back to the infirmary."

Nolan nodded. "I was thinking about grabbing a bite before I head back to Astaria. You hungry?"

A flush crossed the unburnt half of her face, causing his blood to pound through his body. Smiling shyly, she said, "I could eat."

"Come on then," he said, extending his hand. Clutching her unburnt one, he threaded his fingers though hers, squeezing tightly. Leisurely, they strolled through town, coming to a stop in front of one of the Irish pubs.

They sat at the bar, Sadie wriggling her nose at the bartender's offer of a free shot with an appetizer. "Just a beer for me," she said.

"Same," Nolan said, also ordering them some wings and fries.

They chatted, catching up on everything and nothing. Nolan reveled in her genuine laugh and twinkling eyes. It had been like this ever since he'd kissed her that first time. Unable to control the fall, he knew he was tumbling into love with her.

It was quite amazing for someone such as him, who'd been alone and so very unhappy, stuck in a world that wasn't his. Long ago, he'd accepted that was his lot in life. A penance for the mistake he'd made when he discovered the immortal world. And then, out of nowhere, she had appeared. Those tiny hands, that soft smile, even the portions of her that were so badly burned—they all beckoned to him. Causing him to want to wrap himself around her and never let go.

Unable to control his need to touch her, he lifted a finger, tracing it softly over her cheek. "Your skin is healing nicely here."

Her throat bobbled as she swallowed and her tone was just raspy enough to cause him to harden beneath his dress pants. "Yes. The serum is awesome. I can't believe you and Arderin created it for me. It's the most amazing thing anyone's ever done for me."

"We were happy to. You do so much for others. It's nice to have it reciprocated for once, I would imagine."

"It is," she said, nodding against his finger. "Thank you, Nolan."

"You're welcome, sweetie." With one last caress of her smooth skin, he pulled his finger away. Missing that slight contact, he studied her from his barstool. "So, I heard about Evie's ultimatum to Kenden. Sathan told me and swore me to secrecy. Wow. Didn't see that coming."

Sadie tweaked her bottom lip with her teeth. "Seriously. Miranda did the same with me. She and I had a good laugh, but now, I feel bad. I mean, he shouldn't be placed in the position of being with her if he doesn't want to."

Nolan arched a chestnut brow. "I've observed the heat between those two, and if I had to guess, I'd say that it won't be a hardship for him. He's extremely attracted to her."

"Well, she's gorgeous," she said with a shrug, "so it makes sense. We're surrounded by a lot of breathtaking women in this world. It makes me wonder what the rest of us mere underlings are supposed to do."

Their food came, and they arranged their plates, scooping up various pieces and squirting out ketchup. After swallowing, Nolan said, "You're one of the gorgeous ones too, you know? To me, at least."

He could see the pulse pounding in her neck as she gazed at him, her irises full with emotion. "You're the only one who's ever thought so."

"Good," he said, munching on a fry. "It increases my chances of winning you over."

She smiled as she nibbled. "And what happens then?"

Lathering a wing in ranch dressing, he took a bite, contemplating. Finally, his pupils latched on to hers. "Are you open to marrying a human? I think it's time I asked you that. Because I want to continue spending time with you, Sadie, and if that happens, I think that might be where we end up."

Her lids blinked up and down several times as she studied him. "I've never thought about it. I never thought anyone would want to marry me, so it seemed a moot point to waste time contemplating it."

"Hmmm..." he said, finishing the wing and setting the bone on the plate. "Well, maybe you should reassess."

Biting her lip, the flesh squeezed around her teeth. Nolan had to gnaw the inside of his mouth to contain his groan. The action was so sexy.

"Maybe I should," she said, reaching down to grab a wing and dip it in blue cheese. "But not until I complete the regimen with the serum. I wouldn't want to walk down the aisle with anyone looking like I do now."

Anger, swift and true, gripped him as she spoke. It always welled in him when she disparaged herself like that. "I told you, I don't want to hear you say things like that. It's beneath you."

Inhaling deeply, she finished the bite and wiped her hands on the white napkin. "I know. It's just hard. No one sees me like you do."

"I would argue that many do. Starting with Miranda, Arderin, Lila. You're shortchanging yourself."

She scrutinized him, remaining silent as she sipped her beer.

"There's something else you should think about," he said softly. "I can't give you children. Although we know that different species can mate to produce children, especially the purer their blood, a human would never be able to procreate with an immortal. For someone as nurturing as you, it's something to consider."

Her forehead furrowed as she contemplated. "I've never thought of having kids either. It never even seemed a remote possibility. But in my fantasies, I have them. I think I'd be a pretty good mom."

Nolan reached out to tuck a strand of her silky brown hair back between her ear and red ballcap. "You'd be fantastic."

"Thanks," she said, her lids lowering in embarrassment.

"Well, I think that's enough serious talk for today. What do you say? Let's finish up here, and then, I'll walk you to the castle."

After another round of beers, he paid the tab, shoving the bills back at her when she laid them on the counter. Together, they meandered back through town, to the long concrete stairs that led to the main castle's enormous mahogany front doors.

"The health screening went well today. We should do another one soon."

"Okay," she said, nodding. "Thanks for dinner and for walking me home."

"You're welcome." Several soldiers trudged by them, pounding up the steps, and Nolan figured they were heading inside to meet with Miranda or Kenden. Feeling that the moment had passed, he lifted her hand, placing a gentle kiss on the inside of her wrist. "Sweet dreams, Sadie."

Releasing her soft skin, he began to retreat, stopping short when she called his name.

"Yes?" he asked, pivoting.

Her eyes seemed huge as they glowed in the dim moonlight. "Aren't you going to kiss me goodbye?"

The groan escaped his lips before he could stop it. With firm steps, he plodded toward her, pulling her into his arms and cementing his lips to hers. Reveling in her tiny mewls, he plundered her mouth. Pulling off her cap, he tossed it to the ground, moaning as his tongue battled with hers.

"Well, damn," a female voice said beside them. "I'm just in time for the show."

Sadie gasped and pulled back, her face flaming. "Miranda—we were just…"

"Oh, honey, I know what you were doing. Believe me. Good stuff, guys." Miranda winked at Nolan. "It's about time someone made out with our girl."

Nolan chuckled, bending over to grab Sadie's cap and hand it to her. "It was all her fault. I was ready to head to the train, but she couldn't resist me."

"Nolan!" Sadie said, swatting his arm. "I swear, Miranda, I didn't mean to—"

"Mean to, what?" she asked. "Get some action? Why in the hell not? It's awesome. I'm heading in to meet with some of the soldiers. Sorry I interrupted. See ya!" Black hair swaying, she jogged up the stairs.

"Busted," Sadie said, looking up at him with mirth in her brilliant eyes. "Too bad. It was getting good."

He laughed. "Sure was, sweetie." Cupping her cheek, he ran the pad of his thumb over her lips. "See you soon."

"See you soon," she said, her voice gravelly.

With one last peck to her soft lips, he headed for the train, smiling under the moonlight the entire way.

* * * *

On Friday, Kenden headed to Astaria to train the troops. Latimus needed the day off for a parent-teacher conference at Jack's school, and he had no problem covering. Working with the Vampyre commander had become seamless, and they formed an immensely talented team. Kenden had never met a man more dedicated to his troops, nor more skilled in battle. Latimus possessed a general's mind and the physicality of ten men. Together, they led an intensely powerful combined army.

Several hours in to the training, Sathan approached him where he stood on the hill, observing the soldiers perform their drills. The Vampyre king's large body blocked the rays of the sun as he situated beside him.

"It's so beautiful today," Sathan said, lifting his face to the sky, eyes closed. Inhaling a deep breath, he shook his head. "I'm so thankful to Etherya. It's been so long since we've seen the sun."

"Indeed," Kenden said, nodding his head. "I'm thrilled for your people."

"*Our* people," Sathan said, training his black irises on him. "You are as much responsible for lifting the curse as anyone. We truly appreciate everything you've done, Ken. I know Latimus feels the same."

"Happy to do it. We've lived with war and hate for a thousand years. It's time for it to end."

Sathan ran a hand through his thick hair, as he often did when he was pondering something. "Yes, it is. Our final step is to defeat Crimeous. Where do you stand with Evie's proposal? If you won't do it, I understand, but we need to make a decision and strategize how to move forward."

Kicking the ground with the toe of his boot, he said, "I agreed. She came to see me yesterday. We compromised on an...*arrangement* of sorts."

"Really?" A raven-black eyebrow arched. "That's good to hear. I figured the cunning Slayer commander would figure out a way to regain the upper hand."

"She pulled a fast one on me," he said, scowling down at the sparring field. "She's so damn smart. And uses the fact that people underestimate her to manipulate everything around her. I should've anticipated it."

"Then, she seems a worthy opponent for you," Sathan said, his full lips curving into a grin. "For you are the most cunning person I've ever met."

Evie's flawless face flashed through Kenden's mind, reminding him not only of her cleverness but her incomparable beauty. "Perhaps. I'm pissed as hell, but I also recognize that her intelligence and shrewdness will come in handy when we fight her father."

"Let's hope so."

They stood in silence, thick arms crossed, watching the troops.

"Did Miranda send you to speak to me?"

"Yes," Sathan said. "She thinks you're still mad at her."

The corner of his lips curved. "I'm not, but it's fun to see her squirm. I think I'll let her sweat for a while."

Sathan chuckled. "You know she'll give you a few days, minimum, and then come looking for you."

"Can't wait," Kenden said.

"And you're okay with the terms you set with Evie?"

Nostrils flared as he clenched his jaw. "Yes. It's so bizarre, but now that I've had a chance to process it, I see a lot of things clearly. Evie's never had one person who loved her. I think Miranda and Darkrip want to, but she's so closed off, they don't stand a chance. Maybe this will open something inside her. Break down some of the walls she's built to protect herself. Who knows?"

"It doesn't hurt that she's absolutely stunning," Sathan said. "I mean, I love my wife and she'll always be the most beautiful woman in the universe, but Evie's got something. I know she pushed you into it but I can't imagine it will be a chore to sleep with her."

"I was lying to myself and to her that I didn't want it to happen. With anyone else, that wouldn't have mattered, but she can read the images in my mind, so I was fucked." Rubbing his hands over his face, he blew out a breath through puffed cheeks. "It's done now. Might as well make the best of it."

"Truer words, my friend," Sathan said. "Well, don't hesitate to call upon me if you need. It's imperative that we remain in communication while you're, um, getting to know her better."

"Yeah," Kenden said absently. "Thanks. And tell Miranda not to bother me while I'm courting Evie. She's meddlesome, and I don't want her involved in my business."

"My bonded? Meddlesome?" he asked with mock indignation. "Never."

"Right," he said, laughing.

With a tip of his head, Sathan trudged back down the hill toward the main castle at Astaria. Knowing the troops needed a break, Kenden trod down to see what Glarys had prepared for lunch.

"You must not believe that!" the woman cried. "The Universe is powerful and filled with so much goodness. You must have faith, my friend."

Galredad scoffed. "Faith. I have no use for faith anymore. I have lost everything."

"Renewal is a constant theme of our Universe. Although you have lost so much, you must believe in rebirth. Perhaps that is why you were put in my path today. Perchance we were meant to meet."

That caused the man to smile, if only a little. "Perhaps we were..."

Chapter 5

On Saturday, Kenden finished training the soldiers and headed home to shower. As he got ready for the evening, he decided he needed to dress the part to knock Evie's socks off. She always dressed impeccably, making his usual tactical gear look cold and boring. Throwing on slacks, loafers, a buttoned-down, collared shirt, suit jacket and tie, he couldn't tamp down the swell of nerves in his gut. Annoyed, he contemplated why.

Being a man who enjoyed monogamy and intimacy, he hadn't been with a woman in many decades. Although that might seem foreign to another man, Kenden had been so consumed with protecting his people that he'd barely noticed the years fly by. His previous lover, Katia, had been a lovely woman with straw-blond hair and a kind smile. Their couplings had been sweet and slow, scheduled around army trainings and Vampyre raids. Eventually, she'd expressed her desire to start a family. Not foreseeing an end to the War of the Species, they had ended their relationship, Kenden wishing her well.

Never had he felt one-tenth the desire for her that he felt for Evie. In fact, all his former lovers paled in comparison to the intense longing he felt for her. Knowing that, he reluctantly questioned himself. With so much time passing since his last lover, would he be able to please the red-headed temptress? Lord knew she was innately more experienced than him. She'd probably had lovers with moves Kenden had never fathomed.

Shaking his head, as he walked along the grassy field that separated his home from her cabin, he vowed to stop doubting himself. The woman had gone out of her way to corner him into sleeping with her. Hell, it was the stipulation she'd dictated for fighting her evil father and hopefully fulfilling the prophecy. She must want him badly.

Anticipation coursed through him while he imagined caressing her silky skin. Would he be able to love her body without developing feelings for her as well? Not wanting to examine the answer, he continued to her cabin, his soft shoes swishing along the grass.

When he arrived at the wooden steps that led to the front door, it swung open slowly. Filling the doorframe, her slender body was draped in a long, formfitting black dress that showed every minute curve. The flare of her hips; the globes of her perfect breasts, which he knew she'd received via a human plastic surgeon; the paleness of her thigh and knee that were on show through the slit. By the goddess, she was magnificent. Struggling to breathe, he watched her descend the stairs ever so slowly in her red-bottom stilettos.

Eye-level with him, as she stood on the lowest step, her full, red lips curved into a seductive smile. "I can see you like my outfit."

Kenden's throat bobbled as he swallowed. "There's never been any doubt as to your beauty, Evie." Grasping her hand, he lifted the back of it to his mouth. "You look stunning," he said, brushing a kiss against her smooth skin.

"Thank you," she said, dropping her hand. He took solace in the fact that her slender neck pulsed when she swallowed. Although trying to conceal it, she wasn't as unaffected by him as she pretended.

"Ready?"

She nodded. "I can't walk across the grass in these heels, so I'll have to transport us. Where to?"

"The main square at Restia. I made reservations at the expensive steakhouse. Figured I should spend some of the money I inherited but never seem to use."

Her throaty laugh made his dick swell in his pants. Good god, they'd only just begun, and he was hard as an untried teenager.

"Let's get on with it then," she said. Sliding her arms around his neck, she leaned in to him. "I need to hold you close during the transfer."

Nodding, he pulled her against him. "Your brother has transported me before."

One perfectly-plucked scarlet eyebrow arched. "But were you pushing *that* into his hip?" she asked, rubbing against his erection.

Mentally restraining his groan, and telling himself not to rise to her taunting, he clutched her against him. Unashamed, he grinded into her. "I'm only a man, Evie. You know I want you. The fact that I'm aroused shouldn't be a shock."

"Hmmm..." she said, threading the fingers of one hand through the thick hair at the back of his head. "We could just jump to the good part now. If you're so inclined."

"No way," he said, feeling the corner of his lips curve. "You might just happen to think our date is the best part. And then, you'd feel so empty for skipping ahead."

"Boring," she said, rolling her eyes. "But part of the deal, so fine. To Restia we go." Clutching him close, she closed her lids. With a *whoosh*, they were flying, hurtling through time and space, and then, in a moment, they were at Restia.

The town square on the satellite Slayer compound was smaller than Uteria's. Being that Restia was roughly half the size, it made sense. The compound was quaint, possessing a charm that Kenden always felt drawn to. Extending his arm to Evie, she threaded hers through, and he led her to the restaurant.

The cobblestones of the sidewalk felt warm below them as the sun set in the distance. Glancing down, her hair seemed afire in the balmy air. Several passersby nodded their heads at Kenden, and he reciprocated in kind.

"Everyone seems to know you, Commander," she said, grinning up at him.

"Yes. I come here quite often. My mother was from Restia. She moved to Uteria when she married my father."

"How scandalous," Evie said. "Knowing what I do about immortals and their aristocratic bloodlines, I can't imagine your rich father's family was happy about him marrying someone from Restia."

"Uncle Marsias used to tell me that my grandfather hated the idea at first, but I think eventually, my lovely mother won him over. Penethia. That was her name. But my father called her Penny. '*My sweet Penny,*' he used to say. He was head over heels for her."

"Well, well. That makes even my cold, unromantic heart tingle. And what happened to them?"

"They both died in the Awakening. My father, Brenden, always attended the blood-banking festivals. Being brother to King Marsias, Father always tried to help him with the royal duties even though he was the younger son. They were each other's only siblings and were very close. When Valktor slaughtered Calla and Markdor, my parents were nearby. In retaliation, several Vampyre soldiers struck them down. From what I've been told, the bloodshed that day was unimaginable."

Evie sighed. "I'm sorry," she said, gazing up at him. "Everyone always says that dear ol' Grandpa was a good man, but I always questioned the truth of that sentiment. How could it be so if he murdered the Vampyre royals?"

"Miranda saw your grandfather when she was in the Passage. His actions were a twisted attempt to save your mother. Valktor would've done anything for Rina. His love for her was some of the purest I've ever seen."

She wrinkled her nose. "Well, he might have tried to find a different way. What an absolute fool, believing that my father would free Mother. He should've known she was doomed."

"We have the luxury of hindsight now, but who's to say what we would do in the moment, when a choice of that magnitude is forced upon us?"

"Perhaps," she said with a shrug. "No matter. What's done is done. And now, once I collect my...*stipulation* from you, maybe I can finally rid the world of the bastard."

"All our hopes, pinned on your shoulders," Kenden said jovially, trying to lighten the mood. "Hope it's not too overwhelming."

"Not a fucking chance," she said, straightening her spine. "I can't wait to murder that asshole."

Her confidence was bold and extremely attractive to him. "Can't wait to see the day."

They arrived at the thick oak doors of the restaurant. Pulling one open for her, she sauntered inside. Kenden couldn't help but notice the appreciative glances of each of the male staff members as the host led them to the table. From the bartender to the servers to the damn busboys, not one man passed up the opportunity to drink in her beauty. Feeling possessive—and pissed that he was—he shuffled them to the table with a firm hand on her lower back and pulled out her chair a bit roughly.

"Don't worry, darling," she said, patting his cheek. The placating gesture incensed him, and he clenched his teeth to stop himself from telling her to go to hell. "You have to get used to it if you're going to date me. I've spent a hundred lifetimes learning how to make men salivate when I walk by. Just remember, you asked for this."

"Sit down," he commanded, his tone low and firm.

"Oh, Ken. Don't be a stick in the mud—"

"Sit."

Throwing her head back, she gave a silky laugh. The pale skin of her throat glowed, and he wanted to rip every man's eyes out for gawking at her. Sparing him a wink, she sat in the cushy chair, letting him push it in behind her. She was lucky he didn't push her through the damn table. Infuriating woman.

Sitting across from her, they perused the menu, ordering a fancy bottle of red and two steaks. The candle in between them emitted a soft glow on the white tablecloth as they toasted to defeating Crimeous. Watching her full lips caress the glass and imbibe the red liquid made all sorts of things happen inside his trousers. How would those plushy lips feel around his cock? Uncomfortable, he shifted in his seat.

"There, there," she said, her voice so seductive. "We'll get to that part soon enough."

"Stop reading my thoughts," he snapped, taking a sip of wine. "It's obtrusive and beneath you."

"Is it?" she asked. "You don't know what's beneath me, honey. It ain't much."

Unable to help himself, he laughed. Realizing he needed to relax if he was going to enjoy this at all, he forced himself to calm down and breathe. Several minutes later, they were making easy conversation, as if they'd know each other for centuries.

"No!" she said, snickering behind her wine glass. "And you actually broke her nose?"

"Well, what was I supposed to do?" he asked, shrugging innocently. "Miranda told me not to coddle her, and she kept leaving her face unprotected. Eventually, I had to force her to learn."

"Good god, you're a beast," Evie said, shaking her head. "Remind me never to train with you."

Chuckling, he smiled. "We'll get there eventually. I'll need you to do some sessions with the troops, so they learn to trust you. But for now, how are your lessons going with Darkrip?"

"Good," she said with a nod. "He picks up human dark magic like he was made to wield it. It took me several decades to get to the level of proficiency that he's at after several weeks. It's absolutely annoying."

"Well, I'm glad he has a knack for it. We need you both to be as strong as possible to beat Crimeous. What about the joint force-field that you two need to generate to prevent your father from dematerializing? Now that we've come to an agreement, will you start working on that?"

Setting down her wine glass, Evie's features drew together. "Yes. He and I actually began working on it yesterday, now that you've conceded to my terms," she said, her gaze unwavering. "I'll continue to work with him as long as our arrangement is satisfied."

Twirling the wine glass by the stem, she continued, "To be honest, it was a disaster. Conjoining our abilities was much more difficult than I'd anticipated. Our combined powers have a different energy field than our powers alone. It's as if I have a different kind of…I don't know…DNA or something that he doesn't possess. It's quite strange."

Kenden studied her, thinking back to all the old soothsayer gossip he'd gathered over the centuries. One of the oldest tales prophesized that Etherya had injected one of Crimeous' children with her own blood. Contemplating, he wondered if the story could even begin to be factual. Etherya was always so sure to stay apart from her people, knowing the Universe would be displeased if she interfered in their free will.

"It can't be true," Evie said, reading the images in his mind. "No one with Etherya's blood could've suffered the way I did in my youth."

Compassion slammed his solar plexus, and he reached out to cover her hand where it sat atop the table.

"Don't," she said, pulling it away and placing it on her lap. "That was centuries ago. I don't want your pity."

"I don't pity you—"

"Yes, you do. I don't blame you. You're a very empathetic person. But it's a waste of your energy. Use it to defeat my father instead."

Noting her impassive expression, he relented.

Their steaks arrived: hers a filet, his a ribeye. Delving in, they caught up on stories of the past and wishes for days ahead in a world where her father no longer existed. Feeling so comfortable with her, the dinner seemed to fly by, and Kenden found his heart pounding in anticipation of the evening's conclusion.

Once he paid the check, she finished the last of her wine and eyed him seductively. "So, are we done here? Ready for the main course?"

Breathing a laugh, he stood and extended his hand. "Not yet. We're going to walk along the river. It's really pretty. C'mon."

She gave him a droll look from her chair. "While I appreciate this whole seduction track you're on, let me remind you that I'm a sure thing. We are clear on that, yes?"

"Stop being difficult," he said, shaking his hand at her. "The night is young and it's warm tonight. Walk with me."

Standing, she fit her hand into his, latching onto him with her gaze. "If I'm not careful, you might just seduce me into enjoying being courted."

"How terrible," he teased, leading her through the restaurant and outside into the gorgeous night.

Hand-in-hand, they strolled along the stone sidewalk, beyond the bridge that overlooked the river. Under the pale light of the stars, they meandered down the paved walkway that ran parallel to the water.

"It's very serene," she said, closing her eyes and inhaling a deep breath. "Much like the rivers that run through Colorado. I always enjoyed walking along them."

"Tell me about your favorite places in the human world."

Mischief entered her eyes as she arched a brow. "So you can come looking for me in case I defect?"

"So I can get to know you better," he said, tugging on her hand. "Come on. It won't hurt to let yourself get personal just a tiny fraction. Will it?"

"Nothing hurts until you agree to let it," she muttered, making his heart squeeze.

"Tell me about Japan," he said, unrelenting. "It seems like you love it there."

"I do," she said, her tone wistful. "It's just so beautiful, filled with a history of war and harmony, religion and meditation. There's this gorgeous city by the sea. The cliffs have always called to me. Sunsets filled with colors that you never knew existed..."

As she spoke, he found himself entranced by her. By her smile. By her scent. By the longing in her voice as she spoke so reverently about the places she treasured. While they strolled, he listened, engrossed in every fiber of her. An immeasurable time later, they stood back at the bridge, side-to-side, observing the clear water flow beneath.

"It seems like you really enjoyed Italy," he said, gazing down at her as his forearms rested on the railing of the bridge. "Francesco spoke so fondly of you when I met him."

Her features drew together slightly as she absently stared ahead, her face becoming a mask of what he could only discern as remorse. "Yes. He was a wonderful man. Perhaps the one man who understood me above all others in my long, endless life."

Her slender body seemed to pulse beside him, the energy filled with numerous emotions. Understanding washed over him as he watched her silent struggle.

"You killed him," he said softly. "Once you figured out that he told me where to find you."

"Yes," she whispered, her gaze never leaving the gently gurgling river.

"And you regret it."

Inhaling deeply, her eyelids narrowed. "Perhaps. Or maybe not. I'm quite torn about it, which is strange for me. I've never regretted killing, especially men. But I find that things are changing inside me faster than they have in centuries. It's foreign and extremely frustrating."

"I've killed many in my day too. Soldiers have the burdensome task of killing many to save others. It's something that I've struggled with, as many soldiers have."

"Ah, but I'm not a soldier," she said, still staring ahead. "So, what excuse do I have? Except that I'm an evil bitch who revels in the deaths of my victims."

Kenden considered. "From the few statements you've made to me on the subject, men have often tried to harm you. So, in a way, you were your own soldier. Killing them to save yourself."

She shrugged. "And the others? I've killed many, mostly in my youth, for fun and for sport. Don't exonerate me, Ken. It's futile."

"Your brother has embraced his Slayer side for centuries," Kenden said, his tone encouraging. "It's possible that you could do the same."

"And where's the fun in that? I'm just fine, thank you."

Tilting his head to look at the water, he let the silence envelop them, unsure of what to say.

"Does it make it less evil if he was sick?" she asked, her voice scratchy.

"What?" he asked, feeling his brows draw together.

"Francesco. He was riddled with cancer. I could smell it on him, sure as if I saw the tumors myself. They were growing in multiple organs of his body. When I feel regret, I tell myself that I saved him months of suffering with chemo and tubes, nurses and hospitals. He had a granddaughter. An American. I observed her over a decade ago, when she was visiting him in Italy. They sat outside at a café, and I watched them from afar, remembering our time together. She was in her early twenties then, but a little spitfire. She would've never let him die gracefully. She would've tried everything to extend his life, surely causing him to suffer. So, does it make me less evil that I saved him from all that when I snapped his neck?"

"I'm not sure," Kenden said, sliding his hand over hers where it hung over the rail. Threading their fingers together, he squeezed. "But I think it definitely makes you less evil that you're asking the question. So, there's that." Smiling, he bumped her shoulder with his.

"Good god," she said, shaking her head at him. "You're so fucking perfect. How do you do it? Any other man would've told me to go fuck myself. But here you are, courting me so that you can do your duty and save your people. You're a goddamned fairytale prince, Ken."

Feeling his grin widen, he drew her to him, aligning the front of his body with hers. "I'm just a man who wants happiness for those I love. That includes my people. It's easy to fight for them because I care."

Disengaging her hand from his, she slid her palms up his chest and over his neck, causing him to shiver. Landing on his face, she cupped his cheeks. "Well, hot damn," she said, lifting on her toes. "I've never kissed a boy scout. Show me how good it can be."

Slowly moving toward her, he nudged her nose with his. "Don't trivialize this, Evie," he said, exulted at how she shuddered in his arms. "No labels here. Just you and me."

"How positively dull—"

Her words ended in a gasp as he dragged her into him. Snaking an arm around her waist, he fisted the other in her thick red hair. Groaning, he thrust his tongue into her mouth, his heart slamming in his chest when hers jutted back against it. Sliding over her wet tongue, he plundered her, needing to explore the desire that burned for her so intensely.

Thin fingers slid through his hair, scratching his scalp as she drove her tongue through his lips. Melding her body against his, she licked him and then slid her lips over his tongue, back and forth, spurring him to imagine the same motion over his engorged shaft. Growling, he bit her bottom lip and then gently sucked it through his teeth, giving as good as he got, needing her to know that he'd suck her tiny little nub in just that way once they were anywhere close to a bed.

"Oh, god," she groaned, opening wide to slather her tongue over his again. "Take me home and fuck me. Now."

Lifting his head, he studied her as he panted. Olive-green eyes, filled with lust, stared back at him. Cheeks reddened, lips swollen, she looked like a disheveled goddess.

"I can't promise that I can just fuck you, Evie," he said, clutching her hair with his fist. "I'm not very good at doing this without developing feelings. I'm not really wired that way."

"Fine," she said, breathless. "Have all the feelings you want. I don't care right now. Let's go home."

Irises darting back and forth between hers, he contemplated. Knowing he was lost, he drew her in. "Okay," he said, lowering his forehead to hers. "Your place, or mine?"

As her lips curved, she closed her lids and transported them to her cabin.

"So, did all Elves share your traits?" the woman asked, lightly touching his pointed ears with her fingertips.

"Yes," he said, nodding. "We all have tapered ears and thin bodies. I thought us a lovely species."

"How wonderful," she said, giving him a poignant smile. After some time, she stood, wiping the grass away from her white dress.

"I must leave for now, but I wish to see you again. Will you come to this place tomorrow?"

The man stood and gently grasped her thin wrists. "My lady, I would come to this place for a thousand eternities if it meant that I could look upon your face."

Feeling her cheeks grow warm, the woman nodded. "Until tomorrow then..."

Chapter 6

Once beside her bed, Evie cemented her lips to Kenden's, drawing his tongue into her mouth for another deep kiss. Wanting him inside her as quickly as possible, she dematerialized her dress, thongs and heels, causing them to land in a heap on the floor beside the bathroom.

"Whoa," Kenden said, straightening and looking extremely uncomfortable. "Can we slow down a second?"

Something akin to embarrassment flushed through Evie, causing every inch of her exposed skin to feel hot and itchy as they stood by the bed. Reminding herself that it was impossible for her to feel something that ridiculous, she refused to back down.

"Why?" she said, lifting her arms, palms up, as she stood naked in front of him.

"There's no reason we have to rush," he said, disengaging to walk to her closet. Rummaging around, he found a silky robe. Stalking toward her, he draped it over her shoulders, holding one side up so she could snake an arm through.

Shooting him an annoyed glare, she donned the robe and watched in disbelief as he knotted the belt. "Well, I think this is the first time I've had a man put my clothes back *on* before having sex."

Blowing out a breath through puffed cheeks, he regarded her. The brown centers of his eyes were blazing with desire but also with concern. And that made her extremely uncomfortable.

"I'm not like other men," he said, his gaze firm. "Maybe one day, you'll realize that. For now, I want to get to know your body. Slowly, so that I can figure out how to make you feel good."

Evie was slammed with the insane urge to cry. Tears formed in her eyes against her will, and she struggled to keep her chin from quivering. She'd been with so many men, all of them eager and randy. Not one of them had ever taken the time to stop and assess what she might need. And why would they? Long ago, she'd learned that sex was an exchange; her body traded for the moments where her partners were drunk with arousal. Those were her instants of control, where she knew she had the upper hand. Nothing in her world had ever surpassed that feeling.

Until now. Right at this moment, when this handsome-as-sin man with care in his eyes was pleading with her to let him pleasure her. The world had gone mad.

Fear surged through her, threatening to choke her. Struggling to breathe, she stared up at him. No way in hell was she letting him have control. If she slowed down and let him spend time figuring out all the ways to please her with those broad hands, she would never regain her sanity. Terrified to let someone open her up that way, she crossed her arms over her chest. Willing the tears not to fall, she clutched on to the anger that always lived inside.

"What difference does it make if we go fast or slow? We're here to fuck, aren't we?"

"We're here to love each other," he said. His expression was impassive and impossible to read, making her feel as if she was drowning.

"No," she said, shaking her head. "I don't acknowledge that word. Use it again and you'll see how evil I really am."

"Evie—"

"I mean it," she said through gritted teeth. "Now, let's do this, or let's not, but I'm not turning this into some Hallmark movie love scene. I want sex, and you agreed to my terms. Or are you reneging?"

His angular features contorted with fury. "You're determined to control every aspect of this, but it's not happening, Evie. There are two of us here. Or do you not care if I enjoy it?"

She scoffed. "As if a man wouldn't enjoy sex. You're out of your mind."

"I don't enjoy it unless I know my partner is receiving pleasure. That's what turns me on the most."

"Good god," she said, slapping her palm to her forehead. "He's a fucking saint."

"Hey," he said, grabbing her wrist at her forehead and tugging her toward the long mirror that stood beside the dresser in the bedroom. Bringing her to stand in front of him, he locked on to her eyes in the reflection. As his gaze bore into hers, he removed his suit jacket, tossing it on the floor. Unbuttoning his shirt at the wrists, he rolled the sleeves halfway up his arms.

Raising his hands to gently rub her upper arms, he rested his chin on her shoulder, never breaking eye contact. "I know this is hard for you," he said, his voice a deep rumble beside her ear. Hating the goosebumps that rose on her flesh, she refused to look away. "You learned so long ago that men would hurt you if you trusted them."

Opening her mouth to argue, he shifted his hand over it. When she tried to lift her arms to pull it away, he held them down with his thick arm across her waist.

Shaking his hand from her mouth with a violent twist of her head, she warned, "Many men have restrained me like this. Most paid with their lives. You have two fucking seconds to let me go."

His grip gentled but he didn't release her. "I understand," he said, his voice so soothing. "But you're going to have to learn to trust someone eventually, Evie."

"Says who?"

"I say," he said, the dominant words making her shudder. She'd never let a man come close to dominating her. Yet, for some reason, she stood still in his arms. "I want you to trust me. Just for tonight, I want you to let go and let me take care of you. Can you do that for me? I promise, I won't hurt you. It's a vow I take very seriously."

Goddamnit, those fucking tears were back, jeopardizing the thin veil of control she had on her emotions. Opening her lips to tell him to fuck off, she closed them immediately, unable to form the words. Pressing them together, she fought like hell not to cry.

Kenden's thick chest expanded against her back as he inhaled a long breath. Dropping his hands, he embraced her waist with both arms, the thickness of his tan forearms seeming to glow against the purple robe. Seeing his strong arms crossed above her midsection sent a wet rush of desire to her core.

"Yes," he whispered, soft lips brushing her ear as he gazed at her reflection. "That's good. Relax. I've got you."

"I can't," she warbled, one thick tear sliding down her cheek. Mortified, she tried to lift her hand to wipe it away, only to find it encased in his hold.

"You're so damn beautiful right now," he said, kissing a path to the tear and sipping it from her face. "My god, Evie. You deserve to be cherished. Let me love you."

Tilting her head, she stared into his eyes, cursing the emotions that swirled within. He just gazed into her, those chocolate irises so warm and open.

"I can't."

"Yes, you can." Softly, he stroked her bare forearm with his thick fingers. The action was so mesmerizing, so soothing.

Gazing up at him, she realized she had already lost. Petrified, she eased further into him. Swallowing thickly, she nodded. "Okay," she whispered.

Exhaling a breath, he rested his forehead on hers. "Thank the goddess. Am I going to have to fight you this hard every time we make love?"

Something escaped her throat, feeling foreign, and she realized it was laughter. How strange, to laugh when being held by a man who was about to have sex with her. Searching her brain, she wondered if that had ever happened before. Not that she could recall, but she rather liked it. It was quite uncomfortable but also familiar in a strange way.

"I can't vouch for anything past tonight, but for now, I'll relent. Do your worst, Commander. I won't fight it."

Grinning, he touched his lips to hers. It was a sweet kiss, filled with hope and anticipation. Gesturing to the mirror with his head, he said, "Watch me while I touch you."

The directive was so sexy that she almost groaned. Turning to face the mirror, she waited. Ever so slowly, he unlatched his arms from her waist. Running his palms over the silk that covered her abdomen, he slid them over her chest, grazing her breasts. Eyes locked onto hers, his hands roved back down. Caressing, his fingertips grazed up her back until they landed in between her shoulders. With the pads of his thumbs, he began massaging her neck.

The muscles there were so tense, filled with the strain of always having to hold her head high, for if one wasn't aware, they couldn't sense danger. She'd learned that lesson centuries ago.

Unconscious of making the decision, she closed her eyes. Lolling back, her head rested on his shoulder as he massaged away the stiffness.

"You're so tense," he said, his thumbs working magic on her neck.

"Mmmm..." she replied, unable to form any other words. Forget her powers. His fingers were more adept at rendering her motionless than any freezing spell she'd ever placed on another.

"That's it," he soothed. Warmth from his stomach seeped into her back, making her want to melt in a puddle to the floor. "See how good it feels to let go?"

"It's been so long," she said, not realizing she'd said the words aloud until he grumbled in her ear.

"I know, baby," he said, pressing a kiss to her temple.

"I hate that endearment," she mumbled.

"Okay, baby," he said, teasing her.

"Screw you."

The rumble of his deep chuckle vibrated through her. Giving her neck one last squeeze, he threaded his arms under hers, sliding his hands around to the "V" that comprised the opening of her robe. Lifting her lids, she searched the reflection. Brown eyes unwavering, he slowly pulled the fabric apart.

Cold air rushed against her bare breasts, causing her nipples to pebble. Beginning to pant, she watched the mirror with rapt anticipation. The purple fabric sat open, baring her chest and stomach, the silky belt still holding the lower half closed.

His broad hand rubbed her stomach, causing the muscles underneath to quiver. Sliding his hands up, he cupped her breasts, testing the fullness.

"Ken," she whispered, wishing she wasn't trembling beneath him.

"So perfect," he rasped, warm breath heating her ear.

"Touch me," she pleaded.

"Do you want me to tug on those hard little nipples?"

"You know I do."

Lowering a hand, he picked up one of the ends of the tie to the robe. Lifting it, he brought it to one of the straining nubs, gently feathering the soft fabric over it.

Tilting her head back onto his shoulder, she strained toward the material.

"That's it, sweetheart. Reach for it. Does that feel good?"

"Yes," she moaned, looking up at him. "Stop teasing me."

"Look back at the mirror," he said, so confident and sure. "I'll stop teasing when you stop trying to tell me what to do."

"Bastard," she said, following his directive. Body throbbing, she let the feeling take her as he swished the soft fabric over one nipple, then the other. Back and forth, over and over, she thought she might burst with anticipation.

Finally, he lowered the fabric. Skimming the pads of his fingers up her sides, he slid them over to her nipples, latching on with his forefinger and thumb. Watching her in the reflection, breathing hard into the crevice of her ear, he squeezed.

"You're trying to kill me," she moaned, barely recognizing the woman in the mirror with swollen lips and flushed skin.

"I'm trying to please you," he said, tugging the nubs between his fingers in a lazy rhythm. Each tug sent a jolt of moisture between her thighs. "I want so much for you to enjoy being touched."

"I'm enjoying it, believe me," she said, breathing a laugh. "Get on with it. I'm ready to have you inside me."

"Not on your life, sweetheart. We're just getting started."

Groaning, she relaxed into him, letting him tug and play with her nipples. Eventually, he ceased the maddening pulls, skating his hands down to the belt of the robe. Untying the knot, he spread the fabric.

"Red," he said, tracing the tiny strip of hair atop her mound with his index finger.

"Mmm hmm..."

"I was curious."

"I bet you were."

Chuckling, he slid his hands lower. Gripping the inside of her thighs, he spread them slightly. Watching his hand slide toward her core was the sexiest thing she'd ever seen.

With one finger, he traced the lips of her opening. Unashamed, she purred, straining toward him for more.

"I'm barely touching you, and you're soaking my finger. God, Evie. It's so hot."

"I know," she said, panting. "Please, Ken. Make me come."

White teeth glowed as he smiled at her. Goddamnit, his fucking smile was so gorgeous. "Yes, ma'am." Closing his teeth on the rim of her ear, he inserted his middle finger inside her.

Evie cursed, curving her hips to impale him further. Straining up into her, he crooked his finger back and forth. "Where's your spot, baby? Is it there? Or maybe there?"

"Everywhere," she rasped. Writhing in his arms, she jutted into his hand. "More."

Chuckling against her ear, he inserted another finger. Moving them within her, he brought his other hand to toy with her clit. As his thick fingers stretched her, gyrating inside, he rubbed the engorged nub with the pad of his fingers.

"Does that feel good, sweetheart?"

"Yessss... don't stop. Oh, god."

Opening her eyes, she locked onto his beautiful, coffee-colored irises.

"I've seen you like this in my dreams. It's so much better than I imagined. Take my fingers and come for me. I want to feel you gush all over me."

High-pitched mewls escaped her, spurred on by his steamy words. "I'm so close."

"Yes, you are. I can feel your tight little walls choking my fingers." Increasing the pace of both hands, his fingers frenzied on her clit, he demanded, "Come. Now. I've got you."

Flinging her head back, she exploded, every cell in her body shooting bursts of energy to her core. Collapsing in his arms, he held her somehow, still stimulating her as she convulsed. Throbbing and quaking, she gave up control, letting him support her, too raw to care. Even though her legs seemed to be comprised of jelly, she eventually began to feel the floor underneath her feet. Sinking into Kenden's warmth, she reveled in his embrace.

Mustering the energy to lift her lids, she found those arresting eyes in the reflection. They were sated but somehow still filled with hunger. She realized he was happy that she'd found her release first. Something that rarely happened with the men she fucked.

Pulling his hand from her, he brought his fingers to his mouth. Eyes never leaving hers, he closed his lips over his index finger, sliding it out slowly so he could drink her taste from it. Once finished, he lowered his third finger, rubbing it on her lower lip, spreading her essence over the plushy flesh. Parting her lips, he stuck the finger inside, growling when she closed around it. Backing it out slowly, she sipped herself from him.

Placing those fingers on her cheek, he turned her face toward his. Merging his lips to hers, his tongue pushed inside, searching. Making a suggestive noise in the back of his throat, he lapped every inch of her mouth.

"Kissing you while I taste the deepest part of you in your mouth is so sexy," he said against her lips.

"Everything about you is sexy," she said, too replete to come up with something clever. Usually, she was a master at finding the right words to gain the upper hand during sex, but tonight, she was spent. Completely.

"I'm glad you think so. I'm at a huge disadvantage since I can't read your thoughts."

Amused, she nipped at his bottom lip. "I think it's pretty obvious I want you. I mean, I staked the future of two species on it."

His low-toned chuckle washed over her, enveloping her expended frame with its warmth. Walls down, she inwardly admitted how good it felt.

"I'm glad. How about I get out of these clothes so I can accomplish my mission?"

She grinned. "Do you want me to dematerialize them?"

He shook his head. "I want you to undress me. Slowly. Like I'm the first man you've ever undressed and the last man you ever will." Rotating her to face him, he cupped her cheeks. "Got it?"

"Yes, sir, Commander," she said, arching a brow. Excited to see those abs again, she set about following his order.

* * * *

Kenden's blood coursed through his body, thanks to the pounding organ in his chest, as Evie unlaced his tie with her thin fingers. Tossing the silky cloth to the floor, she slowly unbuttoned his shirt. Opening the fabric, she pushed it from his shoulders.

"Good grief," she breathed, raking her red nails over his pecs and stomach. "Your abs are fucking delectable."

"A nice side-effect of my occupation."

"Mmmm..." she murmured, the pads of her fingers brushing over the tiny brown hairs on his chest.

Dropping her hands, she unbuckled his belt, pulling it from the loops and throwing it on the floor. After freeing the button and lowering the zipper, she inserted her hand inside. Grabbing his length, she set him free.

"I love seeing your hand around my cock," he said, his voice seeming to come from far away. Lowering his forehead to rest on hers, he groaned when she began tugging the length, back and forth.

"You're very well-endowed, Commander." Those full lips formed a seductive smile.

"Thank god. I need every advantage with you."

Fusing his lips to hers, he drew her to him, needing to envelop her mouth with his. Shooting high-pitched mewls down the back of his throat, he felt a *whoosh* and realized she'd dematerialized the rest of his attire.

"Sorry, but I've had enough of slow and steady. I need you to fuck me."

Unable to control his growl, he bent his knees and palmed her ass. Lifting her, he rotated and gently threw her on the bed. Tiny giggles escaped her as she bounced, the globes of her breasts moving in tandem with her gorgeous body.

"You look so damn adorable right now," he said, smiling down at her.

"Get over here, you infuriating man." Arms outstretched, she beckoned to him.

Sliding over her, he aligned his body with hers. Balancing his weight on one arm, he reached down with the other to grab her behind the knee. Lifting her leg, he pushed it toward her shoulder. Straightening his arm, palm flat on the mattress, he anchored her thin leg so that she was open to him.

Touching the head of his cock to her slick center, he watched her. Those lips were open, short breaths escaping, eyes heavy-lidded and filled with arousal.

Every muscle of his taut body was on fire as he began to push inside her. Like the sweetest, wettest glove, the plushy walls of her core sucked him inside.

"Yes. Stretch me open," she pleaded below him. "You can go faster."

"No," he said through gritted teeth. Locked on to her magnificent irises, he continued jutting forward, inch by inch. "I want you to *feel* me, sweetheart. Every single bit."

Tossing her head back, her hips undulated to meet him. The action was filled with frustration and desire. Her sultry moans drove him wild as he eased himself into her.

Skin coated with sweat, he finally reached the hilt, cock pulsing as it rested fully inside her warmth. "Look at me," he commanded.

Latching her pupils on to his, she waited.

He withdrew completely and then thrust into her, hard and sure.

"Yessss..."

Increasing the pace, he began fucking her in earnest, making sure to impale her fully each time. Red flushes of fire burned her fair skin, making her look so exquisite in the dim light of the bedside lamp. His shaft was a frayed mass of nerves, the pleasure so intense that he wondered if he'd ever felt anything that compared. Deciding it impossible, he drew her other leg up, anchoring it on his straightened arm. She was fully exposed to him, her legs bent and resting on his arms as her knees stretched toward her shoulders.

Needing to make it good for her, he hammered inside, hitting the spot that sat deep within. Feeling her tense around him, he knew she was close. Fusing his lips to hers, he sucked in her scream before she threw her head back and began to convulse around him.

Wave upon wave of pleasure doused him as her drenched walls milked him. Unable to hold on any longer, he threaded his fingers in her hair, buried his face in her neck and shot into her. Jets pulsed out of him as she throbbed beneath him, both of them finding their release as they shouted words of desire and passion.

Inhaling the fragrant scent of her skin, Kenden held her, loving how their bodies seemed to quake together in the aftermath. Lifting a shaking hand, she caressed his thick hair, causing him to shudder inside her spent body.

They lay like that for minutes, maybe hours, sated and sanguine. Every so often, she would trail her fingertips down his broad back, and his would tangle in her hair. It was lazy, almost gluttonous, and Kenden didn't give a damn.

"I should clean us up and head home but I'm about to fall asleep," he murmured into her shoulder.

"Let's stay here and say fuck it. I feel too good to move."

Chuckling, he pressed a soft kiss on her velvety skin. With strong arms, he repositioned their heads to the pillows, pulling the covers over their bodies. Nuzzling into her, wedged to her side as his thick arm drew her close, he fell into darkness, thanking every god above that she was sated.

And so it went, for centuries in the timeframe of some worlds. The two friends would meet, sating each other's loneliness, as they spoke of days gone by and futures ahead. They formed a strong bond. One of friendship and gaiety.

The woman knew that the man had grown to love her, in the way that a man loves a woman, and her heart hurt at the realization. For, although she loved the man as a dear friend, she did not possess the ability to love romantically. It was something the Universe had not instilled in her when it had conceived her in the moment of creation.

Slowly, her heart began to fill with dread, knowing she would have to eventually tell the man that she could never love him as he loved her...

Chapter 7

Sunlight burned Evie's eyes as she forced them open. Refusing to capitulate to the bright rays, she stared ahead. Kenden snored softly behind her, his arm wrenched around her waist. Warm breath heated the back of her neck as he respired into her, and she realized something extremely important.

She was *pissed*.

Mentally screaming every curse word in her extensive repertoire, she gritted her teeth. The sound of her molars grinding together could probably be heard at the main castle. What in the ever-loving hell had she been thinking?

First, she'd let her guard down, telling Kenden her deepest thoughts as if she was a teenage girl dying to join the popular clique. In a moment of weakness, she'd discussed Francesco's death with him. Stupid and careless.

Then, she'd let him take her home and gain the upper hand. Those strong hands had torn down the seemingly impenetrable walls she'd built long ago. Scoffing, she shook her head into the pillow. Impenetrable her ass.

Next, she'd cried. As in, tears down her cheeks, throat swollen, ugly-cried. Mother of all gods. What otherworldly spirit had invaded her body last night? That was the only explanation that was even remotely possible. She hadn't cried in centuries. Well, for the most part, she begrudgingly admitted, thinking of Francesco again.

And finally, she'd let him stay over. In her bed. Evie usually preferred to stay at her lovers' residences. It allowed her the freedom to disappear whenever the hell she pleased. But no, Kenden had stayed. Cuddling with her like they were high school sweethearts. At one point, he'd woken her, his impressive shaft pressed against her back, and she'd slithered into him. Biting her neck with those perfect teeth, he'd impaled her from behind, giving her another round of exquisite sex. Bastard.

Now, she was lying here in Mr. Perfect's embrace, wondering how in god's name she was going to extricate her body from his.

"If you want to get up, go ahead," he mumbled behind her. The deep timbre of his voice sent all sorts of tingles through her body. "I have to get up soon anyway to train the troops."

"Fine," she said, shrugging off his arm and rising. She absolutely did not miss the heat from his broad body. Nope. Not one bit. Shrugging on her robe, she headed to the kitchen to make coffee. It was early, and Evie didn't do mornings. Not well, anyway, and definitely not cordially.

As the coffee brewed, she inhaled the smell, attempting to calm her jitters. He would leave soon enough. She'd see him out and get back to putting up those defenses that she was so damn proud of. And why shouldn't she be? They'd protected her for ages. This situation with Kenden was temporary. She'd do well to remember that before she fell down the rabbit hole of acting like a complete romantic moron.

"I smell coffee," he said, strolling into the kitchen looking like a bronzed Adonis. Shirt unbuttoned, slacks and loafers on, jacket and tie thrown over his arm. He certainly wasn't worried about making a walk of shame home.

"Yep. I only made enough for myself. Sorry." Pouring some into a ceramic mug, she added creamer from the fridge and came to stand by the small island in the middle of the cramped kitchen. Leaning her hip on it, she smiled sweetly. "Get home safely."

Eyes narrowed as he gave her a knowing grin. "I think there's enough left in the pot for me to have a cup before I go."

"Nope," she said, blinking rapidly. "Too bad. See ya around. Hope the training goes well."

He stood for a moment, a few feet from her, contemplating. Throwing his jacket and tie on the nearby two-seater table, he stalked to the cabinet, pulled down a mug and poured himself a cup from the coffee maker.

Telling herself not to rise to the bait, Evie gave him her most saccharine smile. "Oh, I guess there was enough. Good to know since I didn't offer you any."

Kenden took a sip, chestnut irises observing her over the rim of the mug. Slowly approaching, he set the cup down and faced her, reclining against the island with his hip. There, they stood, mirroring each other as they leaned on the counter, deciding the next move in the game they were suddenly playing.

"So, that's it, huh?" he asked, one eyebrow arched. "We had fun together, and now, you're so anxious for me to leave that you're physically restraining yourself from pushing me out the door?"

"You can stay as long as you want," she said, her tone ever so polite. "I just thought you had stuff to do today. And so do I. I have a session with Darkrip and I need to get ready."

Reaching for the mug, he leisurely swallowed another swig of coffee, amusement pulsing in his eyes. "Your session with Darkrip isn't until ten. It's seven-fifteen."

Of course, the kingdom's commander would know everyone on the compound's schedule. Evie found it infuriating. That, compounded by the fact he was silently laughing at her, made her want to punch him square in his handsome face.

"Well, you're invading my privacy," she snapped. "I should've transported us to your house last night. I'm not sure what sort of temporary insanity made me choose the cabin, but you need to leave. I don't do morning-after bagels and banter, Commander. So, drink up and get the hell out of my house."

Setting the mug on the island, he reached over and attempted to grasp her wrists. Pulling them away, she scowled at him. "Don't touch me."

Gazing down at her, he closed the distance between them until their combined energy seemed to sizzle. Refusing to back down, she lifted her chin, glowering up at him.

"I'm sorry you feel uncomfortable about what happened between us last night, but that's the only apology I'm going to make." Goose bumps washed over her flesh from his silky baritone. "I won't apologize for asking you to open yourself up to me, Evie. It was so beautiful to see you that way, and I wish that you would let yourself be with someone who demands that of you. You deserve to be with a partner who pushes you to be your best self and to be trusting and vulnerable. It's time for you to have that."

What an arrogant bastard he was. Fuming, Evie slammed her mug down on the counter. "Don't tell me what I want or need, you son of a bitch. You don't know the first thing about me. I don't want a partner and I sure as hell don't want to be vulnerable. Now, get the fuck out of my house."

Kenden sighed, long and slow, and shook his head as he regarded her. "Let's talk when I can be assured you won't rip my eyeballs out with your fingernails. I'll text you later." Sauntering over to the table, he picked up his coat and tie. He looked so gorgeous, staring at her as he was framed by the sunlight from the nearby windows. Evie considered that the only reason she didn't hurl the nearby mug right into his attractive face. After all, it would be a tragedy to break that perfect, angular nose.

"Thank you for a lovely evening," he said softly. And then, he was gone.

Evie stood by the counter as the minutes ticked away, each stroke of the second hand another instant to ponder what the hell had happened last night and the grave mistakes she'd made. When the undrunk coffee was cold and her pounding heart had returned to normal, she placed the cups in the sink and headed to shower, hoping to wash it all away.

* * * *

Darkrip watched his sister fail miserably at generating the combined force-field they were working on. Facing each other in the open meadow near her cabin, she stood across from him, frustration lining her expression. From his outstretched hands extended a perfect, solid but almost invisible barrier. From hers, the energy was frazzled and sparking. Realizing they were wasting their time, he dropped his hands, the fuzzy barrier vanishing into thin air.

"What the fuck?" Evie yelled, fisting her hands at her sides so that the hazy plasma around her also disintegrated. "I was getting there. Why did you stop?"

His pupils darted around her face. "You're frazzled. Your mind is somewhere else. It's futile for us to continue."

Almond-shaped eyes narrowed. "Screw you. I'll get it. Let's try again." She lifted her hands and began to generate the block of energy again. Darkrip remained still, eyeing her.

Exhaling a furious breath, she fisted her hands on her hips. "If we don't get this, we're as good as dead. The bastard will chew us up and spit us out. Is that what you want? What will happen to your Vampyre and the little brat she's carrying?"

"I understand the consequences of not generating the force-field effectively," he said, keeping his tone calm. "However, I don't want to waste time practicing with you when you're obviously torn up about fucking Ken last night. Or do you want to deny it?"

Her features drew together, the freckles darkening under the red flash of anger on her skin. "That's none of your business. Stop reading my thoughts."

Lifting his fingers to his chin, Darkrip stroked, looking to the blue sky as he contemplated. "I could use this opportunity to ridicule you as you did me when I fell for Arderin. How positively amusing," he murmured.

"I'm not *falling* for anyone," she spat, thrusting her chin out. "I don't work that way. I didn't think you did either, but the snarky princess must have a golden vagina or something. It's absolutely ridiculous."

Trying to control his mirth, he watched her stomp around the grass, mumbling to herself. "He's a good match for you. I can see these things. Ask Miranda. I knew the night she met Sathan that it was only a matter of time."

Evie crossed her arms over her chest. "Ken's a fucking boy scout who wouldn't last a hot minute with someone as evil as me. Just because you turned into a damn choir boy doesn't mean I will. Let it go. I'm going to grab some water inside. Give me five."

As Darkrip watched her stalk to the cabin, he realized he needed to have a talk with Kenden once the bargain he'd struck with Evie was completed. The Slayer commander was wise but it was important he knew how much he affected Evie. It was imperative that she was one-hundred percent focused when they fought their father. Otherwise, the future of the immortals was doomed.

Sauntering back outside, she thrust a bottle of water at him. "Drink up. I'm ready. I'm actually enjoying the challenge and determined to get this. We'll work on the force-field for another hour, and then, I want to go over the black magic freezing spell."

Deciding not to push her—for now—he took a swig of the water, cherishing it under the midday sun. Sated, they got to work.

After the hour spent on the combined barrier, Evie formed a hexagram in the grass with sticks she'd gathered from the nearby forest. Closing their eyes, they called upon the forces of dark magic and voodoo from the human world. Together, they took turns casting freezing spells upon each other. Since Crimeous was so powerful, they weren't able to immobilize him as they could others. With the human magic, they hoped to enhance their abilities enough to halt him in place, so they could surround him with the force-field that would alleviate his powers. Only then could Evie thrust the Blade of Pestilence into his gristly body, hopefully ridding him from the planet.

As the bright orb above began its daily descent toward the far-off mountains, they sat down on the crunchy grass to assess their progress.

"We're there with the human magic but we have more work to do on the force-field," he said, picking at the grass near his thigh.

"Yes," she said, nodding. "I don't know why I'm having such a hard time with it. I'm used to being excessively more powerful than you."

Darkrip chuckled. "Maybe you're losing your touch now that you're a big softie for the Commander."

Evie rolled her eyes. "Enough. Sex is just another function to me, like breathing or eating. Feelings and emotions have absolutely nothing to do with it. Once we defeat Father, I'm heading back to the human world."

"Well, Arderin and I would love that. I'll be raising the baby while she's completing her medical training and would love for our daughter to get to know her Aunt Evie."

She snorted. "Don't get too excited. I'm okay with kids for a while but then they annoy the ever-loving shit out of me." Glancing over, she pondered. "But maybe I'll like your kid. We'll see. Hope she looks like Arderin. You're an ugly son of a bitch."

His laughter echoed across the open field. "I can always count on you to knock my arrogance down a few notches, sis."

After a moment, he asked, "Would it be so terrible to try something new? To consider attempting a serious relationship with a man? I'm not saying run away and elope tomorrow, but perhaps something more than fucking? I can tell you, from my own experience, opening yourself up that way creates so many new possibilities that I never even fathomed. Arderin was brave enough to love me even with all the terrible things I've done in the past. It's such a gift. I want you to have that, Evie."

"No one will ever love me," she said, drawing her knees up to her chest and embracing them with her thin arms. "I learned that long ago. Even Mother wasn't capable."

Darkrip sighed. "Mother was quite deranged once you were old enough to remember her. He'd tortured every last fraction of spirit from her. But I assure you, she loved you. When you were a baby, she was obsessed with making sure he never hurt you."

Evie scoffed. "Well, she did a piss-poor job."

"Yes. As did I. We both let you down." Straightening his spine, he placed his hand on her shoulder. "But it doesn't mean that we didn't love you." Struggling with feelings that were still so new to him, he said, "I love you now, Evie. I hope you understand that."

Shaking off his hand, she gazed at him, chin resting on her knees. "It's not possible. I'm rotten inside."

Darkrip couldn't control his smile. "Are you really? Is it that bad? I think there's a lot of good in you."

She gave a *harrumph*. "You're delusional."

"Look at you, training to fight with us. Risking your life to save two species. That's pretty amazing. Why are you doing it?"

Her expression was wistful as she stared across the grassy meadow. "I don't know."

"Come on. There must be some reason why you came back. You hate the immortal world, and yet you're jeopardizing your future to fight with us."

Exhaling a breath, her eyelids narrowed. "I guess I'd become complacent with the humans. I'd never really spent any time in the immortal world, outside of the Deamon caves, and I was intrigued. The thought of killing father captivated me, and I was curious to meet Miranda."

"That's a good start," he said, nodding. "But I think you need to identify exactly what you're fighting for. Having clear goals and objectives will help you when things get tough. And I'm sure they will. Father must know you're here."

"I wonder about that as I sit outside my cabin at night sometimes," she said. Straightening her legs, she crossed them at the ankles and rested on outstretched arms behind her back. "He hasn't approached me yet. I don't think he understands the extent of my powers. When he finds out, who knows what he'll do?"

"That's exactly why you need specific goals. To remind you of what you're fighting for. He'll play dirty, and you need to remain true to the cause."

"The cause," she said with a joyless laugh. "Saving tribes of people who want nothing to do with me."

"I want something to do with you," he said, placing his hand over hers. "Miranda does too. And I'm pretty sure Kenden is dead-set on making whatever arrangement you have with him more permanent."

"Not after this morning," she said, her tone wry. "I was an absolute bitch to him."

"Not to be an ass, but he's probably used to that from you, Evie."

Chuckling, she locked her green gaze onto his. "You may be right."

Releasing her hand, Darkrip stood and brushed off his pants. "I have to get home. I told Arderin I'd cook tonight. She's craving food now that she's pregnant."

Evie stood and closed the distance between them. Gently, she brushed some stray grass off his shirt, the absent gesture so caring that he wondered if she even knew how natural it was for her. "You're a domesticated idiot. Mister cook-the-meals and stay-at-home dad. My god, I never thought I'd see the day."

He spiked a brow. "Me neither. Believe me." Placing a kiss on her forehead, he said, "See ya." With a *whoosh*, he dematerialized home to his beloved wife.

* * * *

Moira watched Aron as he directed the delivery men around the park. The council had voted to build an extensive new playground in Uteria's lush main square, and of course, Aron had volunteered to run point. Panting, she lifted the metal container to her lips, chugging the cold water.

She'd come out here for her daily run. It was a great way to start the day before she had to head to the gallery. Smiling, she thought of Tobias. Last week, she'd made a rather large sale to him. That, combined with the amazing show they'd had this past weekend, had led to the highest week of sales since she'd started. Setting an intention that this one would be even better, she stretched against the wide oak tree that stood tall beside her.

Aron must've sensed her watching him from across the park because he lifted his hand in a wave to her. Waving back, she told her stupid heart to stop pounding. He was just about the most adorable man she'd ever met.

Wrinkling her nose, Moira realized it was ridiculous to think a man adorable. Most women wanted someone sexy and hot. Like her bastard ex-husband. He'd been as handsome and charming as a human movie star—until the first time he'd hit her. Narrowing her eyes, she contemplated the memories as she stretched.

The beatings had started out small. A backhand across the cheek here, a forceful shake from his vice-like grip on her upper arms there. Always needing to parade her around as the beauty on his arm, he would become consumed with fury when her face bruised. Much of her stipend, controlled by Diabolos and deposited into her account monthly, was spent buying makeup to cover up the welts. She'd learned very quickly that if she didn't conceal them well, he would beat her more violently when they returned home.

Aron had been around during those decades, never fathoming that his best friend, whom he idolized, could hurt his wife. She'd wanted so many times to run to him, to tell him how terrible Diabolos was. Sadly, Moira never gained the courage, choosing to live with her fear.

She'd known Aron all her life. As a high-born aristocrat, he could've disregarded her, the daughter of their housekeeper. But he'd always accepted her, all those centuries ago, telling her that she was worthy. If only she'd had the guts to believe him.

When Diabolos proposed to her, she saw it as a way out. An opportunity to ascend to a higher station. Never did she think it would instead transport her to a life of so much pain and violence. In the fantasies of her youth, she had often imagined marrying Aron. With his handsome face and kind demeanor, he too could've elevated her position in society. But Aron was quite rigid in his beliefs about bloodlines and heirs. Although he claimed to see her as an equal, she knew he would choose to settle down with a high-born aristocratic woman one day. Diabolos, on the other hand? He'd hated their stuffy, expensive world. His jealousy of Aron had always been clear to Moira, as his bloodline didn't extend nearly as far back. But Aron hadn't seemed to notice, always brushing off her husband's jabs with his affable humor and affection.

The tipping point had come the night of the great feast, over eight centuries ago. King Marsias had gathered all the aristocrats together at the main castle for a grand dinner, hoping to get them to pledge extra money to fund the War of the Species. Diabolos had insisted she wear a low-cut, formfitting dress to show off her beauty and her breasts. He felt that he owned her, sure as the watch or the cufflinks upon his wrist, and he wanted his possession to be paraded for all to see.

The dinner had been quite boring, and she'd struck up a conversation with a nice man seated to her left at the elongated dinner table. Long ago, she'd forgotten his name, but he possessed kind eyes and a quick wit. Moira thoroughly enjoyed their conversation and found herself laughing quite often during dinner.

When the dessert arrived, and the man excused himself to the restroom, she turned to look at her husband. Forcefully, her heart plummeted in her chest. A mask of rage, the likes of which she had never seen, covered his angular features. Fear clasped around her throat, and she dreaded returning home.

She'd said good night to Aron, pleading with him through her eyes. He'd just smiled and given her a peck on the cheek, wishing her and Diabolos a good evening. Her husband's thick body pulsed with fury as he escorted her home in silence, their footsteps ominous on the cold stone sidewalk. Once inside, she'd turned to him, anxious to explain that she'd felt nothing for the man who sat beside her at dinner.

Before she could utter a word, the back of his hand splintered her face. Reeling from the blow, she plodded into the large adjoining dining room and collapsed on the mahogany table. Falling onto it with the top of her body, she felt him behind her, pulling up her dress.

She'd never know where the rush of adrenaline came from that night. Lord knows, she'd let him beat her so many times before. But there, lying across the table, her face throbbing with pain as he pulled at the silky fabric, something snapped in her. With a feral growl, she forced her head back, smacking him in the nose. Cursing, he fell back, holding his hand to his bleeding face.

"You bitch!" he cried, grabbing a chunk of her hair and pulling her to him. Undeterred, she kneed him in the balls, wrenching from his grasp to run away. She made it about half the length of the long table when he seized her again. Fisting her hair in his large hand, he slammed her face into the table. With a mighty roar, he lifted her head again and banged it into the thick wooden chair beside her.

Stars flooded her vision, and she knew that she was dying. Collapsing on the floor, she lifted her hand to her hairline, above her neck, realizing she was gushing blood. Diabolos stood above her, fists clenched at his sides as he prepared to murder her with one last blow.

From so far away, a knock sounded. Was it the Passage? Requesting her to come over to the other side? Surely, she wouldn't hurt so much one she was there. Voices spoke from the front door, Moira only discerning every other sentence.

'Vampyres raiding tonight...stay inside if you can...they're all over the damn compound...'

Grasping on to every last ounce of strength, she rose on wobbly legs. Through the kitchen and out the back door she trudged, until she heard the screams of battle. Desperate to reach them, she slogged until she saw a Vampyre soldier.

His eyebrows drew together as he approached her. "Are you hurt? Our soldiers are under orders not to harm women." Moira found his deep voice so comforting.

"Not from raid..." she sputtered. "Husband hit me. Please, help. He'll kill me."

The Vampyre's almost translucent blue eyes roved over her. "Okay. I've got you."

The large man lifted her, carrying her to one of the metal-barred carriages that the troops used to transport Slayers to Astaria. Sitting her inside, he'd given one of the men orders to clean and address her wounds.

An eternity later, another Vampyre entered the carriage, this one even larger than the one who'd transported her, if possible. "What do we have, Takel?" he asked.

"I carried her here after I found her like this. She says someone beat her."

The massive Vampyre lifted her chin, carefully observing her face. "What is your name?"

"Moira," she rasped.

Ice-blue eyes darted over her injuries. "We can't take you with us, Moira. I'm sorry. You need to go home."

"Please," she begged, knowing this was the one opportunity to save her life. "He'll kill me. Take me with you. I'll perform whatever labor you need. I'll feed your people from my own vein. Whatever it takes."

After a moment of contemplation, his broad arms enfolded her, lifting her and cradling her to his chest. He carried her to a different carriage, this one with a royal crest. Black horses were attached to the front, ready to pull their cargo back to Astaria.

Stepping inside, he lay her across the cushioned seat. With concern in his eyes, he regarded her. "Our king has banned the abduction of women and children. You know this, yes?"

She nodded, praying with everything inside that he would defy the decree.

"I'm reluctant to help you, but you remind me of someone that I...care about very much. I think she would want me to help you."

"Please," she said, tears beginning to fall down her cheeks.

Inhaling a large breath, he nodded. "Okay. Don't move. I'll be back within the hour."

True to his word, the hulking Vampyre had returned and transported her to Astaria. Only later did she learn that he was Latimus, brother to King Sathan and commander of the vast Vampyre army. Thankful for his protection, he'd given her a cabin to stay in on the outskirts of Astaria.

Weeks later, after she'd healed, he'd come to her. With sadness and pain in his blue irises, he'd explained that there was someone he loved and whom he could never have. Understanding washed over Moira as she realized *this* was the woman she reminded him of. Wanting to comfort him, she'd offered herself to him, wanting to soothe the man who'd saved her life.

And so it had gone for centuries. Latimus would come to her when his craving for Lila became too much to bear. He had other women who lived in the cabins, women he had also saved. Moira thought him so kind and often wondered if Lila knew his true feelings. Surely, she couldn't love another over someone as decent as Latimus.

Centuries later, Lila broke the betrothal. Latimus came to her, explaining that he still couldn't have the woman who'd been promised to his brother, but urging her and the other women to return to the Slayer compounds. Moira realized that he couldn't fathom being with anyone else in a world where Lila was free. It was heartbreaking and touching and, after placing a sweet kiss goodbye on his broad lips, she had headed back to the compound she'd called home, all those centuries ago.

First, she'd gone to Aron. She didn't know why he was the one whom she felt comfortable approaching. Perhaps because she trusted that he would protect her from Diabolos once he realized she was alive. With shaking hands, she'd knocked on his door, reveling in the joy on his handsome face when he'd first seen her. Scooping her up in a huge embrace, he told her of Diabolos' passing several centuries ago in a riding accident. He'd had a swift fall and cleanly broken his neck. Bastard. Moira silently wished he'd suffered more.

Afraid to tell Aron where she'd been, she lied to him, telling him that she'd been abducted the night of the raid and escaped, fleeing to live at Restia. She told him that she'd thought Diabolos dead and saw no reason to return to Uteria.

Somehow, Aron bought the flimsy story. Biting her lip, Moira realized it was because he was such a genuine person, always seeing the best in others. It was probably a foreign concept to him that she wouldn't be truthful.

At night, when she lay in the darkness, guilt consumed her for lying to him. But fear of his condemnation as well as a slight bit of shame held her back from imparting the truth. Aron was a traditionalist, believing in the old-school rules for women. He'd told her many times in his youth that he wished to marry a virgin and felt that women should save their virginity for their husbands. She didn't blame him for the views, which she considered stuffy and outdated. He was a product of his upbringing and eternities-old teachings. But she feared what he would think of her, knowing she had traded her body for her safety. Terrified he would hate her and judge her a whore, she decided to stick with the lies.

And now, over a year later, she was also stuck in infatuation. With him. The benevolent aristocrat who'd done so much to help her piece her life back together. Observing him with the laborers as they lined up the various wooden slats and metal bars that would become the playground, she noticed how kind he was to them. Many aristocrats would look down their nose at laborers, but not Aron. Sighing, she reveled in his graciousness.

Longing permeated his attractive features as Miranda approached. Giving him a broad smile, the queen gestured around the future playground, most likely asking him for a progress update. Aron's firm body was slightly tense as he spoke to her, kind and jovial. Love for her seemed to wash off his strong frame in waves. Moira wondered how no one else saw it. He was mad for her.

Moira knew that Aron had proposed to Miranda, only to be shot down when she fell for the Vampyre king. How that must have hurt her proud friend. Rubbing her hand over her heart, she let herself imagine for one moment that he was on his knee in front of her, lifting his mother's ring, asking her to be his wife. How magnificent that would be.

Shaking her head, she mentally scolded herself for living in a damn fairy tale. Not only would Aron never think to marry someone with a servant's bloodline but he was determined to place her on a pedestal as Diabolos' wife. Aron's code of honor would never let him even think of touching his friend's wife, even if he was dead. Frustrated, Moira clenched her jaw.

Done with her stretching, she chugged the contents of her metal canister and decided to head home. She needed to shower and prepare for work. And, if she was honest, she could no longer watch the man she pined for stare at the woman he loved in the way he could never love her.

The woman waited, hoping against hope that the man would release his affection toward her. Sadly, it wasn't meant to be. Knowing she must be gentle but honest, she regarded him under the setting sun.

"I am sorry, my dear Galredad," she said.

"For what?" he asked.

"I have felt your fondness for me and have let it progress too far. I am not like the others of this planet and cannot feel romantic love. I beg you to understand that I care so much for you, in the way that I can, and hope we can remain friends."

The man's face turned cold, causing the woman to shiver...

Chapter 8

Evie's phone buzzed promptly at seven p.m. Monday evening. Glancing toward the device, as she sat at the tiny kitchen table eating a microwave dinner that tasted like cardboard, she scowled.

Kenden: Is it safe to contact you? I want to call but want to make sure you won't reach through the phone and dislodge my testicles.

Oh, so he thought he was funny? Jerk. Picking up the phone, she typed.

Evie: I can't guarantee the safety of your balls. Ever. But you can call me if you want. I'll answer.

Seconds later, the phone buzzed, and she lifted it to her ear. "Hello, Commander," she said, trying to keep her tone light.

"Hello, Evie," he said. Goddamnit, his voice was like warm, melted butter. Maybe she should mentally squeeze his testicles after all. Then, he wouldn't be able to talk in that silken baritone and make her gush in her damn thong. "What are you doing?"

Evie grimaced. "Eating a really shitty dinner. You?"

"Same. I wish I'd learned to cook, but Jana is so great that I always let her cook for me," he said, referencing the main castle's housekeeper.

"I'm actually a pretty good cook."

"No shit," he said, his smile seeming to travel over the phone. "When did you learn?"

"I learned a lot of useless crap over eight centuries in the human world, believe me. I took at least twenty French cooking courses when I lived in Paris."

"Hot damn. I need to see this in action."

Evie chuckled in spite of herself. "Well, maybe I'll cook for you on one of our *dates*." Silence stretched, making her uncomfortable. "I mean, if you still want to continue with the bargain. I was a pretty big bitch to you yesterday morning."

He was quiet, and Evie could almost hear the wheels of his mind churning. "Do I have an out? You were pretty clear in your ultimatum."

A crack shot down her heart that he actually wanted out of their agreement. Self-hate coursed through her, reminding her that this was just one more example of how far decent people would go to escape from her if she gave them a choice. Determined to retain the upper hand, she said, "Sorry, but the deal's still on. Two more dates, or I go back to the human world. I know it's not what you want, but I hold all the cards."

Kenden sighed, sending the sad sound through the phone. "It's not what I want at all—"

"Well, too fucking bad," she snapped, annoyed at him, especially since she'd let herself be so vulnerable with him the other night. "Because it's two more nights of fucking or nothing. Take it or leave it."

"Are you done?" he asked angrily.

She didn't respond.

"What I was trying to say, before someone rudely interrupted me, is that this arrangement is not what I want at all. I'd rather just date you, without there having to be some bargain or timeline."

"Huh," she said, feeling her eyebrows draw together. "Interesting, since you were pretty clear at my brother's wedding that you weren't interested in fucking me."

"That hasn't changed, Evie. I'm not interested just fucking you, as I think I've told you numerous times now. Since that was all you seemed to want, I wasn't interested in pursuing anything further. Now that we've established that we can actually have a good time together, I find myself wanting to spend what extra time I have with you."

Her heart dropped to her stomach, landing in an anxious pit as she absorbed his words. Why in the hell did she react to him this way? Many other men had bestowed beautiful words upon her. None of them had even phased her. But this man, with his sincerity and honesty, threatened to give her a damn heart attack.

"That sounds very serious, Commander, and serious is not on the agenda for me. I assure you, if you give me two more dates, your sentence will be served."

"Fine," he said, sounding resigned and annoyed. "I'm really swamped with the troops, so I'd like to stick to Saturdays if that's okay with you. We can have our second date this Saturday and the last one the following Saturday. Sound good?"

"Sure," she said, trying to sound more nonchalant than she was. "What is it this Saturday? More romantic strolls by the river?"

"I have the day off, so I was thinking we could hang during the day if that works for you. There's a great hiking trail that I'd love to show you. If you like that sort of thing."

"Well, it's your lucky day because I actually love hiking. As I told you, I spent some time in Colorado. The hiking there is fantastic."

"Great," he said. "I'll pick you up at ten a.m. on Saturday. Sound good?"

"I'll be ready. I'll make sure to wear my tightest sports bra so you can ogle my tits and then pretend that you didn't."

His chuckle almost made her squirm. "Now that I've been inside you, I think I can stop pretending. You have gorgeous breasts, Evie, and you damn well know it. If I don't see you on the compound, I'll see you on Saturday. Sweet dreams."

With a click, the phone went dead. As she watched the light of the device fade, she imagined she'd be having very sweet dreams this evening. Of a tall, sweaty man throwing her over a rock by a secluded hiking trail and banging her mindless. Sweet indeed.

* * * *

Kenden entered Miranda's royal office chamber on Tuesday afternoon. The day's training had gone well, and he needed to speak to his cousin about a few things before heading home.

Miranda was sitting at her desk, holding a small square object in her hand. As he sat down in one of the chairs across from the mahogany desk, she gave him a sad smile.

"I found this in the drawer when I returned from Astaria the first time. It's a picture of Mother. Father must've kept it here and looked at it when his longing for her became too much to bear."

"He loved her so much," Kenden said. "Perhaps to his detriment."

Miranda nodded. Sighing, she placed the picture back in the drawer, closing it softly. Lifting her magnificent olive irises to his, they seemed to glisten as they shined with tears. "I can't tell if you're pissed at me or just pretending you are, but I'm ready to grovel."

Kenden breathed a laugh. "Now, that's something I'm dying to see," he said, arching a brow.

Her chin quivered, only slightly, and he felt a tiny crack down his heart. She was the person he'd loved most in the world for so very long. Although he enjoyed teasing her, he certainly didn't want to cause her any pain. Kenden opened his mouth to tell her he'd forgiven her days ago.

"Okay," she said, straightening her spine and lifting her chin before he could speak. "What do I have to do to secure your forgiveness? Public humiliation? A fancy bottle of red? Or...oh—I could chop wood for your fireplace for a month. Am I getting warm?"

Kenden felt his lips curve. "Actually, I really like chopping wood. There's something cathartic about manual labor."

She gave him one of her blazing smiles. "No one would guess you're an aristocrat if they didn't already know it, Ken. You're just a good ol' fashioned guy's guy."

He chuckled. "Yeah, as you always remind me, I'm quite boring."

Love for him swept over her features, causing his heart to swell. "Boring and stable and unfaltering. Thank god. I don't think I would've survived without you.

You're my other half, Ken. I need you." Her throat bobbed as she swallowed thickly. "I'm so sorry. I didn't mean to make fun of the situation with Evie. I really hope you can forgive me. I was just shocked, honestly, and you know I react to tense situations with humor. Please, don't be mad at me."

His eyes narrowed as he debated making her squirm just a bit more. "What kind of public humiliation did you have in mind?"

"Ken," she said, her tone pleading.

Shaking his head, he sat up and reached across the desk. Placing his hand in hers, they laced their fingers. "I forgave you days ago, Randi," he said, genuinely smiling. "I was just shocked and a bit embarrassed, but you know I love teasing you. I could never be mad at you." He squeezed her hand. "But I reserve the right to use the 'public humiliation' card whenever I see fit. One use only, to be fair."

Miranda exhaled a laugh. "Okay," she said, relief evident in her flawless features. "I accept. Those are pretty easy terms. You're losing your edge."

"Never," he said, winking and sitting back in his chair.

"Thank you," she said, running a hand through her hair as she sat back and swiveled in the large chair. "So, what do you need? I know you didn't just search me out to ensure my future humiliation."

"We need to manufacture a hundred more long-range walkies and seven hundred more TECs. I want to make sure we're armed with extras when we attack Crimeous."

"Sure thing. I'll work with Sathan to approve the budget for the laborers on the outer compounds. Just submit a purchase order for me so I can keep track. This war is expensive, especially with the new weapons. I'll be happy when we kill that bastard and can use the funds for the betterment of our kingdom. The new playground's coming along, and we need more improvements like that."

"Agreed," Kenden said.

Miranda gnawed her bottom lip. "So, how are things going with Evie?"

Kenden shot her an acerbic look. "Miranda—"

"I'm just asking a simple question," she interrupted, lifting her hands in the air, palms up, and shrugging.

"No, you're nosy as hell and trying to snoop in my business."

"Of course, I'm nosy," she said, scrunching her features. "Have you freaking met me?"

Laughing in spite of himself, Kenden rubbed his forehead with his fingers. "It's going fine. She's a very complicated woman, and I'm trying my best to understand her."

Miranda studied him, her lips forming a smile. "Well, you're the most patient, understanding person I know, so she's in good hands. I know you're not thrilled with this situation, but I think she's good for you in a lot of ways."

"Is that so?" he asked, lifting a sardonic brow.

"Yes," she said with a confident nod. "It's been a long time since someone has had the voracity to challenge you, Ken. I think she's a worthy opponent for you. I also think that you're very attracted to her and that you're the perfect person to help her recognize the goodness she has within."

"She's convinced she's rotten inside. It's quite sad," he said softly, rubbing his palms together as he contemplated the scarlet-haired beauty who seemed to consume his every thought lately.

"Well, she's no Mother Teresa, that's for sure, but she's my mother's daughter. I have faith that she'll choose the light. The longer she's here, surrounded by people who are determined to make that happen, the better. Although I know you weren't enamored with the circumstances that led to you courting her, I think you two could have something really great together."

"She swears her time in the immortal world is temporary."

"I swore I wanted to kill Sathan with the Blade," Miranda said with a diffident shrug. "Things change. Plus, it doesn't hurt for you to get boned, Ken. It's been a while. She was right about that."

"Okay," Kenden said, standing and running his hand over his hair. "I'm definitely *not* going to sit here and discuss my sex life with you. Let's leave it at the fact that I'm enjoying my time with her and feel a deep well of compassion due to the violence she experienced when she was young. I want to help her understand that not everything that involves emotion involves pain. If I can accomplish that while courting her, then I'll consider it a win."

Affection filled Miranda's features as she stood and walked around the desk. Sliding her arms around Kenden's waist, she laid her head on his broad chest. "You're the best man I know, Ken. She's so lucky to be with you. If anyone can find her goodness, it's you. I love you so much."

"I love you too," he said, embracing her and kissing her on her silky head.

Disengaging, she looked up at him. "I can still find us some really fancy wine, if you like? It's almost dinner time. Jana said she's making halibut and fresh veggies."

"Well, hot damn," he said. "It's my lucky day. Only an idiot would pass on that."

Arm-in-arm, they strolled to the kitchen to devour the sweet housekeeper's delicious food.

* * * *

On Wednesday, Evie dematerialized to the spot where Miranda had texted her. She didn't appreciate being dictated to but figured her sister wouldn't bother unless it was important. Glancing around, she noticed the open meadow under the midday sky. Not a trace of civilization could be seen.

With a *whoosh*, Darkrip materialized, Miranda in his arms.

"Guess you were summoned too," Evie muttered to her brother.

Miranda shot her a glare. "I *asked* you both to meet me here so that I can discuss something important with you."

"Fine," Evie said with a shrug. "What do you need?"

Inhaling a deep breath, Miranda's green irises traveled back and forth between theirs.

"Sathan and I have decided to build another compound here. It will be a joint compound, consisting of Slayers and Vampyres."

"That's great," Darkrip said. "It's nice to see the kingdom growing."

"Yes, it is," Miranda said with a nod. "We also anticipate needing to house Deamons here, after we defeat Crimeous."

Evie's eyebrows drew together. "For what purpose?"

"There will be many women from his harem who have no place to go. We also suspect that several of his men will surrender in exchange for their lives. Although they need to be held accountable for their actions, we wish to start anew. If a Deamon truly wants to atone and is willing to pay his debt to society, we want to offer him a home. Others who won't concede will be placed in the prison that we'll build on the outskirts of the new compound."

"Wow," Darkrip said, his tone cautious. "That's assuming a lot, Miranda. Deamons have been crafted by my father to be extremely malicious. I appreciate your compassion, but we need to make sure it's warranted."

"I understand," she said. "Believe me, we didn't come to this decision lightly. But we've discussed this with many on the council, and Lila has studied human societies extensively. The countries that rehabilitate their prisoners most effectively have the lowest reincarceration rates. Most of those offenders go on to contribute greatly to society. Plus, it's the humane thing to do. We've made our decision."

"Okay," Evie said, crossing her arms over her chest. "So, what does this have to do with us?"

Miranda's features softened. "You both are children of Valktor. You share his blood as much as I do. I was raised to be the Slayer Queen but I don't want to deny you your destiny. I would like to offer you the opportunity to co-govern the new compound. Being the descendants of our grandfather, and half-Deamon, you both would garner a respect from the Deamon inhabitants that Sathan and I never could."

Evie and Darkrip stared at their sister, both a bit stunned.

"Look," Miranda said, lifting her arms at her sides. "I know this is a shock. But we have to think of the livelihood of the kingdom down the road. We can't let the Deamons continue to live in the caves. Ken and Latimus will destroy them all once we win the war. They'll need leaders. You two are the most capable in my eyes. You're both my family, and I want us to build the future of our world together."

"It's a really nice offer," Darkrip said, taking her hand. "I would love to help you, but I made a promise to Arderin, and I have to see that through. Once she's done with her medical training in the human world, I'd be happy to consider this. But for now, I have to decline."

"Fair enough," Miranda said, squeezing his hand. "What about you, Evie?" she asked, pinning her with her green gaze.

"Um, yeah," Evie said, rubbing the back of her neck. "I thought I'd been pretty clear that I'm heading back to the human world after this. No offense, but I hate it here. And I definitely don't want to add Governor to my list of titles. Mean, angry bitch suits me just fine."

Miranda breathed a laugh. "Well, I wouldn't call you mean, exactly…"

They all chuckled.

Miranda grabbed Evie's hand as well. "I understand your reluctance to stay here. You've never had a home or a purpose. That's something I'm trying to remedy. You're a very confident and powerful person, Evie. I think you'd make an excellent leader. I won't push you, but I don't want you to answer now. Think on it. We have time until the battle. Can you at least do that for me?"

"Miranda—"

"I gave you a home, my forgiveness and my best intention to make you my family," Miranda interrupted. "All I'm asking is for you to consider this."

"Fine," Evie said, pulling her hand away. "I'll consider, since you've been so cordial, but don't get your hopes up. I don't see myself staying here."

"Even if the Commander wins you over?" Darkrip asked, arching a brow.

"Screw you," Evie said, scowling at him.

"Hey, it could happen," Miranda said. "Look at Darkrip. He's a lovesick pansy over Arderin."

Darkrip rolled his eyes. "Says the woman who gets googly-eyed when her husband so much as walks into a room."

"Don't make fun of me," she said, swatting him. "My husband is hot. I can't help it."

They all laughed, and Evie realized she was enjoying the moment. Maybe this whole sibling thing wasn't half-bad. Or maybe she was turning into a sentimental prick, living so close to all this lovey-dovey bullshit. Christ.

"C'mon," Miranda said, pivoting and beckoning them with her arm. "I want to show you guys where we plan to build."

For the next several hours, Evie followed her sister around, unwillingly affected by her enthusiasm for the future. Silently wishing she could feel the same.

"Why do you tell me things that aren't true?" the man asked with anger. "I see your cheeks warm from my words and your heart beat fast from my touch."

"I only have the capacity to love those from my womb. It has always been so," the woman said. "But I do feel so warm from your words, and my heart does beat fast, because I consider you such a wonderful friend."

The man's face became a mask of rage. "I do not want a friend," he yelled, his deep voice booming across the field. "I want to love you, as a man loves a woman, and I will settle for no less."

The woman sighed. "Then, I am sorry to say that we cannot see each other anymore. Goodbye, my dear Galredad. I hope you find peace in this world." Turning, she began to walk away.

But not before the man grabbed her arm, halting her retreat...

Chapter 9

On Saturday, Kenden threw on his athletic shorts, t-shirt and sneakers and headed outside to wait for Evie to appear. He'd offered to pick her up at her cabin, but she'd vehemently refused, allowing her to have one more instance of control. Sighing, he sat in one of the wooden rocking chairs on the porch of his house. The sky was a beautiful blue and the day was warm, perfect for a hike. A breeze seemed to ruffle the grass in front of the porch, and suddenly, she appeared.

Like a mermaid rising from the ocean, she was a vision to him. Red hair pulled into a bouncy ponytail behind her flawless face. Black yoga pants hugging her hips and thighs, stopping at her calves. She wore only a black sports bra, her breasts spilling from the top like she promised. The pale swath of skin that comprised her stomach seemed to call to him. Gray sneakers completed her ensemble.

Rising ever so slowly, he ambled down the porch stairs toward her, not stopping until only inches separated them. Pleasure coursed through him when she had to lift her chin to maintain eye contact. At least he had a physical advantage over her, if nothing else.

"Well, I did promise you I'd wear something that showcased my tits," she said, grinning up at him.

"You sure did," he said, allowing his eyes to rove over her. Lifting his finger, he gently traced her collarbone. "Hope you wore sunscreen. Wouldn't want them to burn before I get my hands on them later."

"Lathered and ready," she said. God, he loved the challenge in her voice.

"Then, let's go," he said, extending his hand to her.

Grabbing it, she drew him close. "Where to? I'll transport us."

"Nope," he said, motioning his head toward the four-wheeler. "I'm driving. Hop in. You'll have to throw your leg over the side because the door is welded shut."

She lifted a scarlet brow. "Not the red-carpet welcome I've come to expect from you."

"Shut up and get in the car," he said, playfully biting at her lips.

She nipped right back and then seemed to bounce to the passenger side. Once in, he revved the engine. "It's mostly dirt roads, so things are gonna get bumpy. Hold on."

Kenden drove them along the wall, past the massive doors that led outside the compound, to the open field east of the River Thayne. Riding in silence, he studied her, that silky ponytail blowing in the breeze. Eyes closed, she was magnificent as she inhaled the fresh air. Eventually, they came to the foothills of the nearby mountain range, rolling and gentle above.

"Made it," he said, anchoring his arm on the door and jumping from the four-wheeler. Coming around, he offered her his hand. "Need help?"

"Not on your life, Commander," she said, using her arms to hoist herself out. Landing on her feet, she brushed her hands over her thighs. "Where to?"

"You're going to let me lead? I'm shocked."

"You know the trail," Evie said, holding her hands up, palms facing forward. "I defer to you. Tonight, when we're in bed, I might not be so nice. I'd take advantage while you can."

Chuckling, Kenden reached into the back to grab their supplies. Once his belt was loaded with two knives and a Glock, and they both had water, they began their trudge along the path.

The trail was gorgeous, dotted with various trees and bushes with leaves of green and brown. Dirt and rocks lined the way as their sneaker-clad feet navigated the terrain. A small river gurgled nearby, every so often intersecting with the path. The incline grew steeper as they went, Kenden always reaching back and offering her a hand. Of course, Evie never took it, but a gentleman always offered anyway.

"So, are you always armed?" she asked, making conversation as they trekked.

"Yes," he said, grunting as he climbed over a particularly large rock. "It's been imbedded in me forever. Part of my training."

"Who trained you?" she asked. "After the Awakening?"

"I was distraught that I wasn't at the blood-banking," he said, resignation burning in his chest. "There was a terrible flu circulating around the compound, and I caught it. I was twenty at the time and usually went with my parents but was too sick to go that year. I'll never forgive myself that I wasn't there to save them."

"It wasn't your fault," she said, her tone compassionate. "If you'd been there, you probably would've died."

"Maybe," he said, shrugging as they strolled down a relatively straight part of the trail. "But I still feel responsible."

"I think you feel responsible for a lot of things," she said, those green eyes so deep as she stared up at him. "You can't be everyone's savior, Ken."

"Well, I wish I could've been theirs," he said, sighing. "Regardless, I realized quickly that we needed an army. After the Vampyre's first raid, we were decimated. I'd studied human warfare in school and loved it. All the cunning and strategy, I had a knack for it. Marsias realized it and commissioned me Commander. From there, I set about studying everything I could about warfare and battle. I drafted our strongest men and formed a competent army. So, I guess you could say, I was self-trained. And that consumed my life for ten centuries."

"It's very noble," she said, lifting her bottle to take a sip.

"Want to sit for a minute?" he asked, noticing that she was slightly panting.

"Sure," she said, lowering to a nearby rock. "You're showing me up. I feel inadequate."

Laughing, he took a swig of water as he sat atop a stone on the opposite side of the trail. "Don't worry. I won't tell anyone you couldn't keep up with me."

"Jerk," she teased, smiling at him. His heart slammed at those beautiful teeth and full lips.

"You've protected your people for all these years," she said, shaking her head in wonder. "It's very admirable. I know I like to chide you, but I respect that immensely. I've rarely known a person as selfless as you, Ken. It's amazing that you let me within fifty feet of your humble perfection."

Sorrow choked him, knowing that she saw herself this way. Although she had many flaws, she was the product of so much hurt and violence. It clawed at him, knowing that he'd protected so many but hadn't protected her. It would've been impossible, as he hadn't known of her existence, but his need to save her still scraped at him.

"I'm sorry you had to suffer for all those decades in the caves. I wish—"

"Wishes are for old women at fountains and kids waiting for the tooth fairy," Evie interrupted. "I don't talk about my past with anyone."

Annoyance rushed through him. At her, for being so closed-off. At himself, for caring that she was. They sat in silence, sipping the water, breathing in the air. Suddenly, she stood.

"Do you hear that?" she asked, her head darting to various points behind them.

"Yes," he said softly, standing to assess the situation. "It could be an animal."

"Not likely," she muttered, her jaw clenching. "We need to—"

Before she could finish, the cries of battle overwhelmed them. Deamons, at least thirty strong from Kenden's assessment, swarmed from the trees that surrounded them. Dragging her toward him, he did his best to shield her.

"Give me a break," she said, wrenching her wrist from his grip and glaring up at him in anger. "I'm not one of your meek Slayer women." Pulling a knife from his belt, she turned to face the oncoming soldiers.

The Deamons attacked, strong and sure, circling them as they held various weapons. Guns, eight-shooters, swords—all were on deck for the ambush. Suddenly, the weapons disappeared from the Deamons' grips, and Kenden knew Evie had dematerialized them. Drawing his gun in one hand and a knife in the other, Kenden got to work.

He shot two of the creatures dead between the eyes, turning to plunge the blade into the side of another. Looking over his shoulder, he saw Evie as she fought. By the goddess, she was a machine. Lifting her hand, she drew one of the Deamons toward her with her mind, clutched his throat and gutted him with the knife. The contents of his abdomen spilled onto the ground, and she picked up one of the intestines. Using it like a lasso, she swung it around another soldier's neck, drawing him close and plunging the knife into his genitals. Good god.

"He raped one of the harem women last night," Evie said, daring him to judge her as she looked over her shoulder. "I saw the image in his mind. I'll cut off every one of these bastard's balls who dares to rape a woman. Fucking watch me."

A grunt sounded at Kenden's side, and he resumed fighting, realizing he'd have time to process what an effective and lethal warrior she was later. Together, they fought, determined and solid, until only two Deamons were left.

"Let's knock them unconscious and take them back to Uteria for questioning," Kenden said. "They might be able to give us intel on how much your father knows about your presence here."

"Fuck that," she said, facing him as she held the Deamons frozen with her outstretched hand, palm up. "I'm going to murder these assholes."

"No," Kenden said, trying to keep his voice calm. "We need information, Evie. Sometimes, that's more valuable than death."

"But not as fulfilling. Give me your gun."

"No," he said, clutching the weapon.

Evie's features contorted into something raw and angry. It would've cowered most men. Instead, Kenden stood firm, understanding that she was dangling on a precipice between reason and madness.

"Give me the fucking gun," she said through clenched teeth. "I won't ask again."

"No," he repeated, determined to stand his ground. Wanting so badly for her to choose pragmatism over heated rage.

Those stunning eyes narrowed, and she lifted her other hand, facing Kenden. Suddenly, any feeling that he had below his neck vanished. She'd frozen him, sure as if she'd turned him to stone.

"You're going to learn very quickly that I don't like being defied, Commander," she said, her nostrils flaring. Walking over to his motionless body, she picked up the gun, which had fallen to the ground from his limp hand. The two Deamon soldiers still stood behind her, unable to move. "Now, watch me gut these bastards like the slimy little assholes they are. Then, you can release any notions you have about me being '*good inside.*'" She made quotation marks with her fingers, difficult since she held his Glock in one hand. "And then, you can tell sweet Miranda how I dismembered these soldiers and ensure she stops looking at me through rose-colored glasses as well."

Turning, she sauntered toward the immobile Deamons. Lifting the gun, she ran the nozzle over one of the soldier's cheeks as he shivered with terror.

"Scared little thing, aren't you?" she asked, running the barrel of the gun down his neck. "Were you scared when my father tied up several of the harem women last night and let you and your friend here violate them? Hmmm?"

The Deamon sniveled, baring his teeth to her. "Crimeous will kill you, bitch!" he screamed.

Evie pistol-whipped him, causing his head to fly sideways. "Now, now. I'd shut the fuck up real quick if you want to keep at least one of your balls attached before I murder you. Capisce?"

"Evie, you don't need to torture them," Kenden said, frustrated that he couldn't move a muscle. "If you're going to kill them, do it humanely."

"Humane. Such a nice word. Were these two *humane* when they violated their victims?" she asked, pointing back and forth between the prisoners with the gun. Giving a *tsk, tsk, tsk* with her tongue, she said, "I think not. So, let's dole out the same treatment they gave those women, shall we?"

Kenden proceeded to watch her, his stomach rolling. She cut off the pants of both men, throwing them to the ground. Baring their genitals, she lifted the gun and shot one of them directly in the right testicle. The Deamon wailed in pain, his eyes seeming to pop from his head. Looking to the other man, she dropped the gun and picked up the knife. Extending his flaccid shaft in her hand, she sliced it off with the blade. Never had he heard a man squeal with so much agony.

Kenden had seen the spoils of war. Blood and gore didn't faze him. It hadn't in centuries. But seeing the woman he'd held in his arms only days ago, whom he was coming to cherish and care for, torture these men shifted something inside him. It was dark and dirty, and he wished like hell they'd never been attacked.

"I can read the images in your mind," she said softly, her tone so sad. She still faced the Deamons, now almost unconscious from their maiming. "I know. It's awful. *I'm* awful. I wish I wasn't this way."

He almost missed the gleam from the tear that fell from her face as she stood with her back to him. Almost. It glimmered with the moisture of her despair and the promise that somewhere, deep inside, she still had the ability to feel remorse for her actions.

"You need to kill them, Evie," he said, his throat raw from emotion. "You've tortured them enough."

She scoffed, causing the strands of her ponytail to bob. "It's never enough. That's what you'll never understand about me, Ken." The droop of her shoulders was heartbreaking. "I always need more. I thrive on the violence. On the pain. It's a terrible curse."

Walking toward the soldier on the right, she plunged the knife into his neck. Circling him, she cut a long trail until his entire neck was gaping open. Pushing his head back, it hung, almost swinging from the still-connected spinal cord.

Approaching the other soldier, she grabbed his chin. "Tell me you're sorry. For all the women you raped."

"Never," he said, spittle flying from between his teeth.

Lifting the gun from the ground, she returned to clutch his chin. Sticking the barrel in his mouth, she maneuvered it back and forth, causing the man to groan in pain. "Say it, asshole."

He garbled something unintelligible due to the object in his mouth, but it wasn't what Evie wanted to hear. Cocking the gun, her eyes grew wide as she watched the Deamon tremble. Confident as Kenden had ever seen her, she pulled the trigger. The man's brains spattered to the rocks beyond and everywhere in between.

Pivoting, Evie came to stand before him. Icy, heavy dread began to pulse through Kenden's unmoving body. Never had he seen anything like the sight before him. Evie—gorgeous, flawless Evie—blood-stained and pulsing with rage. Bits of Deamon spatter marred the white expanse of her stomach above the yoga pants, and she still held the gun in her hand.

But none of that made his blood run cold. With what he'd seen in his life, it never could.

No, what rocked him to his core was the look in her olive-green eyes.

Pleasure, pure and limitless, to the depths he'd never seen, glowed in the striking orbs.

As he silently beckoned to her with his eyes, she dropped the gun to the ground, following suit and crumpling to sit on the dirt. Wide, emerald orbs stared up at him as she hugged her knees to her chest.

"I need a moment," she said, her knuckles white as she squeezed her arms around her.

"Okay," Kenden said, his voice scratchy.

As she lowered her forehead to her knees, he watched her tremble violently, wondering the entire time if it was from pleasure or remorse.

* * * *

Evie heaved a ragged sigh into her knees, knowing she needed to stand the hell up. Resolved, she inhaled a deep breath and lifted to her feet. Refusing to meet Ken's eyes, she flicked her hand, giving him control of his muscles.

"Evie—"

"Please, don't touch me," she said, staring at the dead bodies that surrounded them. "I'm not trying to be a bitch. I just can't have anyone touch me right now."

"Okay," he said, his voice so steady and composed. His firm calmness usually rankled her, but she was too raw to muster up the irritation. "We need to clean up the bodies. I'm going to call Darkrip so he can transport some soldiers here."

Evie barely heard the conversation he had with her brother, too entranced by the corpses of her father's soldiers. She'd placed a shield on her thoughts, ensuring

Crimeous wouldn't read them, but his spies were vast. It was only a matter of time before he began tracking her. She thought she'd be scared. Maybe curious. Pissed for sure. She never anticipated feeling the emptiness inside at the discovery that her father knew of her presence in the immortal world. After so many centuries of being fueled by burning rage, it was disconcerting to feel numb.

Her brother appeared, the Slayer soldier Larkin along with him. Darkrip dematerialized again and again, bringing ten Slayer soldiers to the site of the battle.

"We'll get this cleaned up," Darkrip said, patting Kenden on the shoulder. "You two should go back to the compound," he said, gesturing with his head toward Evie.

"I'm fine," she said, although her tone was lifeless. "I can help if you want."

"We've got it," Larkin said. "I'll drive the four-wheeler back. You guys should update Miranda and Sathan. They're at Astaria."

Kenden approached her cautiously. She knew it wasn't because he was afraid but because he somehow understood how dazed she felt. "Can you transport us to Astaria? After that, we'll go home and shower."

Evie nodded, too exhausted to reply. Kenden's firm arms embraced her, clutching her tight. Grasping her hands behind his neck, she transported them to Astaria.

Once in Sathan's office chamber, Miranda rushed to her. "Evie, are you okay? Darkrip updated us."

"Don't," Evie said, holding up a hand. "I can't be touched by anyone but Ken right now. Please."

"Okay." Miranda nodded, backing away. Evie and Kenden stood by the conference table, Miranda and Sathan in front of his mahogany desk. "Can you tell us what happened?"

Kenden recounted the story while Evie rubbed her upper arms, irritation softly pounding through her veins. She'd let the evil take over, unable to stop herself from torturing the bastards. Kenden's chocolate irises had regarded her, filled with disgust and horror. Self-loathing threatened to drown her as she lifted her gaze to Sathan's.

"I'm happy to hear that you defeated them so handily," Sathan said. "Darkrip told me you were a competent warrior and that you've trained with humans over the centuries."

"Yes," Evie said, holding his gaze, pushing away the shame and self-revulsion. "I trained with the samurai of Japan, the armies of Alexander the Great, Attila the Hun and William Wallace. Most didn't welcome women in their ranks, but with my powers, they all thought I was a witch. That made me a potent ally."

"Daughters of Rina know how to kick ass," Miranda said. "I don't doubt you're awesome, Evie."

"I enjoyed it," Evie said, lifting her chin to stare at her sister. "Every single slaughter. Every single death. It's not a hardship for me to kill others. Ken wanted me to kill the Deamons humanely. I'm not capable. You all need to know that."

"She could see images in their minds of them raping Deamon harem women," Kenden said.

"Don't make excuses for me," she snapped. "I keep trying to tell you all how horrible I am. I don't know how to make you believe me."

"Let's table this discussion for another day," Miranda said, shooting a look at Kenden. "You both are covered in Deamon blood and need to wash off the attack. Evie, are you able to transport back to Uteria?"

"Yes," she whispered with a nod.

"Good. You're tough, so I have no doubt you'll be fine. Guys, can you give us a minute?"

Sathan pecked his wife on the cheek and left the room, Kenden following behind as he closed the door with a click.

"Thank you for killing them all," Miranda said. "I fucking hate Deamons. Ken is very pragmatic about war, but I would've done the same. Any man who rapes a woman deserves to get his dick cut off a hundred times. If that makes you evil, then I am too."

"And yet, you want to rehabilitate them," Evie said, confused.

Miranda exhaled a large breath. "There's what I want and what I know is right. Sathan and Ken are good for me. They calm me down so I don't act impulsively. I hate to tell you, sis, but it's a trait of our bloodline. We can't control our impulses sometimes. Perhaps yours is magnified, because of your father's blood, but I'm not going to judge you for having the same affliction I have."

"You people are all so damn forgiving," Evie said. "It's absolutely maddening."

Miranda chuckled. "It's all part of my masterplan to win you over. Don't look now, but I think it's working."

Evie felt the corners of her lips turn up. "Maybe."

After a moment, Evie said, "I cried. In front of Ken. I never cry," she said, shaking her head slowly. "I feel remorse now, every time I kill, even if the victims deserve it. I feel like I've lost my grip on everything I knew. Everything I believed. What the hell is happening to me? I feel like the Earth is crumbling under my feet, and I have no idea how to control it."

Miranda perched on the side of the conference room table with her hip. "Control is a big thing for you. I get it. You've had to grab on to it with an iron fist for so long. If you're going to lose it, Ken is the right person to catch you. He's amazing."

"I know," Evie said, glancing at the floor. "Why does he put up with me? I have nothing to offer him but pain and spite."

"Ken's always been a bit of a savior," Miranda said with a smile. "He has a built-in sense of compassion that drives him to protect those he loves. But he's not without his flaws. He's rigid and set in his ways. If he spends one more hour in that shed of his, he might literally die of boredom. You bring passion into his life, and it's something he sorely needs. Don't sell yourself short, Evie. I think you both have a lot to offer each other if you'd open yourself to him."

"My feelings for him are so different than any other man. It's terrifying."

"Good," Miranda said. "Then, there's hope." Standing, she inched closer to Evie, careful to leave some space between them. "Don't pull away from him today. Let him support you. You're masterful at thriving on your own, but that isolation can fuel your anger. Let it go and let him help you."

"I need the anger," Evie said. "It's the only way I know how to survive."

"Then, perhaps it's time you learn a different way."

Evie studied her sister, speaking words so wise. Not knowing what else to say, she turned to open the door and transport back to Uteria.

"Please, my love," Galredad said, his voice pleading. "I have lost everything. I need your love. Without it, I might as well have perished along with the others."

"I'm so very sorry," she said, cupping his cheek. "But this must be goodbye."

The woman attempted to turn but was restrained yet again. There, under the blazing sun, his face began to contort into a mask of fury and vehemence so dark and sinister that the woman experienced something akin to fear.

"Release your grip," she commanded.

"No," was his firm reply...

Chapter 10

Kenden released Evie as soon as she transported them to his bedroom, acknowledging that they both needed space. Traversing to the mahogany dresser, he turned, leaning his lower back against it as he regarded her.

She stood before him, a war-ravaged beauty, uncertainty swimming in her limitless orbs.

"I need to go back to my cabin and shower," she said softly. He'd rarely seen her so unsure, and it moved something inside his chest.

Exhaling a huge breath, he held up his hand, palm forward. "I'm just trying to process this, Evie. Watching you torture those Deamons was…difficult for me."

"I told you I was evil—"

"Wait," he said, slicing his hand through the air. "This isn't going to turn into a discussion about your Deamon side. I accept that part of you. But what I need to know is if you can embrace your Slayer side. Otherwise, this will never work. And I don't mean you and me," he said, straightening his spine as he stood tall. "I mean you against your father."

Slowly, he began closing the distance between them. When he reached her, he lifted her chin with his fingers. "I want so badly to believe you'll choose the goodness, Evie. But I need you to believe it too."

Her pupils darted back and forth between his. "I'm not sure I can make that promise," she said, her expression so genuine it almost broke his heart. "My evil half has always been my greatest soldier. After so many centuries, it's difficult to push it away."

Sighing, he cupped her cheek. Small splats of Deamon blood marred the smooth skin. "We both need to wash off the battle. Let's do that first." Stepping back, he held out his hand. "Come on," he said, gesturing with his head to the bathroom.

"I should shower at my cabin," she said, rubbing her upper arms with her thin fingers. "I think that might be best. I can't imagine you'd want to be in my presence right now anyway."

"Evie," he said, shaking his head ever so slowly as he regarded her. "I'm a soldier. I've seen the worst displays of torture and death. I'm not repulsed by your actions, although they were gruesome. I'm…disheartened, I guess. I wanted so badly for you to choose rationality over anger. The battle within you is going to be so much harder for you to fight than any skirmish against your father."

"I know," she said. "It's just so hard to side with righteousness when the fury consumes me. No one's ever been there to care that I chose another way."

"I care," he said, his voice almost a growl. "And I need you to trust me on that. I'll support you if you choose the goodness. Always."

"I don't trust anyone."

"That ends today," he said, extending his hand to her again. "Let's wash off the battle."

Green irises searched his, and he thought she might dematerialize away. "I don't understand how you could still want to touch me."

Swallowing thickly, he spoke the truth. "I've never desired anyone as much as you, Evie. I think you could destroy the whole damn planet, and I'd still want you. But I'd rather you just take a shower with me. Let's comfort each other and let the planet survive another day. Come on," he said, shaking his hand. He gave her a gentle smile, wanting to assure her that he supported her, even through her complexity and doubt.

After a small eternity, she placed her hand in his. "Okay," she whispered.

Gripping her tight, he led her to the large master bathroom. Silently, they undressed. Kenden picked up her clothes and threw them in the hamper against the wall. "I'll get them cleaned. Jana is mad for me. She'll do it if I ask her."

That spurred a slight curve of her gorgeous lips. "Should I be jealous?"

"Definitely. I have a thing for housekeepers born centuries before the Awakening."

She smiled then, a bit broken but pure, and he realized that everything might just be okay. Naked, he drew her into the shower, starting the spray so that it sluiced over their battle-rough bodies. Nudging her under the nozzle, he made sure her hair was doused. Grasping the nearby shampoo bottle, he poured a coin-sized amount in his hand and began washing the thick scarlet strands.

With his broad fingers, he massaged her scalp, pulling her back into his body. His erection had appeared the second she'd lost her clothes but that didn't matter right now. What mattered was Evie. It was imperative that she understood that he wouldn't condemn her, even if she made mistakes. He didn't need perfection, he just needed her to strive to be the best version of herself.

Her head lolled back, resting at the juncture of his chest and shoulder. "It feels so good," she moaned, arching toward his fingers as he worked.

"We need to get some of your shampoo for my shower. The scent always drives me crazy. This one won't do it justice."

"Mmmm..." she said. Her gloss-free lips were pink, he noticed as he stared down at her. She always wore lipstick, and he'd rarely seen her without. Lids closed, her face was a mask of pleasure. Knowing that he was giving it to her did all sorts of things to his insides.

"Let me rinse you," he murmured. Pressing her toward the spray, he helped her clean the suds from her hair. With the cloth that hung on the nearby rack, he proceeded to wash her body. Once finished, she repeated his actions, running the cloth over his straining body. Finished, she threw the rag on the tile floor of the shower.

"I think we need to do something about this," she said, grasping his straining length.

"Not right now," he said, kissing her forehead.

Leading her from the shower, onto the plushy mat, he grabbed a towel and dried her off. Wrapping the towel around her, she covered herself while he toweled off. Clutching the cloth where it intersected her breasts, he pulled it away and threw it to the floor. Lowering, he picked her up as if she was made of feathers.

He lay her on the bed, gently urging her to lie on her stomach. "From behind?" she asked with that sultry voice. "I'm quickly realizing that's how you like it best, Commander."

Chuckling, he felt his muscles release at her teasing. They were easing back into their saucy banter; into the place where they were comfortable. Thanking all the gods, he pulled a pillow to each side of her head so she could rest her face in between. "I do like it that way. But for now, I want you to relax."

Straddling her lower back, he began to massage her shoulders with his broad hands.

"*Ohmygod*," she breathed, the words rushing out together. "That's it. You're perfect. I give up."

"Shut up, Evie," he said, smiling as she unwound in his hands. "Let me make you feel good."

Reaching over to his bedside table, he squirted some lotion on his hands. Rubbing them together to warm the liquid, he placed his palms on her lower back. Moving up to her shoulders and back down again, she writhed beneath him.

"Do me a favor and go lower, hmmm?"

Kenden breathed a laugh. "Not yet, sweetheart. You need to release some tension. You're tight as hell."

"Getting attacked by my father's thugs will do that to you."

Feeling his brows draw together, he remained silent, loathing that she'd been spawned by such a terrible creature. He spent several minutes on her back and then shifted to sit on his knees beside her. Intense and thorough, he massaged the backs of her thighs and her calves, eventually coming to rest on the globes of her perfect ass.

Thick fingers maneuvered the tissues there, causing her to purr into the pillows. After thoroughly loosening the straining tension from her cheeks, he parted her thighs. Lowering his hand, he rubbed her wet slit with his middle finger.

Teasing, tantalizing, he rimmed her opening until she began to squirm. Clutching the pillow underneath her head, she looked over her shoulder, slightly resting on her side.

"Please," she begged, undulating her hips toward him.

"Okay, baby," he murmured, inching the finger through her taut opening. "There you are. So wet and snug. Squeeze my finger, sweetheart."

She did, the constriction of her walls causing his erection to harden to the point of pain. If he didn't bury himself into her soon, he might die from unspent arousal.

"I know you want to be inside me," she rasped. "Your hands aren't enough. I need you."

The words tore something inside him, ripping open the cage that held the beast of his desire. Lowering beside her, he aligned her back with his front. Lifting her leg, he slid it over his hip, opening her.

"Is this what you want?" he growled, sliding the head of his cock over her dripping core.

"Yes," she hissed, pleading at him with those gorgeous eyes over her shoulder. "Please—"

She barely finished the word as he impaled her, causing her body to bow back against him. "Too much?" he asked, concerned that he was hurting her.

"Never enough," she said, dropping her forehead to the bed and pushing into him. "Goddamnit, fuck me."

Gritting his teeth, Kenden hammered into her, unable to control the jut of his hips. Her essence slid all over his straining shaft, driving him insane with lust. Grasping her thigh, he moved against her, the primal urge to bury himself deep inside drowning out any other voice in his head.

"I love being with you like this," he growled into her shoulder, biting the skin there. "Fucking you hard, feeling you squeeze my cock. Oh, god, Evie. It's so good."

"I know," she said, reaching up to grasp his hair. The tiny pinpricks of pain from the tugging only urged him on. Sliding his arm around, he found her little nub, nestled below the strip of red hair, with the pads of his fingers. Wanting to make her feel something close to the bliss he was experiencing, he began rubbing in concentric circles while he pounded her from behind.

"Ken," she cried, almost making him come from that sultry voice.

"I'm right here, baby. I've got you."

Her fingers tightened in his hair, magnifying the pleasure to a point so intense, he felt something burst inside. "Come," he commanded, his lips on her ear. "I want to feel your pussy choke me until I can't breathe."

Snapping her head back, she tensed. With a loud wail, she began convulsing in his arms, the shaking so severe that he had to hold her in place with his thick arm.

The feeling of her walls constricting his shaft was too much, and he let go, spurting into her, releasing every bit of arousal into her warmth.

Kenden's hips jerked uncontrollably for what seemed like hours, causing him to collapse behind her once the last pulses died down. "Good god, woman," he said, kissing her neck as he held her close. Reveling in her shiver at the touch of his lips, he grinned. "Sex with you is unbelievable. I've never experienced anything like it."

"Mmmm..." she said, lids closed as she stretched against him like a cat sitting in a sunny windowsill. "It's because of our chemistry. It's off the charts. New for me too. Never been like this."

The fragmented sentences meant she was close to drifting off. No wonder, after the rush of adrenaline they'd both experienced earlier. Compounded by some pretty amazing sex.

Detaching from her, he lifted from the bed as she groaned.

"No. Just a few more minutes. I promise, I eventually hate cuddling. But come back for now."

He leaned down and kissed her by the fiery hair at her temple. "Be right back. Let me get something to clean us up."

Locating the washcloth they'd used earlier, he brought it out, facing her as he lifted her leg and wiped the evidence of their loving. She watched him through slitted eyes, looking content and sated. Depositing the cloth in the hamper, he fell back into bed, hauling her to sprawl across his chest.

"You're hairy," she mumbled, running her fingers through his chest hair.

"Mmm hmm. I never understood why men shaved their chests. Weird, if you ask me." Gently, he traced the pad of his finger over the top of her ear. "They're not pointed like Darkrip's," he said.

"No," she murmured into his pecs. "I had them surgically altered decades ago. Wanted all traces of that bastard erased from my memory."

He held her, skimming his palm over her thick, damp hair. Tightening his arm, he silently acknowledged the strength she'd shown by leaving her terrible past behind to forge a new life in a world that wasn't hers. It was quite remarkable.

"I love your body," she said, her fingers feeling so good as they caressed him. "You're insanely hot."

Chuckling, he kissed the top of her head. "You're the most gorgeous woman I've ever seen, Evie. It's unsettling. I feel inadequate next to your beauty and all those fancy clothes."

"They're just a shield," she said softly as her muscles relaxed into his. "So people don't hurt me."

"I know, baby," he said, running his fingers through her hair. "I wish people hadn't hurt you. I want to protect you so they can't anymore."

"I protect myself. Always have." The words were a bit warbled due to her lips being pressed into his skin. He stroked her, hating how lonely her life had been to this point. Vowing to make sure it never was again.

"You can't be my savior, Ken," she said, her palm coming to rest over his chest. "I'm beyond saving. I'm sorry. I wish I could be the woman you see when you look at me."

"I want you to be exactly who you are," he said, feeling her shudder. Maybe at the baritone of his voice, maybe at his words. "That's enough for me. One day, you'll figure that out."

"Don't count on it," she murmured. And then, she drifted into slumber.

* * * *

Evie awoke with a start, the unfamiliar surroundings causing her heart to pound.

"I'm here," Kenden's deep voice said behind her. Pulling her close with his arm, he snuggled into her side. "You're safe."

There, in the darkness, terror threatened to squeeze every last breath from her straining lungs. He looked so peaceful, already falling back asleep as his face rested on the pillow. Moonlight strayed in from the uncovered window, highlighting his angular features. She'd been fucking him for less than two weeks and was already becoming addicted. Goddamnit.

It was everything she detested. Monogamy. Intimacy. Need. Every word made her shrink further inside herself. As he softly snored next to her, she had the insane desire to strangle him. Not because she wanted to cause him harm but because she wanted to save herself. From him and his beautiful words and his understanding demeanor. No, she couldn't let herself fall for that. In her mind, every outcome of their relationship ended in disaster.

He'd choke on his disappointment. Of whom she couldn't be. Whom she'd never become. She was a demented bitch but she couldn't let that happen to Kenden. He was too good, too noble.

One more date, next week. She'd cherish that time with him since it would be their last. Then, she'd set about defeating her father and getting on with her damn life. There was no future here for her.

Hearing her stomach grumble, she dematerialized to Kenden's downstairs kitchen. Searching the fridge and pantry, she didn't find much, but with her cooking skills, she found enough to throw something together.

Twenty minutes later, he strolled into the kitchen. "Something smells good," he said, walking to the island that sat in the middle of the large room.

"I told you I could cook. Although, you have all the trimmings of a proclaimed bachelor. I could barely find anything to work with but I managed."

Handing him a plate with a steaming omelet, she motioned to the island with her head. "Sit down and eat. It's nine o'clock. We fell asleep for a while."

Kenden sat at the counter, slicing off a large chunk of the omelet with his fork. Shoving it in his mouth, he chewed. "Mmmm..." he said appreciatively. "This is damn good. You're hired. Move in with me and cook. I can pay you in massages."

Laughing, Evie scooped her own omelet from the pan onto a plate. Sitting next to him on the stool, she took a bite. "That's a hefty price to place on one's massages. Sure you're worth it?"

"You tell me," he said, brown eyes sparkling with mirth.

"Hmmm..." she said, chewing. After swallowing, she said, "I guess you're okay."

"Pfft," he said, flicking his hand. "You're insane, woman. I'm fucking awesome. Don't even go there."

They settled into conversation, easy and comfortable. Once the omelets were finished and the dishes put away, Kenden poured them a glass of wine. Sitting on his couch in the darkened living room, they fell into silence.

"Are you having regrets?" she asked softly.

His eyebrows drew together. "About what?"

She rubbed the rim of her glass with the pad of her finger. "Let's see. That you're stuck in a bargain with an evil Deamon? One who revels in torturing and maiming others? I can't believe you still fucked me. Someone as faultless as you shouldn't want to touch anyone as wretched as me."

Inhaling a deep breath, he grasped her wine glass and set them both on the coffee table. Gently grabbing her wrists, he pulled her toward him. Facing her, he stared down into her eyes.

"If you think I don't understand for one second how merciless you can be, you've underestimated me. What you did to those Deamons is child's play for you. I can bet you've tortured others in your past much more vehemently."

"I have," she said, giving a slight nod. "Doesn't that sicken you? To know that you've been inside someone so evil?"

Chestnut irises darted back and forth as he rubbed her wrists with the pads of his thumbs. Evie found the gesture so soothing.

"I've told you this before, in ways that might not have been clear, so let me say it now so that there's no doubt. You have your father's blood. It's malevolent and awful, and I'm sorry that it runs through you. Not because it's a part of you but because it calls you to listen to your worst impulses. That makes it dangerous.

"You've done an amazing job at piecing your life together on your own. I can't imagine how difficult that was. Even though you dismiss your mother's half, it burns so brightly in you. Rina was magnificent. A shining star in our little world. Your brilliance puts hers to shame. Your biggest flaw, at this point in your life, is not allowing yourself to make better choices. Choosing to side with your Deamon half instead of your Slayer half. I see the struggle in you. And the fact that you struggle is all I need. It means there's hope, and I can work with hope. It blazed in me for a thousand years during the War of the Species, and eventually, the tribes reunited. I have enough patience to wait for you, Evie. You're worth it."

She shook her head, the gesture slow and resigned, and whispered, "I'm sorry."

"Why?" he asked, his forehead furrowing.

"Because I'm going to let you down. So fucking hard. It's going to devastate you. I wish I could save you from it."

His gorgeous lips curved as he arched a brow. "I know you're powerful, but even you can't see the future, Evie."

"Sadly, on this, I can." Reaching toward him, she cupped his cheeks. "You deserve a nice woman who will give you lots of babies and a happy home. I truly hope you find her one day." Drawing him toward her, she placed a soft kiss on his lips.

"Don't," he murmured against her. "Don't leave. I want to hold you."

"I'm always going to leave. You're smart enough to know that."

Giving him one last kiss, she dematerialized to the place she felt most comfortable. Her small cabin. Alone and numb.

The woman struck him, hard upon the face, and Galredad gritted his teeth. Fueled by all of the loss and loneliness inside, he threw her body to the ground, climbing on top to ravage her. For in his twisted mind, if he could only show her his love, she would understand.

She struggled beneath him, enhancing his rage, until he felt himself become something rather ugly and squalid. Forgetting himself, his only objective became to hurt her, so she would see how terrible it felt...

Chapter 11

Nolan whistled as he trekked toward the main castle at Uteria. He'd decided to surprise Sadie, securing a reservation at the fancy restaurant that sat in the main square. Clutching the bouquet of flowers in his hand, he noticed how tight his grip was. Similar to the clench of nerves deep in his abdomen.

Being a meticulous person, he had the night planned out, from the first moment he approached her until the end. He was going to ask her to move in with him at Astaria. Knowing that this was the next natural step for them, his heart pulsed blood through his body. If all went well, he'd escort his tiny Slayer home after dinner and finally hold her in his arms as they planned their future.

Nolan knew Sadie was a virgin. He certainly didn't want to rush her. But their increasingly heated kisses had been driving him wild. If she wasn't ready for intercourse, he could at least nibble her small breasts and kiss her deepest place until she writhed under him. Imagining how pretty she'd look when she obtained her release caused his throbbing shaft to twitch in his pants. He'd never wanted a woman as much.

Truth be told, he wasn't that experienced either. He'd only been with a handful of women before he came through the ether. The strict world of Georgian England where he lived during his youth didn't promote promiscuity. It was quite similar to the societies of the immortals in that way. Bloodlines and virgin brides were cherished.

Nolan hadn't been with a woman in over three hundred years. Something that had led to intense loneliness and despair while being trapped in the immortal world. Until sweet Sadie blazed into his sphere. A beautiful savior with a kind smile and generous heart. She'd plucked him from the abyss of lonesomeness and pieced him back into a semblance of a man. Thanking every god that existed, he trekked forward.

Entering the large doors of the castle, he shuffled downstairs toward her infirmary. Approaching the exam rooms, he heard her speaking to someone.

"Everything looks great, Sagtikos. Your vitals are good and your heart is healthy. No marathons for you, but otherwise, you're going to lead a perfectly normal life."

"Thank you, Sadie," a male voice said. Nolan heard a rustling and assumed he was sliding off the exam table. Not wanting to interrupt their appointment, he leaned back against the wall. "I was worried when you caught the heart murmur, especially as an adult. Glad to know my ticker's going to make it."

She laughed. Always so sweet, so soft. "Yep. You're good. Don't go using that heart to break others, okay? I saw you walking with Ariel in the park the other day. She's quite a catch."

Silence echoed for a few moments.

"What if I don't want Ariel?" the man asked. "We've known each other forever, Sadie, but something's changed in you. It's absolutely stunning."

Sadie cleared her throat. "It's my burns. Nolan and Arderin made a salve for me so that my skin would heal. It's amazing, and my cheek is almost completely clear."

"And your arm," the man said, his voice low and almost seductive. Was he touching Sadie? Nolan clenched his teeth, debating if he should intervene.

"Yes," she said, a bit of annoyance in her tone. "Eventually, my entire right side will be healed. I'll look normal again."

The room was quiet. "And then what? Surely, you'll want to marry and have a family."

"I hope so, yes."

"With the human doctor with the fancy accent? He can't give you children, Sadie."

"Not biologically, no. But we have a fully-functioning sperm bank right here. If we choose that route, I could always get inseminated. There are plenty of couples who can't have kids naturally and always find a way."

Nolan heard shuffling again and realized his heart was pounding. He knew he shouldn't be listening to their conversation but he was tethered to the wall by curiosity.

"I could give you children. So could other Slayer men. It would be foolish to tie yourself to a human. I hope you've thought of this. Don't you want to at least play the field a bit before you settle down with the first man who's ever courted you?"

"I...don't know," she said, her tone hesitant. "I've never thought about being with anyone else. Nolan's the only man who's ever been attracted to me."

"*I'm* attracted to you, Sadie. Others will be too. Don't place yourself in a box before you see what's out there. That's all I'm saying."

Nolan's breath caught in his throat. Uncertainty, strong and true, coursed through his veins. Not wanting to call attention to himself, he surreptitiously headed back up the stairs, out of the castle and into the afternoon sunlight. Under the blue sky, he stood, running his hand through his thick brown hair. The scent of the flowers surrounded him, still held in the grip of his other hand.

Thrumming with doubt, as the birds sang above, he replayed the overheard conversation in his head.

What if she wanted to date other men? Once she was fully healed, surely others would want to court her. Since he was pretty sure he was in love with her, he hadn't even considered that she might want to play the field. Cursing himself for moving too quickly, he rubbed his fingers over his forehead in frustration.

Always extremely thorough, Nolan had analyzed their situation methodically, concluding that it was time they cohabitate. Now, he recognized that they both needed more time to decide what was best. He felt compelled to take a step back and deliberate. Asking her to commit to him so soon after her skin was healing was unfair, especially since he couldn't give her children.

"Hey, Nolan," a voice said behind him. "Whatcha doing at the castle?"

"Hi, Moira," he said, straightening to his full height. "Nice to see you again. I, um, was just leaving."

"Beautiful flowers," she said, gesturing with her head. "For someone special?" White teeth glowed from her pretty smile.

"Uh, not really. Here," he said, thrusting them at her. "Please, take them. I don't want them to go to waste."

"Oh, I couldn't—"

"I insist," he said, all but shoving the flowers into her hands. "Now, if you'll excuse me, I have to get back to Astaria. Have a good evening."

Breaking into a full-on speed-walk, Nolan headed to the train station and boarded the next train bound for Astaria. Sitting in the car as it chugged along, worry crept in. Had he overreacted? He was usually so calm and steadfast at giving others relationship advice but realized quickly, as the train approached Astaria, that it wasn't so easy when it was your own heart in the balance.

* * * *

Sadie gritted her teeth, becoming more frustrated by the minute at her conversation with Sagtikos. What an ass, questioning her life decisions. Where the heck had he been when she'd been burnt to a crisp these past centuries? Nowhere. No, the only man who'd ever even thought to look her way when she was ugly and scarred was Nolan. That gift of acceptance was worth so much more to her than having his biological child.

Knowing that Sagtikos would never understand, she shook her head. "Look, we've been friends a long time, but this really isn't your business. I love Nolan, human or not, just as he cared for me when no one else could. So, I really wish you'd stop discussing something that doesn't concern you. In the future, it would probably be best if you saw him for your checkups."

"Sadie—"

"No," she said, shaking off his arm. "Your appointment is complete. Please, leave the gown on the table. I'll see you around the compound, Sagtikos." Giving him a nod, she closed the door firmly behind her.

Frustrated that the checkup with her friend had taken such a turn, Sadie headed up the stairs, looking for Kenden. He was like a brother to her, always so kind and warm. Wanting his advice, she roamed around the castle, entering the large foyer by the front door.

"Hey, Sadie," Moira said, seeming to bounce inside. The woman was quite attractive with her deep blue eyes and thick blond hair. "How's it going?"

"Just great," Sadie said a bit sarcastically. "Gorgeous flowers. Who gave them to you? A suitor?"

Moira laughed. "I wish. No, I saw Nolan leaving here just a minute ago. He kind of just shoved them at me. But I guess I'll take them home and put them in water. It's been about a million centuries since a man gave me flowers. I should probably take advantage of it."

How strange. Nolan had been at Uteria and not told her? And he'd given Moira flowers? Why? Dread filled Sadie as she looked at the stunning Slayer. Was Nolan attracted to her? Sadie had always assumed they were exclusively dating but she'd never asked him. Good lord, she'd never dated anyone until now. In their modern world, was it appropriate to date more than one woman at once? Hurt constricted her throat and tears welled in her eyes.

"Well, they're beautiful," Sadie said. "Enjoy them. I have to, um, head outside for a bit. See you later."

Sadie jogged toward the front door, holding her ballcap to her head so it didn't fly off in the breeze. Reaching the park that sat in the middle of Uteria's main square, she held her palms to her cheeks. There, under the old oak tree, she cursed herself a fool as she somehow managed to hold the tears inside.

* * * *

Moira headed toward Miranda's royal office chamber, not understanding what vibe she was putting off that was causing people to bolt from her presence today. Did she forget to put on deodorant? Looking around the darkened hallway, she quickly sniffed under her arm. Nope. Shower fresh. Deciding that maybe everyone was just a bit insane, she knocked on Miranda's door.

"Come in."

Easing the door open, Moira stepped inside, closing it behind her.

"Did you bring me flowers?" Miranda teased. "You'll have to give notes to my husband. He's been slacking lately."

"Oh, um, I kind of seemed to pick them up on my way here. I'll just leave them on the table while we speak." Setting the bouquet down on the conference table, Moira nervously rubbed her wet palms over her jean-clad thighs.

"Have a seat," Miranda said, waving toward the chairs in front of her mahogany desk. "I was so excited to hear that you wanted to meet with me. Any friend of Aron's is a friend of mine."

"Thank you, Queen Miranda," Moira said, curtsying. "I really appreciate your time."

Miranda's face contorted with distain. Standing, she walked over and placed her hand on Moira's shoulder. "Um, yeah. A few things. One," she said, holding up a finger, "don't ever curtsy to me again. Are we in the fourth century? Good god. And two," she said, holding up two fingers, "it's just Miranda. I can stand the whole *Queen* thing". She made quotation marks with her fingers. Drawing Moira toward her desk by gently tugging her arm, she gestured for her to sit.

"Sorry," Moira said. "I hope I didn't offend you."

Miranda threw back her head and laughed, hearty and bold. "Good lord, no. I'm just a woman who speaks her mind. And I hear you are too," she said, arching a raven-black brow. "Lila told me about your conversation in the gallery when you first met. You're a straight shooter, Moira. I freaking love that."

Relaxing a bit, Moira sat back in her chair. "I needed her to know. That Latimus always loved her. I would've wanted someone to tell me. I know it made her uncomfortable but felt it vital that she understood."

The queen smiled. "That's pretty awesome. Not many women would go out of their way to ensure a man from their past had happiness with his current lover."

"Why not?" Moira said with a shrug. "We're all women just trying to do our best in this world. We need to support each other and lift one another up. It's the only way to be our best selves and find happiness."

Grinning, Miranda sat back in her chair, swiveling absently. "Damn. I like you. Okay, so, let me have it. What do you need? I know it must be important if you asked for one-on-one time with your *queen*." She snickered and rolled her eyes, mocking herself. It was extremely endearing to Moira.

"Aron's birthday is on Thursday. I know this isn't giving you much notice since it's Monday, but I'd like to do something special for him. He's done so much to help me since I've returned. He's very...*fond* of you, so I thought that maybe we could plan a surprise for him. He's super-involved with the playground, and it's almost finished, so I was thinking we could have the unveiling on Thursday and throw him a surprise party. Is that lame?" she asked, feeling like a bit of a dolt in front of the queen.

Miranda shook her head, causing Moira to imagine puffs of steam exiting her ears as the wheels spun in her mind. "No. It's not lame at all. It's fucking brilliant. Aron is a damn saint. He'll only be happy if his birthday is celebrated while he's helping others. Let's throw him a surprise party, and I'll declare it a holiday. A kingdom-wide day of service. We'll name it in honor of Aron and officially open the playground. People can volunteer to clean up the park, do community service, whatever," she said, waving her hand. "Aron and his do-gooder heart will get a kick out of that."

Moira could feel herself beaming. "He would love that. Thank you, Miranda. It's more than I could've even asked."

"Of course," she said with a nod. "Aron was instrumental in cementing my appointment as queen. I most likely wouldn't be here without his support. It's well-deserved."

"You're so kind," Moira said, shaking her head. "I can see why he loves you." Realizing her slipup, she inhaled a sharp breath. "I mean, um, I, uh—"

"You can stop the foot-in-mouth routine," Miranda said, shooting her a droll look. "I'm an expert at it, believe me."

"Sorry," Moira said, rubbing the back of her neck. "Shit. I shouldn't have said that. Aaaaaand now I went and cursed in front of the queen. Crap."

Miranda giggled, her gorgeous green eyes filled with amusement. "Oh, honey, if no one cursed in front of me, I'd never have one damn conversation." They chuckled for a moment, and then, the queen's features softened. "He doesn't, you know."

"Excuse me?"

"Love me," Miranda said. "I know it seems that way, and maybe in his mind he thinks he does. But he loves a version of me that doesn't exist. One that's regal and perfect. Believe me, that sure as hell isn't me. Ask my husband. He'll happily tell you what a pain in the ass I am." Leaning forward, she rested her forearms on the desk. "If you ask me, he might just love you. I've never seen Aron so relaxed and carefree around anyone else. It's awesome for a guy as rigid as he is. It says something about his true feelings for you that he's able to let his guard down."

"Yeah," Moira said, rubbing her palms together between her knees. "I don't think so. He doesn't really see me that way. I was married to his best friend who died centuries ago. I think he just has this sense of protective loyalty toward me. I'd never be equal to him. I'm a servant's daughter. Not one drop of aristocratic blood in me."

Miranda's eyes narrowed. "Do you think that would truly matter to a man as good as Aron? In the end? I don't think it would."

Feeling uncomfortable, Moira shrugged. "I've thought about it a lot. There are a lot of circumstances that will only allow us to be friends. And that's okay. He's been a godsend to me ever since I returned to Uteria. I'm thankful for the friendship we share."

Miranda studied her. "Does he know where you were for the last eight centuries?"

Moira swallowed. Hard. "No," she whispered.

"Ah ha," Miranda said slowly. "I see."

"I'm pretty sure it was wrong to lie to him but I'm also pretty sure he would've thrown me out on my ass if he knew I'd...*given* myself to someone and not tried to work it out with my husband."

The queen chewed her lip. "Lila told me about the scar on your neck. Did your husband give that to you?"

Moira nodded, looking at the floor.

"So, what in the hell was there to work out? I'd have gotten as far away as possible too."

Inhaling a huge breath, she sighed. "It's not that simple."

"It usually never is." Standing, Miranda came to sit in the chair opposite her. Grabbing her hands, she bore her gaze into Moira's. "Let's throw Aron an awesome party and make a goddamn national holiday in his name. What do you say? Fuck all this heavy shit. It'll work out, Moira. I promise." She shook her hands and gave that brilliant smile.

"I say, hell yes," Moira said, beaming back.

And with that, the Aron, Son of Jakal, Kingdom-Wide Day of Service was born.

Regaining her wits, the woman pushed the man away. Summoning the strength of the heavens, she drew a lightning bolt from the sky and shot it into his body. His skin burned, becoming wrinkled and shriveled.

Closing her eyes, the woman called upon the force of the sun. As Galredad lay sprawled on the grass, the bright orb began to singe away his skin.

"Why do you hurt me so?" he cried, struggling to survive the pain.

"I do not wish to," she said, hovering above him as a lone tear ran down her cheek. "But you have become someone quite awful."

Swamped with sadness, the woman vanished...

Chapter 12

On Thursday, Evie took extra time to get ready, wanting to fortify the shield comprised of her expensive clothing and flawless features. She hadn't spoken to Kenden since leaving his house, showing her cowardice. It was appalling. Evie never showed fear and certainly not to men. She should've stayed and let him rock her world another time or two, showing him their connection was only sexual. Instead, he'd dug into her soul, as if he'd taken a damn course on how to swirl her into an emotional wreck.

Not on her fucking life. Evie had no idea when her existence had turned into a bad version of a "very special episode of Oprah" but she was over it. Eyeing her reflection in the mirror, she lifted her chin with resolve. No more crying. No more *intimacy*. Good god. She'd be cordial to Kenden today, at Aron's ceremony, and fuck him on Saturday. After that, they would become soldiers in the same war. Acquaintances who would work together to defeat her father before she returned to the human world. No other option existed.

Anticipating the day, she observed her scowl in the reflection. Miranda had texted her, indicating that she expected Evie to attend. She was getting pretty tired of dear ol' sis dictating orders to her. She'd have a talk with the queen about that as well. Evie didn't follow orders, no matter whose bloodline ran through them.

Slowly scrutinizing her face in the mirror, Evie reveled in her beauty. She'd never been vain. That was for women who craved the attention of men. Instead, she was practical. Her beauty was innate, just as a tree had bark or a bird could fly. It held no value to her, but she understood its importance in controlling her circumstances. Women reluctantly venerated her for it; men salivated over it. And for that, she was grateful she'd inherited her mother's features.

Narrowing her eyes, she ran soft fingers over her hair. The red tresses were an anomaly. As far as she knew, Rina nor Valktor had any trace of the coloring. Perhaps it was inherited from her wretched father. He'd told her once that the scarlet tresses were the same blazing red as Etherya's. As if she'd believe any lies that escaped the monster's reedy lips.

Inhaling deep with resolve, she approached the closet and donned a white cardigan. In the long mirror affixed to the closet door, it looked angelic over the green V-neck, sleeveless silk blouse and dark, thin-legged designer jeans. Slipping on bejeweled sandals, she closed her lids and dematerialized to the playground at Uteria's main square.

Sensations of buzzing sounds and children's amused shrieks greeted her as her feet were tickled by the green grass. There must've been a thousand people milling around the rectangular park, with its thick oak trees, and the nearby town square. The playground was mostly finished. Monkey bars, swings, see-saws—all were currently occupied by energy-filled munchkins under the puffy clouds and warm sunbeams. Picnic tables dotted the perimeter of the dirt-covered swath that comprised the playground.

Evie spotted Darkrip and Arderin sitting with Lila, Latimus and Heden at one of the wooden tables. Miranda sat on a blanket nearby, rubbing Tordor's black hair as he sat beside her. His tiny lips sucked a pacifier as he took in the surroundings, and Evie's heart skipped a beat. Had she ever been as innocent as the little bugger? The chances were slim to none.

Sathan stood behind Miranda, bulky arms crossed in his favorite stance, while Kenden stood beside him. They chatted cordially as Evie reaffirmed her intention to remain emotionless.

"Hello, Evie," a warm voice said from behind.

"Hello, Aron," she said, pasting on a smile. "Looks like we have you to thank for this day of family bliss and perfection."

He chuckled and rubbed the back of his neck, looking slightly embarrassed. "Miranda got some bug in her ear and decided to make a spectacle. I'm always happy to give a speech here and there, but we should be focusing on the kids. I don't mind being the center of attention but it's certainly not something I crave."

"How interesting. I thrive on it," she said, arching a brow.

"I don't mind sharing the spotlight. Never have."

Evie shrugged. "Seems to me, that might push you to the back of the line where it's dark and no one can see you. Maybe it's time you learned to shove up front."

An unreadable emotion passed over his features. "Maybe."

"Aron?" Moira called as she approached. "I think they're ready for you." Gazing at Evie, she said, "I didn't mean to interrupt though. If you want to wait a few minutes…"

"It's fine," Aron said, nodding. "Let's do it."

Evie watched them grin at each other, reading the images in their minds. Their desire for each other was palpable. But there was a man between them, one who was long gone, as well as Moira's lies. Interesting. It moved something in her, watching these almost-lovers who were too afraid to act on their feelings. Strange, since nothing had incited fascination in her for quite a while.

"After the ceremony winds down, perhaps you could give me a tour of your house, Aron?" Evie said. "Miranda told me that it's featured on the walking tours of

Uteria and was built long before the Awakening. And maybe Moira can come along, since she lived there after her father died."

Aron's eyebrows lifted. "I'd be happy to."

"I... Sure, I can come along. My mother was the housekeeper, so she showed me all the secret passageways."

"Great," Evie said. "Maybe after sunset."

Miranda called Aron's name from her now-standing perch beside the blanket, and he headed in her direction, Evie and Moira falling into step behind him.

"You knew I grew up in Aron's house because you can read my thoughts," Moira said beside her as they strolled.

"Yes," Evie said.

"Great," she muttered.

Evie chuckled. "I won't tell him about your time at Astaria, if that's what you're worried about. But take it from me, he wants to sleep with you."

Moira's blue eyes grew wide as she lifted her head. "He's in love with someone else."

"Believe me, sweetheart," Evie said, "this ain't about love. That man wants to bone you until your pretty little head shatters the headboard. You can believe me or not, but it's true."

The Slayer chewed her lower lip. "I was so sure he didn't see me that way."

"Oh, he sees you in a *lot* of ways. Now, I learned a long time ago that I get into trouble when I spread others' thoughts around, so I'll end this conversation here. Take the info and do with it what you will."

"I, um, yeah. Will do. Thanks, Evie."

They came to stand at the front of the crowd, where Miranda had tied a red ribbon from the jungle gym to the monkey bars. Lifting a pair of scissors fashioned for a giant, the queen gave a speech extolling Aron's virtues as he beamed by her side. Evie thought him a handsome man. Short brown hair, mahogany-colored eyes, small but well-proportioned features. He was slight and probably around six feet tall, but that would mean Moira, who was a few inches shorter than her, would fit like a glove in his arms.

Nice, thick lips would be perfect for kissing. He could use them on Moira's mouth...or somewhere more exciting. He'd be tentative at first, but spitfire little Moira would unwind him until he let go and ravaged her. How very exciting.

"He's in love with Miranda," a baritone said softly in her ear. "So, don't get any ideas."

"Well, well, if it isn't the arrogant Slayer commander," she said, looking up into Kenden's melted chocolate irises. "You just know everything, don't you? How awful it must be to deal with us mere minions." She batted her eyelashes, hoping to draw his ire.

Instead, he stayed calm, mired in his always unflappable demeanor. God, she hated him for it.

"I'd be careful throwing accusations of arrogance around," he challenged. "Pot and kettle and all that."

"Arrogance is for fools," she snapped, furious at her pounding heart. "A wasted emotion for people who require adoration. I don't need anyone to think I'm right or intelligent."

"Because you already are?" he taunted.

"Because I wasn't born with the ability to care. About anything. Including what others think about me. It's a powerful trait and one I'm damn proud of."

His gorgeous features softened, filling with the compassion that comprised so much of his nature. "I think you have the ability to care about a lot of things, Evie."

"Then you're a bigger moron than I thought," she said, focusing back on the ceremony.

Miranda handed Aron the gigantic scissors, and he cut the ribbon. The crowd erupted in voracious cheers as they smiled and waved. Everyone began to disperse, and Evie felt Kenden's hand on her upper back.

"Can we talk for a minute?"

"I need to speak to Miranda," she said, turning to face him so that she could pull away from his touch.

"Okay," he said, his eyes darting between hers. "Afterward?"

"Aron's going to give me a tour of his house, and then, I'm heading home."

Kenden sighed and ran a hand through his hair. "You haven't answered any of my texts this week, nor my voicemails. So, are we done here? Do you even want to see me on Saturday?"

Agony swept through her, unwanted and vicious, imagining that last Saturday's grizzly battle would be their last time together. Although she wanted to create space between them, she couldn't let that be the end. Whatever it was that existed between them deserved better. Something they could remember fondly, centuries in the future, when they thought back upon their time with each other. Even her emotionless soul desired that last solemn memory.

"I don't want last Saturday to be the end. If you're willing, I'd like to see our agreement through."

Every muscle in her throat constricted as he studied her, silent and contemplative. God. Fucking. Damn it. The prick of tears began to spark behind her eyes. Willing them away with every cell of her father's malevolent blood, she vowed that she wouldn't let him see her vulnerability.

He remained quiet for so long that she was sure he would say no. Wanting to stave off the rejection, she opened her mouth to tell him that she would release him from their bargain. Although she hated capitulating to him, it was better than having him wring her soul out like a dirty rag.

"I'd like to see it through too," he said, before she could speak.

She closed her mouth. Something so vivid and genuine swam in his deep brown eyes. "Fine," she said, crossing her arms over her chest.

"And after that?" he asked, his tone almost pleading, as if he already knew the answer but wanted to sway her toward a different outcome.

"After that, I'll train with your army. As your comrade and your soldier. I don't renege on my deals, Ken. I promised you I'd fight if you met my ultimatum. After that, I'll become your best warrior. That's all that can be between us. You know deep down, it's true. Smart generals know when to retreat in a losing battle."

He sighed, sad and long. "That, they do." His dejected tone almost broke her unfeeling heart. Encircling her wrist, he drew her hand to his full, sexy lips. "I'll pick you up at your cabin at five," he said, gliding a kiss over her palm. "I have something that I want to show you. I'll drive us there in the four-wheeler. After that, maybe you can show me how to cook in the kitchen I never use? You can text me what ingredients to have on hand. Is that okay?"

Unable to help herself, Evie slid her palm over the soft, clean-shaven skin of his lower jaw. Cupping his cheek, she grinned. "It sounds fucking perfect."

"Great," he said, pecking her hand once more before she dropped it to her side.

"What's up, lovebirds?" Miranda chimed, walking toward them with Tordor on her hip. "Thanks for coming, Evie. It was a nice ceremony, right?"

"Yes," Evie said with a nod. "But I need to have a chat with you about your nasty little habit of thinking you can tell me where to be all the time. It's become rather intolerable."

"Whoa," Kenden said, shooting them both a look. "I think that's my cue to leave. I'll be over there with Latimus. If we see fists being thrown, we're butting in." Giving Evie an endearing wink that absolutely did *not* make her insides melt, he stalked away.

Miranda shifted Tordor to her other hip. "You're really gonna have it out with me while I've got this little monster strapped to my hip? Low blow, sis. Seriously."

"I'm not joking, Miranda," Evie said, attempting to tamp down her anger. "I know you like to joke when things are tense, but I'm not one of your subjects. I don't answer to anyone. Are we clear?"

Miranda stared at her, heat clouding her eyes. She was pissed. Evie thrived on it, as she always thrived on anger.

"Who are you really mad at, Evie?" Miranda asked. "Me? Or yourself, for actually showing up when I ask you? It seems to me, this might be the first time in your life that people care about you enough to want you around. Perhaps that scares the shit out of you."

"One thing I hate more than entitled immortal royals is people who try to psychoanalyze me," Evie said, taking a half-step closer, shortening the distance. "Poor, pitiful Evie, who was raped by her evil father. We just need to love her, and she'll be fine. Well, fuck you, Miranda. Take your self-help books and herbal ginger tea and shove them up your servant-wiped ass. You'll never come close to understanding anything about me but you'd better stop thinking you can boss me around. I'm here by choice and I can leave just as easily."

"Then fucking leave!" Miranda yelled, fury flashing in her grass-green eyes. "You have some nerve calling me entitled, Evie. You waltz in here, after you did everything in your power to almost get me killed and tear my kingdom apart. I hope you're not the one to kill Crimeous because then, I can put a sword in my hand and fight you like I've wanted to every damn time you treat me like shit. Family means something to me, but you shove it back in my face like it's poisonous. If you hate it so much, then go. We'll find another way to kill Crimeous. I'm done putting up with your crap."

Evie opened her mouth to unleash every curse word in her extensive repertoire on her sister, but Lila and Arderin rushed to their sides before she could speak.

"You two are making a scene," Lila scolded in her saccharine voice. Taking Tordor from Miranda's arms, she balanced him on her voluptuous, jean-clad hip. "It's beneath both of you. If you want to argue, do it in private."

"Um, yeah, I'm all for that," Arderin said, standing opposite of Lila so that they formed a haphazard square. "I'll bring the popcorn. It'll be better than Kandi and Phaedra's feud."

The three other women stilled to give Arderin a confused glare.

"Real Housewives of Atlanta?" Arderin asked, lifting her hands and staring at them like they were daft. "Forget it. The point is, I'd like to see you two throw down, but not here. Our people deserve better from their leaders."

Lila gave her a huge smile. "That's so diplomatic, Arderin. Sathan would be so proud of you."

"Obviously," she said, rolling her eyes and winking at Lila.

It broke the tension a bit, and Evie warily regarded Miranda.

"I'm sorry," Miranda breathed, rubbing her fingers over her forehead. "That was uncalled for. Evie, I apologize for *summoning* you or whatever," she said, making quotation marks with her fingers. "I just really want you to be part of this family and I want you to be at every function. Not because I want to boss you around but because I want to spend time with you. I hope you can accept my apology."

Well, shit. Evie studied them, the three stunning women before her. Arderin to her left, with an air of innocence but also a streak of mischief. It was easy to see why Darkrip was wild for her. Miranda across from Evie, their mother's eyes in her striking face, filled with sorrow and remorse. Lila to her right, probably the most beautiful woman she'd ever met, balancing the baby on her hip as if she'd been born with him attached. Never had Evie met a female more destined to be a mother. Too bad her asshole father had maimed her.

God, Crimeous was an abhorrent creature. Evie should've been directing her anger at him, not at the sister who'd welcomed her into her compound with open arms even after Evie's treacherous deeds when she'd lost her child. Unused to regret and guilt, she wanted to melt into the ground. She was no better than her father. A soulless creature who caused everyone pain. Self-loathing threatened to drown her.

"Hey," Miranda said, reaching over to grab Evie's hand. "It's okay. I get passionate. I've cursed Sathan out so much worse."

"True story," Arderin mumbled.

"Please, don't dematerialize," Miranda pleaded. "Stay here and enjoy the day with us. Hang with the three of us. We're super-fun, I promise. Arderin will tell you all about the Kardashians, and Lila can show you what it's like to be perfect."

Lila swatted Miranda on her arm, snickering. "Stop it. I'm only half-perfect."

They chuckled as Evie observed them. The three of them emanated the energy and ease that only close friends shared. Never having close girlfriends, she'd always wondered what that felt like.

"C'mon," Arderin said, threading her arm through Evie's. "Let's share secrets about my husband. I need dirt." Tugging on her arm, Evie let her lead the way to one of the picnic tables. They sat for hours, Evie eventually relaxing as the three of them regaled her with stories from their marriages with their beloved but flawed men.

At one point, Arderin and Lila went to get them a round of beers, leaving her alone with Miranda at the table.

"I don't really feel remorse often, but I'd like to tell you that I'm sorry, Miranda. I misjudged you. I appreciate you asking me to be here today."

"Thank you," Miranda said, covering her hand where it rested atop the wooden table. "And that's all we need to say."

The ladies returned with the beers, and they drank while the setting sun sparked a glow upon their backs. If Evie had been someone even remotely normal, she might have thought it one of the most enjoyable afternoons of her life.

* * * *

After the sun set, Moira walked with Aron and Evie along the cobblestone sidewalk to his house. As they strolled, Moira's heart thudded from the information Evie had given her. Was Aron truly attracted to her? Would he be able to push aside his love for Miranda, and his loyalty to Diabolos, to be with her?

The questions swirled as they entered his large mansion. Together, she and Aron showed Evie the twenty-bedroom abode. From the expansive kitchen to the recently upgraded private movie theater to the spacious master bedroom. Aron was a proud man, and she could sense his pleasure at showing Evie his home.

The estate was immaculately kept by the live-in housekeeper that Aron had hired several centuries ago. Moira had been distraught to learn that her mother had died while she'd been at Astaria. When she'd returned to Uteria, Aron had led her to his back yard, where he'd erected a beautiful headstone for her. Moira visited it often, Aron always allowing her free rein of his home. The gesture of building a memorial for her servant mother was just another example of Aron's kind heart. As they stood in his master chamber, by the large bed, she couldn't focus on their conversation. Longing for him had consumed her, spurred on by Evie's confirmation that he desired her.

"Well, this has been lovely, but look at the time," Evie said, lifting her arm to look at her watch. Except her arm was bare. Locking her stunning green gaze on Moira, she said, "It's time for Cinderella to leave the ball. See you both later." Shooting Moira a subtle wink from her almond-shaped eyes, she vanished.

"That was strange," Aron said, his expression puzzled. "I hope she liked the tour."

"She seemed to," Moira said, her voice sounding like it was trapped in a tunnel a thousand miles away.

"Well, should we head downstairs?" he asked, offering his hand to her.

Moira remained frozen, every cell in her body quivering as she stood by his sizeable bed. Mustering courage from some deep well within, she moved toward him until her body brushed his. Tilting her head back, she stared deep into his gentle brown eyes.

Lifting her hands, she slid them over his clean-shaven cheeks, ever so slowly.

His brows drew together. "Moira?"

Her pupils darted back and forth between his, her throat threatening to cut off every ounce of air. "I want you, Aron," she said, hating the gravel in her voice.

A puff of breath escaped his full lips as he straightened his spine, elevating his height a fraction to look down into her. "Moira—"

"I don't want to live with regrets," she said, cutting off his protest. "I've learned the hard way that life is so precious. Every day we waste is one we'll never get back. I don't want to live like that anymore."

He smiled at her and grabbed her wrists as her hands framed his face. "You're just lonely and tired, angel. The goddess knows, this can be a lonely world. Let's go downstairs and have a drink. We can chat as long as you want."

"No," she said, vowing to stand her ground. Pulling her hands from his face, they formed fists at her sides. "This isn't about loneliness and it isn't about finding a warm body to be with. It's about us, Aron. I trust you more than anyone in the world. I desire you more than any man. It's time I acted on it." Grasping the bottom of her silky, sleeveless blouse, she drew it over her head and tossed it to the ground.

Aron's eyes widened, soaking in the image of her flat stomach and pert breasts, held up by her light-blue lace bra.

Shaking his head, he said, "Diabolos—"

"Diabolos is dead," she said, lifting her chin. "I won't let you use him as a wedge between us anymore."

Inching toward him, she clutched his hands. Lifting them, she settled them around her waist. Reflexively, he dragged her closer. Encouraged, she slid her palms up the fabric of his polo shirt, over his chest, clutching them behind his neck. The bare skin of her upper body bracketed his, and heat seemed to emanate from his toned frame.

"Moira," he whispered, lowering his forehead to rest on hers. Indecision swam in his eyes, so close to hers.

"I don't care if you imagine I'm Miranda. You can call me by her name. Whatever you need to do to be with me."

His features drew together, his expression a mask of confusion. "Why in the hell would I imagine I'm with any other woman when I have you in my arms?" he asked. The growl in his tone sent shivers up her spine. With firm hands, he caressed the soft skin of her back, causing her to purr against him.

Lifting to her toes, she gently touched her lips to his. He stood so very still, panting at the light contact. And then, he snapped. Raggedly moaning her name, he drew her to him with an arm around the waist. Plunging the other into her hair, he opened his mouth over hers.

Moira almost cried at his capitulation, thrusting her fingers into his short brown hair to pull him into her. Their tongues warred as he unclasped her bra, throwing it to the floor. With shaking fingers, she grabbed the hem of his shirt, yanking it from his body.

Unable to contain her moan, as her nipples felt the scratch of the tiny hairs on his chest, she pressed into him, needing more.

"I need these off," she said, maintaining contact with his mouth as she unbuttoned his slacks and began pushing them down his hips. With a frustrated grunt, he pulled them off along with his boxer-briefs. Cementing his lips to hers and bending at the knees, he picked her up and carried her to the bed.

Her back upon the soft covers, he snapped open her jeans, unzipped the metal and slithered them down her legs. Moira noticed his hands shaking as he slid off her sandals, her jeans and thong following shortly after.

Naked, he leaned over her, his gorgeous body in between her open legs. Smiling down at her, he shrugged. "I haven't done this in a really long time," he said. "I'm shaking like a damn virgin."

"It's so cute," she said, palming his face as he loomed above her.

"I don't want to be cute," he said, nipping her lips. "Good god woman, do you want me to lose my erection? I want to be hot and sexy and whatever else you women salivate over."

Moira laughed. "You're so hot." Running her fingers over his toned abs, she grinned up at him while she still held his cheek. "I promise."

Staring into her, his lips curved, and he touched the head of his shaft to her center. Exhaling a breath, he shook his head. "You're so wet," he whispered.

"Only for you," she said, drawing his head down for a kiss. "Please, Aron," she murmured against his mouth.

"I should get a condom," he said.

"I'm on the pill and just saw Sadie recently. Everything's fine. I trust you."

His deep brown eyes, filled with so much emotion, skated back and forth between hers. Lowering his hand, the pads of his fingers pulled at the lips of her core, causing her to mewl. Holding her open, he began jutting into her, panting as he held her gaze.

"Your eyes are so blue right now," he said, his hips pushing him further and further into her. "You feel so good. Oh, god."

With his full length inside her, she threw her head back on the bed, closing her eyes with ecstasy. Relaxing, so that she could open to him more, she groaned as he began to pound her.

Into her he slid, drawing out and plunging in again, in an endless rhythm that threatened to drown her in pleasure. Unable to see him, with her head thrown back on the bed, she felt his palm cover hers as it rested face-up beside her head. Intimate and possessive, he entwined his fingers with hers, clutching her hand as he loved her.

Tears stung her eyes as she trained her gaze upon him. His coffee-colored irises stared into her with such reverence, she thought her heart might burst. Lifting her legs, she surrounded him with them, crossing her ankles across his back. It created a new angle, and he took advantage, hitting a spot with his shaft that drove her wild.

"I'm so close," she cried, locked onto him.

"Me too," he said, clutching her hand even harder as he hammered her. "God, Moira, I'm so deep. Fuck, it feels amazing."

Seeing his thin grip on control shattered something inside her, and her body bowed, convulsing as the orgasm overtook her. He shouted above her, calling her name as he began shooting into her. Together, they crashed, clutching each other close as they fell back to Earth. Shaken and sated, Moira reveled in the weight of his warm body as it stretched over her.

Lifting his head, he gazed into her. With soft fingertips, he stroked her cheek. "Well, I certainly didn't expect *that* on the house tour."

Laughter burst from her throat. She loved how relaxed he was, his handsome face so sweet as he grinned at her. "You mean you don't bone every one of the patrons who tours your home?"

Chuckling, he pecked her on the lips. "No, but it might increase the popularity of the excursion."

She snickered, shaking her head at him. Concern flooded her as his expression grew serious.

"What is it?" she asked.

"Just making sure you're okay that we didn't use protection."

"Yes," she whispered, brushing the pads of her fingers along his strong jaw. "I promise, I just had a physical. Everything was clear."

"Okay," he said, stroking her hair. "I haven't been checked in a few decades, but my last physical was clean, and I haven't been with a woman in over a century. So, I guess I should thank you for breaking my streak."

"You're certainly welcome," she said, absently caressing his shoulder. "I've wanted you like that for so long."

He grinned. "I had no idea. I'm kind of an idiot when it comes to romance." Moira loved the way his fingers threaded through her tresses. "I guess it's been a while for you too. Unless you were with someone at Restia?"

Her stomach dropped to her knees so rapidly that she wondered how the organ didn't shoot from her body altogether. Was this the opportunity to tell him where she'd been? In the aftermath of their lovemaking?

Deciding it would ruin the moment, she tamped down the self-revulsion that threatened to strangle her as she lied to him. "Nope," she said, her voice soft. "I wasn't with anyone at Restia."

Smiling, he kissed her lips and pulled her to stand. After cleaning themselves up in his marble bathroom, he tugged her toward the bed. "Will you stay here tonight?"

Moira studied him, chewing her bottom lip. By the goddess, she wanted to. So badly. But self-loathing at her continued deception led to doubt that was quickly eating her from the inside out.

"Please?" he asked, squeezing her hand.

He looked so adorable, naked longing on his face beside the turned-down bed. Knowing she didn't deserve to be held in his strong arms, she followed him into bed. When he spooned her close, cementing his front to her back in the darkness, she waited until his breathing slowed. Once it was even and steady, she allowed the silent tears to run down her cheeks, wondering how long it would take him to discover her lies.

* * * *

Sadie observed Nolan as he chatted with Sathan under the moonlight. The day was winding down, and he'd be heading back to Astaria soon. She wanted to speak to him, to ask him why he'd been distant lately, but shyness held her back. And a strong dose of fear. What if he'd decided their courtship was over? Best-case scenario? It might break the heart that she'd so tentatively allowed open. Worst? It would completely destroy her.

"You should just go talk to him, you know?" Kenden said, placing a supportive hand on her upper back as he approached. "He's mad for you."

"Yeah," she said, maneuvering her lip with her teeth as she stared absently at Nolan. "He's pulled away a bit lately. I don't know if it's something I did...or said." Blowing out a frustrated breath, she shook her head. "Maybe he wants to be with someone else."

"Doubtful," Kenden said, his hand so soothing as it caressed her through her sweatshirt. He'd always been like a brother, and she loved him immensely. "Although, I'm certainly no expert at love. The woman I'm courting wants to rip my organs from my body half the time. Not an ideal recipe for happily ever after."

Sadie snorted as she giggled. "That's a nice visual."

Kenden smiled. "I'll go distract Sathan so you can corner him. Come on." With a gentle push on her back, they began walking across the park.

"Sathan, before you and Miranda head home, I need to speak to you about next week's trainings," Kenden said.

"Sure," the king nodded. Excusing himself, he departed with Kenden, leaving Sadie alone with Nolan.

"Hi," she said, beaming up at him, determined to put on a brave face. "I feel like I haven't talked to you in a few days. You usually text me so many medical articles I stay up reading way past my bedtime."

"Sorry," he said, grinning sheepishly. "I've been helping Lila run the pop-up clinics for the Slayers that recently moved to Lynia and Naria, and this week has been crazy."

"I can help if you need me to. My schedule's not super-booked next week."

"That wasn't an attempt to guilt you into helping me," he said, winking. The gesture made her insides swirl. "But if you have free time next week, maybe we should have a chat. Do you want to grab drinks? Maybe on Wednesday?"

Little bugs of anxiety swam through her gut at his words. "We can chat now. What did you want to talk about?"

Looking uncomfortable, he ran a hand through his hair. "I, um, I don't know if this is the right place—"

"You're pulling away from me, Nolan," she said, willing away the angry tears she felt forming behind her eyes. "If you want to see other people, just tell me."

He cleared his throat, his Adam's apple bobbing as he swallowed. "I feel like we might have moved too fast, Sadie. That's all. I don't want to deny you anything. You're going to be so beautiful once your skin has healed—"

Pain coursed through her. "As opposed to now?"

His eyes narrowed. "Cheap shot, Sadie. You know I think you're stunning. I always have."

Then, why was he giving other women flowers? She wanted to scream the question at him but knew that if she did, the tears would flow, and she'd look like a moron. "If you think we moved too fast, then I don't want to bother you. I think it's best we take some time apart. You can communicate with me through text or email regarding our shared patients."

"Sadie, I'm trying to do what's best for you," he said, reaching for her arm.

"No!" She slapped his hand away. "I can't do this. I hope you find what you need, Nolan. Good night."

Unable to stomach anymore humiliation, she all but fled to her room at the castle. Once there, she climbed into bed, wishing her clinical skills were extensive enough to piece together her shattered heart.

The man crawled from the meadow to the protection of the forest, away from the murderous sun. Drowning in the loathing and despair from the loss of yet another person he loved, Galredad devolved into a malevolent creature comprised of hate and pain. Needing shelter, he slithered to the caves, knowing they could protect him from the traitorous star above.

Once inside, he seethed, plotting his revenge. For a small eternity, he waited, wanting nothing more than to destroy the woman whom he'd trusted after all others were lost to him. Vowing to never concede in his quest for vengeance, centuries upon centuries passed...

Chapter 13

On Saturday, Kenden showered after training the troops and dressed in jeans, sneakers and a polo shirt. He'd told Evie to dress casually but knowing her, she'd still be draped in designer clothing. Hopping in the four-wheeler, he began the short trek to her cabin.

Once outside, she opened the door and walked down the three wooden steps carrying a small bag. As predicted, she wore designer jeans, a red, silky, sleeveless blouse and fancy-looking sandals. He jogged around to open her door, and she flung the satchel in the back of the vehicle.

"Not that I'll need pajamas," she said, so sexy as she arched an eyebrow. "But I brought some toiletries so I can at least brush my teeth. I plan to spend every second of our last night together rocking your world, Commander."

"So, you're staying all night?" he asked, brushing his lips against hers as she stood beside the vehicle door he held open for her. "Even if I want to cuddle with you and smother you with feelings?"

Throwing her head back, she laughed, the skin of her pale neck calling to him. "There won't be much time for cuddling, but sure, I'll let you smother me in between." Sitting on the leather seat, he closed the door behind her, situated himself behind the wheel, and they were off.

They chatted companionably as he drove, their voices loud over the whipping wind from the open-air four-wheeler. Ten minutes in, they approached the River Thayne, and he cut the engine. Exiting the vehicle, he came around to lead her out.

"*This* is where you wanted to bring me?" she asked, annoyance in her voice.

"Yes," he said, shaking his outstretched hand at her. "Come on."

With a sardonic roll of her gorgeous green eyes, she departed the four-wheeler, grasping his hand. The sun had just set behind the far-off mountains, and dusk surrounded them in its inky glow. Buzzing insects chirped, invisible along the riverbank, as he escorted her to the large tree.

"Isn't bringing me to Mommy's gravesite a little cliché?"

Kenden sighed, the sound flowing around them sure as the gurgling river nearby. "I wanted you to have a part of her. To see the place where Miranda and I remembered her. I thought it might help you connect with her spirit. It runs so deeply through you."

Evie scoffed. "I'm not really in the mood for a 'you have good inside you' speech right now," she said, making quotation marks with her fingers in the air.

"This isn't about that," he said, reminding himself to stay calm. Evie liked to push people's buttons in tense situations, and he refused to rise to the bait. Grasping her hand, he lifted it to the tree, holding her palm to the jagged bark. Covering her hand with his, he gazed into her eyes, still so vivid in the dimness of the rising moonlight.

"This is about your heritage. Your blood. Rina and Valktor. It's a proud lineage for an amazing woman."

"I'm not amazing, Ken," she said, those eyes muddled with confusion. "I don't understand why you insist on seeing something that isn't there."

Lowering her hand from the tree, she turned to face the river. The hunch of her shoulders showed a dejection that he was sure she'd hide from anyone else. Hope surged through him that she'd let him see even that fraction of her vulnerability.

"She always called me Miranda," Evie said softly.

"Rina?" he asked.

"Yes," she said, giving a slight nod. The red strands of her hair glowed as fireflies flamed around her. Kenden found the image stunning, her outline illuminated as he gave her space.

"I was ten when he first raped me." Thin fingers appeared over the backs of her upper arms as she rubbed them. "Rina was insane at that point. A shell of whomever she'd been before he tortured it out of her. He was angry that she didn't fight back. He threatened to punish her by hurting me. I don't think she understood. I didn't blame her for that."

Dropping her arms, she straightened her spine, staring off into the distance. Kenden wanted so badly to hold her but felt she needed space. Inching closer, he made sure not to touch her as her back still faced him.

"That first time was so confusing for me. Crimeous had always been a background figure. Mother raised me and kept me away from him for the first few years of my life. I guess I owe her for that at least." Lifting her chin, she continued. "He tore off the ragged clothes I was wearing and began hurting me, making sure she saw everything. Darkrip was eighteen. He tried to save me, but Father froze him in place. I'll never forget his eyes. There was so much hatred in them for the bastard."

Finally, she turned. Inhaling a large breath, she shrugged. "And so it went. For a small eternity in my mind. Every time he violated me, Rina would beg him not to hurt Miranda. She was too far gone to comprehend that it was her other daughter being victimized. I should've understood. But instead, I was furious. I interpreted that as proof she didn't love me as she'd loved Miranda and never would."

Kenden, usually so calm and composed, was assailed by warring emotions. Compassion that his beautiful Evie had endured such appalling trauma when she was only a child. Heartbreak that she would take Rina's mischaracterization of her as Miranda as evidence that she didn't love her. But most of all, rage at Crimeous for hurting her so badly. He'd never wanted to murder the bastard more. Vowing to crush every bone in his body, he regarded the stunning woman who stood before him on the soft green grass.

"I understand why you would interpret it that way," he said, locking on to her gaze. "But I knew Rina. There wasn't one impure bone in her body. It would've been impossible for her not to love her child."

"I know that now," Evie said, sounding detached from the words. "I've seen the best therapists the human world has to offer. But it doesn't really mean anything. I never knew her. Her spirit was crushed by the time I had any ability to understand the world."

Reaching into the pocket of his jeans, he pulled out a locket. Balancing it on his outstretched palm, he asked, "Do you know what this is?"

She shook her head.

"I found it when we were looking for Darkrip and Arderin. It's from the lair where Crimeous held Rina hostage." Opening the necklace, a lock of red hair sat inside. "The hair is yours. I'm certain of it."

Tentatively, she lifted a finger, tracing the pad over the soft strand. "It looks like my color."

Kenden nodded. "She did the same for Miranda. Before she was taken. She would cut locks of her hair and keep them in little trinkets like this. I think she did the same for you."

Even the threat of darkness couldn't disguise the moisture in Evie's eyes. "It's a nice story."

"And a true one," he said, lifting her hand to place the locket into her palm. "Closing her fingers around it, he held them tight. "I know it with every fiber of my being."

Olive-green irises darted back and forth between his. "I don't know what you want me to do with this."

The corners of his lips turned up. "There's my Evie. Thinking everyone has an agenda. I don't want you do anything with it. Except keep it as a symbol of a mother who loved you very much."

"No one loves me," she whispered. "I'm an abomination."

He gave a breathy laugh. "That terrible, huh?"

"Yup," she said, her lips forming a gorgeous smile.

"I don't think so. You're all bluster and no bite. I've got you figured out, Evie."

She arched a scarlet brow. "Letting you think you understand me might just be right where I want you. Have you considered that?"

"Stop trying to outmaneuver me, woman," he said, drawing her close as he still held her hand. "Haven't you figured out by now, I'm extremely patient and always ensure I get the last move?"

Clutching the locket in her hand, she slid her arms around his neck. "The last move is unforeseeable when you're immortal, my friend." Lifting to her toes, she pressed her lips to his.

Kenden pressed back, needing her to know how wrong she was. How could she think herself unlovable when he was tumbling down the chasm of that very emotion with her more and more each day? Never had he met a more infuriating, frustrating, passionate woman. It was everything he thought he'd never crave and the embodiment of all he now yearned for. She'd pulled him into her abyss, and, Etherya help him, he never wanted to escape.

Thick fingers clutched her silky red hair as his tongue slid over hers. Lost in her, he milked her lips, her tongue, her gorgeous mouth. Like a starved man in search of his last meal, he consumed her, reveling in the tiny purrs that filled him.

Panting, he rested his forehead on hers. Lifting her lids, she stared into him. "I'm determined to be in your life, Evie. You've pushed everyone away so far, but I'm not like the others. You're not pulling one over on me. Get used to that now."

"I'm smarter than you are, Ken," she said, grinning up at him. "I know you've rarely met someone who is. It must drive you crazy."

"It does. Crazy with admiration at how you continue to outfox me. I've never met a more capable opponent. It's so fucking attractive."

"Goddamnit," she said, stealing a kiss from his lips. "I need to fuck you."

"Not yet," he said, gently snipping her bottom lip with his teeth. "I want to sit here with you and let you absorb the energy of this place. You deserve to feel her love for you. I think you'll feel it best here."

"Why are you always telling me to wait to bone you?" she teased. "It could give a girl a complex."

"I don't think there's any swaying your confidence, sweetheart." Giving her one last peck, he pulled her toward the tree. Sitting down, with his back against the thick oak, he held his hand up to her. Grasping it, she sat, enveloped in his embrace.

Surrounded by the symphony of the crickets, he held her, humbled that she'd given him the gift of telling him about her past. Even though it was a small snippet, it was a start. To a forged trust and a tentative tether. A thin, shared understanding that would always connect them.

"Did you erect the headstone for Rina?" she asked, gesturing with her head toward the tiny marble monument beside the tree.

"Miranda and Sathan placed it for their child. The one who died when she fought Crimeous."

Evie stiffened. Wanting to soothe her, he tightened his arms around her.

"How can Miranda still speak to me?" she asked, her tone laced with sadness. "Or Sathan? My actions killed their child. I'm the embodiment of my father. It's revolting."

"Miranda has always had a great capacity for love and forgiveness. It's what makes her such a strong leader. She understands your motivations came from the place inside where you hold your anger and pain."

"Then, she's a fool. I'm capable of so much worse. You all have no idea."

"Capability doesn't mean anything without intent. And you'll never convince me that you wanted to hurt their child. You don't have it in you, Evie."

She opened her mouth to refute him, and he turned her face, his fingers lining her chin. "Don't even try to argue with me on that."

"I was so consumed by anger when you found me. Sometimes, I wonder if I would've made the same choices even if I'd known she was pregnant. What do you say to that?"

"I say that it's really easy to speak in hypotheticals. There's no way you would've hurt their baby."

Her pupils scurried over his face, contemplating. "You're scaring the shit out of me," she said, her voice raspy.

"Because you think I'm wrong?" he asked, his brow furrowing.

"Because I'm terrified you might be right." Cupping his cheek, she shook her head. "I don't know how to live in a world where I'm not evil, Ken. I think it might break me."

The words were so genuine, so raw, that he felt his own heart crumble at her admission. "Then it's a good thing you found someone who's really good at piecing shit back together."

Body pulsing, he stared into her glassy eyes.

"What if all the pieces are too shattered?"

"Then, I'll spend an eternity gluing them until they fit just right. Maybe even better than before."

The lone tear blazed a trail down her flawless cheek. "I've cried more in front of you than I've cried in a thousand years," she whispered.

Capturing the wetness with his lips, he settled them over hers. "I'm honored that you let me see you cry," he said against her mouth. "I want you to give me everything, Evie."

"I can't," she breathed, the words exiting violently from her throat. "But I can give you tonight." Molding her lips to his, she gave him a sweet kiss. "Let's go home."

Lifting them to their feet, he granted her request.

* * * *

Once home, Kenden kicked off his sneakers at the back door and opened the large refrigerator to pull out the ingredients that Evie had instructed him to have available. Evie interrupted him, closing the refrigerator door. Gazing up at him, she gently threaded her fingers through his.

Leading him to the darkened living room, she urged him to sit on the brown leather couch. Green irises swam with emotion as she straddled him, sliding her arms over his shoulders. Full, red lips enveloped his as his broad hands cupped the straining globes of her ass through her tight jeans. The kiss started sweetly but quickly evolved into a warring of tongues and a straining of bodies. Slender fingers pulled his shirt over his head, and she settled back into him, thrusting inside his mouth as she writhed on top of his thighs.

He divested her shirt and almost tore away her bra. Inhaling at the sight of her gorgeous breasts, he palmed them, caressing them slightly. With slitted eyes, she inched toward him, bringing the reddened, pebbled nipple to rest on his lips. Staring up at her, he closed his mouth around the tiny nub.

Her lithe body bowed, fingers clutching his hair as she drew him closer. His tongue teased the sensitive spot, lathering it as he growled against her skin. Sensing she needed more, he closed his teeth around the turgid point.

"Yessss," she hissed, gyrating above him while he loved her. Kissing a trail to her other breast, he gave it equal and fervent attention. Lust racked his muscular frame as his cock pulsed inside his jeans, longing to plunge into her warmth.

Lifting his chin with the pads of her fingers, she latched her mouth to his again. With a stir of air, their clothes were instantly dematerialized, reforming on the floor by the fireplace. Her lips blazed a path over his cheek until they rested on his ear. Warm breath flooded the cavity, causing him to shiver.

"Get ready, Commander. I'm going to show you how sweet surrender can be."

A shudder wracked his body, and he pulled her dripping core over his shaft. "I can't wait to be inside you," he whispered.

Her throaty laugh almost made him shoot his load right there. God, she was the sexiest woman he'd ever touched.

"No fucking way, baby," she said, using the endearment she proclaimed to detest. "Now, be a good boy and clutch my hair. I don't care if you pull it. I like the pain."

Trailing pecs down his neck, over the brown hairs on his chest and down his quivering abdomen, she fell to her knees in front of him. Arching a brow, her lips quirked into a smile. "This hardwood's got to go." Grabbing a pillow from the end of the couch, she tossed it to the floor and situated her knees on top, in between his open legs. "Much better."

Kenden's breath was labored as she grasped his straining length in her hand. "You're hard as a rock," she said.

"Fuck yes," he whispered, threading his hands through her gorgeous hair. "I'm wild for you, Evie." Tugging the strands, careful not to pull too hard, he urged her toward his pulsing phallus.

"Is this what you want?" she asked, swiping her tongue over the sensitive head. Kenden thought his eyes might pop out of their sockets. Never had he been so aroused. Clenching her hair tighter, her olive eyes lit with pleasure. "You're figuring me out, aren't you? Pull even harder, and I'll suck you dry."

Being a smart man, he knew when to listen. Grasping the exquisite red tresses, he jutted his hips toward her face, resting his cock on her lips. Her resulting smile was *everything*. Grass-green irises fastened upon his, she opened her mouth and slid over him.

He couldn't control the undulation of his hips as she consumed him. Every cell in his iron shaft burned with pleasure as her wet mouth created silky pressure on his straining skin. Seeing her like this, on her knees, naked before him, dredged up every possessive instinct inside. So much of her life was spent with defenses held firm and high. The vulnerability she showed as she purred around him was heartbreakingly beautiful. By the goddess, he wanted her like this for eternity. To come home to her, tired and spent, and have her love him.

Telling himself to check the feelings that she so often chided him for, he forced himself to be in the moment. When his balls begin to tingle, he drew her head away.

"Let me get you off," she said, confusion in her eyes as she stared up at him with wet, swollen lips.

"I want to be inside you when I come."

Those lips formed a pout, and he chuckled. Reaching for her, he lifted her under the knees as she wrapped her arms around his neck. Carrying her to the end of the couch, he slid her down his body.

Turning her to face the sofa, he placed his palm on her back and gently urged her to lie on her stomach over the large, leather-covered arm of the couch. Wriggling her perfect ass at him as it lay bare and exposed, she giggled. "From behind again? You're dirty, Commander."

Leaning over her, he covered her body with his. "You like it. Don't deny it, sweetheart," he whispered in her ear. Reveling in her shiver, he traced his lips down her spine until he came to the small of her back. Running the tips of his fingers over the juncture of her lower back and buttocks, he caressed lower, to palm the cheeks. Spreading them open, he kneeled and began kissing the flesh.

She moaned, the sound muffled by the smooth leather of the sofa, driving him mad with arousal. Holding the lips of her sex open, he tongued her there, swiping up every drop of her wetness. Finding the nub at the top of her slit with his finger, he circled it as he impaled her with his tongue.

She cried his name, pushing herself onto his face; into his finger. Unable to wait any longer, he stood behind her. Spreading her legs, he slid the head of his shaft over her wet, sensitive flesh.

Grunting with desire, he thrust into her. Once, twice…until he was at the hilt. The dripping walls of her center clutched him, clouding his vision as she lifted her hips to meet him. Shoving into her, over and over, his broad hands grasped her hips. Needing more, he threaded his arms under her thighs, separating her feet from the floor. Holding her lower body suspended, he pummeled her as she moaned from the couch.

Wracked from the ministrations from her mouth, and now, her tight channel, he knew he wouldn't last long. Reaching underneath, he stimulated her clit as he jackknifed into her.

"Oh god," she called from below, sounding as if she was drowning from the ringing in his ears.

"I'm almost there," he gritted out, the sounds of their bodies slapping together driving him mad with desire. "Let go, baby. Come with me."

By some miracle of the goddess, Evie actually listened to him for once. Her body grew limp as a strained spaghetti noodle, opening to him even more as he pounded her. Reveling in her responsiveness, he clenched his teeth and let himself explode.

Shouting her name, he collapsed over her, spasming as he shot every last drop into her. Their bodies convulsed so violently that they fell to the couch in a heap, Kenden somehow managing to stay inside her as he cuddled her close atop the soft leather of the sofa.

Breathless and panting, he surrounded her, unable to let her go in the intimate moment. And maybe forever. Burying his face in her hair, he closed his eyes and let his muscles shake away the remnants of their lovemaking.

There in the darkness, holding her close, he admitted the truth. If he couldn't figure out how to make her stay, it might just destroy him.

* * * *

Evie slid into consciousness, sure as she slid the skin of her legs over Kenden's soft sheets. Eyes closed, she smiled as he nibbled her neck.

"You taste so good," he murmured, his deep voice causing her to melt against him more. Remembering last night's intimate dinner, the succulent flavor still lingered. The luscious chicken cordon bleu had been perfect. Along with the zesty spread of vegetables, drizzled in olive oil and sprinkled with herbs, and finished with a dash of lemon juice. She'd paired that with a light green baby kale salad topped with fried bacon and goat cheese. Damn, but she was a good cook.

Kenden's face had been a mask of pleasure as they ate at the expansive island in the middle of the kitchen. He'd opened a vintage red, and they'd laughed as they recounted stories from their past. Sated and relaxed from lovemaking, it had damn near been perfect.

Afterward, he'd led her upstairs, into the bathroom, where they brushed their teeth in his dual sinks. Evie had washed away her makeup, usually so careful not to let anyone see her without that shield. Kenden had cupped her moisturized, flushed cheeks, vowing to count every freckle across her nose. She'd always hated her freckles, thinking them ugly, but when he brushed his lips against them, it had liquefied something inside her deadened heart.

He'd carried her to the bed, gently laying her over the sheets, her hair fanning on the pillow. Not from the back again. Not last night. No, he'd slithered over her, aligning his body with hers as he stared into her. Urging her eyes to remain open, he'd loved her as he clutched her hands beside her head on the pillow. Never had Evie experienced something so intimate. To say it terrified her would be an understatement. It *consumed* her, stealing her breath, forcing her to face the fact that Kenden had burrowed not only into her heart but into her blackened soul. And that was something she must remedy, for he deserved so much better than her rotten, malevolent core.

Knowing it was time, she yearned for one more moment. Allowing herself that, she pushed her back into his front, the warmth of his body enveloping her. And then, already hating every piece of herself, she began to draw away.

Sitting on the edge of the bed, she pulled the silky robe she'd packed onto her shoulders. Standing, she tied it at the waist and headed to the bathroom to dress. Once yesterday's clothes were donned, she leaned against the bathroom counter and gazed at her own eyes in the mirror.

It's what's best for him, she silently told herself, knowing it was true. Better that they make a clean break now than let whatever the hell was between them evolve into something even messier. They had no future, and although it was fun to pretend, she had a job to do, and it was time she got around to accomplishing it.

Inhaling a huge breath, she gave her reflection one last nod of confidence and opened the bathroom door. Kenden had slipped on sweatpants that hung low, under his six-pack. The muscles that led toward the waistband formed a "V," causing her mouth to water. *No, Evie!* she mentally scolded. Another round of fabulous sex would just make this harder. After packing her small satchel, she came to stand before him as he waited in between the mahogany dresser and expansive bed. Head tilted back, she locked on to his gaze.

"Well," she said, determined to keep her tone light. "It's been amazing, Commander. You certainly know how to honor an agreement."

His expression was impassive, his brown irises slowly perusing her face. Leaning his hip on the dresser, he crossed his arms over his broad chest. "What are you trying to prove, Evie?"

"Nothing," she said with a shrug. "I named my terms, and you met them. I'll be on the sparring field at eight a.m. sharp Monday morning, ready to train with the troops. It should be fun. I haven't fought with an army in centuries. I'll be rusty but I have quick muscle memory. It will come back in a snap, trust me."

"I have no doubt about your skills as a warrior," he said, his voice so low. "But your skills as a person fucking suck sometimes."

She arched a brow. "Well, don't protect my fragile heart. Give it to me. I think you're looking for a fight here."

"I'm looking for you to care!" he said, the heat in his tone rising as his nostrils flared. "For you to give a shit about me and what we have together. How can you walk away so callously?"

"It's just sex, Ken," she said, lifting her hands in frustration. "I told you that from the beginning—"

"Fuck you, Evie," he interrupted, straightening away from the dresser. "That's bullshit, and you know it. You're a goddamn coward. It's so beneath you, it makes me sick."

"Oh, sweetheart," she said with a biting laugh. "You can't begin to fathom what's beneath me. You look at me with those chocolate-as-sin eyes, dripping with sincerity, and think your goodness can wash my evil away. It doesn't work like that, Ken. I won't taint you with my nature. I'm giving you a gift. One you should thank me for. If I didn't give a damn, I'd use you until you shriveled and throw you out with the trash."

He shook his head. So slow, so sad. The disappointment in his chestnut irises threatened to choke her. "You're lying to yourself if you think we're done here. You know it, and I know it. And I didn't peg you for a person who thrives on dishonesty."

"I don't really give a shit who you pegged me for, you pompous ass. We had a good time together, and let's remember it like adults. We have a war to win, and that won't ever happen if we delude ourselves into thinking this was more than fucking. Get over it, Ken. I already am."

"Liar," he said, inching closer to her. Snaking his hand behind her neck, she gasped as he pulled her face within a hairsbreadth of his. "Stop being a coward—"

Her hand shot to his throat, cutting off his words as he leered down at her. Rage clouded his eyes, his strong jaw clenched. "Don't ever grab me without my consent again. I'll fucking murder you." His pulse was strong under her palm as she held him, also freezing him with her mind. "Thanks for the good fucks and the scenic field trips. Now, leave me the hell alone unless we're training. Got it?" Not waiting for an answer, she brushed a kiss, gentle and brief, on his full lips. Knowing that she needed to let him breathe, she closed her eyes and dematerialized to her cabin.

Once there, she wandered around the tiny space, shaken and restless. Stepping out onto the grass under the bright morning sun, she lay down upon the cushy ground. She'd lain like this so many times, on her back, with men above her. Never, in the long span of her wretched life had any of them meant anything. Never until Kenden.

Under the clouds, she could almost see him above her. Staring into her as he loved her. Whispering words that could never be true. Unwilling to acknowledge her tears, she let them fall, soaking the ground below. And when she was done, she walked back inside, determined to ensure he stayed at arm's length. Using the anger and pain that always existed within, she proceeded to rebuild every wall he'd torn down with his firm hands and tender heart.

The man devolved into an evil monster, forgetting his time in the Elven world and even his wonderful memories with the woman. All that consumed him were feelings of hate and retribution.

Plotting his revenge, he studied the dark forces of the Universe, becoming immensely strong and potent. He developed powers that were unthinkable for other immortals upon the planet...

Chapter 14

True to her word, Evie materialized to the sparring field at Uteria at eight o'clock on Monday morning. The sun was bright in the sky as hundreds of soldiers milled about the turf. Comprised of Vampyres and Slayers, the combined immortal army was vast.

"Good morning, Evie," Latimus said, giving her a nod. "We're excited to have you train with us."

"As am I," she said. "Let's kick that bastard's ass."

Kenden absently listened to their conversation, watching the men stretch in the distance. How a woman who was about to train for battle could look so sexy was something he'd never understand. Scarlet hair was pulled into a thick bun atop her head. Black leggings stopped at her calves above gray Saucony sneakers. A tight black tank top bracketed her perfect breasts.

After their argument Sunday morning, he'd been a wreck. He'd shuffled around the house, trying not to smell her perfume in every corner. Sadly, the effort had been futile. She lingered in all the places they'd touched and every room where she'd given him her gorgeous smile. Today, the smile was gone, replaced by an expression of resolve and fortitude.

"Hello, Commander," she said, chin lifted proudly.

"Good morning," he said, hating her. Loving her. Not knowing what the difference was anymore. "Ready to meet the men?"

Her grin almost buckled his knees. "You bet your perfect ass, I am. Let's go."

Kenden and Latimus walked her toward the open field. Addressing the soldiers, Kenden explained that Evie was the newest member of their team and was to be accepted immediately. Informing the men that they were to treat her as an equal and spar with her using their full effort, the soldiers cheered and saluted in approval.

"You're not trying to get me killed, are you?" she asked, gazing up at him.

"You'd be pissed if I told them to go easy on you," Kenden said.

"So fucking true. Hand me a sword." Thrusting out her hand, Latimus stepped forward and armed her with the weapon she requested. Waggling her eyebrows, she said, "Let's have some fun, boys. Hmmm?" Pivoting to face the troops, she sauntered toward the first group of men, ready to train.

"Damn," Latimus said, rubbing the back of his neck. "She's something else."

"Tell me about it," Kenden muttered.

"Are you guys okay?"

"Not even close," Kenden said, staring abstractedly at the field.

"Is this going to fuck up your head?"

"No," he said, staring at the ground as he kicked it with his army boot. "There's too much on the line to lose it now. I'm straight. You have my word."

Latimus patted him on the back. "Never doubted you, man. Come on. Let's get down there and prepare to kill that asshole."

The two commanders strolled down the hill, onto the meadow, and dispersed to work with different bands of men. For hours, they practiced and sparred, Evie fighting along with them. She never showed one sign of fatigue, impressing him as the soldiers towered over her slight frame. Although she was slender, she was mighty. She had the power to kill them all with a flick of her wrist. It would be a huge advantage when they fought the Deamons, and for that, Kenden was grateful.

He'd agreed to her ridiculous ultimatum with the understanding that having her powers available alongside his soldiers would be invaluable. At least, that's what he told himself. Otherwise, he would have to admit that he'd accepted her terms for other reasons. Ones that had to do with emotions and feelings. All the things that threatened to drown him, and repulsed her. Pushing those thoughts away, he focused on his army.

After lunch, Darkrip materialized for the afternoon session, his morning comprised of a visit to see Nolan with Arderin.

"How's your wife doing, man?" Kenden asked him.

"Great," Darkrip said, beaming with pride. "She's five and a half months now, and the bump is so damn cute. I'm a fucking wreck, but she's a rock. We're having a little girl. It's unbelievable."

"Miranda told me," Kenden said, his lips curving. Who would've thought that the man he met so recently, who professed to be evil, would've turned into such a caring bonded mate and father? Love really was miraculous. Would Evie be able to make the same transformation? The question filled him with doubt, but he still clung to hope. Only time would tell if she could transform that intensely. It was a huge gamble but one that Kenden felt was important.

Reprimanding his drifting thoughts, he focused back on Darkrip. "I'm really happy for you guys. Arderin certainly seems to keep you on your toes."

"She's infuriating. Stubborn woman," he muttered, shaking his head. "I'm obsessed with her. I'll never understand why she loves me but I'm so fucking honored."

Kenden smiled, crossing his arms over his chest as they observed the soldiers returning to the field from lunch.

"Enough about that though," Darkrip said. "I vomit in my mouth when I hear myself talk about her." Patting Kenden on the shoulder, he asked, "What's going on with you and Evie?"

Kenden sighed. "Our agreement has been honored. She's going to train with us and attack when we're ready."

"Right," Darkrip said, his tone flat. "I think you and I need to talk. How about tomorrow? At the pub in Uteria's main square after training?"

"Sure," Kenden said, wanting so badly to know the parts of Evie that she kept closely hidden. Darkrip would be able to shed some light, if small, and that comforted him somehow. "Seven p.m. I'll meet you there."

Darkrip gave a nod and one more pat of solidarity on the shoulder. Plodding down to the sparring turf, he joined Evie's group of men. For the next several hours, they proceeded to practice forming the joint force-field as soldiers fought to disarm them. They needed the experience if they were going to surround Crimeous while his Deamon soldiers battled to protect him.

Watching from the hill, Kenden couldn't help but admire what a strong warrior Evie was. He knew she'd fought with many human armies over the centuries, and it showed. She was deft with a sword and most likely with other weapons. Those skills combined with her powers made her almost invincible.

Increasingly liking their chances against the Dark Lord, he trekked down the hill to implement some afternoon drills.

* * * *

Kenden walked into the quaint Irish pub promptly at seven o'clock on Wednesday. Darkrip's broad shoulders were hunched over the bar as he lifted a pint to his mouth.

"You started without me?" Kenden teased, sliding onto the stool beside him.

"Sorry," Darkrip said, smiling. "I got here early and was ready for a beer."

The mustached bartender appeared, and Kenden ordered an IPA. Lifting it, he clinked his glass with Darkrip's. "To your wife and child. Congrats, man."

"Thanks," Darkrip said, grinning as he sipped. "Weird. Still so fucking weird," he said, setting down the glass. "I'm going to be a father. Good lord, I hope I do a good job. I'm terrified."

Kenden felt the corner of his lips curve. "You've got this. You're going to do great. And if you suck, Arderin will pick up your slack."

Darkrip chuckled. "Thank god."

They caught up on life, chatting cordially. Kenden hadn't spent much time with Miranda's brother but he found that he liked him immensely. His transformation to living by his Slayer half was commendable, and he was quite curious as to how he made the choice.

"It was my mother," Darkrip said, his elbow resting on the lip of the bar. "She appeared to me centuries ago and asked for my word. I gave it to her and vowed to honor it. It was the only thing that kept me going for so long."

"You loved her very much," Kenden said.

"Yes," he said with a nod. "My love for her was strong enough to motivate me into action. Sadly, Evie didn't experience the same connection with her. I wish she'd known Mother when she was still cognizant. She loved her so much, even though Evie won't let herself believe it."

"She told me the same thing," Kenden said, taking a sip of his beer. "She's convinced that she only loved you and Miranda."

Darkrip's brows drew together. "I can't believe she told you about Mother. She rarely opens up about the past."

"I know. She told me about the first time your father violated her too. It was a huge step for her to tell me. I was surprised but extremely honored that she trusted me enough to talk about it."

"Wow," Darkrip said, shaking his head. "She cares for you more than I thought if she spoke to you about the past. That's usually extremely off-limits."

Kenden sighed. "I think she cares for me, but who knows? She's built so many walls that every time I tear one down, I'm met with a hundred more. It's so damn frustrating."

Green irises probed his own. "Why do you care about her so much? Not to be an ass, but she can be a huge bitch sometimes."

Kenden laughed. "So true. It started out as attraction. When I first saw her in France, I was floored. I mean, socked-in-the-chest, unable to breathe, floored. She's the most stunningly beautiful woman I've ever seen." Rubbing the glass with the pad of his thumb, he stared absently at the liquid inside. "But then, I began to realize how broken she was. How much she'd been violated and how torturous it must've been. She told me she'd never had anyone who cared for her, nor had she cared for anyone else. It moved something in me. I felt empathy to depths that I'd never felt before. I found myself wanting so badly to show her that someone could care for her."

"That's admirable. It reminds me of Arderin. She cared for my blackened soul even though I didn't deserve it and probably never will. It's hard for creatures like me and Evie to understand how you guys can feel sympathy toward us."

Kenden's brow furrowed. "I've always been this way. Miranda says I have a savior complex. She's right, although I'd never admit it to her," he said, grinning.

"Evie doesn't need saving," Darkrip said, understanding in his olive eyes. "She needs an equal. Someone who will challenge her and bring out her goodness, against her will if needed. I think you're the right person to do that. I hope you won't give up on her. She's beginning to change, although it's hard for her to accept. I think a lot of that has to do with her feelings for you."

"She swears she doesn't have any feelings for me at all," he muttered.

Darkrip scoffed. "Uh, yeah, I can read the images in her mind. She's quite preoccupied with you. It's very interesting. I don't think she has any idea how to handle it. It throws her off-balance, and that's just what she needs. Being uncomfortable will help her push through and become the person she's meant to be. She reminds me so much of Mother. I think she would want me to help Evie live by her Slayer side."

"Your mother was remarkable," Kenden said. "I loved her very much. She always challenged Uncle Marsias, that was for sure. He was insanely devoted to her."

"I wish I could've known her when she lived here," Darkrip said, swallowing thickly. "But I can at least honor her by helping Evie. I wanted to talk to you, so that you understand how deeply scarred she is. Her anger and pain are so imbedded in her psyche that you're going to have to battle to pull the goodness out of her. It won't be easy, but I'm hoping that you can care for her enough to help her. I think you might be the only person who can."

Kenden blinked, looking at the stained wood of the bar. "I care for her. Very deeply. It's frustrating, since she's determined not to care for me back, but it's there, and I'm too much of a straight-shooter to deny it."

"Good," he said, giving a nod of his raven-black head. "I want to tell you a bit about what she experienced in the caves and some details that I think will help you. I don't want to violate her privacy but I think that having a better understanding of her will help your cause."

"Okay."

Inhaling a deep breath, Darkrip began to tell him bits and pieces from Evie's two centuries in the Deamon caves. Compassion, deep and true, swelled in Kenden's heart as he learned of the numerous violations and brutalizations she'd experienced. It was a miracle that she'd even survived. The fact she'd gone on to piece together a successful life in the human world was astounding. Admiration for her coursed through his veins.

"That's good," Darkrip said, patting his shoulder. "The feelings you're having. Remember those when she pushes you away." Standing, Darkrip threw some bills on the counter. "I've told you all I can without infringing on her privacy more than I already have. The rest is up to you. I want so badly for her to find happiness with you. I think that will solidify her reason to fight with us."

Chugging the last of his beer, Kenden stood and shook his hand. "Thank you. I appreciate everything you've told me and promise I'll do my best to take care of her. Even though she's determined to push me away."

Darkrip smiled. "Man, you and Arderin are two peas in a pod. It's amazing. Evie and I are very lucky. Now, speaking of my wife, I need to get home and cook her dinner. I've figured out that the better the food tastes, the more she wants to thank me later, if you catch my drift."

Chuckling, Kenden nodded. "Loud and clear. Thanks, Darkrip."

"Anytime." Closing his lids, the Slayer-Deamon disappeared.

Sitting back down, Kenden ordered another drink and allowed himself to absorb the information that Evie's brother had given him.

Eventually, the wicked creature began to grow an army. Vast and sinister, they would help him in his efforts to destroy every fragment of the immortal world. For agony had become his existence and he would not rest until every other being in the realm felt his unassuageable anguish...

* * * *

**Archived in the hidden files by King Valktor, never to be released again. This decree recorded on the first day of the ninth month of the thirty-seventh year of the fourteenth century after Creation.

*Archivists note: The King has become quite insistent that we do not tell this story to our children. It is imperative that our world-balance is kept in order and that none surmise the true origin of the creatures that dwell in the caves. Ergo, this will be the last entry shared.

Chapter 15

By the week's end, Evie's body was tired and battered. It felt magnificent. She'd always loved fighting in battle, and Kenden's soldiers held nothing back. As the training finished up, she studied the handsome commander. He was collecting the SSWs from the remaining soldiers, compiling them into a four-wheeler. Once they'd all been loaded, he jumped inside and revved the engine. Dusk had fallen, and she watched his hair whip in the dim light as he drove away.

Left alone on the sparring field, she rubbed her upper arms. A chill ran down her spine as she found herself wondering what Kenden was doing for the weekend. Where was he headed? To spend time with Sadie perhaps? She knew he had a close relationship with the Slayer physician.

Deciding she'd like to find out, she transported to the main square and perched on the stone wall. It gave her a nice view of the castle and she'd be able to see Kenden when he returned from the barracks to eat dinner.

Twenty minutes later, he appeared, sauntering from the barracks behind the castle. Approaching the massive wooden doors that led inside the large mansion, Evie admired his confident swagger. God, she hated how handsome he was. It was extremely unfair.

Suddenly, his broad lips curved into a smile, the whites of his teeth almost blinding under the just-risen moon. Was he smiling at her? Feeling her heartbeat quicken, she lifted her hand to wave. And then dropped it just as quickly.

A perky little blond jaunted up to him, her wavy hair bouncing behind her. Kenden enfolded her in his strong arms, causing Evie a moment of panic. Who in the hell was this woman, and why did Kenden feel the need to touch her?

Releasing her, he grinned down at her as they spoke. He appeared so relaxed in her presence, his hands now resting on his waist as the woman gestured with her arms while speaking. Evie imagined cutting them off and shoving them down her throat.

Narrowing her eyes, she entered Kenden's head, reading his mind. *Katia*. The name appeared to her, dragged from his thoughts, along with several images of Kenden entwined with her perfect little body. Goddamnit. Jealousy snaked its way through every cell of Evie's frame, almost choking her with its viciousness. How dare the little bitch smile up at her man like that, with that innocent face and come-hither expression. Visions of murder flashed through Evie's brain, and she struggled to tamp them down.

Kenden was anything but *her* man. She'd do well to remember that. Fury bubbled inside as she watched them, almost drowning her in its grip. Knowing that she needed to calm down, she closed her eyes and transported back to her cabin. To be alone, like she wanted. Yes, she wanted to be alone and untethered and solitary. Reminding herself of that repeatedly, she began to cook dinner as she stewed in her anger.

The stir-fry she whipped up was unappealing, probably due to the insane jealousy sweeping through her veins, and she only ate a small portion. Once the leftovers were stowed and the kitchen cleaned, Evie pulled on her silken pajamas and prepared for bed. As she rubbed the fancy night cream into her freshly-washed cheeks, she couldn't shake the rage of her jealous resentment. Staring at her reflection, she wondered if she'd ever felt the emotion. Unable to recall anything remotely close, she admitted that this was her first experience with the green-eyed monster. It was rather annoying and stirred up every ounce of virulence that dwelled within.

In that moment, she made the decision to confront Kenden. Tomorrow, she would search him out at his shed. She knew he liked to spend his weekend mornings there when he wasn't training the troops. There were things that needed to be said, especially after the disastrous way they'd ended their sexual relationship. Evie hated loose ends and vowed to tie up every dangling, complicated one with the alluring commander.

Feeling her eyelids narrow, she realized she'd probably be unable to contain the fury of her jealousy. It was so potent as it coursed through her body. Deciding that he was strong enough to take it, she pledged not to sugarcoat her words. After all, Kenden seemed unfazed by her vitriolic moods, something that impressed Evie, knowing how they'd cowered so many before him. Feeling her lips curve, she admitted that his calm demeanor in her worst moments was extremely attractive. Rarely had someone been able to handle her fits of wrath.

Rubbing the soft bedsheet with her palm, she imagined, for one moment, that he was there beside her. Holding her after one of their bouts of passion. Forming a fist, she pounded the mattress, giving a *harrumph* as she turned on her side. Letting the emotions war within, she closed her eyes, wondering if nightmares would haunt her sleep, as they so often did.

* * * *

The next morning, Kenden was holed up in his shed studying blueprints of the Deamon caves. The tiny shack was his absolute favorite place on the planet. A thoughtful and curious student of war, he loved studying maps of the terrain where future battles would occur. It only heightened his chances of success, and that was greatly needed against someone as powerful as Crimeous.

Kenden smelled her before she appeared at the door of the shed. The fragrance of her perfume was all-consuming. Clenching his teeth, he vowed to remain calm. Curiosity had him wondering why she'd decided to approach him. They'd spent the week barely communicating.

He'd helped Evie train with the troops and then left her alone. Needing to thoroughly prepare before confronting her, if they were going to have any chance at a relationship or a future, he'd decided to give her some distance. Hell, maybe she'd miss him a fraction of the amount he missed her. Doubtful, but a guy could hope. Regardless, she was after something. Evie always was. He was determined to retain the upper hand here, in his shed. The one place he'd sought solace for a thousand years.

Slender body silhouetted by the morning sunlight, she lifted her arms, placing her palms flat on each side of the shed doorframe. It was the pose of a Greek goddess, stone-like and magnificent. Wanting to appear nonplussed, he lowered his eyes back to the map he'd been studying.

"I'd give you the line about 'all work and no play' but I think that might be futile with you, Mr. Serious." Her voice was sultry, the come-hither tone causing him to stiffen in his faded jeans.

"It's imperative that I know every inch of the Deamon caves where we plan to attack," he said, striving to keep his voice even. "Although you profess not to care about anyone but yourself, I'd like to prevent as many of our soldiers' deaths as possible."

"Ah, yes," she said, sauntering into the shed. "The noble commander. How tedious it must be to be so exceptional all the time." With her slender arm, she closed the door, the soft click making an ominous sound.

Kenden stared at her from the stool where he sat, behind the wooden table. Upon it rested the map, the paper spread under his forearms. "I'm right in the middle of this, Evie, and not quite sure why you're here. I met the terms of your demand, and you've made it very clear that our relationship only exists on the battlefield. Unless I'm missing something."

Ignoring him, she walked slowly around the small cabin. Weapons lined the wooden walls, collected by him over the centuries. Always an inquisitive scholar of war, he'd studied as many weapons as he could—human, Vampyre, Deamon and Slayer—so that he could strategize effectively.

Her white slacks and blue silk, sleeveless blouse somehow seemed too pristine for his shed. Although clean, it was sparse. It was no place for her expensive tailored clothes and much more suited to his jeans, t-shirt and sneakers.

In curiosity, her thin fingers tinkered with one of the metal weapons. "A musket," she mused, her voice quiet.

"Yes," he said, setting down the pencil he'd been using to make notes on the map. "From eighteenth century America."

She nodded. "I used one of these to shoot a man who got a bit too friendly a few centuries ago. It felt magnificent in my hands."

Kenden felt his eyes narrow. "I imagine you've used quite a few armaments on many men who've tried to take the upper hand."

The corner of her gorgeous lips turned up. "You imagine correctly." Turning to face him, those olive-green eyes bore into his. "Men have a nasty habit of thinking they can have control with a pretty woman. I consider it a duty and a privilege to prove them wrong."

Compassion coursed through him as he remembered the stories that Darkrip told him the other evening. Crimeous had repeatedly raped her for years. Once Rina perished, he'd thrown Evie to his Deamon soldiers, letting them violate her for decades until she'd realized her true power. And then, as Darkrip had recounted, she'd made each and every soldier who'd violated her pay. First, with torture. Ultimately, with their lives.

"Your pity is wasted on me," she said, inching closer to the table. Resting her palms flat on top, she leaned forward, gazing into him. "I'm just fine and I don't need the superhero routine. You play the knight in shining armor well, but I'm no damsel in distress."

Slowly, he stood, placing his palms flat on top of the drawings. Closing in, he brought his face within inches of hers, their bodies separated by the two-foot-wide table. "I'd never mistake you for someone who wanted or needed anyone, Evie. Let's be clear about that."

Her perfect scarlet brow arched. "Good." Tilting her face toward his, she brushed her lips across his mouth. Fuck. He wanted her so badly.

"No," he said, his tone gruff. "We want different things, Evie. I can't just have sex with you and move on. I'm sorry, but I can't."

Rolling her eyes, she straightened her spine. Crossing her arms over her perfect breasts, she regarded him. "You're hard as a rock right now. It's futile for you to deny it."

"I won't deny it," he said, keeping his voice steady. "But I won't be another man who just fucks you. You deserve better, and so do I. So, we do it my way, or we don't do it at all."

"*Your* way," she said, scoffing as she shook her head. "Candles and late-nineties R&B? Or warm baths and massages? Am I close?"

Gritting his teeth at her sarcasm, Kenden felt the anger well in his gut. Striding around the table, he grasped her upper arms and drew her to him. She crashed into his body, and he threaded his fingers through her soft hair. Tilting her head back, he latched on to her with his eyes.

"With *emotion*," he said, hating that she'd gotten a rise out of him. "With caring and feeling. That's how I want to make love to you. Otherwise, leave me the hell alone."

Desire flashed in her eyes. With her thin hand, she palmed his length where it threatened to burst behind the fly of his jeans. "But you're so ready—"

"No," he said, pulling her hand away. Inhaling, he took a step back, creating distance. "Not like this."

"Like what?" she asked, her chiding tone infuriating him. "Like *Katia*?" she asked, the woman's name spouted with vitriol from her lips. "Should I let you smother me in tender kisses and whisper words of love?"

"I did love her," he said, shrugging. "Like I've loved every woman I've been intimate with. I told you that."

"Did you fuck her last night?" Evie asked.

"That's none of your business."

"You'll never feel one ounce of desire for her like you feel for me," she said, lifting her hand to caress his cheek. "Admit it."

He grabbed her wrist, prompting anger to flash in her eyes.

"Let go of me."

Furious, he squeezed harder. Those almond-shaped eyes widened, filled with rage.

"Let. Me. Go." The words were mangled through clenched teeth.

Heart pounding, he held fast onto her wrist. Lifting her other hand, she crashed the palm into his cheek. Growling, he latched onto that arm as well. Yanking her around, he rotated her so that her back slammed against the wooden wall of the shed.

Arousal quickly replaced the fury in her green irises.

"Yessss," she hissed, disengaging her wrists from his grasp and sliding her palms down his abdomen. Deftly, her fingers attempted to unzip his pants. "Take me hard, against the wall."

He stilled her hands with his own. Lifting her arms above her head, he held them prisoner, with one hand around her crossed wrists. "You'd like that, wouldn't you?"

"Yes," she said, panting.

Realization coursed through him. "You want me to hurt you," he said, sadness swamping him.

"God, yes," she said, a pleading tone in her voice. "Pain feels so good to me. You have no idea."

Staring down at her, he felt the animal inside him roar. He'd always kept it restrained. Hidden. Vowing to be cool and collected. What would it feel like to free the beast of his lust for this complicated woman? Many in his life had told him he was too controlled; too unspontaneous. Capitulating to the arousal pulsing within, he clamped his jaw with resolve.

Using his free hand, Kenden yanked her shirt out of her waistband. Releasing her wrists, he grabbed onto the collar with both fists and ripped it down the middle. Throwing the tattered silk to the floor, he unbuttoned her pants. After lowering the zipper, he inserted his hands in between her hips and the lacy material of her thong. Pushing them to the ground, he growled, "Step out."

She nudged out of her sandals and kicked the pants away. "I could've just dematerialized my clothes—"

Standing to his full height, he stuck his fingers in her hair and pulled her head back. "Shut up," he said, lowering his mouth to hers.

Inhaling her gasp, he thrust his tongue into her mouth, slathering it over hers. Blood coursed through his muscled frame as he gyrated his hips against her body, clad only in her silky pink bra.

"You want me to make you feel pain?" he asked, biting her lower lip and then sliding his tongue over it to wash away the sting.

"Yes," she whimpered. "It always feels so good."

"Of course, it does," he said, tilting his head to devour her mouth from a different angle. The tiny responding mewls that escaped her throat drove him mad. Disengaging from her, he gazed into her as they panted. "If someone hurts you while loving you, it makes it easier for you to dismiss them when it's over."

Anger flashed in her stunning eyes. "Don't psychoanalyze me, you son of a bitch."

"It's true," he said, reaching down to unbutton his jeans and lower the fly. Pushing them and his boxer briefs to his knees, he bent down. After grabbing the luscious globes of her ass, he picked her up. Instinctively, her legs wrapped around his waist.

Holding her, he aligned himself with her dripping core. Locking his eyes onto hers, he thrust her back against the wall, simultaneously thrusting his turgid cock into her wetness. Caught up in his burning arousal for her, he'd forgotten that two nails protruded from the wall behind her. A weapon had once hung there that had recently been taken down for polishing.

Her body stiffened as the nails impaled her back. Those magnificent emerald irises filled with pleasure-pain as she opened her mouth wide and gasped.

Cursing, he started to pull her away, hoping to save her from the pain.

"No!" she cried, clutching him tighter. "It doesn't hurt. Please. Like this."

Hesitating, he studied her, as the lush walls of her center still surrounded him.

"Please, Ken."

The soft cry shattered something inside him. Capitulating, he began sliding within her.

"Darkrip told me that you feel pleasure from pain," he said, slowly pulling his shaft out of her wet channel and then inserting it fully again. "So I'll give it to you, Evie, even though it kills me." Grunting, he increased the speed of his strokes, the plushy folds of her core choking his cock.

Her head lolled back as she moaned, consumed by passion. "Faster," she commanded, clutching her arms behind his neck.

Using his hands, he moved her slender hips up and down in a mindless rhythm. His balls slapped against her as he hammered into her flushed body. Knowing that the barbs that protruded from the wall were lodged in the frail skin of her back made him want to retch, but she plodded on, seeming enthralled by the multiple sensations. Not even beginning to understand how something that painful could cause pleasure, he tried not to let his self-revulsion at hurting her choke him.

"It feels amazing," she said, lifting her head to lock her gaze on to his. Threading her fingers through his hair, on both sides of his head, she held on for dear life as he jackknifed into her.

"I hate hurting you," he said through gritted teeth. "Can't you see that, Evie? I don't want to be another man who hurts you."

Emotion entered her eyes, so vibrant and true. Sure that she'd never intended for him to see it, he realized how vulnerable she was at this moment. How raw.

"Don't you understand?" he pleaded, bringing one hand up to cup her cheek. "I want to love you. I don't want to cause you pain."

"No," she said, shaking her head violently, forcing his hand away. "No one loves me. Just fuck me. Oh, god." Tilting her head back, her body went limp. Unable to deny himself the pleasure of being inside her, he continued, his body at war with his mind. Groaning, he slid both hands further under her, lifting her up and down on his thick cock.

Continuing to pound her, he lowered his head, burying his face in her neck. Sweat poured from him as he inhaled the sweet scent of her skin. Kissing a path up her neck, he placed his lips on her ear. "This is more than fucking. You can try to deny it but you know it's true."

She moaned, shaking her head against the wall, her fire-read hair creating a blaze against the wood. "There's nothing more than fucking. There never will be for me."

"Goddamnit," Kenden said, moving his face so that his forehead rested on hers. "Look at me."

Opening her lids, she complied. "Do you not *feel* this?" he asked, needing her to understand how special the energy was between them. By the goddess, he'd never felt anything as consuming as what he felt with her.

"It feels so good," she said. His heart threated to shatter when wetness entered her eyes. "It always feels so good with you."

"Let yourself feel it, baby," he said, rubbing the skin of his forehead against hers as he loved her. "It could be like this forever."

"No," she said, her voice strangled. "I don't want that."

Snarling at her, he bared his teeth. "Liar."

Pulling him to her, with her fingers still clutched in his hair, she kissed him. Jabbing her tongue in his mouth, she drew his out to war with hers. Figuring that she was trying to silence him, he let her.

Battling with her tongue, he moved her upon him, fucking her as if it were the last time he'd ever do the deed. Hell, it was so good, maybe it would be. The tip of his shaft threatened to explode as he connected with the spot deep inside her that he knew would send her over the edge. Tiny purrs escaped from her, into his mouth, and he growled in approval. The muscles of his thighs and calves quivered as he felt his balls begin to tingle.

Unlatching from him, she threw her head back and wailed, calling his name in the dim light of the shack. Convulsing around him, he felt the rush of moisture from her climax wash over the straining nerve-endings of his shaft. Cursing, he began to come, holding on to her for dear life as he jetted his release into her. Burying his face in the juncture of her neck and shoulder, he spurted into her for what seemed to be a small lifetime. Eventually, his cock slowed its pulsing, relaxing and softening in her sweet, luscious warmth. Sated, he clutched her close, needing to inhale her scent.

Evie trembled as he held her, her supple body wrapped around his, her gorgeous hair falling over his shoulder. Her quivering shook him to his core. He loved nothing more than to see her vulnerable and open.

The drops of their loving slowly began to drip down his upper thighs, drawing him slowly back to Earth. Lifting his head, he brought his hand up to caress her cheek.

"Are you okay?" he asked, his voice scratchy.

She nodded, those magnificent eyes filled with so many emotions that he had no idea how to differentiate.

"Let's get you cleaned up," he said, rubbing the pad of his thumb over her swollen lower lip.

She didn't speak. Instead, she just watched him, her expression wary. Still inside her, he separated her from the wall. She hissed a breath through her teeth as the soft skin of her back disengaged from the nails.

Hating that he'd hurt her, he stared down into her eyes.

"I'm okay," she said. "Like I told you, pain hurts for me but it also courses pleasure through my body. I'm fine."

Gazing into her, he questioned the truth of her statement. She didn't look fine. She looked shaken...and guileless...and beautiful.

Nudging off his sneakers, he used his feet to pull off his jeans and underwear. Tossing them on the floor by kicking them, he turned away from the wall. Holding her tight, he carried her to the tiny cot he kept in the shed. He'd sometimes slept there, before he'd built his house, on nights he was too tired to walk back to the main castle. It rested against the wall, opposite the door, behind the wooden table.

Sliding out of her, he set her on her feet. Reaching for the box of tissues on the small table at the head of the cot, he grabbed several and lowered in front of her. Crouching down, he gently rubbed away the evidence of their loving from her thighs.

"Lie down on the cot, on your stomach."

She arched a brow. "Are you going to take me from behind? I thought you might need at least a few minutes of recovery time."

From his kneeling position, he shot her a glare. "I'm going to clean the wounds on your back. Lie down, Evie. And take off your bra."

"Wow," she said, reaching behind to unclasp the garment. "I'm pretty sure that's the most unromantic way any man has ordered me to remove my bra." Pulling it off her breasts, she threw it on the floor.

Kenden slowly stood, running the tip of his nose up her stomach and between her breasts, until he came to his full height. "Don't throw your other lovers in my face. I don't like it." Gently, he nipped at her lips.

"Well, look who's possessive." The always-present glint of mischief was in her eyes as she chided him, but they were also still bursting with unnamed feelings. She was rattled, even though she was trying to hide it.

"Right now, I'm the only one sharing your bed. It's going to stay that way until we both decide that we're ready to move on. Got it?"

She breathed a laugh. "I dictate the terms of who shares my bed."

"Oh, I know it," he said, rubbing his lips against hers. "But you came here looking for me, sweetheart, so I'm in charge of this negotiation. Now, lie the hell down."

"God, you're so sexy when you boss me around," she said, giving him a sultry smile. "Fine. Stitch me up if you must." With a dramatic sigh, she lowered onto the cot, crossing her arms underneath her head as she watched him mill about the shed.

After wiping his release from his shaft with the tissues, Kenden stalked over and grabbed his boxer-briefs, shrugging them on. Locating the first-aid kit, which he kept in the file cabinet by the front door, he walked to her and sat down on the hard floor. Opening the kit, he pulled out the travel-sized bottle of alcohol, cotton swabs and bandages.

Two quarter-sized lacerations marred her flawless skin, one inside each of her shoulder blades. Wetting a cotton ball with alcohol, he held it over one of the wounds. "This will probably hurt."

"Good," she said, the word slightly garbled as her cheek rested on her arm.

Lowering the soft swab to her skin, his heart clenched at the rasp of her indrawn breath when it connected with the wound.

"You okay?" he asked softly.

She nodded, her eyes seeming to glow in the soft light that emanated from the lightbulb hanging from the ceiling in the middle of the shed.

Kenden commenced cleaning the lacerations, ensuring they wouldn't be infected, and then covered them with two large bandages. Putting everything back in the first-aid kit, he closed it and pushed it aside. Lifting his broad hand, he stroked her silky, scarlet hair as she gazed at him.

Silence pervaded the room but instead of being stifling, it was welcome. There, in the dim light, he caressed her while she watched him, her lids growing heavy. Content to just observe her breathe, he reveled in her beauty. Never had he met a woman more exquisite.

Letting her fall into sleep, he sat by her side as long as his body allowed. Then, exhausted by their lovemaking, he let himself fall as well.

Chapter 16

Evie gasped a breath, coming into consciousness as her eyes darted around the small space. Then, she remembered. She was in Kenden's shed, recovering from what was probably the most intense sexual experience of her life. Letting her pupils settle on him, her heart constricted in her chest as she rested on her stomach.

There on the dirty floor he lay, snoring softly as he slept. Aching to touch him, she slid her fingers into his hair. Gently, she soothed him, waiting for him to rouse. Those lids opened slowly, and he regarded her with his always-sexy deep brown eyes.

"Why are you sleeping on the floor?" she asked, a slight teasing in her tone.

He shrugged. "I didn't want you to wake up somewhere unfamiliar. I wanted to be here, so you'd see me when you awoke."

Emotion clawed at her throat, threatening to close it as she reeled from his words. He was such a good man. One who deserved a woman who would give him everything he desired. Something pulsed inside her as she stared at him, her fingers never ceasing their ministrations on his thick hair. Terrified that it was love, she pushed it away. She'd never felt anything remotely close to that emotion and vowed she never would.

"Thank you," she whispered, humbled by him. "I like seeing you when I wake up. It's the first time that's ever happened to me."

"I like it too," he said, reaching up to caress her cheek with the pads of his fingers. "It could happen every morning if you moved in with me. I have so much space, and I'm sure you're tired of living in that tiny cabin."

The hand in his hair froze. "Ken..." she said softly, struggling to find the right words to deny his ridiculous request.

"Don't say you don't want to. I've always appreciated how straightforward you are, sweetheart. It's beneath you to lie about this."

Inhaling a deep breath, she felt her irises darting over his face. "I'm a nightmare, Ken. A goddamn nightmare. You don't want to live with me."

His thick lips curved into a smile. "Um, I'm pretty sure I just indicated that I do."

Sliding her hand from his hair to his cheek, she cupped his face. "I'm a monster in the morning. Bitchy as hell until I've had several cups of coffee. I use too much hot water and leave a huge clump of hair behind each time I shower."

He chuckled, the sound so deep it sent shivers through her body. "Well, I'm pretty handy. If you clog the drain, I'll snake it."

Fear lodged in her gut as she tried to think of more excuses. Better excuses. There were so many, weren't there?

"I know you're scared, baby," he said, his thumb so soothing as it caressed her cheek. "I am too. I've never felt about anyone the way I feel about you."

"I don't want your feelings, Ken. I've tried to tell you that."

"I know," he said, looking like a sad puppy. "But they exist, and I'm a straight-shooter. It's one of the many things we have in common."

Evie scoffed. "We don't have anything in common."

His eyebrow arched as he grinned. "Wanna bet? We're both competent soldiers, enthralled by war. We thrive on honesty and candidness and both love a good steak. You cook a mean chicken cordon bleu, and I'm a whiz at washing the dishes. I think we have to live together just to streamline efficiencies. We'd have the most proficient house on the compound."

She laughed in spite of herself. "A compelling argument, but wasted. I can't move in with you. I don't want that level of commitment."

"I don't need any level of commitment from you, Evie. I just want you. Let's keep it simple and not define it. Having you in my home will mean you can sleep with me anytime you damn well please. That has to be somewhat enticing, no?" His smile was so adorable that her heart threatened to burst in her chest.

"If I was going to be enticed by anything, it would be unlimited access to your gorgeous cock. It's fucking magnificent."

He breathed a laugh. "Then, move in with me. No timeframe, no restrictions. Just you and me and unlimited sex."

Evie was thoroughly enjoying their banter. He was so captivatingly charming.

"I can't," she whispered.

Sitting up, he slid his arms around her and pulled her off the cot to straddle his lap. She wrapped her legs around him, loving the feel of his erection on her naked core through his boxer briefs.

"Yes, you can." Gently, he nibbled her lower lip. "Move in with me."

"No," she said, shaking her head as her arms surrounded his neck.

Reaching down, he pulled himself through the hole of his underwear. Lifting her by the globe of her butt with his other hand, he positioned the head of his shaft at the delicate skin of her deepest place. Ever so softly, he rubbed the sensitive tip against the wet lips of her core.

"Move in with me," he said, his voice gravelly.

"No," she said, almost moaning from the sweet contact.

Slowly, he began to nudge himself into her. Clutching onto his hair, she bit her lip to contain her groan. The soft skin of his straining cock felt so good as it stretched her. Eventually, he reached the hilt. Touching his forehead to hers, he jutted back and forth, stimulating the spot that brought her so much pleasure.

"Move in with me," he repeated, his gaze locked onto hers.

"Oh, god," she wailed, gyrating her hips to magnify the contact. "You're not playing fair."

"I never cheat but I always make sure the odds are in my favor." Nudging his nose with hers, he drove into her channel in short bursts that felt amazing. "Move in with me, and I'll make you scream."

"What if you end up hating me?" The question was wrenched from her pleasure-drenched body, too aroused to care how vulnerable it made her.

"Won't happen," he said, his tone confident. "Say yes, sweetheart. You can do it."

Purring with desire, she placed her lips against his, her lissome frame shuddering. "I'll stay with you this weekend. It's all I can give right now. Now, fuck me like you mean it."

"I love the way you compromise," he said, gently biting her plushy lower lip. Pushing her back to the floor, he began hammering into her, honoring his word to make her scream. It felt so good, she damn near forgot to be terrified that she'd been handled. Even if there were concessions, he'd gotten her to capitulate. And damn, if that wasn't hot as hell. Loving his brain almost as much as his cock, she let Kenden bone her into senselessness.

* * * *

They spent the weekend together, Evie cooking dinner on Saturday and Sunday. Both afternoons, while preparing the food, she stared out the window, watching Kenden chop wood that would be used for their evening fire. Muscles, tanned and bulging, stretched under the buttery sunlight, causing Evie intense pangs of longing in her gut.

Every so often, he would lift the metal container to his mouth and drink, his thick throat bobbing as he swallowed. Wiping his lips with the back of his arm, he smiled at her through the window and gave a wave. Annoyed that she was even considering waving back, she would scowl each time and curse him in her head. How dare he look at her with those gorgeous eyes and tan, sweaty skin? Bastard.

At night, after dinner, they sat by the fire. Kenden rubbed her feet while they chatted about life and war and the upcoming battle they faced. It was all too surreal for Evie. She'd lived alone for so long, never needing companionship, and was terrified that this display of domestic bliss was going to gestate into something more. It couldn't happen. Their time together was limited. It had to be.

Good grief, he'd want her to have a hundred babies. Impossible, since they'd have her father's blood. She knew that Kenden understood this, somewhere deep inside. That their situation was all too temporary. But he seemed to carry on, not willing to acknowledge their lack of a future.

At night he pulled her close, clutching her to him after they loved each other. Never being a cuddler, she let him hold her anyway. Where was the harm in that? He was so patient and kind to her, she could at least let him smother her with his strong body. The warmth from his solid frame would wash over her as they drifted, causing Evie to take a mental snapshot. Although never a sentimental fool, she did want to remember their time together when she returned to the human world. She would recall these moments, when they were sated and content, so fondly.

Monday came, and a new week of training along with it. Evie fought tirelessly with the troops, returning to her cabin on Monday evening. Rubbing her upper arms as she stood beside the lonely bed, she admitted that she missed him. It was unwelcome and rather annoying.

By mid-week, she was struck with a yearning so intense she could actually feel it throbbing in her stomach. Brushing her teeth under the florescent light of the small bathroom, clad in her silky robe, she ached for him. Unable to stop herself, she transported to his house.

Kenden didn't seem fazed as she appeared from thin air. His eyes met hers in the reflection as he slid the brush over his teeth. Leaning over to rinse, he deposited the toothbrush in the nearby cup and rested his palms beside the sink. "Hello, Evie," he said, his irises locked on hers in the mirror.

Unable to form words, she slowly approached. Placing her palms on his back, she caressed his straining muscles. Sliding her arms around his waist, she rested her forehead between his shoulder blades. There, they stood, breathless, motionless, in the white marble bathroom.

Eventually, Kenden turned, picking her up and carrying her to the four-post bed. Discarding her robe and his underwear, he loomed above her, magnificent and striking. Entering her, inch by inch, his melted-chocolate eyes communicated emotions that she craved against her will. Afterward, he pulled her limp body to his side, surrounding her with his corded arms.

"For someone who doesn't want to live with me, you sure show up here a lot," he murmured into her hair.

Evie didn't answer. How could she? Instead, she ran her hand through the thick hairs on his chest, loving how they tickled her palm. Nestling into his side, she gave way to her dreams.

Chapter 17

Thursday, alone in her cabin after the day's training, Evie looked at the text from Miranda, expecting to feel another wave of anger at her beckoning.

Miranda: We're having a joint Slayer-Vampyre BBQ tonight so the species can mingle. Hope you'll come. NOT summoning you. Just really want you there so we can hang.

Inhaling a deep breath, Evie searched her feelings. Not only was she not incensed, but she almost felt a sense of elation that her headstrong sister seemed determined to spend time with her. The joy at the text was ridiculous, but what did she expect with the shit show her life had recently become? She'd turned into an emotional sap, craving Kenden's company and crying like a teenage girl in line for a Shawn Mendes concert. It was so absolutely frustrating that Evie gave up trying to push it away. At this point, she was too tired to fight the insane sentiments. Giving in to them, she prepped to head to the barbeque.

Throwing on jeans, so she could sit in the green grass if needed, a loose tank and sandals, she materialized to the playground at Uteria's main square. Right away, she saw Jack's red hair swishing as he jumped around the monkey bars, daring the other kids to traverse them as quickly as he did. Feeling her lips twitch, she admitted that she liked the little tyke. Lila and Latimus' adopted son had a competitive spirit that was admirable, especially for a kid who'd been through what he had.

Kenden approached her, handing her a red solo cup. "It's beer from the keg. We don't really get too fancy during these barbeques."

"Who needs fancy?" she asked, taking a sip. "It tastes fine to me. I've always loved a good beer."

"Be still, my beating heart," he said, sipping from his own cup. "You're adding to the tally of things we have in common. Careful."

Chuckling, she beamed up at him. "I guess there are worse people I could share similarities with." Glancing around, Evie noticed members of the royal family lounging around the picnic tables under a large redwood. "I need to grab some food. I'm starving."

"Come on," he said, offering his hand to her.

Evie hesitated, staring at his broad hand.

"The whole compound knows we're sleeping together. I think it's okay if you hold my hand."

Scowling up at him, she grabbed his hand and interlaced their fingers. The challenge in his voice had rankled her, which she was sure was his intended consequence.

Tugging her gently, Kenden led her to where the royal family was sitting. Arderin, so beautiful with the flush of her pregnancy, was in the middle of stealing Darkrip's fork and eating the large bite of meat he'd procured on top.

"Good grief, woman," Darkrip said, shooting her a light-hearted glare. "You don't even need food. Why do you insist on eating mine all the time?"

"Because it drives you nuts," was her good-natured reply as she waggled her eyebrows.

"You'll pay for that later," he murmured into her ear.

"God, I hope so," she said, fangs squishing her bottom lip as she gave him a come-hither smile.

Evie set her cup on the table and headed to the line of grills to get some food. Scooping some on top of the thick paper plate, she noticed Sathan cooking behind one of the large metal grills.

"Didn't know Vampyres knew how to barbeque," Evie said to him.

He grabbed a piece of grilled chicken with large metal tongs and deposited it on her plate. "Miranda says it makes me more approachable to our people, doing everyday tasks like grilling. Let me know what you think. I hope it's not too dry."

"I'm sure it's fine," she said, continuing down the line to spoon some macaroni salad onto her plate. Pondering, she admitted that she was thankful for the Vampyre king's cordiality toward her. They certainly hadn't gotten off to the best start, and Evie assumed that he was making his best effort to tolerate her due to Miranda's urging and the fact he needed her to possibly fulfill the prophecy. Inwardly, she hoped she was the descendant of Valktor to kill her father. It would be a great service to both species and would perhaps exonerate Evie from the disastrous decisions she'd made when Kenden first found her, if only slightly.

Heading back to the table, she sat across from her brother and Arderin, Miranda to her right.

"How's my husband doing up there?" Miranda asked, surreptitiously glancing over her shoulder. "He's not thrilled that I made him cook, but I'm the boss." She flicked her glossy hair over her shoulder as she grinned.

"Pretty well," Evie said, cutting into the chicken with her plastic fork and knife. Ingesting a bite, she chewed. "It's quite tasty. Don't think it will kill me, maybe to your husband's chagrin."

"No way," Miranda said, squeezing her wrist. "We're happy to have you here, Evie. *All* of us."

"Thank you," she said softly, humbled by her sister's acceptance.

Kenden sat down to Evie's left, his plate heaving with food.

"Careful, or you'll lose those abs you're so proud of," Evie teased.

"Not on your life, sweetheart," he said, grinning. "I need them to tempt you when you want run away from me."

Stuffing a huge bite of food into his mouth, situated atop the plastic fork, he chewed. The muscles in his jaw, sinewed and corded, strained as his mouth worked. For the love of all the gods, Evie was marveling at his jaw muscles. This really had to stop. She'd gone fucking insane.

"Okay," Miranda said, standing and tossing her plate in the nearby trash can. "I'm gonna go mingle. Anybody want to come with?"

"Yep," Arderin said, bouncing up from the table. "I need to roam around. This baby's having a dance-off in my stomach."

Darkrip's face clouded with concern. "Do you need to see Sadie?" he asked from his perch on the picnic bench.

"No," Arderin said, bending to give him a peck on the lips. "She's just cantankerous like her dad, being all cooped up in there. Can't wait to meet her. She's going to be a handful."

"Don't I know it," Darkrip muttered. "I'm terrified."

Arderin laughed, the sound melodious and sweet. "Don't worry, I'll save you. Thank the goddess you bonded with someone who's tough."

"Tough as nails," he said, squeezing her hand. "I'll finish up and come find you guys. Love you."

"Love you," she whispered, giving him an absent kiss on the forehead before walking away with Miranda.

Evie smiled, finding that she was truly happy for her brother. How amazing. It had been so long since she'd felt happiness for others. It was foreign yet somehow welcome. Kenden's knee brushed hers under the table, and she stared up at him, realizing he'd bumped her intentionally. Love, deep and true, glowed in his gorgeous eyes. Starting into them, Evie could only form one thought: *Holy shit, I am so fucked.*

As the three of them were finishing the last of the scrumptious food, Lila sauntered over to sit beside Evie, Jack at her side. Her face glowed as she gave a gorgeous smile, although it was a bit hesitant and shy.

"Hi, Evie," she said in her melodic tone. "I hope you don't mind, but I have a favor to ask you."

"Shoot," Evie said, her gaze traveling to Jack, who was beaming up at her, his crooked teeth somehow adorable between his tiny red lips.

"Jack is enthralled by the samurai he learned about in school. It's become a bit of an obsession. Latimus told me that you trained with the samurai in Japan for many decades. I was wondering if you could tell him a bit about your experience."

Evie eyed the little scamp, unable not to smile back. Something about his red hair and freckled face called to her.

"Better yet, why don't I show you?" Standing, Evie rubbed her palms over her thighs. "Got a sword lying around anywhere?"

Pleasure burst in Jack's wide brown eyes. "Yes!" he said, nodding furiously. "Give me a sec, okay?"

"Okay," Evie said, chuckling as he ran toward the playground. Thirty seconds later, he returned triumphant, two toy swords in hand.

"Come on," she said, motioning him toward the open grass a few feet away from the picnic table. Facing him, she grabbed the base of one of the plastic swords. With the respect that one would employ when addressing a master samurai, Evie began showing Jack different stances, lunges and methods she'd learned in her extensive training. Once she'd explained the basics, she began sparring with him.

The plastic blades clanked and shuddered as they fought, the boy determined to best her. Brow furrowed, he jousted and grunted as she skated around his weapon, dodging his jabs.

"Whoa, there," she said, leaning over to rest on her knees. "You're playing dirty. You almost stabbed me in the liver."

His eyes grew round as saucers. "Are you okay? I'm sorry. I didn't mean—"

Evie sliced her sword through the air, cutting off his words as she knocked his weapon to the ground. "First lesson of warfare, kid. Don't get distracted."

Jack stared up at her, his chin trembling slightly. *Shit.* Of course, she'd scared the crap out of the little bugger. Evie had always been terrible with kids. Yet another reason why she'd never let Kenden tie himself to her. No way would she deny the certain future 'Dad of the Year' the opportunity to have children. It would be the height of selfishness to taint his offspring with her father's awful blood.

Leaning down, she reached toward Jack, hoping to soothe him by ruffling his thick hair, the color so like her own. "I'm sorry, Jack—"

Bending down, he grabbed his sword from the grass and thrust the point into her midsection. Not too hard to hurt her, but enough to spur a large exhale from her shocked body. The rascal had taken advantage of her lowered position to regain the upper hand. To say she was impressed would be an understatement.

"I surrender," she said, laughing as she held up her hands and dropped her weapon. "You're a smart one, aren't you?" Arching a brow, she reveled in his huge smile.

"Did you think I was gonna cry?" he asked, excitement in his tone. "I wanted to trick you, so you'd underestimate me. Latimus always says that having your opponent underestimate you is the best way to gain the advantage."

"He's absolutely right," she said. "You're a pretty awesome warrior, Jack. I assume you want to be a soldier one day?"

"Yep," he said, eagerness evident in his nod. "Latimus says I can join the army when I'm eighteen, and I'm going to work my way up to be his second-in-command one day."

"Well, he'd better watch out, or you might usurp him and become the commander yourself. You're pretty sly."

"What does 'you-syrup' mean?" he asked, his brow furrowing.

Evie snickered. "It means you'll take the position of commander from him against his will, because your skills will be better."

"Oh," he said, shaking his head. "I wouldn't do that. He's awesome. I wouldn't take anything from him. I don't mind sharing."

"What a sweet boy you are," she said, reverently stroking his head. Had she ever had the ability to be so open and loving? It moved something in her as she stared into his deep brown eyes. "Well, then, maybe you can be co-commanders. How's that?"

"Perfect," he said, grinning from ear-to-ear.

"Okay, sweetheart," Lila said, seeming to float over toward them. "It's getting late, and we need to say our goodbyes. I think Aunt Evie has shown you enough for today. What do you say?"

"Thank you, Aunt Evie," he said, the tone of his voice so sincere.

"Just 'Evie' is fine, kid," she said, shooting Lila a good-natured glare. "And you're welcome. We'll train again one day soon, okay?"

"Okay," he shouted, rushing toward her and throwing his arms around her waist. Feeling extremely uncomfortable but also a bit overwhelmed by her affection toward him, she hugged him back. Sparing a glance toward Kenden, still sitting at the picnic table with Darkrip, she could see he was transfixed by the scene. Great. Just what she needed. The noble Slayer commander bombarded with images of her loving interactions with a child. Good lord. Stiffening, she pulled away from Jack.

Unable to bring herself to sit beside Kenden, she walked toward Latimus, who was standing under the large elm tree several feet away. Making up some unnecessary question to ask him about the next morning's training, she cowered to her fear, too afraid to face the only man who, in ten long centuries, made her crave things deep inside that could never become reality.

Chapter 18

Darkrip heard the shrieks as soon as he stood up to throw his empty plate in the trash. Off in the distance, they pierced the night, ominous and shrill. Deamons rushed toward the park, what seemed like hundreds of the beady-eyed creatures, and his brain locked on to her name: *Arderin*.

Turning, he searched for her in the distance, throat choked by fear. She carried their babe, so powerful inside her womb, and it made her a prime target for Crimeous. The Dark Lord vowed that he would abduct the child and raise it to be evil; an undefeatable warrior in his army due to the offspring's combined bloodline from her powerful grandparents. Determined to never let that happen, Darkrip closed his eyes, locating Arderin on the outskirts of the main square with Miranda.

Transporting to them, he pulled her slender body close.

"I'm taking you to Astaria," he growled. "Hold on."

Clutching his beloved wife, he conveyed to the main castle at the Vampyre compound. Releasing her, he observed her ice-blue irises, filled with fear. Not for herself, but for those she left behind.

"Stay here," he said, kissing her on her pink lips. "I'm going back to help them."

Astaria had an impenetrable wall built by Etherya. One that Crimeous had never succeeded in breaking through. His bonded would be protected while he fought with the others at Uteria.

"Please, be safe," she whispered, tears swimming in her eyes.

"I will, princess. I'll be back before you know it." With one last brush of his lips to her cheek, he materialized back to Uteria.

The battle was raging now. Clashes of swords sounded in tandem with pops from machine guns and discharges from TECs. Darkrip spotted Kenden, surrounded by Deamons, fighting each one off with an SSW. Evie stood to his side, wielding her powers to disintegrate their weapons and help the powerful Slayer commander.

Latimus was yards away, working in tandem with Larkin, battling the creatures with a knife in one hand and a Glock in the other.

"Hey!" Miranda yelled, running up to Darkrip, Tordor on her hip. "Materialize a sword for me, will ya? Then, I need you to transport Tordor, Lila and Jack to Astaria. After that, come back here and help me kick these bastards' asses."

Darkrip smiled, reading the excitement at getting to fight again coursing through his half-sister's veins. Miranda was a competent warrior and had laid down her weapons since becoming a mother. Sensing she needed the tussle, he grabbed Tordor from her and envisioned a sword, which promptly appeared in her hands.

Sathan appeared beside her, breathless, with a knife drawn from his belt.

"You need to go to Astaria, Miranda," he said in his deep baritone. "We can't lose you."

Grabbing his t-shirt by the neck, Miranda yanked him to her. "No offense, but no fucking way. I'm tired of letting everyone else fight these assholes." She placed a firm kiss on his lips. "Are you gonna fight with me, or not? Because I seem to remember we make a pretty great team."

Sathan snarled, Darkrip sensing that he was both frustrated and extremely aroused by his wife's question. "Get Tordor to Astaria," the Vampyre said, his eyes never leaving Miranda's. "And give me a sword too. I want to slaughter these bastards."

Darkrip complied, the object appearing in Sathan's hand, and then closed his lids to transport Tordor to Astaria. Handing the toddler to Arderin, he returned to Uteria to look for Lila and Jack.

Miranda and Sathan were sparring with a group of Deamons to his left, Latimus and Larkin still fighting off in the distance. Evie and Kenden seemed to be holding their own as numerous Slayer and Vampyre soldiers battled across the expansive field of the park.

"Jack!" Darkrip called, unable to locate the boy anywhere in the main square. Several of the soldiers were herding people toward the back of the castle, hoping to shield them from the skirmish.

Suddenly, he saw Lila's blond hair flash as she ran toward the playground. Jack squatted behind the see-saw, hiding from the fighting. Closing his eyes, Darkrip transported to him.

"Jack!" Lila cried, crouching beside her son.

"Let me transport him to Astaria," Darkrip said. "Then, I'll come back and get you."

"Okay." She nodded, fear latent in her lavender irises.

Darkrip grabbed the child, closing his eyes to transport them. Unable to dematerialize, his heart filled with dread.

Crimeous appeared atop the dirt-covered ground, cackling as he sauntered toward them. His long robe was black, one of the many colors he draped himself in when he chose to leave the caves. Hate for his father consumed Darkrip, and he knew the bastard had rendered him powerless.

"Well, well," the Dark Lord said in his malevolent tone. "How gallant you are, son. After all those centuries of killing alongside me, you still pretend to be good. It will never be your true nature. You know that as well as I do."

Darkrip handed Jack to Lila and pushed them behind him. "You just can't leave us the hell alone, can you, old man?" Lifting his hands, he formed fists. "If I have to, I'll fight you hand-to-hand, without my powers. I won't let you hurt the people I love."

Crimeous threw back his head, the escaping laugh awful and wicked. "Love. What a wretched word spawned from your worthless mouth. You'll never be one of them," he said, gesturing to the nearby battle with his head. "Come back with me and train. It's only a matter of time before everyone you profess to care for is dead. Don't you understand, son?"

"Don't call me son," Darkrip said through clenched teeth. "Now, fight me if you want but leave the boy and the woman out of it."

Scoffing, Crimeous lifted his hand and sliced it through the air. Darkrip felt his body flying and he landed with a thud several feet away on the dirt. Lila clutched Jack tight, turning away to shield him with her body.

"Now, now," the Dark Lord chided, approaching them slowly. "It's okay, my beauty. I still imagine raping you in front of Latimus. I never even thought of doing it in front of your child. How magnificent."

Lila sat Jack down and turned to face Crimeous while the boy clutched her waist from behind. Pulling a knife from her belt, she lifted it in anticipation. Darkrip thought the action so brave for someone raised as an aristocrat, far away from war. He desperately wanted to help her, but his father had frozen him to stone.

When Crimeous was within inches of her, Lila jabbed with the knife, and his father swerved easily. "I'm glad to see that Latimus has armed you. A smart yet futile attempt to save you. What a waste of time, but I admire the effort."

Grabbing Lila's thick flaxen hair in his fist, he violently tossed her to the ground. Jack stood immobile, cowering in front of the Dark Lord. Chin quivering and brown eyes wide, Darkrip felt agony at his inability to help the boy.

"Now, now," Crimeous said, lifting Jack's chin with his reedy fingers. "Which way do I want to kill you? Hmmm..."

"You're really tough when you're hurting kids, asshole!" a voice shouted from the edge of the playground. Thanking every god that existed, Darkrip saw Evie jogging toward Jack. Latimus was behind her, SSW drawn, and he began striking Crimeous with the always-lit blade. As his father wailed, Evie disappeared with Jack in her arms, only to return a moment later to grab Lila from the nearby ground and evaporate again. With a *whoosh*, Evie reappeared, an SSW materializing in her hand. The glowing blade emerged from the Solar Simulator Weapon, casting an ominous luminosity under the now-darkened sky. Teeth gritted, she began attacking the Dark Lord alongside Latimus.

His father fought back, a sword in his hand, and Darkrip realized it must've been fashioned from poisoned steel. Not only would it decimate a Vampyre's self-healing body but the metal was strong enough to withstand the solar power of the SSW. The three of them fought, metal clashing against blade, in a circling dance of determination and skill.

Suddenly, Evie stood tall and lifted her hand, palm facing out. Both Latimus' and Crimeous' weapons disappeared. She spoke softly, her face illuminated by the yellow light of the SSW, still extended in her hand.

"It's time you and I had a talk," Evie said to Crimeous, holding the weapon firm. "Latimus, step away. This is between us."

Latimus' ice-blue irises darted between Evie and the Dark Lord. Giving her a nod, he backed away several feet. Still close, lest she need him if Crimeous conjured another weapon in his hand.

Clutching the hilt of her weapon with both hands, Evie retracted the glowing ember of the SSW and threw the armament on the ground. "Hello, Father."

"Hello, Evie," he said, his expression pensive and thoughtful. "How interesting. Darkrip's thoughts indicated that your powers were greater than his, but I see I've underestimated you. I can't interfere with them at all."

"Your knowledge of human dark magic is vast but it will never equal mine. I've studied it for centuries, never really comprehending why I was so enthralled by it. Now, I understand that it was because I'm meant to kill you."

Crimeous chuckled, the sound quiet. "Is that so?"

"You can't escape the prophecy, Father. It will be me or one of Miranda or Darkrip's children. You know that as well as I. You're living on borrowed time already."

"Etherya is a liar, and her prophecy is nothing more than a fairy tale. I believe in it no more than I believe these people truly accept you. You're rotten inside, child. An abhorrent manifestation of me. They tolerate you because they desperately want to rid the world of me. Once they realize you haven't the voracity to kill me, they'll cast you out like the abomination you are." He stretched out his hand, the wrist thin and pale under the sleeve of the robe. "Join me, Evie. Together, we could rule the Universe. Our combined powers would be unstoppable. You're nothing to these immortals."

"That's not true," Kenden's baritone voice called from beside Latimus. The words were laced with determination and a hint of fear. Darkrip wasn't sure if he was scared that Evie would be hurt or afraid that she would defect with his father. Or perhaps both.

"Evie is loved by every member of our family, and we honor her presence here," Kenden continued. "Your hateful words have no place here." Training his gaze on Evie, Kenden said, "The Blade is in Miranda's office."

Nodding, Evie closed her eyes. A moment later, the Blade of Pestilence appeared in her hand. Motionless, she stared at Crimeous.

"I see your struggle, child," the Dark Lord said as he stood before her. "So many emotions war within you. Your hate for me is nothing compared to your hate for yourself. You will never be able to choose the light. Killing me would be futile, for a happy existence can never be the destiny for someone like you, riddled with my blood. You take hope from Darkrip but know that you won't be able to choose the same path. Come," he said, shaking his hand. "Accompany me back to the caves, and we will combine our powers to kill every last immortal."

Evie's leaf-green eyes studied their father, blazing under the light of the full moon. Darkrip could feel her struggle, the war within magnified on her flawless face. Nostrils flared as she panted, contemplating his words. Darkrip had felt the same recently, when he'd let his father's feelings of viciousness and supremacy course through him. They were glorious, and his body pounded with terror that Evie would choose to align with him.

"We love you, Evie," Darkrip gritted from his frozen spot on the dirt. "Don't listen to the bastard. Strike him!"

The words must've snapped something within her because her chin lifted with resolve. Raising the Blade, she swung it forcefully, attempting to slice Crimeous through the neck. The Deamon screamed, rotating to materialize a sword in his hand. One-on-one, they fought, metal clashing, neither one seeming to tire. Pulling back, Crimeous held up his hand, stopping the scuffle.

"You are a competent warrior, child," he said, breathless.

"Stop calling me that," she said, jaw clenched.

"I see that I might not be able to best you hand-to-hand. Therefore, why don't I do some damage where it will hurt you the most?"

Her eyebrows drew together as she warily regarded him, hands clutched around the handle of the Blade. "What the hell does that mean?"

Throwing the sword to the ground, Crimeous materialized a knife in his hand. Quick as lightning, he rotated, throwing the knife across the ten-foot space that separated him from Kenden.

In a flash, Evie evaporated, appearing in front of Kenden to take the blow. Her gasp could be heard across the expanse of the park as the dagger entered her throat.

"No!" Kenden screamed, clutching her to his body as she collapsed on the ground. Latimus drew the SSW from Kenden's belt and charged Crimeous, Larkin and several other soldiers close behind. Within seconds of being battered by multiple solar weapons, the Dark Lord wailed and threw back his head, disappearing into thin air.

Darkrip regained movement thanks to his father's maiming and rushed to Evie's side as Kenden rocked her in his arms.

"She's bleeding out!" Kenden yelled, holding his hand across the massive injury as blood spurted around the still-inserted knife.

"Let me transport her to Sadie's infirmary."

"I'll meet you there," the Slayer physician said from above them. Darkrip knew she'd been in attendance at the picnic. "And then, can you transport to Astaria and bring Nolan and Arderin to help me? I'm going to need every hand to save her."

"Yes," Darkrip said, drawing Evie close. She was unconscious, her head lolling to the side as crimson rivulets gushed from her neck. Closing his eyes, he conveyed her to the pristine white bed of the clinic, praying for dear life to Etherya that she survived.

Chapter 19

Nolan was with Arderin, Lila, Jack and Tordor when Darkrip materialized in the sitting room. He'd been in the infirmary when Arderin had called to tell him of the attack. Unable to face Sadie, due to the absolute mess he'd created, he'd decided to forego the barbeque. Upon hearing that Uteria was raided, he headed upstairs to console the others as they waited.

"Evie's badly hurt," Darkrip said. "Sadie needs both of you. I'll take Nolan first and then Arderin."

"Okay," Nolan said, rising from the couch. "Is the battle over?"

"Yes," Darkrip said. "They're defeated for now, and Crimeous has returned to the caves. Come on."

The Slayer-Deamon whisked Nolan to one of the sterile ORs of Sadie's infirmary. Seconds later, he appeared with Arderin.

Sadie was already leaning over Evie, compressing blood-soaked gauze pads to her neck.

"Approximate five-inch laceration of the neck," she said, her speckled eyes focused and solid. "I need you to hold pressure so I can seal the edges and begin suturing. She's struggling to breathe on her own, and we'll need to insert a tube once I've closed the lesion."

Jumping into action, Nolan donned two plastic gloves from the box affixed to the wall and applied pressure. Arderin worked with deft movements behind them, loading supplies onto a sterile tray and wheeling it over. For minutes, they worked furiously, unable to control the bleeding.

Kenden ran into the room, breathless. "What can I do?" he asked, his tone distraught.

"Get Sathan in here now. I have an idea. Hurry! We must act quickly." Sadie said.

Kenden ran from the room as Nolan held his fingers to the spurting arteries and veins on Evie's throat. Unwilling to imagine the worst, Nolan clung to hope as the woman he loved stood across from him, small hands furious in their movements, proving once again how magnificent she was.

* * * *

Several hours later, Nolan was exhausted. Arderin, tired from being on her pregnancy-swollen feet, had returned to Astaria with Darkrip. Evie's prognosis was fair, thanks to Sadie's quick thinking. A miracle, considering how severe her injury was.

Miranda and Kenden were chatting by Evie's bedside. The queen looked pensive, the Slayer commander distressed. Judging by Kenden's reaction as they treated Evie, it was obvious to Nolan that he was in love with her. He hoped like hell that the woman who'd saved so many this night would be able to recover enough to accept it.

"I don't want you to have to go to Astaria tonight," Miranda said, placing her hand on Nolan's shoulder. "We need you here anyway, in case her condition worsens. I asked Jana to prepare the room next to Sadie's for you. You should have everything you need up there. Toothbrush, change of clothes. If you need anything, just call Jana from the phone in the room. Sadie, you can walk him up, right? I think we all need to get some rest."

"I'm staying here," Kenden said. "I don't want her to wake up alone. You all go to bed." Approaching Nolan, he held out his hand. "Thank you for saving her, Doc. I'll never be able to repay you."

"We don't do this to be repaid," Nolan said, shaking his hand. "I'll say a prayer for her."

Nodding, Kenden drew Sadie into his embrace and whispered words of thanks into the shell of her ear. Disengaging, she came to stand before him, staring up at Nolan with her stunning eyes. The vibrancy of the hues took his breath away.

"Come on," Sadie said in her soft voice. "I'll show you to your room."

Nolan followed behind her, up the large carpeted staircase, until they were walking down the darkened hallway. Silence, thick and heavy, surrounded them as their feet padded on the hallway floor.

"Here you go," she said, turning to face him where they stood in front of the bedroom door. "Mine's next door. If you need anything." Shifting her gaze down, she kicked the rug with the toe of her sneaker. "See ya in the morning."

Frozen, he watched her walk to the next door on the right. Turning the knob, she entered, closing the door behind her with a gentle click.

Sighing, Nolan entered the chamber. Removing his clothes, he pulled the t-shirt over his head, noticing how large it was. It must've been Sathan's, brought to his room by Jana when she prepared everything. Throwing on the black shorts, also a few sizes too big, he walked into the sparse bathroom to brush his teeth.

The mundane action seemed wrong. Hell, everything seemed wrong. Sadie was only feet away, but inside, he felt they were worlds apart. How had he messed everything up so terribly? He'd only wanted to give her space. To give her time to think of all she would be sacrificing if she settled for a life with him. Instead, he'd made her doubt herself all over again, causing him to want to murder himself. Nolan had worked so hard to pull Sadie from her shell of self-doubt. To make her realize how beautiful and remarkable she was. Frustrated at his stupidity, he ran his hands over his face.

Exhausted from the night's events, he slid under the covers, aching for her as she slept only feet away. Physically so close, but light-years away from where they'd been. Where he wanted to be. Sighing into the pillow, Nolan cascaded into a fitful slumber, filled with nightmares of his beloved Sadie marrying another. One who could give her everything he couldn't.

Chapter 20

Evie swam into awareness, feeling as if her legs were weighted down by a thousand anvils. Unable to inhale, she clutched at her throat, pulling the vices that strangled her there. Someone restrained her wrists, drawing them away, and she fought like hell to kill whoever was harming her.

"You're safe," a voice called through the plasma in her brain. A familiar voice, one that she trusted. "It's okay, baby. I've got you. Please, stop struggling."

Her lids were glued shut, and she wished she could get the damn things to separate. Finally, by some miracle of Etherya, she was able to open them. Kenden loomed above her, concern dripping in his stunning brown irises.

"You're safe," he whispered, still holding her wrists. Gently, he lowered them to her sides. Cupping her cheeks, his eyes welled with tears. "I'm here, Evie. Always. I promise, you're okay. You're not going to be able to talk, so I need you to calm down and focus on breathing. Sadie took out your breathing tube a few hours ago, but if you reopen the wound, she'll have to insert it again." Calmly, his hand stroked her face, so soothing as her heart pounded within.

"That's it," he said, smiling at her with those perfect white teeth. "I'm here."

Unable to wrangle her warring emotions, a tear slipped down her cheek. Catching it with the pad of his thumb, Kenden rubbed the wetness over her skin.

"I know, baby," he said, his tone filled with understanding. "It's awful. You must feel so helpless. I know you hate that more than anything. I promise, I won't let anyone hurt you. Now, close your eyes and get some rest." The metal legs of the chair made a scraping sound as he pulled it toward the bed and sat down. "I'm not leaving until you're well enough to tell me to go to hell," he said, his wobbly smile so endearing. "It's three a.m. and everyone's sleeping. I promise, you're okay. Close your eyes, and I'll be here when you wake up."

She blinked up at him, hating that she clutched onto his words. Inwardly admitting that she didn't want him to leave, she pleaded to him with her gaze.

"Trust me," he said, stroking her cheek. "I promise, I won't leave. Not even to go to the bathroom. I'll find a bucket if I have to."

A laugh lodged in Evie's chest, unable to exit her throat due to the massive gash in her neck.

"See how funny I am?" he asked, his other hand fingering through the hair at her temple. "One more reason to move in with me. I'll make you laugh for eternity.

You have to tell Miranda though. She always says she's funnier than me. No way in hell."

Evie thought the conversation so ridiculous but understood what he was doing. If she focused on his musings, she might just forget that her father had maimed her and she was vulnerable in the infirmary. How bad was her injury? Would she regain the ability to speak?

Unable to keep her eyes open, she closed them as the questions whirled in her head, and Kenden dribbled on above her with his low-toned voice. Eventually, she conceded in her battle against unconsciousness.

* * * *

The next time Evie awoke, she was able to clear her throat. Kenden sat beside her reading a book. Knowing him, it was a detailed history of some long-ago human war. Lifting his gaze to her, he smiled.

"You're awake." Setting the book on the floor, he scooted to the edge of the chair and clutched her hand. "How are you feeling?"

She tried to speak but found it impossible. Pain coursed through her body as well as the accompanying pleasure. The sensations were hellish, causing her skin to prickle. She felt like someone had rammed a truck into her body and left her muscles to disintegrate into jelly. Helplessness swamped her as she stared at him.

"Sadie said you might not be able to talk for a while. That bastard's knife hit you right in the middle of the throat. But she swears that with enough time, you'll be able to speak again." His brown irises darted over her face. "Are you thirsty?"

Realizing that she was, Evie nodded. Releasing her hand, he walked to the counter and poured some water in a plastic cup. Sitting by her side again, he lifted it to her lips. Not wanting to appear like a dying invalid, she took the water and sat up against the pillows. She might not be able to speak but she'd be damned if she couldn't hold a freaking cup to her mouth. It was extremely difficult to swallow, but she was determined. Regarding him, she sipped, wishing she could ask him the questions that were swirling within.

"You've been in and out for about two and a half days," he said. "It's almost noon on Sunday. You were amazing, Evie," he said, admiration strewn across his handsome face. "You fought him like a champ. And then, you jumped in and saved me. It was so brave. Thank you."

Evie recalled the battle and the jolt of terror she'd experienced when her father had thrown the knife directly at Kenden's heart. There'd been no other choice in her mind. She'd acted without thinking. Narrowing her eyes, she pondered that sentiment. Never had there been anyone in her life whom she'd put before herself. It was disconcerting and made her extremely uncomfortable.

"Okay," Kenden said, taking the empty container from her hands. Her throat felt raw where she had swallowed the water. "Let me have the cup before you crush it. I take it you're not thrilled that your first reaction was to save me. Sorry, sweetheart, but I think we've crossed the 'no feelings' line. It's time to admit that you're crazy about me." His lips were so full as he teased her, curved into a sexy smile. Nostrils flaring, she imagined throttling him.

"That's good," he said, winking. "You're getting your snark back. I think it's one of the things I love most about you." Her stupid heart slammed at his words. "What other questions can I answer for you?" he asked, sitting back in the chair. "Everyone is fine. You were so smart to transport Jack and Lila to Astaria—thoroughly debunking your theory that you only care for yourself, by the way," he said, lifting his finger in the air.

Evie scowled.

Kenden chuckled, shaking his head as he grinned at her. "Man, I am so going to pay for this later, aren't I?"

Unable to control the twitch of her lips, Evie gave a subtle nod.

"Worth it if it makes you smile, baby," he said, scooching forward again and cupping her cheek with his broad hand. "I thought I lost you," he almost whispered. "It tore apart something inside of me that I don't want to put back together. I'll need to explore that with you when you're ready."

Evie's breath caught, and she struggled not to pant as he stared into her.

"For now, you need to rest. I've been here for days watching over you but I'm pretty sure I stink and need to shower. Miranda offered to come hang with you when you were awake enough. I'm going to send her down." Standing, he stretched, the corded muscles of his arms making her mouth water. Pulling his phone from his belt, he shot off a text, most likely to Miranda. Replacing his phone, he contemplated her.

"Sathan gave you a blood transfusion. Being the purest-bred Vampyre, his self-healing abilities are off the charts. Sadie performed the transfusion just in time. Any later, and it wouldn't have worked. It helped save your life, and Sadie says you'll heal quickly. I know you think that Sathan doesn't care for you, but you need to know that. You're part of our family now, Evie. Prophecy or not. When you're ready, we're going to discuss that too. Your father tried to plant some pretty absurd bullshit in your head, and I'm not letting that seed grow one fucking bit. Do you understand me?"

Evie just stared at him, unable to nod. Didn't he realize that Crimeous was right? She was rotten, down to her very core. No one in this inane world needed her or cared for her. How could they? They couldn't understand the evil that churned within. Hell, she barely comprehended it herself.

"Don't go there," he said, lowering his face to within inches of hers. "It's beneath you." Placing a kiss on her forehead, he gave her jaw one last caress.

Miranda plodded into the infirmary, a huge beam strewn across her face. "Hey, sis! Thank god you're okay." Striding to the bed, she held Evie's hand. "You saved a bunch of people, including Lila and Jack. I can't even begin to thank you."

"Told you," Kenden said to Evie, squeezing her upper arm as Miranda clutched her hand. "I'll be back in about an hour," he said to Miranda.

"Take your time," she said, drawing the chair forward to sit down. "I'm sure Evie's already tired of your savior complex, right?" she joked, arching an eyebrow.

A breathy laugh escaped Evie's throat, and she nodded against the soft pillow.

"See? She's over you. Get the hell out of here. We'll see you in a bit. I'm going to regale my darling sister here with stories from your youth and how awkward you were when you used to address the troops." Looking at Evie, she said, "He was as nervous as a virgin on prom night. Our fearless commander hasn't always been so confident, believe me." Her tone was filled with mischief.

"Can you please not tell the most beautiful woman I've ever seen stories that will make her never want to kiss me again? I've grown to like kissing her very much." With one last wink at Evie and a peck to Miranda's forehead, he exited the infirmary.

As Miranda began chatting away, Evie watched the door, blood coursing through her frame at his words. She found herself unable to let go of the image of his broad back as he left the room, or the hope that he would return to her soon. Tamping down the fear of needing him so fiercely, Evie let her sister talk her to sleep.

Chapter 21

On Monday, Aron headed to the playground to assess the damage. The recent battle had wreaked carnage on the play area, the surrounding park and the main square. Frustrated at the frequent attacks by Crimeous, he rubbed his fingers across his forehead. The park was lined with downed trees, discarded swords and triggered TECs. Remnants of the scuffle also marred the main square where many vendors' tents had been damaged.

The playground, which had been enveloped in an atmosphere of hope and peace during the coronation in Aron's name, was now decimated. The see-saw lay tilted off its axis. The monkey bars and carousel were scattered in pieces across the dirty, grassy ground. Vowing to never let the bastard dissuade him, Aron began forming a plan to resurrect the entire main square.

Sensing someone behind him, he turned his head to see Lila floating toward him, coming to a stop at his side.

"Crimeous just keeps destroying everything we build," she said in her soft voice. "I want so badly for Evie to be the one who murders him."

Aron studied her pensive expression as she observed the wreckage. He'd never heard Lila speak so frankly about death but the bastard had rendered her barren. She must want him annihilated more than anyone.

"We'll defeat him," he said, grabbing the woman's hand, whom he'd come to admire considerably as he'd gotten to know her during their shared council meetings. Squeezing, she smiled, acknowledging his comforting gesture. The action contorted her face into something more glorious than it already was, if that was possible. Lila was an extremely stunning woman.

Releasing his hand, she sighed. "I rode the train with Latimus today, so I could help you start the clean-up and restoration while he trains the troops. Miranda said she's assembled a team of fifty volunteers who will be here shortly."

"Yes," Aron said with a nod. "We'll rebuild, stronger and better than before. We always do. Moira will be here soon. We closed the gallery today so that she and Preston could help."

"Wonderful," Lila said, her perfect pink lips curving as she observed him with her lavender gaze. "She's such a nice woman. Although we got off to a bit of an...*uncomfortable* start, I like her immensely."

Aron's eyebrows drew together. "Why would you get off to an uncomfortable start?" he asked, wondering why there was a slight ringing of alarm in his head.

Her eyes grew wide, filling with anxiety. "I, um...you two are together now, right? I was sure that Miranda told me you were."

"Yes," he said, annoyed for some reason.

"Okay, I, uh..." She chewed her bottom lip. "I just assumed that she would've told you about her time with Latimus. She's very direct."

Aron felt his heart plummet to his chest, wondering what in the hell the Vampyre was talking about. When did Moira spend any time with Latimus? He'd been with Lila pretty much since Aron had known him, and Moira had been at Restia for the past eight hundred years. Hadn't she?

"What time with Latimus?" he asked, his tone filled with warning and a bit of anger.

"Oh, dear," Lila said, bringing her hands to her burning cheeks. "I thought she told you, knowing that you were together. Latimus and I tell each other everything. I—" She shook her head, sorrow blazing in her purple irises. "I'm so sorry, Aron. It wasn't my place to tell you. I...I don't know what to say."

Rage coursed through Aron's toned frame, seething within as he thought of the last weeks he'd spent with Moira. She'd been staying at his house every night, sharing the intimacies of a monogamous relationship. Dinner, lounges on the porch, reading by the firelight on rainy nights. Sexual encounters that would make a young buck blush. Moira was a firecracker in bed, pushing the limits of his desire and opening him to experiences that he'd never had. But she'd had them all, hadn't she? Looking at Lila's flushed face, the extent of Moira's fabrications began to wash over him. How could he have been so blind? And why would she lie to him so extensively?

"Aron," Lila said, clutching his forearm. "You don't know the whole story. She was with Latimus for reasons that were very important. I don't want to betray her trust any further, but you need to talk to her with an open mind. Please. She deserves that."

He yanked his arm away, angry that she knew secrets he'd never even fathomed. How many others knew? Miranda? Sathan? The entire compound? He felt like the biggest fool who'd ever walked the Earth. What a massive mistake he'd made to trust Moira.

"Don't tell me that a woman who lied repeatedly to my face deserves *anything*," he spat. "I can't believe you all kept her secrets and enabled her deceit!"

"It wasn't like that, Aron." Lila's magnificent eyes welled with tears. "It was devastating for me too, when I found out about their history, but now that I know why she left Uteria, I understand. You need to give her the benefit of the doubt."

"Don't talk to me about her time at Uteria. She was married to the best man I know. The fact that she would attempt to leave him tells me all I need to know about her character." Feeling his nostrils flare, he inhaled a deep breath, attempting to control his anger. "I'll ask you to never speak about this to anyone. This is between me and Moira, and I won't have everyone in the kingdom gossiping about my personal business."

"I won't," she said, swallowing thickly. "I'm so sorry, Aron."

Moira chose that moment to bounce up to them, filled with the vibrant energy that she always seemed to possess.

"Hi, guys. I'm ready to start the clean-up. Where do you want me?"

Aron and Lila stared at her, immobile, and the realization that something was terribly wrong seemed to wash across her face.

"Aron?" she called softly.

"How could you?" he gritted, hating how gorgeous she looked under the morning sunlight. Ocean-blue eyes glowed as she gazed up at him, slowly filling with dread.

Heaving in a deep breath, she shook her head. "This isn't the place. We have a job to do. Let's discuss this tonight, when we can talk in private."

"Tell me one thing," he said, the words laced with fury. "Did you, or did you not lie to me about where you've been for the past eight hundred years?"

Moira's irises darted between his, then looked to Lila. Moving her pupils to lock back on his, Aron sensed her defeat and eventual capitulation. "Yes," she said, straightening her spine. "I lied to you. I was with Latimus for the past eight hundred years at Astaria. He kept me safe, and I gave myself to him. Being angry at me won't change it, and we have work to do. So, you can sit there and stew, or you can help me rebuild the playground for the kids. What's it going to be?"

Well, he admired her gumption if nothing else. Although she'd been the transgressor, she was daring him to shelve it so they could work toward a common goal. Appreciating her ability to compartmentalize, he caved in.

"Fine," he snapped, wishing to all the gods that Lila hadn't arrived early that morning. Then, they could go back to where everything was normal. Where Moira was the woman he'd fallen head over heels for. The one he wanted to ask to marry him and build a life with.

But no. That life was shattered now. Moira was a liar. A schemer who'd betrayed his best friend and manipulated everyone around her. If his veins weren't coursing with loathing, he might just admire how brilliantly she'd pulled it off.

"We'll clear the park and help our people. But know that I won't tolerate being deceived, Moira. It's the manifestation of everything I detest. You're not welcome at my home anymore. I'll have a courier send over any of your things that are there. And you're fired from the gallery. I don't trust you with the money anymore. Lord knows how much you could've stolen, right from under our noses. You're never to set foot in there again. Are we clear?"

"Aron," Lila said, her soft voice pleading as she grabbed his forearm. "I don't think you understand—"

"It's fine," Moira interrupted. He expected some fight out of her, since she was always so strong and determined, but she seemed utterly defeated. "I'm just a servant's daughter after all. And a whore. You're right not to trust me. I won't bother you again."

Aron couldn't understand why he felt an overwhelming sense of compassion for her in that moment. He should hate her with his entire soul for the deception she'd executed. Instead, he felt the insane urge to comfort her. Pushing it away, he made sure his voice was gruff.

"Good. I never want to speak to you again. Stay the hell out of my way." Needing to distance himself from her crushed expression and the smell of her shiny hair, he went to join the group of volunteers that had gathered in the middle of the park.

* * * *

Moira watched Aron walk away, willing the tears to stay inside her rapidly-filling eyes. After all, this was bound to happen and no less than she deserved. She'd known, somewhere deep inside, that he would hate her when he discovered her lies. Oh, how badly it hurt to have him affirm how he really saw her. A lowly servant who would steal from his gallery and portray herself as a whore to the world.

"Moira," Lila said, dragging her from her thoughts. "I'm so very sorry. I thought you'd told him. I don't know what to say. What can I do to fix this?"

"Nothing," Moira said, swiping a tear from her cheek. Vowing that would be the last one that fell, she lifted her chin defiantly. "He's right. I'm beneath him. I always have been."

"That's not even close to true," she said, empathy in her stunning irises. "You're such a wonderful person, Moira, and I've come to consider you a friend. Something I thought impossible when I first met you, considering your history with my bonded, but it happened anyway. Mostly because you're really amazing."

"Thank you, Lila," Moira said, feeling her throat close up. "I really like you too. And I don't blame you for telling Aron. I should have. I just knew that he would react exactly as he did. So, I guess it sucks to be right sometimes," she finished with a sad shrug.

"He's angry now but that will pass. You need to tell him about your husband, Moira. It's obvious he doesn't know."

Moira sighed. "He'll never believe me, especially now. He idolized Diabolos."

"You need to give him the benefit of the doubt, as much as he needs to do the same to you. Your assumptions about each other will destroy you. Believe me, I'm an expert in disastrous assumptions. They kept me and Latimus apart for a thousand years."

"But you guys always loved each other," Moira said. "Aron could never love a servant's daughter, not for the long haul. He wants an aristocratic wife. He used to talk about it when we were young."

Lila's blond eyebrows drew together. "I've never once heard him say that. And believe me, if you love someone, that stuff just doesn't matter. Latimus gave up having biological children to be with me. He didn't see it as a sacrifice at all, even though his bloodline is the purest on the planet. You need to have faith in his love for you, Moira."

"Sadly, I think I've destroyed any emotion he might have started to feel for me." Holding up a hand, she prevented Lila from answering. "What's done is done. Let's get to cleaning this playground up, huh? I find that I feel better when I have a dirty task to complete."

"Okay," Lila said, enfolding her hand. "Please, call me if you need to talk. I'm so sorry that I spilled your secret. I feel terrible."

"It's okay," Moira said, unable to be upset with the woman before her, who was always filled with such genuineness. Together, they strolled to remedy the destruction Crimeous had rendered.

Chapter 22

Nolan scribbled in Evie's chart while Sadie spoke soft words to her. She wanted Evie to stay one more night in the infirmary to monitor her vitals and would release her in the morning barring any further complications.

"I know you're tough, Evie," Sadie said, squeezing her hand as she lay in the hospital bed, "but your body has been through significant trauma. It's going to be hard to eat for several days, and I recommend soup and soft food. Otherwise, it will be difficult to swallow. I'm prescribing bed rest for a few days at Ken's house. I'd suggest you follow it. He's already sworn that if you try to go back to your cabin, he'll just drag you back to his house."

Evie scowled and wrote something on the pad that they'd given her to communicate. Sadie glanced at it and breathed a laugh.

"Yes, he's a caveman sometimes. But he wants to take care of you. Let him, okay? He's not so bad most of the time. I promise," she said, giving Evie a wink.

Evie nodded, and Nolan noticed the faint curve of her lips.

Sadie approached him and stared at him with her gorgeous, prismatic irises. "I'm heading to bed. You can file the chart before you go back to Astaria. Thanks so much for staying here over the past few days. Good night." Her warbled grin almost splintered his heart. Padding across the floor in her sneakers, she exited the room.

Nolan sighed and finished the notes. Filing away the manila folder, he turned to tell Evie goodbye.

"I'm glad you're okay, Evie," he said, smiling as he regarded her. "If you need anything, please, let me know. I'm only a phone call away."

He turned to leave but was stalled by her firm grip around his wrist. Tilting his head, he looked into her olive eyes. She seemed to be trying to speak, although he knew she hadn't quite regained the ability to talk.

Frustration surrounded her as she gripped the pen in her hand. Jotting something on the pad, she lifted it to him.

She loves you.

Nolan exhaled a ragged breath and shook his head. "I can't give her children. I don't want to make her an outsider or deny her the opportunity to marry one of her own. I'm...torn," he said, running his hand over his face. "I just want to do what's best for her."

Evie's pupils darted between his. Lifting the pad, she scribbled again.

You're enough for her. I know it's hard to believe. Maybe if you can do it, I can too.

"Maybe," he said, his heart welling with compassion for her. She probably felt like as much of an interloper in the immortal world as he often did.

"Thank you, Evie," he said, squeezing her wrist. "Get better soon. We're all rooting for you." With one last nod of his head, he left her to heal.

Upon exiting the infirmary, Nolan couldn't stop the pounding of his heart. Drawn by an invisible force, he quietly climbed the carpeted stairs that led to Sadie's room. Knocking softly on the door, he heard her voice, garbled through the wooden door. Did she say, "Come in?" Unsure, he slowly creaked open the hinges.

She was topless, standing in front of her dresser mirror, her feet bare below the cuff of her jeans. Left arm slung awkwardly behind her back, she was attempting to rub the burn-healing salve on her right side, near her shoulder blade. When she saw him in the reflection, she yelped.

Lifting her t-shirt from the dresser, she covered her breasts. Nolan had caught only a glimpse—one so supple and perfect, the other almost non-existent due to the charring. "I said, 'Don't come in!'" she yelled, her expression furious.

Knowing he was invading her privacy but powerless to do anything to the contrary, he closed the door and ambled toward her.

"Please, don't," she said, eyes locked on his in the mirror. "I don't want you to see me this way."

Pain slammed through his body at her solemn words. How could she still believe, after all this time, that he saw her as anything but gorgeous? The one woman who epitomized beauty above all others, inside and out.

Inhaling a deep breath, he laid his hands atop her bare shoulders, hating her resulting flinch.

"You can't reach your back on your own," he said, the pads of his fingers rubbing her soft skin, ever so gently. "Why didn't you ask me or Arderin for help? We could've been helping you to apply the serum this whole time."

Her chin quivered in the reflection, sending a crack so wide down Nolan's heart that he thought it might break in two. "I didn't want to bother you guys."

"Sadie," he whispered, rubbing her shoulders in earnest now, reveling in being able to touch her, if only that small bit. "Don't you know, I would do anything for you? All you have to do is ask."

Blazing irises darted between his. "I don't know anything anymore. I'm terrible at this. I wish you'd never kissed me."

Nolan felt little pangs in his eyes and realized they were filling with tears. How strange. He hadn't had the urge to cry in centuries, not since he'd realized that he could never return home. But his emotions for the woman before him were complicated, turning his stomach into a mass of knots.

"Kissing you was the only thing I've done right in three hundred years," he said, his voice gravelly. Reaching down to the dresser, he picked up the tube that held the formula. Squirting some of the clear gel on his index and middle finger, he began to massage it into the skin beside her shoulder blade.

She stood so still, her head dropping forward as his ministrations continued. Nolan worked for several minutes, covering every inch of her upper back with the healing salve. When he was finished, he pulled a tissue from the box beside the mirror, wiping it from his hands.

"See?" he asked, unable to read her since her eyes were still downcast. "That wasn't so hard. I'd be happy to help you apply the formula anytime." Grasping her thin upper arm, he turned her toward him. Placing his fingers under her chin, he tilted her head so that she was forced to meet his gaze.

"I'd do anything for you, Sadie," he said, the words laced with sadness. "It's not fair to you. I want you so badly that I would deny you a full life. One where you could marry a Slayer and have his children. I'm such a selfish bastard that I'd even do that. And you deserve so much better."

Breath exited her throat in choppy pants as an expression of extreme confusion crossed her face. Shaking her head, she asked, "What in the hell are you talking about?"

Expelling air through his puffed lips, he lifted his hand to cup her unburnt cheek. Sliding the pad of his thumb over her bottom lip, he said, "I heard you talking with your patient a few weeks ago. I shouldn't have been listening but I couldn't stop myself. You deserve to be courted by a plethora of men who will shower you with flowers and gifts. But I find myself wanting to claim you, to beg you to choose me, to never let another man love you. I should care enough for you to let you experience everything you're worthy of."

Her forehead furrowed as tears glistened in her eyes. Angry at himself for making her upset, he dropped his hand. "I'm heading back to Astaria. I just...I don't know...I needed to see you. To talk to you." Dejected, he began to turn away.

"Wait!" she called, grabbing his forearm. "Look at me, Nolan."

Lifting his irises to hers, he noticed her fist held a death grip on the t-shirt that she still had across her breasts. He would've teased her for being nervous if the situation hadn't been so tense. Chest rising and falling with anxious breaths, she slowly lowered the shirt back to the dresser.

Standing before him was the most magnificent image he'd ever beheld. His beautiful Sadie, one perky breast on her left side, a maze of scarred tissue where the other should be. Although she'd been using the serum, the skin wasn't fully healed. Her chest had experienced extreme damage and would need several months of consistent application of the formula to mend. The mass of her breast had been charred off in the flames, all those centuries ago. Knowing how hard it must be to show him such vulnerability, he yearned to touch her. To show her with his body how magnificent she was. Inching toward her, as if pulled by an invisible tether, he slowly lifted his hand. Cupping the globe of her breast, he tested the weight in his palm.

Her gasp unleashed something inside him, causing him to want more. Lifting his thumb, he swept the pad over the pebbled nipple, the skin there so smooth and taut. Bringing his index finger to the tiny nubbin, he squeezed the sensitive point.

Sadie gave a little mewl, the sound so sexy in the quiet room. Need, swift and true, clenched inside him. Sliding his hands down her sides, he palmed her jean-clad bottom, lifting her and carrying her to the bed. Laying her across the purple comforter, he placed his forehead against hers as he sprawled over her.

"Is this okay?" he asked, not wanting to push her if she wasn't ready.

The bob of her throat was so cute as she swallowed, obviously anxious at what was surely her first sexual encounter. "Yes," she whispered, her brown hair sliding across the bed as she nodded.

"You know, I'm not very experienced either," he said, hoping to put her at ease. "I was in my early twenties when I came through the ether, and my experiences were short and clumsy. I hope I'm able to please you. I can recite every bone and muscle in the body but strictly for surgical purposes. And I'm pretty sure you'd rather I kiss your sensitive spots than perform a procedure on them."

Sadie snickered, breaking the tension a bit. "Yeah, I'd rather you kiss them. I don't know a lot either, but what you were doing to my breast felt pretty good." She bit her lip, the innocent action remarkably adorable.

"Like this?" he asked, slipping his hand down to cup the small globe again. With his fingers, he pinched the nub, causing her hips to buck against him.

"Yes," she whispered.

"Or maybe like this?" he murmured, trailing a line of kisses to the pale curve, prodding the ruddy tip with his nose. Opening his lips, he pressed them over her sensitive nipple, drawing it back in between them as he sucked.

"Oh, yes," she said, writhing beneath him. "It feels so good."

Sliding his hands under her, he lifted her lithe torso to his mouth, lathering her nipple with his tongue. Wanting so badly to satisfy her, he tuned in to her breathless reactions. Seeming to like when he sucked her deep, he closed around her again, pulling her entire areola into his mouth as the tip of his tongue flicked the pebbly nub.

She cried his name as he loved her, making his muscles shake with desire and lust. Wanting her to understand that every part of her body was beautiful, he traversed his lips across to where her other breast would be, kissing the flat center.

"Oh, Nolan," she said, threading her fingers through his hair. Her eyes shined as she stared into him. "You don't have to kiss me there."

"Yes, I do," he murmured, placing butterfly pecks all over her burnt skin. "Every part of you is desirable to me, sweetheart. I wish you could understand." Swiping his tongue over the mangled tissue of her nonexistent breast, he felt her shake with arousal.

Moving the palm of his hand to the snap of her jeans, he hesitated. "Can I take these off? If you're not ready, I understand. I don't want to do anything you don't want to do."

Reaching down, she ran the tips of her fingers over his jaw, the gesture so loving. "I've been ready since you kissed me. How could you not know that? I think that if you don't take my pants off, I might just die right here."

Chuckling, he placed a kiss on her flat abdomen. "I think Arderin's dramatic temperament is rubbing off on you."

Her resounding laugh was like a beautiful aria. Standing to his full height, he undid her jeans and slid them and her panties off her legs. Always the observant physician, he ran his hand over her right thigh. "You're healing nicely here."

Slender shoulders shrugged atop the comforter. "I can reach my thigh way better than my back."

"Well, I'm applying to be your back-salve applicator from now on," he said, waggling his eyebrows. "If it leads to getting to see you like this, I'm so in."

White teeth flashed as she smiled shyly at him. Placing his palms on her thighs above her knees, he skimmed them up the silky flesh until his thumbs brushed the lips of her sex. Small whimpers escaped her throat as he lightly feathered her there.

Sliding the pads of his thumbs over the swollen flesh, he realized how wet she was. The moisture gleamed in the pale light of the dresser lamp, beckoning to him. Rimming her opening with the tip of his index finger, he gently began nudging it inside her.

"Nolan," she pleaded, squirming on the soft bed. "Please. I want you inside me."

"Are you sure?" he asked, slowly moving his finger in and out of her tight channel. "I can kiss you here first, to get you ready."

"Um, I think I'm ready," she said, almost giggling. "I mean, I want you to kiss me there, but we can do that next time, right? I'm ready to give myself to you." Locking on to him with her kaleidoscopic eyes, fresh with shades of newly-turned autumn, her lips curved into a heartbreaking smile. "I love you, Nolan."

Every single cell in his pounding heart shattered. It was the most wondrous moment of his life, hearing those words from her stunning lips in her sweet voice. Oh, how he wanted to say it back, but his throat had closed up, and he was having a terrible time breathing. Letting instinct take over, he pulled the shirt over his head and discarded his dress pants and underwear.

Gliding his body over hers, he palmed the back of her head as he pushed her thigh open with his other hand. Grasping his straining shaft, he aligned the engorged head with her slick opening. Gazing into her, he began sliding in, the pressure on his straining shaft giving him immeasurable pleasure.

"I love you too," he whispered, the words torn from his chest as he jutted into her. "More than I ever thought possible. You're everything, Sadie," he said, groaning as the wet tissues of her tight channel choked him. Lowering his forehead to hers, he gritted his teeth. "*Everything.*"

Throwing her head back, she opened to him, the gesture such a gift as she gave him her innocence. Body relaxed, she bestowed her trust upon him, knowing he would do his best not to hurt her. Tightening his fingers in her hair, he struggled to retain his composure, wanting so badly to give her pleasure.

"I love you," she whispered against his lips, the words giving him permission to fully claim her. "I love—"

The fragment ended in a gasp as he sheathed himself completely, claiming her for what he hoped was forever. Clutching her close, he branded her with his body, the thrill at being the first to hold her like this overwhelming. Wanting to ease her pain, he placed his finger on the nub below her triangle of hair, rubbing it in concentric circles as his shaft slid through her wetness. Having been alone for so long, Nolan reveled in the beauty of making love; the pounding heartbeat of the amazing woman below him; the almost unbearable pleasure at loving someone more than himself.

Sensing she was close, he increased the pressure on her clit and lowered his mouth to suck her succulent nipple into his mouth. Drowning in the multiple sensations, her slender body bowed under him. Lids closing with desire, her mouth opened, and she screamed his name, consumed with her orgasm.

Feeling the drenched tissues of her core spasm against him was Nolan's undoing. Threading his arms under her, he pushed his hips into her once, twice...and then exploded into the most intense climax of his long life. The jets of his release pulsed into her, marking her as his, consuming him. *Mine*, his brain echoed, as his hips bucked against her. Replete, he collapsed, hoping he wasn't squashing her. He just couldn't find the energy to move. It was as if his body had lost all muscle control.

The realization that Sadie was shaking violently brought him to his senses. Worried for her, he lifted his head and cupped her cheek. "Sadie?" he asked, concerned. "Are you okay, sweetheart?"

Opening her mouth and expelling a large exhale, her lids blinked open. "Am I okay?" she repeated, an expression of wonder spread across her pretty features. "You just told me you loved me and gave me the first orgasm of my life. Uh, yeah, I think I'm going to be fine."

Chuckling, he shifted to place a kiss on her lips. "I do, Sadie. So much. I wish I could give you everything you deserve."

"Nolan," she said, threading her fingers through his hair, the action so soothing. "I don't need to have your biological children. Of course, I wish I could, but it's certainly not a deal-breaker for me. If you're open to me getting inseminated, I think that's what I'd like to do. In the future, I mean."

"I would be thrilled at that, sweetie," he said, resting his head on his hand as his elbow perched on the bed. "To see your body grow full with our children." His hand ran over her smooth stomach. "But I want you to be sure. It's still a huge sacrifice."

"It's not a sacrifice at all," she said, her hair fanning out on the bed as she shook her head. "You should have told me you eavesdropped on us," she said, scrunching her features as she shot him a playful glare. "You must've missed the end, where I told Sagtikos to go screw himself."

Laughing, he nipped at her lips. "Did you now?"

"Yep," she said, her smile so endearing. "I told him that I loved you, and he needed to stop meddling in my business."

"I should've had more faith in you. I'd brought you flowers and was going to ask you to move in with me. When I heard your conversation, I freaked out."

"That's why Moira had your flowers!" she said, realization crossing her face. "I saw her in the castle, and she said you gave them to her. I thought you were trying to court both of us."

"Seriously?" he asked. "I can barely court one woman, much less two. You're giving me way too much credit."

"Man, we were such idiots. I thought you didn't want me anymore. It broke my heart."

Crushed by her admission, he wanted to strangle himself. "I'm so sorry. I was trying to give you space while your skin healed. I didn't want to tie you to me and deny you the opportunity to find someone who could give you children."

Her lips twitched. "Can we make a pact to communicate better? Because the last few weeks have sucked. I was a wreck."

"Yes, let's do that. This has been a huge wake-up call for me. I'm always so great at giving relationship advice to everyone else but realized recently that I'm terrible at giving it to myself. Good grief. I created a mess."

"Well, thank god you busted into my room tonight," she said, entwining her arms around his neck. "And now, I'm not a virgin anymore. Holy crap."

"No, you certainly are not," he said, rubbing his nose against hers. "That was amazing, Sadie. I've never felt anything like it. I can't wait to make love to you for eternity."

A huge red splotch appeared on her unburnt cheek. "Neither can I. That was awesome, Nolan."

Basking in the glow of their coupling, they lounged for a while before prepping for bed. Nolan didn't return to Astaria that evening, preferring to hold the woman he loved in his arms as he slept upon her smooth sheets.

Chapter 23

Sadie released Evie from the infirmary early Wednesday morning. Sathan's blood had contributed to her quick healing, and Evie found herself grateful to yet another person in the immortal world. How absolutely annoying. She was becoming more and more ingratiated to the people whom she swore she didn't need. It was enough to drive her insane.

Kenden insisted on driving her to his house even though her ability to materialize was uncompromised by her injury. Once he'd carried her inside and laid her on the couch, he covered her with a fluffy blanket, tucking the corners around her.

"This is ridiculous," she muttered, scowling at him. "I'm perfectly fine." The impact of the words was weak, however, considering the scratchiness of her voice. It would still be several more days before she could speak without a rasp.

Sitting beside her, Kenden grinned as he rubbed her hair with his fingers. It absolutely did *not* feel amazing, being soothed by him. Nope. No way.

"I'm wondering if this is the first time in your life that people have gone out of their way to help you," he said in his always-calm tone. "I can't imagine how foreign it must feel."

"It feels fine," she snapped, hating every single person who'd helped her. It wouldn't matter when she returned to the land of humans. Once that happened, she'd be able to retain her footing and live in an environment she understood. Thank god. She couldn't wait for that day.

The human world certainly wasn't perfect, but it was the only place where she'd felt a sense of peace. Humans were messy creatures, extremely flawed and capable of making great mistakes. Something about that comforted Evie and pulled at her during some of the loneliest moments she'd experienced since returning to the land of Slayers and Vampyres. In the mortal world, she wasn't overwhelmed by self-doubt and fear. Although they existed, she could temper them so much easier in that environment. For some reason, now that she was back in the land of her origin, the unrest crowded her, and she often questioned herself. For someone so sure, it was disconcerting. Being in the land of humans would restore her to solid ground, even if it was isolated and solitary.

A slow burn of anxiety began to glow in her gut as she imagined living on her own, alone in the human world. Letting the images form, she imagined leaving those whom she'd come to know. Of not hearing Miranda's throaty laugh as she approached the castle at Uteria. Not seeing Jack as he grew into the competent warrior he was sure to become. Denying herself the luxury of being held in Kenden's strong arms.

Pushing the musings away, she cursed herself. Her brain was probably just on overload from her injury. Clutching the darkness within, her eyes narrowed.

"You all just need me to fulfill the prophecy," she said, unwilling to discuss everyone's sudden desire to help her any further. "Once I do that, or once I fail, you all will get over it. Believe me. You're better off without me."

His handsome features seemed overcome with sadness. "I hope that's just the drugs talking, because I don't want to have to argue with you when you're recovering."

"I'm not on any drugs," she said sullenly.

"Because you're so strong," he said. Adoration swam in his eyes, and she hated that he was placating her when she needed him to understand how futile it was to care about her. It was an absolute waste of his time. He needed to be out training the troops, not helping her heal.

"I don't want you here," she said. "I'm going to transport back to my cabin. I can't distract you, especially now that my father has attacked. We need to be as strong as possible to defeat him."

"We will be," he said, stroking her face. "Latimus is training the soldiers today. Let me be here for you. I don't want to play games, Evie. It's not who we are. Don't denigrate us to that. I want to help you recover, and you like having me around. Stop being a coward and admit it."

"I don't—"

"Stop," he said, placing two fingers over her lips. "You can pull off that crap with every other man you've been with but not me. We care about each other, Evie. And a lot more that I'm ready to say, but you're not ready to hear, so I'll keep my damn mouth shut. But you need to stop fighting me. I need you to just accept that we're in each other's lives. For now, and if I have anything to say about it, forever. I'm just as stubborn as you are. You don't want to get into a battle of wills with me, especially not when you're injured. It won't be pretty for you."

Evie scowled, hating how her heart thumped at his words. "Fine," she said, too exhausted to argue. She'd barely regained the ability to speak and still felt like someone had run over her with a snowplow. "But I'm *not* moving in with you," she said. "I'm just staying here so you won't drive me crazy. I know you'll never give up if I try to head back to my cabin."

"You're right. I'd just come over and drag you back here. I'm not letting you go, Evie. Maybe one day, if I say that enough, you'll start to believe me."

In spite of herself, she breathed a laugh. He was infuriatingly persistent. "Maybe one day, I will."

"Now, what do you want for dinner? Our lovely Jana has stocked my fridge with soup. Tomato, broccoli and cheddar, or chicken and wild rice. What will it be?"

"Tomato. I can help you cook it—"

"No way," he said, standing and shaking his head. "I know I'm an idiot in the kitchen but even I know how to use a microwave. Give me a few." Leaning down, he kissed her forehead before heading to the adjoining kitchen.

They ate in companionable silence, Evie struggling to swallow when she ingested heftier spoonfuls. Once finished, Kenden made sure soft music was emanating from the surround system speakers he'd installed upon building the house. As the classical symphony soothed her to sleep, he went outside to chop wood and work in the yard.

That evening, he led her upstairs, relenting when she told him she'd dismember him if he tried to carry her. Clutching her hand, they prepared for bed and climbed under the silken covers. Evie slid her palm to his shaft, becoming frustrated when he pulled it away and cuddled her firmly into his side.

"I don't want to open your stitches. Let's wait until you get them out on Friday," he said, placing a peck atop her red hair as her cheek rested on his chest. "We need you, Evie. It's important that you heal properly. It's okay if we just hold each other until we fall asleep."

"I don't see any reason to sleep with someone if there's no sex involved. What a waste of a perfectly good opportunity to get some action."

Kenden breathed a laugh. "You're a pain in the ass, Evie. Let me hold you. I promise, it won't be as bad as you think."

"We'll see," she said, throwing her thigh over his and spreading her fingers wide over his pecs. Moments later, his breathing began to even out, and she felt him drift into slumber. Wide awake, the tips of her fingers made lazy circles through the prickly hairs on his chest.

There was no denying that his words bothered her. *We need you, Evie.* Yes, they needed her badly. To fulfill the prophecy and save the immortal realm. But was that all? Would they ever truly need her? Just Evie, in all her fallible complexity and simmering darkness. Doubtful.

There were only two possibilities. If she killed Crimeous, they'd respect her for a while, sure. But how many years or decades would it take to forget? For the viciousness of her anger and the truth of her heritage to remind them all how terrible she truly was?

And what if she wasn't the savior? What if that burden fell to Tordor or the child Arderin was now carrying in her womb? Would they cast her back into the human world once they understood that Crimeous' child would always taint the pristine atmosphere of the land they called home?

Kenden cared for her. Hell, he most likely loved her. The descendant of Valktor who would save them all. But if she failed, if Crimeous survived, how could he stay with her? Knowing the children he so vehemently craved would have the blood of the monster they sought so doggedly to destroy?

Evie couldn't let him make that choice. Perhaps her one last act of kindness could be extricating herself from him and pushing him into the arms of Katia or someone like her. Someone who shared his desire to build a home and a family. Yes, she thought, feeling herself begin to drift. There were ways to care for someone. Sadly, the best way for her to care for Kenden would be to ensure their separation, no matter how much it hurt.

* * * *

Returning from her Saturday afternoon walk, Evie shrugged off her sweater and caught her reflection in the mirror that hung by the coat closet. Fingering the reddened scar on her neck, she contemplated. Sadie had removed the stitches yesterday, the tiny pricks of the scissors along her skin thrilling. The pleasure from the small stings reminded her how much power she wielded inside her nearly-healed body.

Kenden was cataloguing the weapons with the troops, preparing the ones that would be used in their upcoming trainings. Feeling restless, Evie stepped back outside, leaving her arms bare.

Approaching Kenden's stump where he split the logs used for the fireplace, she spotted the squirrel. It sat atop the weathered stub, furiously munching an acorn from a nearby tree. Focusing on the animal, she narrowed her eyes.

The freezing spell took hold immediately. The squirrel pondered her, his beady pupils locked on to hers. Did it comprehend the supremacy she held? That she could squash his furry body with barely a thought?

Closing her lids, she tilted her face to the sky, keeping the animal immobile. Inhaling, she finally let the true strength of the evil she'd felt from Crimeous during their battle at the playground saturate her bones. Clenching her teeth, she fisted her hands, imagining crushing the necks of Vampyre and Slayer soldiers, faceless and weak. This is what would happen if she joined her father in his quest to defeat his enemies. She'd murder so many, and the extreme pleasure she would feel would be beyond compare. By the goddess, she could feel it now. It was exalting.

Her phone vibrated in her back jean pocket, pulling her from her thoughts. Scowling, she released her hold on the squirrel and watched it scurry away. Lifting the phone, she spoke.

"Hello," she said, her voice quiet even though she'd mostly regained the ability to speak normally.

"Hey," Kenden's warm voice replied. It was so serene against the raging emotions coursing through her body. "I'm almost done here. Miranda wants to know if you'd like to have dinner at the castle."

Evie deliberated, kicking the grass with the toe of her sandal. Her sister could read her well. Would she suspect the direction that Evie's thoughts had strayed since her injury? Not wanting to find out, Evie cleared her throat.

"I'm good, but you should stay. She loves spending time with you. I'm tired anyway and will probably go to bed early. I want to be ready to fight again next week."

Silence stretched, causing Evie's pulse to quicken. Kenden had become so adept at understanding her moods. Did he suspect her musings? What would that mean for the fledgling trust they'd begun to develop?

"Okay," he said, the word crackling through the device. "But please, don't go to your cabin. I'll be home in a few hours. I want to be with you tonight."

Hating how her heart slammed at his words, she lightened her tone. "Only if you promise to fuck me. Otherwise, I've reached my cuddling limit."

The reverent timbre of his chuckle enveloped her, causing her to shiver. "I'm going to make you feel so good, sweetheart. You'll be begging me to give you a break."

"Deal," she said, her lips curving. "See ya in a bit."

"See ya," he said.

Disconnecting, she noticed the little acorn-eating bugger was back, perched on the stump, taunting her. Tamping down the desire to snap its neck, she realized it reminded her of Kenden. Too trusting of her nearness; too open to her presence. Lifting her hand, she drew the squirrel toward her with her mind.

Clutching the fuzzy body in her hand, she gazed into its eyes. "Careful, little rodent. Trusting souls are always the first to be tempered by evil witches." The animal wriggled in her grasp, its claws scratching the skin of her hand, causing her to bleed in several places. Reveling in the pain of each one of the welts, she eventually threw the creature to the ground and watched it run away. Hopefully for good this time. Because next time, she might not be so nice.

Heading inside, she found Kenden's first-aid kit and cleaned the wounds, deciding she would tell him she hurt it cooking. Yes, he would believe that. For he was just as trusting as the tiny squirrel.

Chapter 24

On Monday morning Miranda called a combined council meeting. The members sat around the large table in her royal chambers, the mood somber.

"Thank you all for coming," Miranda said from her perch at the head of the table. "I've asked Evie to join us so that we can discuss next steps. It's time for us to plan the final assault on Crimeous. First of all, I'd like to thank Evie for stepping in and saving our asses during the last attack. We're all grateful to you and hope you're feeling better."

Evie regarded them from the leather seat at the opposite end of the table. Extremely uncomfortable with the unwanted gratitude, she gave a curt nod. "Good to go. I'm ready to form a battle plan and fight with you all."

Kenden's gaze was filled with concern as he sat to her right. "If you need more time, we can give it to you. I don't want you to reopen your wound." He covered her hand with his.

Drawing it away, Evie narrowed her eyes. "I'm fine," she said, trying to keep herself from snapping. Nothing would be accomplished if she let the always-boiling anger inside get the best of her. "I'm ready to attack the bastard."

Heden stood, holding a TEC in his hands. "I've revamped the TEC so that it has a bunch of new features." Maneuvering the weapon in his hand, he showcased the differences as he spoke. "The blade it deploys is now an inch longer and releases a half a second quicker. It won't seem like much, but in a battle where every moment counts, it can save lives."

"Sweet," Miranda said, lifting one of the prototypes that Heden had brought with him from the table. "And you worked on adding a solar component?"

"Yup," Heden said, nodding as he rotated his wrist and pointed at the now-deployed blade. "Each edge of the updated TEC is now embedded with the solar components of the SSW. They're not as potent as the SSWs, since they're smaller, but they should be able to maim Crimeous now. I'm hoping that they can paralyze him long enough for Evie and Darkrip to generate the barrier they need to surround him."

Darkrip spoke from his seat between Kenden and Lila. "Evie and I have had an extremely difficult time generating the combined force-field. I think that we need to spend the mornings working on that. In the afternoon sessions, we can spar with the troops and have them try to disable and disarm us. If we can't figure out how to immobilize Crimeous and stop him from interfering with my powers, then Evie won't be able to strike him down."

"Agreed," Latimus said in his deep baritone. "I think we need three solid months to form a perfectly executed battle plan. We'll alternate training weeks at Uteria and Astaria, so the soldiers can see their wives on alternative weeks. The visiting soldiers can bunk at each compound. Sound good?" he asked, training his ice-blue irises on Kenden.

"Absolutely," Kenden said with a nod. "Three months is a perfect timeframe. It will also give soldiers time to get their affairs in order. Although we're going to try our best to lose as few as possible, there will be casualties." Settling his forearms on the desk, he leaned forward to make eye contact with each of the council members. "You all should do the same. This will be the biggest attack we've ever staged upon Crimeous. His army has grown exceptionally large. If we fail, there is a possibility that he will find a way to overtake the compounds and begin systematically murdering our people. He'll start with aristocrats and work his way down. I don't want to be morbid, but we have to be realistic about what's ahead."

"No fucking way," Miranda said, her hands forming fists at her sides. "I appreciate your attempt at foresight, Ken, but there's no way in hell that bastard is going to beat us. You all can prepare if you want, but I'll never allow that thought to enter my mind. It's just not happening."

Sathan stood and placed his arm across Miranda's shoulders, drawing her in to his side. "Well, you all heard my wife. I've learned not to argue with her when she's dead-set on something." Miranda scrunched her features at him, causing him to give her a good-natured peck on the lips.

"Seriously, guys," Heden said, relaxing back into the leather chair. "I have no desire to be the last of the Vampyre royals. Ruling would force me to get married and produce an heir, and I have other priorities. There are so many new compounds of hot women that I haven't had the opportunity to, um, spend time with."

"Could we possibly have one meeting where you don't turn everything into a joke?" Latimus grumbled.

"Honestly, I'm kind of digging the comic relief," Miranda said, smiling at Heden. "Let's all remember that this is what we're fighting for. The ability to live our lives the way we choose, unaffected by evil and war. Even if Heden's jokes are terrible, I'd sure miss hearing them." She winked at Heden, causing him to wink back as he smacked his gum between his teeth.

"The plan is set," Sathan said. "Three months of extensive training followed by a well-planned attack. Let's get started. Latimus, I'll meet you at the battlefield after Miranda and I finish the budget," he said, motioning toward her desk with his head.

With that, the meeting came to an end. The members dispersed, and Evie followed her brother, Latimus and Larkin to the Uterian sparring field, Kenden at her side.

"I don't want you to fight yet if you're not ready," he said, taking her hand as they walked. Evie resisted the urge to pull it away. His concern was choking, and she did her best to remain nonchalant.

"I'm fine," she said, smiling up at him with false confidence. "Let's do this."

They made it to the meadow, Evie grabbing a sword and proceeding to spar with a group of soldiers. The exertion of physical energy was exactly what she needed and she reveled in it under the bright morning sun.

* * * *

And so it went, the days of training and preparation turning into weeks. Evie fought like a champ, working with her brother on the combined force-field in the mornings and sparring with the troops in the afternoons. The mindless scuffling was soothing to her somehow, considering how restless she'd grown at Uteria.

Although she hadn't yet given up her cabin, she found herself staying with Kenden most nights. It was just easier since she could transport them from Astaria the weeks that they trained there. Once home, they fell into a seamless rhythm. She would cook, always something succulent and amazing. Kenden would clean the pots and pans, load the plates in the dishwasher, and they would share a glass of wine by the fire.

It was comfortable. Familiar. Easy. And that scared the living hell out of Evie.

Some nights, she would need space. Kenden seemed to sense that and would stay out of her way. She would walk under the stars to the wooden swing-bench her handy man had built. It sat under a large oak tree, and Evie would sip her wine as she soaked up the silence.

Her father's words had rankled her. As the weeks passed, she couldn't seem to get them out of her head. They burrowed inside, threating to drown her in self-doubt. Increasingly becoming convinced that she wasn't the savior, she contemplated what this would mean. It would be a huge letdown and leave her without a clear path forward. Would anyone even tolerate her presence if she failed?

And then, there were the feelings of viciousness and supremacy she'd felt when she let her father's true essence run through her veins. They were so appealing; so utterly magnificent. They embodied true authority, the likes of which she'd never known. If she did choose to join Crimeous and let him combine his wicked powers with hers, they would be unstoppable. The indomitable strength she would have was unimaginable. No one would dismiss her then, would they?

"Whatcha thinking about, out here all alone?" Kenden's deep voice asked behind her.

"Nothing," she said, noting how the swing creaked as he sat beside her. Stretching his broad arm across her shoulders, they wafted back and forth under the gorgeous night sky, filled with numerous twinkling stars.

"I can't give you a life as exciting as the one you had in the human world," he said, grasping her hand atop her thigh as her other one clutched her glass. "I know it's hard to imagine what we could build together, but it could be exciting in its own way. You could govern the new compound, and I'd transition the troops from combat to a law-enforcement body. Your father would be gone, and we'd be free to make a life together. Make a family together. If you're open to that."

Evie inhaled a deep breath, the resulting sigh sad and slow. "I don't want those things, Ken." She stared at the moon-glistened grass, unable to meet his gaze.

"Not even with me? You seem to like spending time with me. I can't get you to leave my house most of the time." He bumped his shoulder against hers, acknowledging his teasing.

Tilting her head back, she closed her eyes, breathing in the fragrant air of the immortal world's balmy evening. "If it was going to be with anyone, it would be with you. But I'm too restless. Too unpredictable. Your children would have my father's wretched blood. It's unthinkable."

He didn't answer. The warmth of his hand seeped into hers as they rocked back and forth. Eventually, he spoke.

"I don't mind if they have his blood. It's something I've thought about a lot. If it means I get to build a life with you, then I accept it. It won't be easy, raising children with your powers, but it will be worth it. You're worth it, Evie."

Unable to comprehend how he could make such a sacrifice, she turned her head, locking on to his eyes. "No, I'm not."

His gorgeous smile was immediate. "Yes, you are."

"God, you're infuriating," she said, shaking her head. "Why do you love me, Ken?"

The time for skirting around the truth was over. She knew it as well as he did. He loved her, sure as the day was long. A fact that stunned the hell out of Evie.

Lifting their joined hands to his mouth, he kissed the back of hers. "We just fit, Evie. In every damn way. I'm a steady war commander who possesses a deep well of compassion with a hefty side of savior-complex. I lived for so long without passion and spontaneity, telling myself I didn't need them, but that wasn't true. You're the first person who's ever gained the upper hand on me. Every smart general understands the importance of aligning with someone who sees their vulnerabilities. It only makes them stronger. *You* make me stronger," he said, squeezing her hand.

"You're a frustratingly complex woman who needs to be challenged and loved by someone who's not afraid of you. It's time you had a partner who sees past your beauty to the remarkable woman inside. I can't imagine two people who need each other more than we do. It's meant to be."

"I won't be able to make you happy," she said softly. "And I won't consider having children. I would be a terrible mother."

"I've seen you with Tordor and Jack. You're a natural, sweetheart."

"Jack is pretty damn awesome," she said, feeling her lips curve. "That kid would challenge my father to a fight if he thought he had a chance to win. I admire his spirit."

"See?" Kenden asked, lacing his fingers with hers. "We could have a bunch of little Jacks, running around and driving us nuts. I'd love that."

"Good grief," she said, chuckling in spite of herself. "You're living in a fantasy world."

His arm tightened around her shoulders, drawing her close. "Don't knock it till you try it. I won't make you decide anything now. Let's focus on defeating your father. But, as I've stated to you before, I'm not like the other men you've been with. I'm stubborn and I'm not letting you run away from me. You can try, but it's not happening."

"I'm pretty good at hiding," she said, resting her head against his shoulder. He felt so solid, so sure. "If I don't want to be found, you won't find me. Believe me."

"We'll see, sweetheart," he said, placing a kiss on her hair. "We'll see."

There, under the moon, they swung slowly. Evie thought about telling him how far her mind had been wandering lately, relishing the evil she could possess if she united with her father. Then, she dismissed the notion. She would never align with the bastard who had harmed her so violently, all those centuries ago. Her hate for the vile creature was so much greater than her lust for ultimate supremacy. Wasn't it?

Hoping with all her might that it was, she relaxed into Kenden's body under the darkened sky.

Chapter 25

Aron awaited Max at the small table in the coffee shop. Looking at his watch, he hoped the man arrived soon. He'd requested to meet here early, and Aron had a council meeting to get to.

Maximillian breezed through the door, the tiny bell ringing behind him. Giving Aron a wave, he sauntered to the counter to order a coffee and then approached the table. Sitting down across from Aron, he pulled an envelope out of his pants pocket.

"Great to see you, Max," Aron said cordially. "You look well. How's the new baby?"

"Wonderful," the man said, eyes shining as he sipped the coffee that the barista brought over. "She's a handful though. Now that we have three kids, I've decided my wife has formed a master plan to drive me insane. She's already talking about having a fourth. I don't know where she thinks we'll fit another one." Amusement sparkled in his eyes.

"You come from a long line of aristocrats who own half the real estate in Uteria's main square," Aron said, sitting back in his chair and crossing his arms. "I'm sure you'll find some space."

"Well, you know what they say, 'Happy wife, happy life.' I don't really have a choice."

Aron chuckled. "You love Bonita to pieces and you're a great father. Another child will be a welcome addition."

"And what about you?" Max asked. "You haven't married after all these centuries. The only woman you've shown interest in is the queen, and unfortunately, she's taken."

"Yes," Aron said, frustrated yet again at what a disaster his love life was. "Maybe I'll become a monk."

"Don't be silly," Max said, waving his hand. "You're going to be a great father. What about Moira? You two were spending so much time together. I was sure you were going to court her. She's quite beautiful."

"Yes, she is," Aron said solemnly. Moira's face blazed through his mind, causing the resulting pain that he always felt when he thought of her betrayal. "But she will always belong to Diabolos."

"Well, it's too bad," Max said, pushing the envelope across the table to him. "Now that she's leaving Uteria, you've most likely lost your shot anyway."

"What do you mean?" Aron asked, picking up the envelope and opening it to observe a check.

"That's your security deposit. The lease on her apartment is up, and she's moving to Restia. She didn't tell you?"

"No," Aron said, hurt slicing through him that she would leave without telling him. But what did he expect? He'd reacted so angrily and told her never to speak to him again. She was only following his directive.

"She still doesn't know that you gave me the deposit," he said, stirring his coffee. "You were clear that you didn't want me to tell her. It was a nice thing to do for someone in her position."

"And what position is that?" Aron asked, not liking the tone of his aristocratic friend's voice.

"You know," Max said, shrugging. "A poor servant's daughter. Although she married Diabolos, she'll never be one of us."

"One of us," Aron said, his voice flat.

"An aristocrat with a proud lineage. We're the true bloodline of the Slayers, Aron. You know this. Moira's a very nice woman but she'll never rise to our status."

Blood boiled inside Aron's veins as he listened to the man across from him, whom he considered a friend. He absolutely detested the classism that existed in their kingdom and had always done his best to squash it. How dare he speak of Moira that way? Aron had never known a woman kinder and humbler, or more fun and full of life. Aching for her, he realized how much he missed her. By the goddess, he had dismissed her without a thought, not even giving her the opportunity to explain. Someone as guileless as Moira must've had a reason to lie to him so vehemently, no?

Standing, the legs of Aron's chair made an abrupt scraping noise on the tiled floor. "I don't appreciate you speaking of Moira or anyone with a laborer's bloodline that way. You know that type of prejudice is everything I abhor. Do better, Max. You sound like an ass. Thanks for the check." Giving him a nod, he exited the restaurant.

Walking under the bright morning sun, Aron allowed himself to contemplate all the scenarios as to why Moira would deceive him. Unable to come up with anything, he jogged up the stairs to the main castle at Uteria. Entering Miranda's royal office chamber, he sat down for the combined council meeting.

The attack on Crimeous was two weeks away. Latimus and Kenden had been training the troops extensively for two and a half months. They were prepared and ready. Evie and Darkrip updated everyone on their progress with the combined force-field. Although it wasn't perfect, they felt they had progressed enough to generate a barrier strong enough to immobilize the Dark Lord while Evie struck him. Evie explained that Sadie and Nolan had tested her blood, and there was indeed a different DNA imprint than Darkrip's preventing the shield from being seamless. It was a mystery to them, as the two siblings should've shared the same DNA.

Resigned to the battle, Evie still appeared confident that she would succeed. Aron hoped so, as he was ready to rid the world of the evil Deamon. He craved peace so badly and wanted to help Miranda build their kingdom to the preeminence it should have as one of Etherya's species' domains.

When the meeting was over, Miranda asked Aron to hang back so she could speak with him privately. Once everyone had exited the room, she sat on the edge of her mahogany desk, her leg swinging over the side. Aron stood a few feet from her, his back to the open window. A soft breeze blew against his neck as he waited for her to speak.

The queen's almond-shaped green eyes studied him as she seemed to struggle with what to say. Straightening her spine, she inhaled a deep breath.

"What the hell are you doing, Aron?" she finally asked.

"Excuse me?" he asked, confused by her slightly angry tone.

"With Moira," she said, looking quite disappointed in him. "What are you trying to prove? Yes, she lied to you. And yes, it was a huge deception. But have you ever asked her why? Or do you expect everyone to be perfect like you? Believe me, none of us have a shot. I'm sorry to tell you that." She lifted her arms and shrugged.

Sighing, Aron turned to the window, looking out over the green meadow behind the castle. "I'm nowhere near perfect, Miranda. You know that. I never claimed to be."

"Well, you're pretty damn close. Unfortunately, the rest of us fuck up. A lot. Moira should've told you where she was for the past eight hundred years. I'm not exonerating her for that. But you didn't even give her the benefit of the doubt. It's so unlike you. I don't understand why."

"I should've never touched her," he said, his hands resting in his pockets. "I always felt quite guilty about it. She was my best friend's wife. I coveted her even though I shouldn't have, and now, I've betrayed him so viciously for a woman who blatantly deceived me."

"I didn't know Diabolos well," Miranda said. "I hated those royal fundraising dinners my father threw and rarely attended them. But I do remember the reputation he had. It was as a vain man who liked to show off his money and possessions."

"As does every aristocrat in our kingdom," Aron said, turning to face her. "They're all pretentious assholes. If I didn't speak to those who flaunted their worth, I wouldn't have any friends at all."

Miranda smiled. "That's probably true. But you seem to hold him on a pedestal. I know you grew up with him, but have you ever considered the possibility that he wasn't as good a man as you thought?"

Aron felt his brow furrow. "Why would I ever consider that possibility?"

Miranda drew in a deep breath, rubbing her upper arm. "When you were with Moira, did you ever happen to see a scar by her hairline, above her neck?"

"No," he said, searching his brain to see if he recalled such a thing.

Miranda nodded and gnawed her bottom lip. "I don't want to betray Moira's trust but I think you need to ask her to show you her scar."

Aron's heart started to pound in his chest. "And why would I do that?"

Standing, Miranda approached him and clutched his hands. "You're a very intelligent man, Aron. I think that if you search really hard, you're going to find the answer. I don't think you'll like it but I think that somewhere, in a place you don't want to acknowledge, you know the truth."

Realization flooded Aron as he stared down at the queen. Flashes of memories from all his centuries on Earth.

The night when Moira had worn the large hat to one of their formal balls, commenting that Diabolos liked how she looked in it. She'd worn it the entire night, covering her forehead and temples.

The hot summer days where she'd worn long sleeved sweaters when they'd gone walking by the river. Aron had always chided her for not dressing appropriately for the climate.

The times when she'd winced when sitting down at the large dining room table where the three of them had dinner. She would laugh in her always affable way and tell the latest story of how her clumsiness had led to her obtaining a rather large bruise on her leg.

They were covers. All of them. Shields and stories to hide her wounds. A wave of nausea consumed Aron as the awareness set in. Diabolos, the man he'd trusted most in the world, had beaten his wife.

"It sucks," Miranda said, squeezing his hands. "To realize that someone we trust is a terrible person. I went through it when I discovered Sathan's letters to my father, buried in his desk for so many centuries. It's heartbreaking. And a good reminder that things aren't always what they seem."

Lifting a hand to his temple, Aron rubbed his forehead with the pads of his fingers. "How could I have not seen it?"

Releasing him, she perched back on the side of the desk. "Sometimes, we aren't ready to see things that are painful. But at least now, you know the truth. She ran away to escape her husband, Aron. Latimus protected her. I think they found comfort in each other during a time that they both severely needed it. I can't fault her for saving herself. Can you?"

"Damn it!" he said, running his hand through his hair. "I feel like such a fool. This whole mess has been awful and extremely embarrassing. You'd think I would've gotten smarter after you rejected me cold."

Laughing, she stood, looking at him with such admiration. "I care for you so much, Aron. I always have. But we were never quite right for each other. I know you realize that now. Sathan is my match in every way. Just as Moira is yours. It's so clear to me. I don't understand why you would throw that away. If Sathan lied to me, I would be pissed for sure and I'd give him hell about it. But I'd also give him the benefit of the doubt because I love him so damn much."

"I need to do the same," Aron said, looking dejectedly at the floor. "God, I'm such an idiot."

"Well, there's still time if you hurry. She's moving to Restia today. I tried to talk her out of it, but she's convinced she has nothing to stay here for. If I were you, I'd hurry up and change her mind."

"Thank you, Miranda," he said, pulling her in for a hug.

"You're welcome," she said, placing a kiss on his cheek. "Now, go get your woman."

Not needing any further urging, Aron fled the room.

* * * *

Moira's eyebrows drew together at the knock on the door. Were the movers here already? They weren't supposed to come for another hour. Lila and Miranda had insisted on hiring professional movers for her trek to Restia, although Moira didn't want their charity. Eventually, she'd realized that arguing with the two women was futile and she'd let them hire the men. Walking over to the door, she pulled it open.

"I still have a few boxes to pack, but you can start on those—"

Her hand stilled in mid-gesture as she realized who was at the door. "Aron?"

His expression was impassive, his face too handsome for words. Mentally cursing her pounding heart, she stepped back to let him in. "Why are you here?"

His eyes darted around the room as he entered, over her half-packed boxes in the small, one-bedroom unit. Locking on to her with his gaze, he studied her.

"You're moving," he said, his tone unreadable.

"Yes," she said, nodding. "I can't afford the rent here anymore, now that I don't have the job at the gallery, and there's a restaurant that will hire me as a server at Restia."

His demeanor seemed to turn sad, along with an air of frustration. Of course, he was frustrated with her. She'd repeatedly lied to him and deceived him terribly. Understanding that she deserved no less than his vitriol, she closed the door and came to stand before him.

Staring down at her, he slowly crossed his arms over his chest. Brown irises darted back and forth between hers. The silence seemed to stretch forever, until Moira thought she might go mad.

Finally, he spoke. "Why didn't you tell me?" he asked, his voice so deep and slightly morose.

Inhaling a large breath, Moira struggled to find the courage to speak. "I thought you'd think I was a whore—" she said quietly.

"Not about your time with Latimus," he interrupted, anger flashing in his eyes. "Although, you should've told me about that too."

"I should have," she said, swallowing thickly.

"Why didn't you tell me about Diabolos?"

Moira fought to catch her breath as tears welled in her eyes. Fighting to hold them in, she clutched onto the lie she'd told for so long. Shame that she'd let her husband beat her for all those years coursed through her body, spurring the deception. "There was nothing to tell."

"No!" Aron yelled, causing her to flinch as she stared up at him. "No more lies, Moira. I'm so fucking sick of them." Uncrossing his arms, he reached for her, sliding his hands to cup her cheeks. Craving his touch for so many weeks, she couldn't stop the tears from falling. They glided over his hands, wetting them as he stared down at her. "Why?" he whispered.

"Because I didn't think you would believe me!" she cried, the words ripped from her throat. "He was your friend, wealthy and revered. I was no one."

Aron shook his head, appearing so disappointed as he stared into her. "You foolish woman. I swear to the goddess, you might just drive me into the nuthouse."

Moira was extremely uncomfortable and so shocked from his presence that a short laugh escaped her, breaking the intensity if only slightly. "You were right to be upset with me. I don't know what to say."

"I should've known when you didn't put up a fight. You *never* miss an opportunity to fight and scrape, Moira. But you let me dismiss you so easily. So fervently. I should've fucking known."

Her brow furrowed. "I don't think I've ever heard you use that word. I'm not sure what's happening right now."

"Well, I'm pissed. That happens when the woman you're crazy about spins a web of lies to protect someone who's been dead for seven centuries. I don't understand what's going on in that brain of yours."

"I didn't want to ruin your image of him," she said, pleading with him to understand. "He was your dearest friend."

"Who *beat* you," he said, clutching her face. "All those times, when you told me how clumsy you'd been. He did that to you, didn't he?"

"Yes," she whispered, closing her lids as the tears fell.

"And this," he said, sliding his hand to lift her hair. Aron sucked in a breath as he traced his fingertip down her long and ugly scar, adjacent to her hairline. "My god, Moira. How did you even survive?"

"Barely," she said, opening her eyes to look at him. "The night he gave me this scar was the night I left. I ran straight into the raid and found Latimus and never looked back. I'm so sorry, Aron. I just...I didn't know what to do."

Lowering his forehead to hers, his eyes seemed to glisten with their own unspent tears. "My god. All those years. All this time. I should've never let him have you. I should've fought for you and married you when we were young. I was trying to give you what you wanted, but Evie's right. It's time I stepped to the front of the damn line. To hell with being courteous and polite. I'm done with that."

"You couldn't have married a servant's daughter," she said, shaking her head against his.

"Says who? Some old curmudgeon who wrote a soothsayer manual a hundred centuries ago? Give me a break, Moira."

"But you always said you wanted a virgin with a pristine bloodline."

"I can't help how I was raised, Moira. I'm sure I said those things in my youth, when I was inexperienced and stupid. But you of all people should know that I don't see bloodlines when I look at people. How can you not have faith in me on that at least?"

"I should've had faith in you," she said, palming his cheeks as she drowned in remorse. "I should've told you about Diabolos and my time at Astaria and believed that you wanted me for me. But it's too late. I messed everything up."

"Did you?" he asked, his lips curving. "Are we that far gone?"

"How can you want me now? My deception was unforgivable."

"I'm so pissed, angel. At myself and at you and at this whole situation. But there's one thing I'm very clear about. I'm bone-deep in love with you. So deep that if I lose you, I don't know how I'll go on in this lonely-as-hell world. So, yes, we have a lot to figure out, but I need you to stop doubting that I want you. I've always wanted you, somewhere inside. It just took me a few centuries to figure it out."

"Aron," she breathed, aligning her body with his. "I'm not good enough for you."

"Shut up, Moira," he said, dropping his arms to clutch her around the waist. Drawing her in to his body, he placed his lips over hers.

Sinking her fingers into his hair, she moaned, lifting to her toes to meet his questing tongue. Sliding over each other, they devoured the taste of their love and desire. Moira had missed him dreadfully, and her body trembled as he kissed her so passionately.

After a small eternity, he lifted his head. "I'm pretty terrible at this romance thing and already have a complex. So, if you love me back, could you do me a favor and tell me? Because I'm really bad at getting women to say it back to—"

"I love you, you daft man," she interrupted, the waves of her laughter surrounding them. "I love you so much it hurts."

"No more hurt," he said, rubbing her nose with his. "No more pain, angel. We've had enough. I want to make you happy."

"I want to make you happy too. I promise, I'll try. I don't know if I can but I'll do everything in my power to be someone you deserve. No more lies. I promise. I'm so sorry, Aron."

"No more apologies either," he said, brushing the pad of his thumb over her lip. "Today, we're starting fresh. The past is behind us. I want to build something new with you. Are you ready for that?"

"I'm so ready," she said, her mouth almost hurting from the width of her smile. "I want to give you babies and laughter and love and whatever else I can. I want to give you everything, Aron."

"All I need is you," he said, giving her a sweet kiss. "But babies will be nice too. Making them won't be half bad either."

Moira giggled, feeling so giddy as he held her. "Oh, yeah. Making them will be awesome. Can't freaking wait."

Bending his knees, he lifted her by her butt as she squealed and wrapped her legs around his waist. "When will the movers be here?" he asked.

Moira glanced at the watch on her arm. "Forty minutes."

"Plenty of time to start baby-making," he said, carrying her to the bed. "And then, we'll have them transport your stuff to my house."

"I don't have any sheets on the bed," she said, as he threw her down gently.

Sprawling over her, he laced his fingers through hers, one on each side of her head.

"Then, we'll have to be sure not to make a mess."

Cutting off her snickers, he cemented his mouth to hers. And proceeded to show her how much fun two people could have on a sheetless mattress.

Chapter 26

Evie sat at the dressing table in her tiny cabin, applying makeup for the day's attack. One might find it strange that she would paint her face for battle, but her beauty had always been an armament for her. It gave her confidence, and the goddess knew, she needed it in spades for the feat that lay before her. For if all went well, she would kill her father today.

It was still pre-dawn, the sun not due to appear over the horizon for a half hour yet. The plan was for the troops to gather upon the sparring field at Uteria, seven hundred soldiers strong. They would load into the various hummers and tanks and head to the Deamon caves. Once inside, they would attack her father, not resting until he was dead.

Finished with her makeup, Evie stood and sheathed the Blade in the holster between her shoulder blades. The weapon felt firm upon her back, and she lifted her chin with resolve. Staring into her mother's eyes in the reflection, she vowed to be successful.

Closing her lids, she materialized to the field. Kenden jogged up to her, a huge smile on his face. "You look absolutely gorgeous," he said, admiration in his eyes as he ran the tips of his fingers over her cheek. "If they ever do a *Soldier's Weekly* magazine, you'll be the cover model for sure."

Arching a brow, she gave in to his teasing. "As I always say, it's okay to die but never okay to die ugly."

He was so achingly attractive as he grinned down at her, the curve of his lips wistful. "You're not dying today, baby," he said, lifting her chin with his fingers. "Count on it." Lowering to brush a kiss over her lips, he whispered against them, "I missed you last night."

"I needed to clear my head," she said, drawing back to stare up at him. "And besides, I'm sure you're tired of me invading your house at every turn."

"Never," he said, winking. Her damn heart almost melted at the gesture.

"You guys ready?" Latimus asked, approaching them.

"Yes," they responded, voices firm with resolve.

Miranda and Arderin stood off to the side, clutching their husbands to them as if it was the last time they'd ever see them. Evie hoped to god it wasn't.

"What is Arderin doing here?" Evie asked. "She should be at Astaria. I'm sure my father knows we're coming."

"Darkrip said she was adamant about sending him off in person. And then, he mumbled something about it being futile to argue with her." Kenden said. "We immortal men seem to find ourselves entangled with a lot of hardheaded women."

"Damn straight," Evie said with a nod.

Miranda and Arderin released their husbands, and Sathan and Darkrip began to trudge across the field to join the troops.

A jolt of lightning bolted from the gray sky, still darkened as the sun lingered below the horizon. Fire flashed, and the grass began to burn around them. Soldiers lifted their weapons, ready to take on their surprise assailants, but none could be seen. The usual war cries of the Deamons were missing.

As if in slow motion, Evie turned her head to search for Arderin. Knowing how much her father coveted the babe growing in her womb, fear slammed Evie's chest. Sure enough, Crimeous had appeared behind her, clutching him to her as he held a knife to her throat.

Darkrip screamed, his body overcome with rage and fear, and began to run toward her. The Dark Lord must've impeded his ability to dematerialize. It was the only reason he'd be approaching them on foot. Suddenly, her brother stopped short, falling to the ground, frozen.

"Call the physicians!" Crimeous yelled, his voice deep and reedy as he held the dagger to Arderin's throat. "The burned one and the human. I want the baby extricated from her body. If you do as I ask, I'll consider letting her live."

Evie slowly began approaching Crimeous across the meadow. She somehow felt it smarter to approach him slowly, rather than materialize in front of him. Any sudden movements might cause him to slash Arderin's throat. The Dark Lord seemed quite deranged as he held her, possibly from the knowledge that the vast immortal army would soon be executing an intensely skilled attack on his domain. Kenden grabbed her forearm, dragging her back a step. Staring up at him, she shook her head.

"Let me go, Ken. I have to help her. You know that."

Terror and concern swam in his coffee-colored eyes. Eventually, he released her arm. Resuming her approach, she came to stand two feet in front of her father, admiring how Arderin struggled against him although her efforts were futile.

"Let her go, Father," Evie said, trying like hell to keep her voice calm. "She's barely nine months pregnant. The child will be much more powerful if you let it gestate fully. Being a Vampyre, she needs at least two more months for it to be close to full-term."

"No!" he screamed. "She will bear the spawn now, and I will incubate it in the caves. You know nothing of my plans, you hateful child."

Drawing the Blade of Pestilence from her back, Evie clutched it with both hands. "Maybe I'll just kill you now, and the Vampyre and her spawn along with you. We certainly could use less creatures with your vile blood roaming the Earth. There's no dispute about that."

"No, Evie!" Darkrip yelled behind her. "Please, don't hurt her." Annoyed at his interference, Evie turned to give him a furious glare. Waving her hand in the air, she denigrated his ability to speak.

"That's enough intrusion from the peanut gallery," she said, making sure everyone on the field could hear. "This is between me and my father. If any of you tries to interfere again, I'll murder you. Don't test me." Sending one last determined glare across the meadow, she rotated to face her father again.

Tilting her head, she observed the creature as he clutched Arderin to his chest. Never had she seen him so unhinged; so disjointed. It was a rare crack in his usually unflappable armor, and Evie seized the opportunity to change course.

"Take me instead," she said, throwing the Blade to the ground and stretching her hand out to him. "I'm the one you want. Combining your powers with mine will make you undefeatable. We could work together to destroy Etherya's tribes in a matter of days. The babe in her belly will take decades to become that strong." Shaking her hand, she lifted her chin. "Take. Me."

"Don't do this, Evie!" Kenden yelled behind her, his voice seeming so far away. "Don't align with him. I see your struggle, but it's not you. There's another way."

Clenching her teeth, she turned to face him. His eyes pleaded with her as he stood across the meadow. "I told you *not* to interfere," she said. Jerking her head, she froze him to stone, watching him crumble to the ground. "It was inevitable that I would join him, Ken. You always knew this, somewhere deep inside. I'm sorry."

She gazed into him, willing away every scrap of emotion she'd ever felt for the kind and stubborn commander. Kenden just stared back at her from the springy grass, his eyes shining with moisture and love and silent pleas for her to make a different choice. Sighing, Evie turned back to her father.

"Well?" she asked, shrugging. "What's it going to be? The Blade is on the ground, and I'm willing to unite our abilities. The sun will rise soon and burn you to death, so you must decide quickly. Let her go, and you can have it all, Father. Are you strong enough to make the right choice?" She lifted her arm again, hand outstretched.

Crimeous' dark, beady pupils darted between hers. For one moment, Evie was sure that he'd deny her request and kill Arderin anyway. And then, with a flash of movement, he pushed Arderin to the ground. Grabbing Evie's hand, he closed his lids, dematerializing them to the main lair at the Deamon caves. Kenden's screams echoed in her head as she vanished into thin air.

Once in the lair, Evie looked around, documenting the surroundings. It wasn't so different from the space he'd held her and Rina captive, violently torturing them all those centuries ago. Light burned from torches along the rock walls. A desk sat atop a rock slab, the stone twenty feet wide and ten feet long. A bookshelf held jars with liquid in them, severed body parts floating within. Curious, Evie approached them and touched one of the jars with her finger, the glass cold and squalid.

"It's a trophy case of sorts," her father said behind her, causing her to shiver.

"How exquisite," she said, tracing the jar with the pad of her finger.

"Why did you decide to join me, child?" he asked, genuine curiosity in his gravelly voice.

Pivoting, she stared at him. This creature who had so vehemently hurt her so long ago. She thought she'd feel rage at being in his presence; instead, she just felt numb. Not a drop of emotion filled her, not even the constant wrath and anger that had churned inside her for her entire squalid existence.

"I don't know," she said, shrugging. "I think I'm curious about the evil you possess. I'd never felt the extent of it until you attacked Uteria. Mother's blood prevents me from experiencing the malevolence that deeply."

Crimeous gave a slow nod. "You've only just begun. There are so many facets to my evil. They're magnificent."

"What can I do to enhance your blood in my system more than Mother's? Surely, you have some idea."

"I could bank my blood and transfuse you. Over time, it will temper Rina's blood until there are only traces of it left. You'll become extremely powerful."

Evie nodded. "Let's start today. The immortal army will still attack, especially now that I've defected. It's imperative we work quickly."

"I have a makeshift infirmary set up where I perform the cloning of my soldiers. We can perform the first infusion today."

"Fine. But I need to get one thing straight. You were able to hurt me when I was a child because I didn't realize the scope of my capabilities. I'm not that person anymore. I'm sure you realize the extent of my abilities. You can't disable them like you can Darkrip's. Be wary, Father. I didn't fight back when I was young because I didn't know how. That's not the case anymore. Are we clear?"

"No one will attempt to lay a hand on you, child," the Dark Lord said. "I will make sure that every last Deamon receives the order."

"Good. Tell them that I'm your right-hand. We can't have any confusion on that. I need them to follow my orders if we're going to fight together."

"It will be done," Crimeous said.

"Excellent," Evie said, straightening to her full height. "Now, show me this infirmary."

* * * *

Kenden regained his ability to move shortly after he watched Evie disappear with Crimeous. Screaming at the top of his lungs for her to stay, she dematerialized away. Anguish, so vibrant and true, coursed through his muscular frame. Sitting up on the soft grass, he pulled his knees to his chest, resting his elbows atop them, and thrust his fingers into his thick hair. Cradling himself, he rocked back and forth, trying to understand why his beloved Evie would make such a choice.

"Ken," Miranda called softly, her thin hand resting on his shoulder.

"No!" he cried, the magnitude of the pain he was experiencing unlike anything he'd ever felt, even when his parents died all those centuries ago.

Expelling a large breath, Miranda sat on the ground, encircling him with her arms. Together, they rocked, contemplating the huge loss that had just occurred.

Latimus wrangled the men in the background, telling them to take an hour's break before returning to the field to train. The battle would be postponed, all their plans destroyed, now that Evie had defected.

Defeated, Kenden raised his head to look at his cousin. "How could she join with him, Miranda? I don't understand."

"She saved Arderin. Maybe she saw it as the only way to accomplish that. I don't know."

Giving a ragged sigh, he ran his hand through his hair. "I need to think. I can't do it here. I need to go to my shed." Standing, he pulled Miranda up beside him by her outstretched hand.

"Can you train the troops on your own today?" Kenden asked Latimus as he approached them.

"Yes," Latimus said, concern in his expression. "But if you need me, I'm here."

"Thanks," Kenden said. "I just need some time alone to process this. Give me a few hours. I'll come find you after lunch."

Dejected, he hopped into a nearby four-wheeler and drove to his shed. It had always been the place where he could think clearly. The one point of solace where his fastidious mind could brainstorm a solution to any problem. And boy, did he need a solution now.

Entering the shack, he closed the door behind him and switched on the lightbulb that hung overhead. Walking to the wall, he gently touched the nails that protruded from the wood. He'd hurt Evie with them although he hadn't meant to. Remembering the passion that they shared in the small space threatened to rip his heart open.

Walking over to the table, he sat on the stool. The maps of the Deamon caves were spread out before him, and he slid his palm over them. Studying them, he visualized where Evie was now. Pointing to a certain spot with his finger, he trained all his energy on that one point. It was Crimeous' main lair, the one he'd been using after Kenden and Latimus destroyed so many others when they were looking for Arderin and Darkrip. Evie was there now—of that, he had no doubt. Rubbing the map with his fingers, he felt tears well in his eyes. Wanting so badly to see her and ask why she'd chosen her Father over them, he concentrated on the spot.

Slowly, as if in a vision, the tip of his finger seemed to warm. Feeling his eyebrows draw together, Kenden resumed stroking the paper, amazed that it continued to grow hot under his touch. After a moment, the site began to shoot sparks, and then, a small piece burst into flames. Unable to believe the spontaneous combustion, Kenden grabbed a nearby water bottle, dousing the fire.

"It is a sign, my child," an airy voice said.

Lifting his head, Kenden regarded Etherya. Unsure what to do, he observed her with wide eyes. The Slayers had disowned the goddess after the Awakening, and he hadn't worshipped her in centuries. Was he supposed to bow? Or kneel?

"It is okay, son," Etherya said, floating toward him as long, red curls stretched behind. "You do not need to address me in any certain way. Goddess is fine."

"Hello, Goddess," he said, giving a reverent nod. "I'm a bit shocked at your presence."

Black irises studied him as she hovered in front of his body. "You lost your faith in me, child, but I never wavered in my faith for you. Your protection of your people is honorable. I am so proud of you."

"Thank you," he said, swallowing deeply. Always a straight-shooter, he asked the question burning in his mind. "Why did she defect, Goddess?"

"These things are always unclear. She has been struggling with her desire to align with him since he attacked Uteria months ago. She wanted to tell you but was afraid. Evie has much fear when it comes to you."

"Why?" he asked. "When I love her so much? She knows this to be true, I have no doubt."

Etherya sighed. "There is a difference between what one knows and what one believes, deep within. She is consumed by fear that your love for her is conditional."

"Upon what?"

"Many things," Etherya said. "Whether she is the one to fulfill the prophecy. Whether you'll love her once you realize how evil she is inside. Whether that malevolence will destroy all that she loves, especially any children she would have with you. Her terror fuels her doubt; her doubt fuels her self-hatred. Eventually, it will destroy her."

"I won't let that happen," Kenden said, so firm in his belief of Evie's goodness. It had always been there, located under all the internal armor she'd built. He wouldn't give up until he extricated it fully and succeeded in his efforts to help her live by it.

"That is good, Commander," Etherya said. "Your faith in her makes her strong. Things are not always as they seem. She sent you a message. One of fire, through the map." The goddess gestured to the table with her fiery head. "You need to be smart enough to listen."

Creating distance between them, the goddess began to float away. "I have already angered the Universe enough. You must discern this on your own. But you are on the right path. Stay true in your belief of her. It is warranted."

"Wait," Kenden said. Slowly, he approached the goddess. Lifting one of her long strands of hair, he ran his thumb over the silken lock. "It's the same color as Evie's," he said, his tone contemplative. "I would know it anywhere after all the times I've held her. You infused her with your blood. When?"

Etherya seemed to smile, although he couldn't be sure. "Very good, Commander. You are cunning, indeed. You will do well with my Evie. She has so much of my magnificent Valktor in her. Help her use it to make the right choice. To destroy Crimeous, once and for all. Do not wait. The time to attack is near. I will be watching over you all." Lifting her airy hand, she pulled the curl from his fingers. With nary a sound, she vanished.

Shaking his head as if it was all a dream, Kenden glanced at the table. The map sat atop, a hole burned where he had touched it earlier. It was the sign he needed. Grabbing onto hope that Evie could still be turned back to their side, he ran into the morning sunlight to tell Miranda of his encounter with the goddess.

Chapter 27

Three weeks later, the immortal army was ready to attack again. They'd needed the time to prepare an assault that wasn't centered around Evie. The new strategy was to charge forward with their massive militia, Darkrip carrying the Blade upon his back. Once he, Kenden and Latimus isolated Crimeous and Evie, they would do their best to sway her back to their side. If she turned, Darkrip would generate the force-field with her and hand her the Blade to strike down the Dark Lord.

If she didn't make the choice to reenlist with them...well, Kenden wasn't sure he would survive. All his love for the glorious beauty was entangled in the belief that she had goodness inside; that she would choose her Slayer half when everything was on the line. If she didn't, their world would be plunged into chaos. The immortal army would never be able to defeat the father-daughter powerhouse. His people would suffer, centuries upon centuries of war, until they would most likely be exterminated.

Kenden stood atop the hill that crested over the sparring field at Uteria, the just-risen sun shining upon him as his hair blew in the breeze. Arms crossed over his broad chest, he observed the soldiers. They were ready. All his centuries of training had come down to this one battle. Clenching his jaw, he hoped like hell they would succeed.

"The men are prepared," Latimus' baritone voice chimed as he came to stand beside him. "We won't fail."

"We can't fail," Kenden said, gaze trained on the troops. "It's time for our people to live in a world without war."

They stood silent, bodies firm, arms crossed, as they observed the massive army they'd built.

"How's Adelyn?" Kenden asked, tilting his head toward Latimus.

The hulking Vampyre, known for being so brooding and curt, broke into a beaming smile. "Amazing. When Lila brought her home a few weeks ago, I was a bit shocked. But we'd been discussing adopting an infant for a while. She's the most adorable thing I've ever seen. I'm already in love with her."

"That's great, man," Kenden said, patting him on the back. "I'm so happy for you guys."

"Yeah," he said, his grin comprising the width of his face. "It's unbelievable. I never thought I'd have anything like this. Lila is the most incredible person on the planet. I'm a lucky bastard."

"She's pretty awesome," Kenden said with a nod.

Latimus blinked down at him. "I'm sorry about Evie, Ken. I really am. I hope we can turn her."

"We can," he said, so confident that Evie still possessed righteousness within. "I won't contemplate anything else. She's going to join us today and murder that bastard. I feel it with everything I have."

"Okay, then," Latimus said. "Let's get to it. I'll lead the troops attacking from overhead in the Hummer, and you'll lead the ground troops with the tanks."

"Ten-four," he said.

"Once we hear you charging, we'll detonate the explosives and enter from above. He'll know we're coming, but we're equipped. I've never seen the men so determined."

"Me neither," Kenden said. "Let's go."

Knowing that all the words had been said, they plodded down the hill to meet their army. Wrangling the troops, they bounded into their armored vehicles and led them to battle.

* * * *

Evie milled around the quiet cave, situated down a long hallway from Crimeous' main lair. The troops were on their way to attack. Evie could see this, as she knew her father could, and she prepared by donning her war clothes. Black yoga pants, sneakers and a thin turtleneck. She'd placed a spell upon them, so if she was struck, the blades or bullets would bounce off. The high neck was so that she didn't get her throat sliced open again. It had been rather uncomfortable, and she'd like not to repeat the experience, if possible.

Sighing, she gathered her thick hair in a ponytail, securing it so that it bobbed behind her head. Ready as she'd ever be, she transported to the main lair to join her father.

"You are ready for battle," Crimeous said, his pointed teeth glistening with saliva from the nearby torchlight. "It will not be easy. Latimus and Kenden have built a strong army."

Evie shrugged. "Nothing will ever be as strong as our combined powers. You know this, as I do. We'll decimate them. There's no other option."

Her father's pleasure at her words coursed through her. Now that she'd been banking his blood for several weeks, she could read his thoughts so well. He was mad with power, drunk with vengeance and starving for destruction. It was a potent combination of extreme maliciousness that Evie had never experienced. It made her both nauseous and exulted. A dangerous amalgamation indeed.

From high atop the rock slab, she pivoted to observe Crimeous' Deamon soldiers. They were a mighty force but not as strong as the immortal army. Many were evil, as wicked as her father. But some carried flashes of emotion and surges of conscience, causing Evie to remember her sister's wish to allow those who genuinely wanted to repent a chance at reformation. If, by some small chance, Crimeous was defeated, it would be those soldiers who benefitted from her sister's wise benevolence.

Closing her eyes, she sensed their approach. Waves upon waves of Vampyre and Slayer soldiers, charging to destroy the most spiteful creature who'd ever walked Etherya's Earth.

"Are you ready, child?" her father asked behind her.

Gritting her teeth at the term he insisted on calling her, she nodded, not bothering to turn around. "I'm ready. Let's kick some ass."

"Good. They're here."

Straightening her spine, Evie readied for the attack.

Chapter 28

Kenden marched the troops through the mouth of the cave, feeling confident as five hundred strong paraded behind him. Latimus would lead two hundred more through the holes that he blew open in the ground above, and together, they'd set about decimating the Dark Lord.

"I'll materialize to the top of the slab when I see an opening," Darkrip said beside him. "My father and Evie will be up there, letting the soldiers below take the brunt of the battle. Once you see me ascend, it's imperative you climb up and join me. We have no chance of swaying her without you. You're the only person still capable of turning her."

"I'll be there," Kenden said, observing the light from the lair begin to shine in the darkened cave. "May the gods be with you."

"I think we might need more help than even they can give, but what's the hell in asking?" Darkrip said. Gritting his teeth, he began to jog forward. Kenden yelled, "Charge!" and the cries of war erupted behind him. Resolved, he trudged into battle.

Metal clattered and shots sounded as the Deamons retaliated. Every clank that Kenden encountered as his sword struck against another enthralled him. Pulling a TEC from the arsenal around his waist, he attached it to a Deamon's head and detonated it. The slimy creature collapsed to his death on the squalid ground.

For minutes, they fought, hand-to-hand, sword against sword, fist against TEC. Some of the soldiers had guns, but Kenden never once felt the spray of bullets. Was it too much to hope that Evie was disintegrating them from her perch atop the slab, secretly helping their cause?

Pulling his thoughts back to the battle, Kenden clenched his jaw as he proceeded to destroy several more Deamons. Latimus was fighting off to his far right, his soldiers engaged and determined as Sathan fought by his side.

Approaching the slab, Kenden spied Evie. She fought the few Vampyre and Slayer soldiers who crested the stone, pushing them off as their weapons vanished to thin air. She wasn't killing them, and suddenly, he knew.

She'd defected to deceive her father. This entire time, she'd been on their side. He remembered her olive orbs, latched on to him before she disappeared. He'd been too consumed by fear to read the message in them: *Trust me.*

Filled with more love for her than he'd ever envisioned, he blazed a path toward the slab, striking Deamons along the way. Darkrip materialized to the top and began fighting his father with the Blade of Pestilence. Evie watched them from feet away, frozen, unsure whom to help.

Crimeous' sword, forged from poisoned steel, clashed against the Blade as father and son fought. Sheathing his sword in the carrier upon his back, Kenden scaled the large rock. Finding his footing on the surface, he drew a TEC from his belt. Approaching Crimeous, he saw an opening and attached it to his head, deploying it immediately.

The Dark Lord wailed in pain, dropping his sword as he clutched his forehead. Thanks to Heden's improvements, it was capable of harming Crimeous, but Kenden knew they only had moments before he recovered.

"Form the force-field!" Kenden yelled. Evie jolted at his voice, her wide eyes locking on to his. "You can do this, Evie," he said, his voice calm amidst the terrible clanking below. "I believe in you. I always have. I know you didn't betray us."

"I've been banking his blood, Ken," she said, swallowing thickly. "It's changed something in me. I did it to read his thoughts. To gain an advantage. But I think it's turned me into something even more sinister." Her gaze fell to her father struggling beside her and then landed on Darkrip. "I don't know if I can end him. My body is craving more of his blood. More of his evil. It's...*glorious*," she almost whispered, closing her eyes and tilting her face toward the heavens.

"I don't care how much of his blood you infuse," Kenden said, slowly closing the distance between them. "You will always be Rina's daughter and you will always have goodness inside." Reaching her, he placed his fingers under her chin. When she opened them, his eyes bore into her. "I love you, Evie. No matter how much of him is inside you. It's time for you to fulfill your destiny and kill him." Thrusting his hand toward Darkrip, he accepted the weapon that the Slayer-Deamon handed him. Wrapping her hand around the handle of the Blade of Pestilence, he clutched it with his own. "I believe in you."

"How sweet," Crimeous chided, recovering from the blow from the TEC and giving a malicious cackle. Picking up the poison-tipped sword beside him, he lifted it for battle. With a vicious cry, he swung his arms behind his head and attacked Kenden.

Quick to react, Kenden pulled an SSW from his belt and extended the glowing blade. The armaments clashed against each other as they fought, a battle of good and evil exemplified in the squalid lair.

Darkrip extended both hands, a cloudy plasma forming around them and extending out from his body. Latching his gaze on to Evie's, he implored her. "Form the barrier with me, Evie," he said, his deep voice rock-solid. "You can do it."

She stood for so long, a century might have passed. Forests might have grown over, civilizations might have fallen, worlds might have been destroyed. For what seemed like forever, she contemplated her brother. Ever so slowly, she sheathed the Blade in the holster upon her back. Extending her hands, the murky substance appeared. Stretching from her thin arms, it joined with Darkrip's ether. Unfortunately, after several seconds, it fizzled out.

"Fuck!" Darkrip cursed, grabbing the SSW from his belt and extending the shining ember. Crimeous gave a low chortle, pulling another weapon from the sheath on his back. The sword's blade was lined with tiny spikes dripping with poison, ready to kill any immortal with only a glance against the skin.

"The force-field won't work if you're torn, Evie!" Darkrip shouted, grunting as he battled his father. "You have to be all-in. Otherwise, we have to drag him outside and try to burn him in the sun."

Sathan crested the stone, screaming as he charged Crimeous with his SSW. "You fucking bastard!" he screamed. "You killed our child. I'll murder you!"

As they scuffled, Kenden grabbed Evie's shoulders. "Evie!" he screamed, terrified at the dazed look in her eyes. "You're too strong for this," he said, shaking her with his firm grip. "Don't choose the evil. It's not who you are anymore."

Those leaf-green orbs lifted to his, swimming with uncertainty. "I can't—"

Her words were interrupted by the sound of bullets whizzing around them. Ducking, Kenden pulled her toward him, hoping to shield her.

Disengaging from him, she lifted the Blade of Pestilence from her back, gritting her teeth as she fought the assailant: a Deamon soldier with a Glock in his hand.

Throngs of Deamon warriors began to swarm atop the slab. Lifting his SSW, Kenden attempted to hold them off. Blinded by rage against the hateful creatures, he fought tirelessly. Out of the corner of his eye, he spotted Sathan and Darkrip sparring with Crimeous. Realizing that Latimus was still leading the troops below, unless he'd been injured by an eight-shooter, he swung his weapon. There was no second chance this time. His future and that of his people depended upon his success.

Evie fought off several Deamons and pushed quite a few more Slayers and Vampyres from the elevated stone. Turning to face him, she yelled, "I'm ready! I'm not going to die today. Isolate Crimeous and stun him with a TEC. I'll form the barrier with Darkrip!"

Nodding, Kenden rushed toward the Dark Lord, waiting for an opening in between Sathan and Darkrip's blows. When he spotted one, he pounced, deploying the TEC on the pasty skin of Crimeous' forehead.

Kenden stood back as Evie jogged over. She and Darkrip extended their arms, and Kenden observed the cloudy plasma encircle the Dark Lord. Terror slowly marred Crimeous' hideous, wrinkled face as he halted, immobilized and unmoving, realizing the strength of his offsprings' combined energy.

"I'll hold the force-field, Evie," Darkrip said. "I've got it. Take the Blade and strike him."

"He's the only one on this wretched planet as evil as I am," she said, her voice so ragged it shifted something in Kenden's soul. "Once he's gone, I'll be the worst amongst us. How can I live with that?"

"I'm here, Evie," Darkrip said, his tone soothing in the dirty cave. "I have those same fears, but they're not real. Mother gave us everything we'll ever need, deep inside. You know this somewhere within but you need to have the courage to believe it. I have faith in you, and so does Ken. So do Miranda and Arderin and every single person you've drawn under your spell. You're a part of us now, and even though you're pretty damn powerful, you'll never change that."

A tear slid down her cheek, gleaming in the torchlight as she wavered.

"We can't hold him frozen forever, Evie," Darkrip said, his arms quivering with the strength he was expending to generate the barrier.

Lifting her gorgeous irises to Kenden, she asked, "How did you know I didn't defect?"

He smiled, so sure that she was going to make the right choice. "Because you love me too. And that will always outweigh any choice your Deamon side wants to make. It's so beautiful, Evie, and I'm so honored to have it."

Her nostrils flared, chin lifting slightly. Reaching behind her head, she drew the Blade from the sheath. Clutching the hilt, she swung her arms behind her head.

"Goodbye, Father," she said through clenched teeth.

Kenden waited, anxious to see her slice the Blade through his neck.

Arms held high, she stood still. So very still.

And that's when Kenden realized. Crimeous had rendered her immobile. The bastard had figured out how to manipulate her powers as he had Darkrip's. Lifting his SSW, Kenden screamed toward Darkrip and Sathan, "He's frozen her! Hold the force-field as long as you can, Darkrip!"

The laugh that enveloped the cave was so malevolent it made the hairs on Kenden's arms stand to attention. Stepping through the energy barrier that Darkrip so tenuously held, Crimeous flitted his hand through the air, effectively dispelling it.

"Did you really think it would be that easy?" Crimeous asked. "Did you truly think I wouldn't anticipate that she would choose you?" Kenden lost control of his limbs as the disgusting creature approached him, the clattering sounds of war below dulled by the ringing in his ears. Sathan and Darkrip were immobilized to his right. Staring into irises so evil, above the Dark Lord's thin nose and reedy lips, Kenden felt the loss overwhelm him. They were going to die here, in this squalid cave, at the hands of this wicked creature. He'd never get to hug Miranda again, or kiss Sadie on her beautifully imperfect cheek, or hold his gorgeous Evie in his arms.

Shrouded in despair, he stood motionless, except for the pounding of his nearly-broken heart.

Crimeous seemed to glide toward Evie as they all watched, held stationary by his immense power. Surrounding her neck with his gray hand, his thin fingers squeezed.

"Good," he said, watching her struggle to breathe. "I remember when you used to squirm like this, all those centuries ago. Perhaps I'll take you once more, to show you how stupid it was to defy me. Here, in front of the man who professes to love you. How splendid." Extending his nail, he ran it down her body, neck to abdomen, slicing the fabric of her turtleneck. Pulling the cloth from her body, he tossed it on the ground. Grabbing the Blade, he threw it to lie upon her tattered shirt. Pulling her arms to her side, he regarded her, venomous energy seeming to emanate from his lean body.

Bile rose in Kenden's throat as the monster traced the pale skin of Evie's stomach below her black sports bra. How had it come to this? He'd wanted so badly to protect her, and now, she would perish after reliving her worst memories, once more, before them all.

"There, there," Crimeous said, scratching her abdomen with his nails, filed into sharp points. "It won't be so bad. I think it will hurt the Slayer commander more than you. We'll see."

Evie's eyes darted toward the Blade, causing Kenden to notice the trembling of her fingers. How was that possible if she was immobile?

"Come closer," she said, her voice garbled. "Before you rape me, I need to tell you something."

Leaning down, his forehead almost touched hers. "What is it, child?"

Her jaw clenched so tightly that Kenden thought it might smash. "I hate it when you call me that," she said through gritted teeth.

"Then, what shall I call you, child? I'll give you that last concession before I torture and murder you."

"How about, 'Your worst fucking nightmare?'" she spat.

Opening her fingers, the Blade of Pestilence shot from the floor, straight into her palm. With a mighty yell, she thrust it into his abdomen. Crimeous cried in agony, falling backward a few steps.

"Burn in hell, you fucking asshole!"

Lifting her arms, she swished the Blade through the air, chopping off his head with one strike.

The Dark Lord's skull fell to the dirty floor, his body collapsing behind it. Heaving air through her lungs, Evie dropped the Blade to the ground, seeming shocked that she'd bested him.

"How did you regain your powers?" Kenden asked, rushing over to her.

"I'd placed a spell on my clothes. When the Blade landed on top of my shirt, I was able to pull enough energy from the magic it held to regain my abilities. Is his head reattaching?" she asked, an expression of worry overtaking her face.

Kenden, Evie, Sathan and Darkrip loomed over the severed body, watching to see if the parts congealed back together. Although Crimeous' head had been separated, his lips were still moving slightly, as if he was trying to speak. The remaining sounds of war ceased below, the troops understanding that something of great significance was occurring on the slab.

Suddenly, an enormous flash of light appeared. The goddess Etherya materialized in front of them, collapsing on her knees beside Crimeous' skull. So very gently, she picked up the cranium, placing it in her lap and stroking the gray, smooth skin at the temple.

"Etherya," the grisly whisper sounded from the barely-alive severed head. "What happened? I haven't seen you in so long."

"My beautiful Galredad," she cried, cloudy tears falling onto his face. "You lost your way so very long ago. It filled me with so much anguish. But now, you will be released from this world and can find some peace in that."

"The Passage?" he asked, blood spurting from his mouth.

"No, my friend. You have hurt too many for that. You will suffer in the Land of Lost Souls. But eternity is long, and perhaps the Universe will allow you to repent. One never understands the workings of the fickle Universe, even one as omnipotent as me. Know that I will think of you often and go knowing that you left two magnificent children behind. It is time, Galredad. Close your eyes." Lifting her cloudy hand, she gently closed his lids as the last breath exited his lips.

"All this time," Kenden said, barely able to believe the sight in front of him. "You've had a history with him all this time."

"Yes," the goddess said. Cradling Crimeous' head, she gradually set it upon the dirty ground and rose. "It is a long chronicle that you need not be bothered with. It is imperative you destroy his body, so that no others clone it." Floating over to Evie, she cupped her cheek. "Well done, my child. When I infused you with my blood, so long ago, I had hoped this would be the result. You are too brave to let your self-loathing destroy you. Please, don't let that happen. Your grandfather, mother and I love you very much." Placing a kiss to Evie's forehead, Etherya disappeared.

Kenden watched a stunned Evie lift her gaze to his, a question in them.

"I'd already figured it out," he said. "She came to see me when you defected. Her hair is identical to yours."

Evie inhaled a huge breath. "Holy shit."

"Holy shit is right," Darkrip muttered, stunned as well, as he stood beside them.

"We need to dispose of his body in the Purges of Methesda," Evie said, chin lifting with resolve. "Darkrip, you can transport the body, and I'll transport the head."

"Yes," Darkrip nodded. "Let's do it now. Ken, you'll clean up the blood? We have to make sure not one drop is left, lest someone finds it and clones it."

"Latimus, Larkin and I will take care of it," Kenden said. Strutting to Evie's side, he pulled her into his strong arms. Lowering his lips to hers, he devoured her mouth, so grateful that she was alive and unharmed.

After ending the kiss, he placed his forehead upon hers. "Wow. You just saved the world of immortals, Evie. I'm a bit in awe."

She shook her head against his, her almond eyes wide and stunned. "I've never been more overwhelmed. Maybe I'll enjoy it once we dispose of the body. I was so sure we were defeated."

"That bastard didn't stand a chance against you. You're so fucking amazing. Thank you for saving our people."

"*Your* people," she said.

"*Ours*," he corrected, placing a soft peck on her lips. "You'll realize that one day." Drawing back, he assessed her stomach and collarbone, the skin blemished with abrasions around her black sports bra. "Are you hurt anywhere?"

"No," she said, shaking her head. "Only minor scratches. I'm fine. We need to destroy the body. Come on, Darkrip. Let's do this."

She and Darkrip proceeded to pull the various parts of Crimeous' limp body close. Before they could materialize, a sound came from below. They pivoted to face the soldiers, whose fighting had ceased minutes ago.

Deamon soldiers, at least three hundred strong, simultaneously took a knee. Planting their weapons on the ground, they all trained their gazes upon Evie.

"Hail, Queen Evangeline," they said in unison.

If the situation hadn't been so tense, Kenden would've laughed at her stunned expression. Lifting her gaze to his, she gave a reluctant shrug. "I told my father to tell them I was in command. I thought that if we won, it would come in handy. Didn't really think that one through."

A large Deamon soldier crested the slab, coming to kneel in front of Evie as she held Crimeous' head in her arms.

"Stand, soldier," she said.

Rising, he saluted her. "I am Rekalb, captain of your father's ground troops. We had orders from our leader to accept you as Commander if he was to perish. My men and I pledge our loyalty to you. Several soldiers who only would serve your father ran from the caves when you defeated him. They will need to be reined in. For now, those of us that remain are your humble servants."

"Thank you," Evie said. Although Kenden knew she was floored, she retained her ever-present confidence and grace. She would make such a magnificent leader, he thought as he observed her. "We are going to dispose of my father's body. I would like you to help the immortals clean up the battlefield. Then, we will work with my sister to find you lodgings. I am grateful for your loyalty and do not accept it lightly."

"Yes, ma'am," Rekalb said, saluting her again. "It will be done."

Giving him a nod, she looked at Kenden. Those beautiful lips curved into a heart-wrenching smile. Then, she closed her lids and dematerialized, her brother close behind her.

Allowing himself to accept that Crimeous was finally gone, Kenden got to work spearheading the clean-up.

Chapter 29

Evie appeared at the top of the cliffs above the Purges of Methesda, her brother emerging shortly thereafter. Silent, they watched the boiling lava below, clutching parts of their father's body.

"It's time," Darkrip said, after they'd had their moment of reflection.

Nodding, Evie inhaled a deep breath and plunged her father's head into the molten plasma below.

Feeling his nostrils flare, Darkrip followed suit, flinging his father's lifeless body into the blazing ash.

Placing his arms over his sister's slender shoulders, he pulled her close. Together, they stood, watching the Dark Lord's corpus disintegrate into nothingness.

"All that death and destruction from one vile creature," she said.

"Yes," he replied, resting the side of his head against hers. "I feel the worst for Mother. She endured so much violence from him. Followed only by you. You two experienced the brunt of his viciousness."

"That's over now," she said, sliding her arm around his waist. "We have a chance at a life without his presence in the world. You're going to have a baby and be a father. How remarkable."

"Remarkable and strange as hell," he muttered, causing her to chuckle. "And you'll build a life with Ken, maybe even have a few rug rats of your own."

She stiffened against him. "That's not my path. It seemed so easy for you, but it's not for me. I wasn't lying about banking his blood. I did it to gain an advantage but it courses though me so much stronger now. I can't saddle Ken with someone so much like Father. It wouldn't be fair to someone as good and decent as he is."

Turning her with his arm, Darkrip placed both hands on her shoulders. "First of all, making the choice to be with Arderin wasn't easy for me at all. I struggled with it terribly and hurt her very much. I still don't understand how in the hell she loves me, but she does, and I'm enormously grateful for that.

"Second," he said, squeezing her shoulders tight, needing her to listen, "Father is dead. Any traces of his evil are gone along with him. You have a chance to make a choice. To be with the man you love and who loves you back with all his heart. Don't waste it. There's good inside you, Evie, just as there is inside of me. Whether we want to believe it or not, it's there."

"I don't believe it," she whispered.

"Well, I'm pretty sure Ken does. So does Miranda, and I sure as hell do—so, sorry, sis, but you're outvoted. You're a good person, whether you want to believe it or not."

"I've done so many terrible things in my past," she said, her gaze falling to the ground.

"As have I," he said, lifting it back by placing his fingers under her chin. "They're awful, and I feel extreme guilt over them and probably always will. But every religion on the damn planet preaches atonement and forgiveness. I'm going to do everything in my power to atone for my sins for the rest of my days and hope that the Universe forgives me. I choose to live by Mother's blood and know that has to mean something. You can do the same. After all, you've always been more powerful than me, so if I can do it, then you definitely can do it." He smiled, thrilled that she grinned back at him.

"It won't be easy," she said.

"Nope," he said, shaking his head. "Never said it would be. But it will be worth it. Give Ken a chance, Evie. Give happiness a chance."

"I have absolutely no idea how to be happy."

"Well, maybe it's time you figure it out," he said, placing a sweet kiss on her forehead. "And you just saved an entire kingdom full of people. I mean, wow, there's got to be some good karma in that, right?"

Laughing, she nodded. "I studied Buddhism quite a bit in the human world and I have to say, there is a lot of karma in saving two species."

"Three species, actually. Isn't that right, *Queen Evie*?" He couldn't control his snicker.

"How insane was that?" she asked, looking genuinely perplexed. "Miranda's great at the queen stuff, but I'm not cut out for it at all."

"I would beg to differ, but my wife has taught me never to argue with a woman dead set in her opinion." Evie breathed a laugh. "But you should think about Miranda's offer to govern the new compound. I think you'd be great at it."

"Right," she said, rolling her eyes. "I'm not a leader, Darkrip. I've been hiding in the human world for centuries."

"Well, maybe it's time you came into the light. You're pretty magnificent, Evie."

Placing her palms on his cheeks, her eyebrows drew together. "Damn. I think I love you. Like, from the bottom of my heart, genuinely love you. It's so strange."

He smiled, exhilarated to hear the words from her. "I felt the same when I realized I loved Miranda. And Arderin. And you," he said, shrugging. "It's really fucking weird but also quite amazing."

"It is," she said hesitantly, shaking her head. "So damn weird. Holy shit."

Breathing a laugh, he drew her in for a hug. Drawing back, he looked into her eyes, blazing before him as brightly as Rina's had all those centuries ago. "Come on. I need to get home. Someone's got to cook for my wife."

Snorting, Evie patted his shoulder. "You're a sap, bro. It's so absurd."

"Shut up."

Joining hands, they grinned at each other. Closing their lids, they materialized back to Uteria to find their family.

* * * *

Miranda enveloped Evie in the most smothering embrace of her long life when she and Darkrip appeared in front of the castle at Uteria. Noticing that her brother was being enveloped in a fervent hug of his own by his sassy Vampyre, Evie let the joy overtake her and hugged her sister back.

Hordes of people stood along the road that led to the castle, Slayer and Vampyre alike. Cheers and whistles sounded as Evie regarded them, drawing back from Miranda to absorb the enormous waves of positive energy. As someone who'd so often lived in shadows and solace, it was strange to be the object of mass adulation, but Evie figured she'd dammed well earned it.

"Holy crap, Evie!" Miranda said, grabbing her hands. "You did it! It's unbelievable. I'm floored. You saved every single one of our people. I don't know how I'll ever begin to repay you."

"I'm still a bit shocked myself," Evie said, unable not to smile back. "It will be so freeing to live in a world without him."

"Yes, it will," she said, squeezing her. "Ken, Larkin and a few of the troops are hanging back to make sure they clean and disinfect every drop of his blood from the lair. In the meantime, we need to ensure that the Deamon soldiers who want to repent are housed in the abandoned hospital. We stationed the Vampyre troops there when they first came to Uteria, and it's the perfect place for them until we build quarters for them at the new compound."

"I'll be happy to help you with that," Evie said.

"Thanks, *Queen Evie*," Miranda said, holding her hand over her mouth as she snickered. "Whether you like it or not, you're a royal now, sis."

Evie scrunched her nose. "How do you deal with it? It's so formal."

"Oh, I don't let anyone call me that. Except my husband, when we're in the bedroom and we're roleplaying..." Waving her hand, she bit her lip, looking guilty. "Shit, he'd kill me if I kept talking, so I'd better shut up now."

Evie arched a brow. "Really?" she asked. "Our buttoned-up Vampyre king?"

"You have no idea," Miranda said, threading her arm through Evie's as they began to walk toward the hospital, located several hundred yards behind the castle. "He's an absolute tiger in bed."

The crowd had calmed a bit, although the vibrant energy remained. There would be a celebration to rival all others in the main square of each immortal compound tonight. Of that, Evie was sure.

Darkrip appeared in their path, clutching Sathan. Evie realized he must've transported to the cave to grab the king. Miranda launched herself at her bonded mate, wrapping her legs around his waist as she devoured his mouth.

"It's so gross," Arderin said, coming to stand beside her. "Like, get a room already."

"I could say the same about you and Darkrip," Evie teased.

"Sweetie, you don't want to know what we'd do if we got a room. Believe me."

Chuckling, Evie accompanied them to the abandoned hospital. The Deamon troops arrived, led by Latimus, and they proceeded to help them get acclimated. Miranda decided to station soldiers around the perimeter. Although the Deamons professed loyalty to Evie, and all expressed their desire to align with the immortals, it would take time to build trust. In the meantime, extra laborers would be dispatched to build the new compound. Not needing to focus on manufacturing weapons anymore, their entire workforce would be dedicated to creating the new establishment.

After a long day, Evie returned to her cabin. Entering the small shower, she washed away the battle. Running her fingertips over the scratches on her abdomen, left there by Crimeous' pointed nails, she realized they were the last scars her father would ever bestow upon her. Physical or mental. Unable to cope with the gravity of that thought, she let the tears well in her eyes. Then, she stuck her face under the spray and let them fall away. They would be the last she'd ever shed as a result of the vile creature. Inhaling a deep breath, she turned the knob and dried off, dressing herself in jeans and a loose, comfy sweater.

Once finished, she felt restless and poured a glass of wine. Knowing others were surely celebrating brought a smile to her lips but she didn't feel like joining the revelry. Instead, she grasped the wine bottle and headed outside. Sitting on the green grass, she sipped from her glass as the sun began to dip below the horizon.

As if she'd conjured him into existence, the man of her dreams appeared atop the far-off hill. Noticing he'd showered and was dressed in fresh clothes, he must have stopped home first to rinse away the grime of war.

Approaching her, he blocked the low-hanging orb at his back as he smiled. "You bring a glass for me?"

Closing her eyes, she materialized one in her hand. "That's the great thing about dating Crimeous' daughter. You won't have to ask him for her hand in marriage, and she can make a wine glass appear on a whim."

Laughing, he sat beside her as she poured him a glass. Taking it from her, he took a swallow. "Best damn glass of wine I've ever had. Damn, but victory is sweet."

"A thousand years," she said, so comfortable with him as she leaned into his muscular frame, the wine glass hanging from her fingers as her arm dangled over her knees. "He kidnapped Mother a thousand years ago, initiating so much hate and destruction, and now, it's over."

"Thank the goddess," he said.

"So, you're an Etherya worshipper again?" she asked, arching a brow.

He shrugged. "She's growing on me. Especially now that I know she infused you. Loving her is like loving a small piece of you."

Evie nipped his shoulder. "That's sweet."

Placing his arm around her, he held her close. "I'd be content to sit here with you like this forever, Evie. I hope you know that."

Feeling her lips curve, she rested her head on his shoulder. "Then, let's do that. I don't want to discuss serious things right now. Let's just enjoy each other's company and a nice glass of wine."

"Sounds perfect."

They finished the bottle, slow and languid, until the sky had long turned dark. Clutching each other's hands, they walked inside her tiny cabin. Divesting their clothes, they loved each other, ardently and passionately, whispering words that were still too new to say vociferously. Once their war-ravaged bodies were spent and sated, they fell asleep, wrapped in each other's embrace.

Chapter 30

Miranda awoke with a start. Something was wrong. She'd always listened to her gut and did so now with anxious concern. Throwing off the covers, she disentangled herself from her husband's thick body and rose to dress.

"What is it, sweetheart?" Sathan called from the bed.

"Something's going on, but I think it's fine."

Her bonded sat up, a vein pulsing in his neck. "What do you need me to do?"

"Nothing," she said, kissing him on his broad lips. "I'm heading downstairs. Evie's down there. She needs me. Give me ten minutes. If I'm not back by then, come find us. Okay?"

"Miranda, I'm not letting you walk into danger—"

"She won't hurt me, but she's in intense pain. I feel it. It's so strange." She ran her hand through her hair. "I'll be fine. Ten minutes. Love you."

Leaving her confused husband on their rumpled sheets, she hurried down the stairs.

Throwing open the massive wooden doors to the castle, she saw her sister standing outside. The faint glow of pre-dawn flamed off in the distance, and Miranda came to stand before her.

"Evie?"

"I'm leaving," she said, swallowing thickly. "I have to. I need to think and I can't do it in the immortal world."

Miranda felt her heart crumble. "Ken will be devastated."

Evie sighed. "I know. But it's what I have to do. I came back here to defeat my father and I'm not sure what comes next. The human world is where I feel comfortable, and I need to go there."

Miranda rubbed her hands over her thighs, covered in the yoga pants she'd thrown on. "He'll come looking for you."

"Maybe," she said, lifting her hands to rub her upper arms. "But he won't find me. I'm untraceable when I don't want to be located."

"Ken's the best tracker I know. You might have met your match, Evie."

She breathed a laugh. "Perhaps. Regardless, it's what I need to do." Extending her arm, she clutched Miranda's hand. "Thank you for your offer to govern the compound. It's extremely generous, but I wouldn't even know how to go about leading people."

"You'd be fine," Miranda said, feeling her lips form a wide smile. "I'm no expert either but I seem to do okay."

"You're great at it, Miranda." Looking at their joined hands, she seemed to hesitate, and Miranda wondered if she was fighting tears. Lifting her head, her green eyes seemed to glow. "I can't give him what he wants or what he needs. I want so badly to be the person who can but I can't, Miranda. I transfused my father's blood when I stayed in the caves, and it's warped something inside of me. I feel the struggle between his evil and her goodness," she said, referencing Rina. "It's consuming me. I can't do anything until I figure out how to remedy it."

"Okay," Miranda said, understanding how difficult the battle within her must be. "But I need to say something, and I want you to listen. Daughters of Rina are extremely hardheaded but you *need* to hear me on this."

Grinning, Evie nodded. "Okay,"

"You are always welcome here. Always. Your struggle only means that you have so much good inside you that it's battling to break through. I have faith that you will defeat the darkness that comprises your father's blood and emerge more victorious than ever. When that day comes, know that you'll have a home here. The offer to govern the new compound is always on the table, even if it takes you several centuries to accept it. Do you understand me, Evie?"

"Yes," she said, the word gravelly and filled with emotion. "I've never understood what it's like to have family, but your acceptance of me is humbling. Thank you."

"You're welcome." Drawing her close, they shared a hug. "Please, be careful out there," she whispered into the shell of her ear.

"I will."

Sathan's voice called from behind. "Miranda? Are you okay?"

"Goodbye," Evie garbled, tears glistening in her eyes.

"Goodbye."

And then, she was gone. Vanished into thin air, as if she'd never existed. Miranda felt Sathan's warmth behind her, drawing her into his front, as her heart splintered.

"She'll be back, little Slayer," he said, kissing her silky hair. "Don't worry."

"I know," Miranda said, emotion clogging her throat. "But will it be soon enough to repair Ken's heart?"

Sighing, he clutched her close. "Only time will tell, sweetheart."

Turning in his arms, she slid her hand over his face. "Carry me inside and make me forget for a minute, will ya?"

Chuckling, he fused his lips to hers. "I am the queen's humble servant and will do my best to follow her command," he mumbled against her mouth.

"God, yes. We're gonna play that game. Take me upstairs. We have at least half an hour before Tordor wakes up. An hour if we're lucky."

His deep laugh reverberated through her body, shooting daggers of desire to every limb. Loving how he swung her into his broad arms, she buried her face in his neck, anticipating every sexy thing her husband was about to do to her. Squealing as he carried her up the stairs, he silenced her with his mouth, surrounding the hallway in silence so they didn't wake their son.

* * * *

Kenden awoke, alone in her small cabin, already understanding that she was gone. As he'd held her last night, he'd felt the struggle within. In between their bouts of passion, she'd lain in his arms, explaining why she'd infused Crimeous' blood. Not only had it given her the ability to read his thoughts, which she couldn't do through the shield he'd erected, but it also made him trust that she'd defected.

He understood why she did it. The action was warranted and so very smart. Yet another cunning move by the remarkably astute woman he loved with his entire heart. Placing his hands beneath his head on the pillow, he realized he wasn't even angry. He'd known, somewhere deep inside, that she would leave. She needed to process the sweeping changes that had comprised her life recently. Killing her father. Her slow but steady evolution toward choosing to live by her Slayer half. Her acceptance of her love for him, Miranda, Darkrip and others. It must be intensely overwhelming for someone who'd thrived in solitude, needing no one for centuries.

Aching for her, he lifted from the bed, resolute to let her stew for a bit before finding her. And, oh, he would find her. Of that, he had no doubt. Walking into the small kitchen, he noticed that the coffee pot was on and half-full of steaming coffee. Plodding toward it, he pulled a mug from the cabinet above. Pouring himself a cup, he lifted it to his lips, sipping the warm liquid.

Lifting the note she'd left beside the pot, he read her sweeping scrawl:

Ken,
I'm sure you're not even surprised that I left, for you knew I had to. Hell, you probably know me better than I know myself at this point. It's a hard thing, when you realize that someone understands your fears, doubts and insecurities better than you do. It makes me want to curl up into a ball and forget that I ever met you. Or held you. Or let you look at me with those sexy-as-sin eyes.

But I can't forget, as much as I want to, so I'm going to remember. I'm off in search of answers and will do my best to recall our time together fondly. I don't think it will be hard, considering that I feel more for you than I've ever felt for anyone. It's annoying and disconcerting and makes me hate you, just a little bit.

You can try to find me but, as we've already discussed, it will be a waste of your time. I want you to be happy, Ken. Marry a woman who can give you babies and love; who isn't filled with evil and memories of past atrocities, both received and committed. I deceived myself that I was good enough to be touched by you for as long as I could. You will do a disservice to yourself if you continue the same deception.

If I ever do see you again, perhaps centuries down the road, know that I will embrace you and feel true joy at the family you've built. I only want you to be happy, and this is why I can't stay.

I made coffee for you, to soften the blow. At least we overcame the hurdle of me being able to share the coffee pot. You changed so much in me, Ken, and for that, I will always love you.

Be happy,
Evie

Kenden finished the letter, smiling as he sipped his coffee. Man, the woman was head over heels for him. How magnificent. But she had another thing coming if she thought for one second that he was letting her go.

Pondering how much time he would give her before he started looking, he leaned on the counter. He'd give it a few weeks, to let Evie roam the human world and to help Miranda transition the kingdoms to a realm without Crimeous.

And then, when everything was in place, he'd travel to the land of humans to claim his woman. He didn't care if it took him days, years or centuries. He'd locate her and drag her back with him, kicking and screaming if he had to. Chuckling at the image, he finished his coffee.

Making sure all the lights were off in the cabin, he shut the door behind him and headed home to start the day.

Chapter 31

Miranda stood at the wall of ether, hugging Darkrip tight. Unable to stop the tears pouring down her face, she disengaged from him and clutched Arderin close.

"We're going to be fine, Miranda," Arderin said, running her hand over her glossy hair. "I'll only be gone a few years and I think I can finish medical school pretty quickly. We'll come back to visit as much as we can. I promise."

"I can't believe I'm gonna miss this little munchkin growing up," Miranda said, kissing the forehead of the baby girl Arderin held in her arms. Straightening, she swiped at the wetness on her cheeks. "I wanted to be there to help you."

"I've read every baby book imaginable," Darkrip said, hugging Arderin to his side. "My wife has been diligently quizzing me on what I've retained, and I'm pretty sure I can keep the little monster alive."

Arderin punched his upper arm, scrunching her face at his teasing. "Don't call our daughter a monster."

Chuckling, Darkrip pecked her pink lips. "The cutest monster I've ever seen."

Arderin beamed up at him, joy evident in the tiny new family.

"I've already had Sarah Lowenstein make some calls," Sadie said, Nolan's arms around her waist as he stood behind her. "The OB-GYNs and pediatricians at UCLA are top notch. If there are any emergencies, they'll take care of Callie as if she was their own. I see no reason why they would even begin to suspect that she's not human. But her self-healing abilities should keep her healthy."

"Okay," Miranda said, leaning back into Sathan. "Are you going to survive this, darling?" she asked, rubbing his face with her palm.

"I'm not thrilled but I trust Darkrip to take care of them," he muttered.

"Thanks, Sathan," Darkrip said. "You have my word."

"Okay, little one," Latimus said, "we already said our goodbyes to you yesterday. I'm sure Lila's a mess right now because she already misses you so much, and I need to get back to her and the kids. Be safe over there."

"I will, old man," she teased, ice-blue eyes twinkling in the sunlight.

Heden gave her one last firm hug and then shook Darkrip's hand. Telling Arderin not to be a pain in the ass, they all laughed when she stuck her tongue out at her younger brother.

Then, they waved, watching as Darkrip, Arderin and Callie entered the ether and disappeared. Sighing, Miranda turned to look at Kenden, who'd been quite somber during the exchange. As the others headed to the four-wheelers, she placed her hand on his chest.

"Whoa, there. Someone's awfully quiet today. You okay?"

"Yeah," Kenden said, his lips forming a half-hearted smile. "I just miss her, Randi. Two more weeks, and then, I'm heading to find her. We need to finish the transition of the soldiers to law-enforcement as much as we can before I leave. I don't want to saddle Latimus with all the work."

"Always such a boy scout," Miranda said, linking her arm with his as they sauntered toward the vehicles.

"Evie called me that. You two must've been sharing notes."

She laughed, the sound wafting along the gentle breeze. "Maybe we were. Regardless, I've got your back. As we discussed, a quarter of the troops will remain combat ready. You and Latimus have already done a great job destroying the Deamon caves and rounding up the Deamons that need to be imprisoned. The remaining troops will be transitioned to law-enforcement, security and construction for the new compound at double their army salary, if they so choose. Not to toot my own horn, but I'm pretty awesome at this 'ruler' thing." She made quotation marks in the air with two of her fingers.

"You're remarkable," he said, placing a kiss atop her head. "You always have been."

"But you've found another person," she said, beaming up at him. "I'm so glad, Ken. I've always wanted so badly for you to find someone who would challenge you and love you and drag you from that ridiculous shed."

"Hey," he said, his eyebrows drawing together. "My shed is awesome."

She snorted. "Not even close, buddy."

Reveling in their closeness, he helped his cousin into one of the four-wheelers. True to his word, Kenden fulfilled his duties for another two weeks. And then, he traveled through the ether to locate the other half of his heart.

* * * *

Kenden walked along the pebbly trail, the rocks crunching under his feet. Eventually, he came to a parting of the trees and stepped onto the stony shore. The beaches in this region of Italy were all made of tiny rocks. So different from many of the sand-splotched coastlines he'd visited recently, trying to find her.

Eventually, he'd located this small island. Only accessible by boat, it had a steep hill in the center lined with green bushes and was rarely visited by humans. It had taken several months for him to track her down but he'd anticipated that before beginning his search. Kenden was nothing if not patient and he'd systematically and methodically tracked her every movement until he'd found her here, in this place of such tranquil beauty.

She stood tall and solemn as she watched the sun tangle with the horizon. Hands thrust in the back pocket of her designer jeans, she wore a loose t-shirt and sneakers. Red hair blazing down her shoulders, she looked comfortable and peaceful. It made him happy, since he wanted peace for his beautiful Evie more than anything.

She knew he was there. Of that, he had no doubt. Evie was powerful and could see many things. Needing to touch her, he slowly approached her lithe body, sliding his hands around her waist. Clutching them across her abdomen, he waited, resting his chin on her shoulder.

She relaxed into him, causing Kenden to thank every god in the heavens. For he was holding her again, something that always drove his system into overload. Blood coursing through his veins, he inhaled her scent, closing his eyes as he exhaled. Love for her, so vibrant and true, pervaded every cell in his muscular body.

There, they stood, watching the gorgeous sunset as it dipped below the darkened ocean. Somewhere along the way, she brought her hands to rest on his forearms. Locked in the gentle embrace, they marveled at the dying embers of the bright orb.

Once the sun set, he buried his face in her hair, nuzzling the side of her neck with his nose. She shivered, the small movement giving him hope that she'd missed him at least half as much as he'd pined for her. The sensation of having her in his arms again was overwhelming.

"I missed you by two days in New Zealand," he said, loving the tiny bumps that rose up on her neck at hearing his voice. "By one day in Japan, and by only hours in North Carolina. When you said you were good at hiding, you weren't kidding, sweetheart."

Her lips twitched, eyes closed as she burrowed into his nestling. He placed a soft kiss on the sensitive skin of her neck and swore he felt her tremble in his embrace.

"Well, you found me," she said, her tone sultry and oh-so-sexy. Kenden felt himself harden in his jeans and clutched her closer. "Now, what are you going to do with me?"

Breathing in the smell of her shampoo, he grasped her closer, unable to imagine ever letting her go again. "I'm thinking I'd like to marry you, make you happy and raise a lot of babies with you."

He'd expected that would start the debate. About futures they couldn't share and things they didn't want. Instead, she tensed but only slightly. Perhaps they were making progress after all.

"If you truly don't want to have children, I won't push you, Evie. I believe that a woman should always have the ability to choose whether motherhood is something she wants or not." Drawing back, he gently spun her so that he could look into her stunning green eyes. "But if you're open to it, I'd love to have babies with you. Ones with red hair and blazing tempers and, yes, with your father's blood. I don't enter into decisions like this lightly. You're my person, Evie. Miranda will always hold such a special place in my heart, but you're the one. I love you, with everything I am and everything I aspire to be."

Those magnificent eyes filled with tears, brimming over until they began to silently slide down her cheeks. Cupping her face, he swept them away with the pads of his thumbs. "Don't cry, baby. This is a good thing. I want to build a life with you."

Evie stared into him, not bothering to hide her tears or the trembling of her chin. He was so honored that she would open herself like that to him, knowing how terribly she detested vulnerability.

Lifting her hand, she palmed his cheek. Running her thumb over his bottom lip, she gave a warbled smile through the emotions that were raging across her face. "I'm terrified," she whispered.

"I know," he said against her thumb, pulsing at her reverent admission. "So am I. I have no idea how to give you a life as exciting and fulfilling as the one you could have here. I'm so scared I'll bore you to death. I'm used to hanging in a dirty old shed for fun. Not exactly fast-paced excitement."

Her smile was blindingly vivid as she chuckled. "Excitement's overrated anyway."

"Yeah?" he asked, grinning back at her.

"Yeah," she said, smoothing her palm over his clean-shaven cheek. "You're so worried that you can't give me an exciting life when all I think about is how miserable I'm going to make you if I let you convince me to marry you."

"That bad, huh?" he teased. "I've seen you in the mornings, and it's no picnic, but I think I can handle it. I also have a pretty good eye for knowing when you need your space. I'll let you have it, Evie. I don't want to smother you. I just want to love you. Forever, if you'll let me."

She breathed a disbelieving laugh. "When you say things like that to me, my heart shatters. What in the hell did I do to deserve you?"

"You suffered so much pain and hurt for so long. It made you undeniably strong, but there's a place, deep inside you, that needs to be loved. All this time, you thought you were unlovable. It's not true, sweetheart, and I'm going to prove that to you. Every damn day, until you believe me."

"I can't promise that I'll want to have kids, Ken," she said, her irises darting back and forth between his. "I might eventually but I don't want to lie to you. I know you want them so badly."

"I do, but I want you more," he said, needing her to understand how profoundly he loved her. He would sacrifice having children to be with her. Although it was an incredibly tough decision, he knew he'd never come close to loving another woman as much as he loved Evie. "And if that's your decision, I'll accept it. But I hope that one day, once you finally acknowledge how much I love you, you'll change your mind. Because I think you and I would slay parenting together."

The corner of her full lips curved. "We'd kick ass."

Chuckling, he pulled her close and rested his forehead upon hers. "We sure would. We're unstoppable together, Evie."

Staring into him, she sucked in a huge breath. Olive-green eyes swam with fear and contemplation as she regarded him. Finally, when he felt he would die if she didn't speak, she opened her mouth and tore his heart apart.

"I love you too," she whispered.

Breath, slow and steady, departed his lungs in an enormous exhale. "Good grief, woman. Everything with you is a damn struggle. It took you long enough."

"Get ready, big boy," she said, waggling her eyebrows against his brow. "If we're going to do this, it's probably going to be a bumpy ride."

"I wouldn't have it any other way," he said, sliding his arms down her sides to pull her into his body. "I love you so damn much." Lowering his lips to hers, he opened her mouth with them, sliding his tongue inside. Groaning, he twined his fingers in her hair as she tangled her tongue with his. The taste of her, so sweet and sultry, after such a long drought brought him endless pleasure.

There, under the starlit sky and half-risen moon, they devoured each other. Lifting his head, Kenden panted softly as he gazed down at her.

"Ready to go?"

Separating from her quivering body, he stretched his arm across the small distance between them. Opening his hand, he waited.

Evie stared at his exposed palm, the debate at whether to take it warring across her flawless face. Kenden stood firm, willing to wait for centuries if it meant she would place her hand in his at the end.

When they finally left the island, it was together, hand-in-hand, taking the first steps into their shared eternity.

Epilogue
Five Years Later...

The members of the secret society gathered around the wooden table. Hidden deep within one of the few caves the immortals hadn't located, each participant took their seat. The light from the lone candle in the middle of the table cast a pallid glow upon each of their faces.

"Thank you all for coming," the leader said in his baritone voice. "I have called you all together because we share a common goal: ultimate defeat of the immortal royals and all who are loyal to them. They have grown bold in their arrogance and careless with their heritage. They procreate with children of Crimeous, denigrating the pristine bloodlines that the Universe intended. My aim is only to restore the preeminence of the immortals to the glory they once had. Do you all concur?"

"Aye," came the hushed replies.

"Very well. Please, introduce yourselves. We all must understand each other's strengths and weaknesses if we are to succeed."

"My name is Vadik," one of the men said. "I was Crimeous' second-in-command, behind Rekalb. It is appalling that so many Deamons pledged loyalty to the red-haired usurper. I will stop at nothing to murder her and restore the Deamons to their true dominance, as children of Crimeous. I will always worship Crimeous as Lord. I know you do not share that belief," he said to the leader, "but I am willing to align with you to destroy the Vampyres and the Slayers. I am prepared to overlook our differences to accomplish our common goal."

"Welcome, Vadik," the leader said. "I appreciate your candor and understand the terms of your alliance. I believe that together, we can both accomplish our objectives."

"My name is Sofia," a woman said. Easing the hood of her sweatshirt off her head, black, springy curls bounced in its wake. "The red-haired bitch killed my grandfather, Francesco. I'm sure of it. I've spent the last few years tracking her. Her bastard brother broke into a lab in Houston several years ago, and that led me toward finding the ether. Once I came through, I began studying your world. Since I'm in between realms, I'll do my best to attend these meetings but I'm not always on this side."

Lifting her black cloth backpack to the table, she dumped out several devices. Sliding one across the table to each of the society members, she said, "I'm a competent hacker and have programmed these phones so they can send texts through the ether. If you need me, use these to contact me. And I suggest using them for all of our shared communications moving forward. I've installed spyware and security protection on all of them. The only person in the immortal world even close to being as skilled a hacker as I am is the youngest Vampyre sibling, and he's still leagues behind me. Regardless, I would urge caution."

"Thank you, Sofia," the leader said. "We are honored to have you on our team."

"I am Ananda," another woman said.

"And I am Diabolos," the man beside her said. "As you already know, Vadik was able to transfuse our corpses with Crimeous' blood and bring us back to life. My wife and best friend have betrayed me, and he is extremely loyal to the Slayer queen. I want nothing more than to ensure their demise."

"And the Vampyre royal family has always treated me with extreme disrespect," Ananda said. "The king banished me from the royal compound, and his younger brother put his filthy hands all over my niece, ensuring her degradation. It is a disgrace to her dear parents, and I won't stand for it."

"The Vampyre royals are garbage," a nasty, slightly higher-pitched voice chimed. "Although my husband Camron has forgiven them for causing us extreme embarrassment in public many times over, I do not share his sympathetic heart. My name is Melania, daughter of Falkon and Marika, and I won't stop until I see the bastard Latimus, his tramp bonded mate and his entire family murdered." The woman gave a nod, her silky black hair shining by the light of the flame.

"Understood," the leader said. "You all are valuable members of our society, and I'm pleased that Vadik was able to bring Diabolos and Ananda back."

Heads tilted in agreement.

Straightening his spine, long and firm to accommodate his six-foot, seven-inch height, the leader spoke. "I am Bakari, middle child of King Markdor and Queen Calla, born in between the Warrior and the Princess."

Making eye contact with everyone in the room, he let the admission float between them to have the fullest impact. "My mother and father were told that I perished when I was a babe. As you can all see, I am alive and well. The story of where I've been for a thousand years is best left for another time. Rest assured, I have a deep understanding of both this world and the human world. Over the centuries, some humans became aware of my presence, spurring the creation of the character we now know as Count Dracula. However, they are still too stupid to fathom that our world exists."

"Hey," Sofia muttered.

"Present company excluded," Bakari said with a bend of his head.

"So why do you want to fight?" Vadik asked. "You weren't loyal to Crimeous."

"No," Bakari said, "but I see the future so clearly. The immortals will rise to their full power again, now that Crimeous is gone. The royals of both species are filled with notions of democracy and freedom." His tone was laced with vitriol. "That is not what Etherya intended when she created my parents and Valktor. She wanted imminent rulers who would enforce stability and lawfulness upon her people. As a child of Markdor and Calla, I cannot stand by and watch my siblings ruin the immortal world. Therefore, I will fight to defeat them and rule the kingdom in their place, ensuring that true order is established."

"And will you be able to kill your own family?" Sofia asked.

"The Vampyre sovereigns mean nothing to me. I will systematically decimate each one of them and any subjects who pledge loyalty to them, one by one if I have to. I am something close to a god in the human world and I wish to be so here. I assure you, I know what is best for my people. My arrogance might be offensive to you, but it fuels my desire to fight."

"Fair enough," Sofia said. "We need to be smart but we need to work quickly. Some of us here aren't immortal. That bitch killed my grandfather when I was thirty-one, and I'm almost thirty-eight now. Time's ticking for me. Unfortunately, Crimeous' blood has no effect on a human body, so if I die, you can't bring me back. If you want my help, I would urge you all to get serious."

"Agreed," Bakari said. "Let's plan to meet again in three months' time. By then, we all will have had time to sufficiently brainstorm. After combining the best of our ideas, we will prepare to implement the plan to ensure the ruin of the immortal monarchs and their families. Every last one."

Eyes met, expressing acknowledgement, as they cemented their allegiance to each other.

Upon exiting the cave, they destroyed it, vowing to leave no trace behind.

* * * *

Evie sat at the vanity in her bedroom, smoothing cream onto her just-washed face. Her husband entered the room, looking tired yet gorgeous as always. Sauntering toward her, he bent to kiss her hair.

"Hey, baby. How was your day?"

"Good," she said, rubbing the lotion into her hands. "Aron and I did the orientation for the new Vampyres that are moving over from Valeria. It will be nice to get some aristocratic blood on Takelia," she said, referencing the compound that was reverently named after the strong Vampyre warrior who'd perished in one of their battles. "We have a lot of laborers and prisoners but having some stuffy aristocrats to annoy is always so much fun." Her eyes sparkled in the reflection.

"There's my wife," he said, removing his shirt. The muscles in his abs seemed to ripple, causing Evie to clench her thighs together. Good lord, but her husband was *hot*. "Always looking for mischief."

"And I always seem to find it," she said, smiling at him in the mirror. "How was your day?"

"Good," Kenden said, pulling off his pants one leg at a time. "The police force on each compound is great, but the recruits at Lynia need a bit more training. We'll get there. Now that Latimus has three kids, I find myself covering more than ever."

"You should tell him if it's too much."

"You know I don't mind," he said, coming to stand behind her. Placing his hands on her shoulders, he gently began massaging them.

Studying his chocolate irises in the reflection, she sensed his anxiousness.

"What?" she asked, although she could read the images in his mind. *Shit.* She should've known by now that the powerful Slayer commander knew everyone's schedule down to the last detail.

"I was going to tell you," she said, her lips forming a pout.

"Is that so?" he asked, lifting his brows. "Because imagine my surprise when Sadie bounced up to me today, pregnant as a jaybird, and asked me if I was coming with you to the appointment tomorrow."

"Why would you come with me to a GYN appointment?" she snapped, trying to tamp down the temper that still seemed to violently flare even though she tried her best to live by her Slayer half.

"Um, maybe to accompany you to Uteria to see Miranda and Sadie? You know I don't get there as much anymore. Now that we live on Takelia, and Sadie and Nolan have taken our old house, I always look for opportunities to spend time there."

"And maybe visit your shed?" she asked, arching a scarlet brow.

"Quiet about my shed, woman," he said, scrunching his face at her. "It was my only love until you came along."

Chuckling, she regarded his reflection. Rising, she turned to face him and slide her arms around his neck.

"Oh, no, sweetheart," he said, those perfect white teeth flashing. "You're not seducing me into letting this go."

"Letting what go?" she asked innocently, moving her palm down his body until it clutched his hardened shaft.

"Evie," he said, a warning in his tone.

Closing her lids, she dematerialized his underwear. As he stood magnificently naked before her, she dropped to her knees. Opening her mouth, she placed the engorged head of his cock over her lips and drew him deep inside.

"You're not off the hook," he growled, thrusting his fingers into her thick hair. Groaning up at him, she purred.

He jutted his hips into her until he was screaming her name. Popping from her wet mouth, he lifted her to the bed and impaled her body, naked beneath her robe.

Together, they rode each other, clutching sweaty skin, until they collapsed in a heap of spent desire.

"My god, woman," he said into the soft comforter, his face buried beside her head. "If you want to kill me before I can interrogate you, fine. I surrender. You're an animal."

Giving a sated chuckle, she ran her nails over his back, causing him to shiver. "You don't need to interrogate me. Just trust your wife. I do think that was required in our vows, no?"

Lifting his head, he gazed into her, placing a soft kiss on her lips. "I do trust you," he said, running his fingers through the hair at her temple. "But I had to beg you to marry me for four years. When you finally relented, I asked you to consider having kids, and you said you were open. I thought you might be going to see Sadie to possibly discuss that tomorrow. And if you are, I'm sad that you wouldn't tell me."

Inhaling a deep breath, she studied him. This beautiful man whom she was so lucky to call hers. He always challenged her to be her best self, and perhaps, in this instance, she hadn't been as forthright as she could've been.

"I'm sorry," she whispered, lifting her hand to rub his cheek with the pads of her fingers. "I was going to discuss possibly removing my IUD during the appointment tomorrow." Kenden's eyes lit with pleasure. "*Possibly*," she cautioned. "And this is exactly why I didn't tell you. You get all revved up about things and move too fast. I mean, for god's sake, you asked me to move in with you when we'd only been fucking for a month."

"But you wanted to," he said, nipping at her lips. "Admit it."

"Beside the point," she said, standing her ground. "I knew that if I told you I was considering getting pregnant, you'd have me knocked-up and on bed rest within the week."

He chortled, the sound bursting from his throat. "Is it that bad?"

"Terrible," she teased. "I can't keep up with you."

"I know I push you, baby," he said, rubbing the tip of her nose with his. "It's because I love you so damn much. You have no idea how often I think about the children we could have. The girls would have red hair and tiny freckles, and the boys would be so strong. We'd raise them to be good men, worthy of loving a woman as resilient and beautiful as their mother one day."

Evie felt the prick of tears behind her eyes. Not surprising, since the man had always possessed the ability to tear down every wall she'd erected. "Goddamnit," she whispered. "Why do you have to say stuff like that? It reminds me of how amazing you are and how I'll never deserve you."

"You deserve it all, sweetheart," he said, kissing her again. "But if you're not ready, I won't push."

"Right," she said, rolling her eyes.

"I won't," he said, his grin wide. "But you'll decide to have babies with me one day. I know it. Until then, we can just keep having mind-blowing sex. I'm one-hundred percent okay with that."

Lips twitching, she caressed his hair. "I'm going to tell her to remove the IUD."

She'd never seen him smile so broadly. "Are you sure?"

"I'm sure," she said, the words warbled since her throat seemed to be closing up.

"You're so incredible," he said softly, nuzzling into her. "I'm so in love with you, Evie. Thank you for everything you've given me. I know it's not easy for you."

"Are you seriously thanking me right now?" she asked, not comprehending how he couldn't see that she was the lucky one. Grasping his face between her hands, she spoke words so genuine and true. "You saved me, Ken. Don't you understand? You challenged me to become the person that I never even fathomed I could be. You saved my life in so many ways. I love you with my entire soul."

Lowering his lips to hers, he moaned as their tongues warred and mated. Their life together wasn't easy and would never be perfect but it was *theirs*. Something they'd built concurrently that they both so reverently cherished. Although she knew there were unseen threats looming on the horizon, Evie held fast to hope. She'd learned that after tranquility, there was always more hardship. It was the yin to the yang of life. Living for eternity, they were sure to experience as many peaks as they would valleys.

But with Kenden as her partner, she knew she would always choose light over darkness. Though she may be tempted, his love, so steadfast and sure, would always direct her to make the right choice. There was comfort in that, along with the reassurance that she'd do everything in her power to make him happy. Snuggling into her husband, she enjoyed the bliss of the moment, understanding how precious it truly was.

Before you go...

Well, guys, that ending was a doozie, huh? I mean, another Vampyre sibling?!?! Who knew? For those of you wondering about the future of the Etherya's Earth series, rest assured I'm not done yet! Obviously, our amazing and loveable jokester Heden needs a HEA. And wouldn't it be wonderful to see Jack, Callie, Tordor and others as adults, helping their parents fight the obstacles that will surely occur? I will be working on Book 5, which will be Heden's book, along with some other projects over the next year. The best way to stay updated on when Heden's book will be available is to follow me on social media (see links below). Also, please tell everyone you can about these books (and you can ask your library to order them too!) They make great summer reads and I'm always looking to spread the word. Thanks for accompanying me on this journey so far. Can't wait to see you in Book 5! ☺RH

Acknowledgments

Finishing this book was bittersweet. Although I'm not done with the series, I knew that I would take a break after Book 4 to evaluate the next steps on this awesome, winding and sometimes scary journey of being an author. Tears streamed down my face as I wrote the letter from Evie to Kenden and I hope that you all feel as emotionally connected to these characters as I do! Thanks to each and every one of you for taking time out of your busy lives to read these books.

Several friends whom I've yet to mention have been extremely supportive and I'd like to shout them out.

Thanks to Eva for loving the series and saying that it should be made into a Netflix show. I can only hope, sister! Thanks to Liz and Sharan for sending me pictures of my books as they lounged on the beach. To Kristen for snapping a pic from a plane. To Nikki for the pic of her reading in FL. To Judy for texting me from a plane while she was crying reading TES & wondering if the guy next to her thought she was nuts...haha! To Tara for showing me the pic of her reading TEoH at jury duty. That one was great!

Thanks to Tara in CT (yes, I know two awesome Tara B.'s ☺) for leaving a review even though Amazon doesn't make it easy. Reviews are so important to authors and I appreciate everyone who takes the time to leave one.

Thanks to Colleen and Misty, my OGs who read and reviewed these books. Thanks to Susan for loving steamy books like I do, even though we grew up in BM...hee hee! BM book signing, here we come!

Thanks to the book bloggers who've taken a chance on me over the past few months: Rose, Karen Jo, Bonnie, SP and so many others. You'll never know how thrilled I am when you message me that you like my books. It's absolutely amazing!

Thanks to the awesome people I've meet through the #WritingCommunity on Twitter. Special shout out to amazing author Sarah Bailey who also writes steamy novels. Our discussions about our mothers reading our books are hilarious!

Thanks to Megan McKeever for the wonderful editing, as always. I feel so lucky to have found you! And thanks to Susan Olinsky for the steamy cover!

Wishing you all a wonderful summer and remember that even through our flaws and mistakes, we all still have so much to give. If Kenden can love Evie for who she is inside, then we all can love ourselves too! Be kind to yourself and to others. Share your wisdom. Laugh freely and choose positivity over all. Hoping you find your Zen until we meet again!

About the Author

Rebecca Hefner grew up in Western NC and now calls the Hudson River of NYC home. In her youth, she would sneak into her mother's bedroom and raid the bookshelf, falling in love with the stories of Judith McNaught, Sandra Brown and Nora Roberts. Years later that love of a good romance, with lots of great characters and conflicts, has extended to her other favorite authors such as JR Ward and Lisa Kleypas. Also a huge Game of Thrones and Star Wars fan, she loves an epic fantasy and a surprise twist (Luke, he IS your father).

Rebecca published her first book in November of 2018. Before that, she had an extensive twelve-year medical device sales career, where she fought to shatter the glass ceiling in a Corporate America world dominated by men. After saving up for years, she left her established career to follow the long, winding and scary path of becoming a full-time author. Due to her experience, you'll find her books filled with strong, smart heroines on a personal journey to find inner fortitude and peace while combating sexism and misogyny. She would be thrilled to hear from you anytime at rebecca@rebeccahefner.com.

If you liked this book then *please* leave a review on Amazon, Goodreads and/or BookBub. Your friendly neighborhood author thanks you from the bottom of her heart!

FOR MORE ON THIS AUTHOR:
www.rebeccahefner.com

Facebook: https://www.facebook.com/rebeccahefnerauthor/

Twitter: https://twitter.com/RebHefnerAuthor

Instagram: https://www.instagram.com/rebeccahefner/

Amazon: http://author.to/RebeccaHefner

Goodreads: https://www.goodreads.com/author/show/18637390.Rebecca_Hefner

BookBub: https://www.bookbub.com/authors/rebecca-hefner

Book 5 (Heden's book!!) will definitely be coming soon! Make sure you follow Rebecca on social media to hear all of the announcements and updates.

Made in the
USA
Middletown, DE

76036684R00146